Devoured by Shadows

Copyright © 2025 by Entice Publishing LLC
www.RosalynStirling.com

Devoured by Shadows
The Wild Shadows, #2

All rights reserved. No parts of the book may be used or reproduced, transmitted, stored in, or introduced into a retrieval system in any form or by any means (including but not limited to electronic, mechanical, photocopying, and recording) without written permission from the author or publisher nor otherwise circulated in any form of binding or cover other than that in which it is published without a similar condition being imposed on the subsequent purchaser. The exception is for the use of brief quotations in a book review.

This book is a work of fiction. Names, characters, establishments, organizations, and incidents are either products of the author's imagination or are used fictitiously to give a sense of authenticity. Any resemblance to actual persons, living or dead, events, or locales is entirely coincidental.

For every woman who's longed for a man (or partner) who'd do anything for her... But realized you were the one in the relationship who'd burn down the world for him.

Be you. Be fierce.

And never apologize for it.

In Case You Missed It...

Witness the moment when Arabella gets her memories back in an exclusive bonus chapter to *Kissed by a Demon*.

Click here to download (e-book only) or go to: **bit.ly/KBAD-bonus-chapter.**

Trigger Warnings

This novel contains mature elements and themes, including (but not limited to) explicit sexual content, graphic violence, sexual assault (not between the main characters), and torture. Reader discretion is advised.

Chapter One
ARABELLA

To have found her mate and lost him in the same instant was as unfathomable as time itself.

Arabella stormed out of the library and down the castle halls—shadows in her fists, fury in her heart, and her memories returned to her.

My mate did this for me.

Somehow, Elias had found a way to get her memories back.

The shadows rumbled, stirring and ascending from the deep. They rolled like lapping waves at her feet—appearing as twisting, thorned vines when they emerged far enough to take on a corporeal state. She breathed in, feeling power surge in her veins.

Something in her had awakened. And there was no putting it back to sleep.

She was no longer just an enchantress.

Now, she was something more.

The clicks of several pairs of boots on the stone floor echoed behind her. Waves of power filled the hallway as she strode around a bend and down the stairs toward the main entryway and the castle's front doors.

Even without looking, she knew who followed her by the feel of their magic.

The three enchantresses had magic as bright and golden as the late summer sunshine, while Breckett bore a darker energy, like a mist along a blackened forest floor far beyond civilization.

Breckett was an erox, a type of demon who looked like men and sustained their immortal life by feeding off the sexual pleasures of mortals. Her mate was such a demon.

Her demon.

Of all the creatures existing in the mortal or fae realms—humans, vampires, shape shifters, witches, sorcerers, enchantresses, the fae courts, and more—somehow, she'd fallen for a demon.

The very being she'd vowed to protect the human race from.

"Wait, Arabella," a female voice called from behind her. "Where are you going?"

It was Jessamine, one of the most powerful warriors among the enchantresses. But even the sound of worry in her friend's voice didn't slow her pace.

Arabella had already packed her bags.

They had been planning to leave Elias' castle to return to Shadowbank, their home and a remote human village. That was before Arabella had been struck with some strange magic and her memories had returned to her.

In a desperate bargain with the Witch of the Woods, she'd given up her memories in exchange for an amplifier, a rare magical artifact that stored a limited amount of energy within it. That power could amplify a magic wielder's ability—and do the impossible, such as repair or build a magical ward.

Her bargain with the witch had been to protect Elias' castle from a sorcerer's amassing army of erox, ogres, gargoyles, and other dark creatures by strengthening the magical ward around it. But his castle wasn't the only place with a ward that desperately needed to be reinforced—or recreated. Shadowbank was vulnerable to the demon-infested forest just beyond its stone walls and weakening ward.

As Arabella walked through the castle, she wove her hair into her customary long braid and tightened the empty sheaths along her waist and arms.

First, she needed to find her swords, and then she'd find Elias.

He'd only been gone for a day. To return her memories, he'd given himself to that sorcerer, Magnus. But now, he was in danger. She could sense it.

Something tugged at her chest, pulling her toward the dark forest that stretched on for countless miles beyond the castle. It was a sensation unlike anything she'd ever felt—like a chord had wrapped around her heart and was tethered somewhere beyond the horizon. A sharp, fathomless fear echoed down it, snaking up her chest before embedding into her thoughts. There was endless pain, too. It was like a deep chasm had yawned open and threatened to pull her into its depths and engulf her.

Elias needed her.

The forest demon she'd been taught to fear during her upbringing in Shadowbank.

The Devourer.

My mate.

"I'm going to find him." Arabella didn't look back at Jessamine or the others as she strode into the castle's entryway and headed for the large oak doors. The walls and floors were made entirely of stone, and the lanterns along the walls had gone dark.

There was no reason to linger for a moment longer.

Arabella was dressed in the black leathers all enchantresses wore, which were imbued with protective magic. She also wore a head chain with the teardrop gemstone that hung down to the center of her forehead.

"Do you know where he is?" Jessamine pressed.

"Yes."

Somehow, Arabella knew that the tugging in her chest would lead her to him.

Before she could reach for the cast-iron door handle and make for the stables beyond it, pain shot down the bond.

She staggered forward, clutching her stomach.

It felt like a blade had been submerged in fire and then sheathed in her gut. Agony exploded in her mind, consuming every sense. She cried out, tears streaming down her cheeks. Grasping at her stomach, she was surprised when her fingers came back bloodless.

Blinking, she stared at her hand and swallowed back bile.

What are they doing to you?

Magnus had Elias. And he was hurting him.

The hairs along her arms stood on end as though lightning were about to strike.

Heart racing, she ignored the hands on her shoulders and the worried looks of her friends. She had to move. *Now.*

I need to learn how to control what I feel down the bond, she thought. *And soon.*

When her memories returned and the mating bond had snapped back into place a few minutes ago, she felt Elias' emotions with such clarity. In an instant, her mind was no longer her own. Her fate had become entwined with a demon. It was already a struggle to tease out what she was feeling from Elias' experiences, especially as his pain and fear mingled and crashed down on her.

There wasn't time to sort that out now.

A hand caught her wrist, forcing her to stop as she reached for the door handle again.

"Stop," Jessamine said, her voice unyielding. It was a tone that Arabella knew all too well. It brooked no argument. "If your memories are back, then you'll also recall there's a fucking *army* beyond the ward. As powerful as you are, even you can't single-handedly face down an army of dark creatures. None of us can."

Gritting her teeth, Arabella turned on a heel and faced Jessamine.

There was an unparalleled fierceness in Jessamine's gaze. She was short in stature and as fearless as the dragons of legend. Like Arabella, she wore enchantress leathers with countless knives sheathed throughout her armor. But her blonde hair was loose, hanging in long waves.

Beside her stood Cora and Brynne, two other enchantresses from Shadowbank and some of Arabella's dearest friends. They'd come with Jessamine to Elias' castle to try to help Arabella regain her memories.

Now, the three enchantresses all had varying expressions of concern on their faces.

For the first time, Arabella wondered if the worry wasn't for Elias' safety but instead what she might do with her new shadow magic.

Breckett stood very still behind them, his face devoid of expression.

She didn't bother to wipe her tears away as she looked at them.

"You can feel him somehow. Can't you?" Jessamine said, her eyes fixed on Arabella's face—and the devastation that was likely as plain as the dawn. In a quieter voice, as though speaking to herself, she said, "What are they doing to him?"

Arabella's gaze turned to Breckett. The demon was tall with light brown skin and eyes as dark as night. Like all erox, he possessed an unearthly beauty and magnetism that had her heart pattering at his nearness. Her body would desire any erox she was near, but the pull wasn't anything like what she'd experienced with Elias. What she felt with her mate was electric—as though they were ocean currents flowing toward each other, drawn ever closer and set to collide.

Breckett's short black hair was in complete disarray as though he'd been running his hand through it repeatedly. There were purple smudges beneath his eyes, and for a moment, she wondered if he'd been crying.

She looked directly at him, and he returned her gaze with equal ferocity.

"Magnus," she said at last, voicing the name of the sorcerer who'd captured her not long ago—the sorcerer who would have allowed his erox to feed on her until she died if Elias and Breckett hadn't saved her. "That's who Elias is afraid of. Isn't it?"

In the time she'd spent with Elias, she'd gleaned one thing with utter certainty.

There was someone who terrified him more than the inner demon that threatened to consume his humanity.

If erox didn't feed enough, their memories would fade until they were nothing but a mindless demon, intent on feeding upon anyone they came across. And they could never again return to the males they once were—lost to an eternity of gluttonous hunger.

It was a fate Elias had feared fiercely.

But even more than the prospect of losing himself, he'd lived in fear of someone finding him. It had made him desperate to reinforce the ward around his castle and remain in hiding.

Elias had never been able to name Magnus as the source of the fear piercing his brown gaze. But the fear that rippled down the bond now... It was deeper than anything she'd experienced. He was terrified to his core of whatever was happening—or would soon happen—to him.

"Yes," Breckett answered simply. "Magnus is our maker and the first erox."

She blinked. "Your what?"

Only erox could create other erox, and they needed a magical blade called a syphen to do it. But Magnus was a sorcerer. While his abilities far exceeded Elias' dark magic and likely even rivaled or surpassed the fae... How was it possible for a sorcerer to create an erox?

Breckett's eyes grew distant. "Magnus experimented with vampire, demon, and fae blood centuries ago and found a way to create a demon that feeds on sexual desires."

Realization dawned.

That was why fangs appeared when Elias had gone too long without feeding—why he craved her blood. Some part of him was vampire. Or perhaps the origin of his power was from vampires. How had she not put that together?

"Now, you know the truth," Breckett said with narrowed eyes—as though she were the one who'd caused all this.

Only men could become erox. For reasons she didn't understand, women died in the transition to become this kind of demon. That meant for centuries, Magnus had been preying on vulnerable men and experimenting on them.

Like what he'd done to Elias.

And for some reason, her mate was his favorite subject.

Jessamine dropped Arabella's wrist and paced in the castle's entryway, hand on her forehead and muttering obscenities that would have had the head enchantress blushing.

Brynne ran a hand over the back of her neck, her muscled arms near to bursting through her leathers. She was tall and had a tongue as sharp as the two-handed longsword sheathed on her back.

Her smaller counterpart, Cora, fixed her gaze on the floor, shaking her head. Like Jessamine, her hair was the color of summer sunshine. Though hers was far shorter, and she'd braided the hair at her temples back.

Arabella sighed.

They were right.

Outside the ward were hundreds of erox, ogres, gargoyles, and who knew what else. Not long ago, she'd been captured by Magnus' army—and that had been with an amplifier in her possession. Even with her new shadow abilities, which had been awakened the moment she used the amplifier against the ogres, she'd be little more than a helpless rabbit. The moment the erox drew too close to her, she'd be under their spell. There was no way for a mortal to fight an erox's magic.

They were all in over their heads.

"I can't do *nothing*," she said, desperation seeping into every word. "He's my—"

Mate.

The word caught in her throat.

She'd never voiced her feelings for Elias or what they were to each other. The thought of putting words to it when he was far away, likely being tortured, made her throat constrict and her mouth go dry.

Somehow, a magic usually reserved for the fae had touched them both, binding them to each other.

Before she'd lost her memories, the mating bond had clicked into place. Then it had disappeared when her memories had been taken by the Witch of the Woods. The moment her memories came back, the bond had settled in her chest once more.

"I can scent it on you," Breckett said. "The mating bond."

Arabella crossed her arms. "That's gross."

The erox rolled his eyes.

"Elias got my memories back," she said. It wasn't a question. Somehow, he'd done something to return her memories. As she spoke, her eyes never left Breckett. "How?"

"Magnus."

Of course.

There was no bargaining with the Witch of the Woods to get her memories back. So, to free them from one of the most powerful witches on the continent, Elias must have sought out another magic wielder—one strong enough to simply *take* the memories from the witch.

"If I know anything about Elias, he would have given his freedom in exchange for Magnus' help to return your memories," Breckett said. "Magnus would have accepted nothing less. He'll likely be..." He swallowed. "Performing research."

Tears welled in her eyes, and the castle entryway's stone walls swirled around her as though she stood in the center of a tempest.

Something hard cracked against her knee, and she realized her legs had given out and she was kneeling on the stone floor. It felt as though a great weight had settled on her. Taking a single breath felt like an insurmountable impossibility. She brought a hand to her chest, pulling her leather jacket open. Her hands shook as she tried to loosen it.

"I... can't... breathe..." she managed between labored gasps.

The agony that had been flowing down the bond crescendoed. For a moment, she thought she could hear Elias' scream. The soundless cry pierced her thoughts like the fracturing of the night sky. It was ragged and infused with desperation.

"The bond." Breckett's voice echoed as though he spoke from down a distant corridor. "Whatever is happening to him, she feels it, too."

She clawed at her corset, desperate to get a full breath as her heart pounded. Her entire being felt as though it was entwined with his and submerged in flames. She could sense his emotions and the endless tides of agony. With sudden clarity, she knew Magnus was pushing Elias to the brink of what his body could withstand.

Please, she thought desperately. *Let it stop.*

How long would Magnus torture him? Surely, he knew Elias couldn't take it much longer. If he didn't stop, he'd kill him. Would that kill her, too? Did one mate die if the other perished? She had no idea.

But in that moment, it didn't matter.

All she knew was Elias' terror and pain, and her own desperation to protect him.

Tears fell onto the stones beneath her. Her shadows rippled, twisting and agitated, clawing at anything that drew near.

She had to do something. Her mate was in danger.

Shadows sunk barbed vines into the walls, sending pebbles clattering to the floor.

Suddenly, Jessamine and Cora were before her. Their lips moved, but she couldn't hear their words. Cora clutched one of her hands, but Arabella couldn't feel it. Her body was no longer in this castle. She was leagues away—trapped, tied down, and unable to run away as a sorcerer plunged something into Elias again and again.

A shriek pierced the air. The sound was like the tolling of broken bells.

The castle trembled as though it felt the agony interwoven into that cry.

It was then she realized the sound was coming from her.

More shadows erupted.

Inky blackness cascaded in the entryway, as wild and untamable as the forest itself. Chunks of stones fell from the walls and the ceiling.

Let all who walked upon the earth feel fear for what was being done to her mate. She would take down the sky itself to get him back.

She was the wild shadows.

She was the night, itself.

Something struck her face, *hard*.

Air spewed from her lungs as her teeth clacked together, and she tasted blood. Her shadows writhed, stunned, but they didn't yield. Something struck her across the opposite cheek, snapping her head in the other direction.

She managed to catch herself before her face collided with the ground.

As though a bubble had popped, the agony she'd been drowning in faded to the back of her mind.

It was still there. But her pain, her thoughts, were hers once more.

"Did you just hit me?" Arabella managed, spitting blood as her eyes narrowed on Brynne.

"You're welcome." Brynne dusted her hands, a vein ticking in her jaw. "Seemed the most efficient way to bring you back."

"I've never seen anything like that. The shadows... They were alive," Cora said from where she sat on the ground a few feet away.

When had Cora gotten on the ground? Arabella vaguely recalled Cora and Jessamine coming to kneel before her. Had Brynne pushed them out of the way to get to Arabella?

It was then she looked around.

Chunks of stones were scattered across the entryway. Some of the stones on the stairway had broken free, and sections of the railing were missing. Farther up, there were pebbles across the landing—the very same place Elias had pinned her down and nearly fucked her. That felt like an eternity ago.

With a sigh, she accepted Brynne's outstretched hand and rose to her feet.

At once, Brynne, Cora, and Jessamine surrounded Arabella, their hands on her shoulders. Their gazes felt like the warmth of morning sunshine in the heart of winter.

Her family. They were here. They were safe.

They hadn't abandoned her once they'd learned she'd fallen for a demon.

"We're going to get him back," Jessamine said, determination filling her eyes. "We won't stop until we do."

"You're not alone," Cora added.

"And you're no use to anyone dead or out of control," said Brynne, her tone matter-of-fact.

"I missed you all, too," Arabella said, new tears filling her eyes.

For several long moments, they just stood in the hallway.

If she let herself, she could pretend they were back in the Quarter, the headquarters and home of the enchantresses in Shadowbank, holding each other close after a long day of training.

So much had changed since Arabella had offered herself to the Devourer.

Now, she had two homes to protect.

"Do I want to know what that shadowy shit was?" Brynne asked as she, Jessamine, and Cora stood before her once more.

Awaiting orders.

Once, Arabella had been the second-in-command to the head enchantress. The enchantresses had looked to her for direction and obeyed her command. But even when she was no longer in

Shadowbank, these women prepared to follow her wherever she may lead.

It had something twisting in Arabella's chest.

"I'll explain about my magic later," she promised to Brynne and the others. Then she turned to Breckett, a thought occurring to her. "Vorkle and the other goblins. Where are they?"

Breckett crossed his arms. "Most left the moment Elias did. They know what comes next, even with the repaired ward."

Swallowing thickly, she managed a nod.

Elias would be tortured, and he could be forced to reveal that the goblins had been hiding in the castle.

Goblins were the only mortal beings who could portal from one location to another within the mortal and fae realms, even long distances. Over the centuries, they'd been hunted down for this gift. Most believed them to be extinct. But Elias had hidden a small group of goblins in his castle, using the ward to shield them from prying eyes.

"Are any of them still here?" Arabella asked.

When Breckett shrugged unhelpfully, she turned and strode down a nearby hallway that led toward the kitchens. If they were lucky, maybe one of the goblins would still be in the castle and could help them.

"Vorkle!" she shouted, calling for the goblin who'd helped her get the amplifier from the Witch of the Woods. The stone walls somehow both absorbed the sound and had her shout reverberating. "Vorkle! We need to talk." But even as the echoes of her words fell to silence, the goblin didn't appear.

She cursed before turning back to the others and saying, "Time to come up with a plan."

"The five of us can't face down Magnus and his army single-handed," Jessamine said.

"Yes," Arabella interrupted. "Got that."

She didn't dare ask the other enchantresses at Shadowbank for help—not when everyone was needed to protect the village if demons broke through the ward. Losing even one enchantress was a heavy toll on their defenses. It was bad enough that Jessamine, Cora, and Brynne were here with her.

She turned to Breckett, nodding to a knife sheathed at Breckett's side. "How many syphens does Magnus have?"

Syphens were magical blades created by the now-extinct shadow fae. New erox could be created—and controlled—through the power of these blades. Erox could also be killed with this blade by one swipe to the heart.

"Once, he had two syphens. Elias stole the first when he escaped. I have the second," Breckett said, his hand resting protectively on the blade at his hip.

Breckett had stolen one of the syphens that Magnus used to create many of the erox in his army. Before setting his sights on Elias, the sorcerer had been hunting down Breckett to get the blade back.

"He shouldn't have any," Breckett said, his tone wary. "Unless he found the one you dropped in the forest."

Arabella bit the inside of her cheek.

When she'd been desperate to protect Shadowbank, she'd stabbed Elias with his own syphen, stolen the amplifier, and fled the castle. She'd intended to give the amplifier to the enchantresses in Shadowbank so they could fix the failing ward before she'd return to the castle to fulfill her time as Elias' offering. Instead, she'd been captured by Magnus' ogres and lost the syphen in the woods during the fight.

Fear filled her at the idea that Magnus might have the syphen that created Elias and could force him to do anything with it.

She had to focus on the present—on what she *could* do.

"So, you're telling me that Magnus can't control his erox," Arabella said.

If the sorcerer didn't have either of the syphens, he couldn't *make* them do anything.

Breckett laughed humorlessly. "There are ways he can control erox without a syphen."

She tilted her head to the side, weighing his words. "Are there any erox who'd stand with us?"

Breckett shook his head. "None that would dare stand up to Magnus."

And face his wrath, he didn't need to add.

"Not without... encouragement," she said, her eyes snapping down to the syphen at Breckett's hip.

"No," Breckett said, his body angling away from her.

It was clear in the way he stood, body lowering into a defensive stance, that he wasn't sure he'd be able to get away from her even with his invisibility. While he was more powerful than the average magic wielder, she wasn't just any enchantress. Now, she was also a shadow whisperer.

One who'd caused stones to crumble with a mere thought.

Just what was she capable of?

"No one should have their free will taken from them," he said.

She took a step forward. "Magnus has my mate. I intend to take him back, and I will use any weapon at my disposal."

Somehow, she'd found her mate in this life. And she wasn't about to lose him. She didn't care if she had to single-handedly face down a sorcerer and his army.

There was nothing she wouldn't do for Elias.

She would burn down the world and cast it into shadow to get him back.

"Elias taught me that some demons can be good," she said, taking another step toward Breckett. "That demons aren't all enemies to mankind. But the way I see it..." She let her voice trail off, let Breckett see the severity in her gaze. "Anyone who stands between my mate and I is the enemy."

Breckett's eyes narrowed. "That makes you no better than Magnus."

"I'm nothing like him," she said. "I'll wield the syphen long enough to get Elias back. After that, they're free to go. I don't intend to demand eternal servitude—like Magnus."

While she didn't like the idea of taking anyone's free will from them, she would protect those she loved at all costs. If growing up in a village at the edge of civilization had taught her anything, it's that this world was a violent one. To survive meant to fight for every breath. And there was no protecting everyone. If she had to choose who to keep safe, she would always choose her family and Elias.

Which meant that Breckett and the other erox were a barrier in her way that needed to be removed.

Jessamine glanced between them. Then she angled toward the erox, hand on the hilt of her sword.

No matter what was happening, she would have Arabella's back.

Brynne and Cora did likewise, turning toward Breckett in a single motion.

Breckett glanced between the enchantresses before taking a step backward. "I won't let you have it."

Arabella raised a brow. "Are you telling me you'd rather protect the other erox than your friend? Some of those erox are murderers and rapists. You should know—you helped Elias rescue me from them."

For the first time, uncertainty filled Breckett's gaze, and he shook his head.

Shadows traveled up her legs, her sides, before trailing in circles in the palm of her hands. "I'll return the syphen once Elias is safe. You have my word."

Breckett's eyes flickered between hers and the hissing shadows in her palm. "Magnus will rue the thing he awakened in you."

She smiled. "I'm relying upon it."

Breckett winked out of existence.

For a moment, she considered what to do. But then she realized she didn't need to see him—not when his body's shadow remained when he'd become invisible. Bands of black wrapped around the blade and tore it free of its sheath. In an instant, the blade snapped through the air and landed in her hand.

Her home and her people would forever be her priority.

But now, so was Elias.

She would stop at nothing to protect him and get him back.

Breckett dropped his invisibility cloak. His eyes narrowed as he stood with tensed muscles, ready to move. Likewise, Jessamine, Cora, and Brynne all lowered their stances, prepared to attack at her word.

Four magic wielders, all poised to strike.

The erox was outmatched, and he knew it.

With a flick of her fingers, she sheathed the syphen at her side before turning from him. Her shadows moved around her shoulders as she strode toward the castle's front doors, flanked by the three enchantresses.

"It won't be enough," Breckett called from behind her. "Have you forgotten about the ogres, gargoyles, and other creatures that follow Magnus? What of the erox who were created with Elias' syphen?"

For a moment, she hesitated, her hand on the door's cool metal handle.

He was right.

This syphen was a start, but it wasn't going to be enough.

Something dark moved through her thoughts, sharpening her anger. It felt like a flower made of blades bloomed in her chest. For a moment, she wondered if this was another effect of her new shadow magic. It was unlike anything she'd experienced before, but she let it fill her. Let the anger strengthen her.

Throwing the doors wide, she walked out into the cool autumn air.

The castle was nestled deep within a mountainous forest and had a small clearing around it on three sides and a lake on the other. A translucent gray ward sprouted from the earth and encased them in mist, forming a barrier between the castle and the dark forest beyond it—and the demons that never ceased searching for their next prey.

Without the collar suppressing her magic, she could see the ward clearly. The color was so unlike the purple-blue hue of the ward surrounding Shadowbank. Whoever created this one had not used earth magic.

She made it only a few steps beyond the castle doors before pain sliced through her.

The suddenness of it stole her breath away. It felt like an earthquake had caused a fissure in her very being, fracturing all that she was and engulfing her in agony.

Her vision blurred, and she could no longer see the castle grounds before her or the trees beyond them.

Knees buckling, she collapsed onto the ground, eyelids shuttering.

Before blackness took her, one name lingered in her thoughts.

Elias.

Then she succumbed to the torrent and knew no more.

Chapter Two
ARABELLA

Arabella floated in a fathomless darkness before her feet touched down.

There was no ground beneath her or anything to indicate there was any substance in this place. But she was able to stand on her own.

Where am I?

She glanced around into an endless void.

There was nothing in any direction. No people, no buildings, no land. In the darkness, there was a deeper black, branching all around like creeping, leafless vines with large, protruding thorns.

Glancing down, she studied her hands, which glowed faintly with a gray-white light. She realized it wasn't just her hands that glowed. It was all of her skin that appeared above her leathers.

How strange.

She wondered just how she'd gotten here. Last she knew, she'd been standing outside the castle before pain struck her.

Had Breckett struck her down when her back had been turned? Even with the others guarding her back, she'd been foolish enough to turn from him when he was furious. Did he have some secret power he'd been hiding from her and used it when she'd taken the syphen from him? Or had it been something else?

Another thought struck her.

Was Elias being tortured again? Did she black out from experiencing his pain? If that had been the reason for her passing out, she needed to learn how to separate the sensations and feelings of her mate from her own. Or else, she'd risk fainting at any moment. If she blacked out in the middle of her journey through the forest when they left the castle, she'd be demon fodder. But she wouldn't remain in the castle for any longer than she had to. The moment she was conscious again, she'd set a course for Elias.

It didn't matter if she was outnumbered by Magnus' army even with the help of the syphen. Facing Magnus was still worth the risk.

She couldn't do *nothing*.

Suddenly, a gray-blue light shimmered on in the distance. It wasn't a true horizon, as there was no true beginning and end to the darkness. But far away, the light shimmered as it descended before disappearing.

She began to raise her arm to wave but hesitated.

Whatever it was could be an enemy—some monster seeking to consume her soul. It could also be her ticket out of here. Maybe it was someone who knew what this place was and how to get out. More likely, it was just some phantom in a dream she'd soon wake up from.

The light was gone as quickly as it had appeared.

Sighing, she tugged her braid, wondering what to do next.

Was this just a dream, and she simply needed to wait until she woke up? Or had Magnus summoned her here, and this was some strange place between realms where he could take her out? She wasn't sure whether the sorcerer was possessive enough of Elias that he would go out of his way to take her out just to ensure he'd have Elias forever.

Casting her thoughts out, she allowed her senses to spread into the endless dark. Doing so had become instinctual. As a magic wielder, she could sense when another being with magic was nearby. When her mind scraped against something, she started. She hadn't expected to actually sense anything in this place.

There was something—or someone—out there that possessed magic.

It wasn't alive, exactly. But it wasn't *nothing*. It was like some dark vortex lurked somewhere just beyond her sight.

Suddenly, a second presence blossomed behind her. Then desire swirled through her so strongly that her breath hitched.

The world stilled as the tugging in her chest—the one that she'd felt since the moment her memories returned—went slack. She breathed a sigh of relief at the lack of pressure, which was replaced by an urgency to *move*.

Again, lust swam through her, so thick it was hard to think straight.

She'd only felt this type of carnal attraction with one demon.

Arms wrapped around her middle, enfolding her in a larger body that smelled of citrus and pine.

"Elias?"

The word escaped her lips, sounding like a prayer.

For a moment, it was all she could do to breathe, to remain standing and not fall to her knees.

Some part of her had wondered if she'd ever feel this attraction again.

This was an illusion, a conjuring of her mind, surely.

Glancing down, she watched as one of those muscled arms skirted up until a hand wrapped around her throat, tightening. Her mind swam in just the way she liked, and she leaned back into strong shoulders, eyelids fluttering closed.

She realized she didn't care if this was an illusion so long as it didn't stop.

His other hand skirted lower until it was between her legs. A single finger ran over her pussy, and quite suddenly the feel of clothes against her skin was too much. She needed to feel his skin against hers, to feel his body everywhere—wrapping her in his warmth.

Then the arms turned her so she faced him, and her breath hitched.

The illusion looked just like Elias.

Dark curls fell to his shoulders, and a thick beard covered his handsome, angular face. Eyes with widening pupils soaked her in. It was as though she was the light of day in deep, fathomless space.

Like his arms, his thighs were thick with muscle. His light brown skin was as smooth and rich as she remembered it. But as her eyes roamed over him, she thought she saw slashes along his arms. Before she could truly look, his hands were at her corset, untying the laces.

Distantly, her mind registered how unlike him this was. In the past, he'd used his magic to undress her. Why wouldn't he do that now?

But his fingers moved swiftly. In moments, her corset was undone, and he pulled her undershirt down. Cool air kissed her breasts, and she longed to have him squeeze them until it hurt, until she screamed his name and begged him to stop.

This could be a trap, some distant part of her thought. But after everything that had happened with Magnus, the Witch of the Woods, and losing her memories, she wanted a moment to pretend Elias hadn't sacrificed himself for her. That he wasn't out of her reach and being tortured by a sadistic sorcerer. She wanted to allow herself to believe that he was here, with her. That they had all the time in the world to explore each other and learn just what it meant to be mates.

Soon, all worries faded to the back of her thoughts as she let herself be swept up in the dream.

She wanted this mirage to ravage her. To fuck her until there was nothing left so that when she awoke, she wouldn't have to feel the chasm that had opened in her chest the moment she'd realized he was gone.

"Please," she begged, uncaring of the desperation in her voice. "Take me. Take all of me."

A snarl escaped his lips before he tore the rest of her shirt away, pulling her free of the rest of her leathers until she was utterly naked before him.

He guided her until she was lying in the darkness. It didn't feel like cold, hard ground. Instead, it was soft as the clouds of night.

The phantom Elias tore his shirt and tossed the fabric aside. Had there been streaks of blood on it? But she wasn't thinking straight, couldn't focus on anything but the male before her—or the mirage of him.

Something buzzed in her chest at his nearness. It was as though something in her came alive, and she wanted to lose herself in the feeling.

He lowered himself between her legs until he knelt.

Rather than running his tongue over the length of her, he trailed kisses along her inner thigh—moving slowly from her knee to her hip. Then he moved to her other leg and did the same. Only, as he drew closer to her hip, his soft kisses turned to licking and nipping. She craved him even as she felt him, needing him to drive into her.

He stopped, and his eyes fixed on her. She felt his warm exhale on her clit, and she bit back a whimper. His lips moved, but no sound emerged. Then he leaned down and licked her from her pussy up to her clit.

Grasping at the darkness around her, her fingers slipped through the shadows as a moan escaped her lips.

Again, she watched his lips move as he stared longingly at her pussy. Like if he looked away, even for a moment, she would disappear.

As though he didn't think any of this was real either.

She opened her mouth to speak, but then he was moving. He turned his body around so that he kneeled over her—his cock above her mouth and his mouth over her pussy.

Oh *fuck*.

He wanted to eat her out while fucking her mouth.

She felt herself grow wet with desire, instantly ready for him. Ready for anything he gave her. At that moment, she'd say yes to anything he asked.

She needed him more than she needed her next breath.

Then he descended on her.

Opening her mouth, she took in his wide cock, grabbing him around the base. She worked her hand in time with her mouth's movement along his shaft. As she did, his tongue glanced against her clit in a single flick. Slowly. As though to tease her. Then he was moving, giving her the pressure she craved as he licked in the long up-and-down motions she loved so much.

Their desire entwined in the quiet darkness.

Neither stopped moving, eager to please as much as receive. It was as if this mirage actually wanted her.

His cock pressed deep into her throat, pulsing and hardening further as he moved. She could feel veins bulging and tasted the faint saltiness of his precum. His hips moved as though he were desperate for more of her. To plunge into her until he found her center, and they were no longer two separate bodies but a single soul—intertwining, bonding, *mating*.

Her hips began moving of their own accord, thrusting against his mouth, eager for even more pressure. His tongue focused on her clit, and her entire body hummed. But she longed to be filled, and not by his tongue or fingers. She wanted him to fuck her until she forgot her name.

Breaths ragged, her moans against his cock turned into whimpers as her pleasure arced. She wasn't going to last much longer. And neither was he by the way his hips hitched as he fucked her mouth.

Suddenly, his body went taut as a bowstring. He froze, his cock deep in her throat. But he didn't come. It was as though he was trying to keep from falling over the edge, to stretch out this moment. His chest heaved as he gasped.

Then he was moving again, fucking her mouth in vicious strokes. It was all she could do to take everything he was giving her. He fell upon her pussy once more, ravishing her as though he were a starving man.

Then she was coming undone.

Delicious pressure blossomed from her core, spreading out as waves of pleasure crashed over her. He thrust into her mouth—once, twice, three times—and he was coming. Warmth splashed in the back of her throat, and she swallowed him down, enjoying the feel of his body trembling with pleasure. Enjoying that she could give him this release.

If this really was Elias, she thought, *he'd have consumed my essence when I came.*

But this wasn't her erox.

It was merely some strange dream she'd found herself in. Though her orgasm felt far more real than any ordinary dream.

He pulled out of her mouth.

Some part of her had prepared herself for this Elias to rise and leave—perhaps to dissipate into the darkness now that this part of the dream had finished. Instead of getting up or disappearing, he rotated his body so that he kneeled between her legs once more. Then he leaned down and pressed kiss after hungry kiss on her neck.

He just came.

Surely, this phantom was sated.

As she blinked back the remnants of her pleasure, she glanced down.

His cock was hard. Fuck. He wanted her—again.

His hand enclosed around her neck as he sucked and nipped down her chest. He pulled one of her nipples into his mouth, and she cried out, back arching.

Instantly, she was ready to go again. She was far from done with him.

She'd never get enough of him.

Even as she had the thought, the humming in her chest swelled.

His hand was on his cock as he notched himself before her entrance. All the while, he didn't release her neck.

His mouth moved, and she thought he might have formed the words, "You're mine." But any response she might have made escaped her as he thrust.

Pleasure cascaded through her at that first connection.

She never wanted this moment to end. She wanted to feel him like this, buried inside her—their bodies entwined—forever.

He was hers. Her mate.

Then he fucked her with abandon. She felt every inch of him as he plunged into her. Her pussy clenched around him as though to hold him there. But he never stopped moving, claiming her with every stroke.

Leaning down, he pressed his lips to hers while increasing the pressure on her neck. Mind swimming, she opened her mouth to him—submitting to him fully.

Never in her life had she wanted to give control to anyone else, to relinquish the power she had over herself. This demon had stolen her heart, and all she wanted now was the chance to have him back—to tell him how she felt and hope he felt the same for her.

His thrusts slowed, and his tongue arced across her mouth.

She was a breath away from coming again as pleasure tightened her core.

His eyes flashed with blue flames, and she could sense the unfettered hunger in them. When he was about to feed, his brown eyes changed and glowed a brilliant blue—the color of the essence he could wield at will.

Reaching up, she laced her fingers into his hair as he thrust into her with those vicious, claiming strokes.

A single tear fell from his eyes.

She watched it trail down his cheek before plopping onto her lower lip. Slowly, she licked, tasting the saltiness.

This is too real.

A second tear slid down his cheek, and her chest squeezed at the sight.

Not releasing her neck, his thrusts slowed until he sat upright. Their bodies were still joined, but he looked down. His eyes soaked in the sight of her like this was the last time he'd ever see her.

On instinct, she wrapped her legs around his back, pulling him back down so that he was on his hands and knees above her, his cock sheathed inside her.

He was just a phantom.

None of this was real.

But she needed him to be well—even in this place.

"Use me," she said, desperate to eradicate the desolation in his gaze. "Sate your hunger."

His blue irises shrunk as his pupils swelled. While she could still sense his despair, she could also feel his desire—his *need* for her.

Then he descended upon her.

He thrust into her with everything he had, his cock filling her, spreading her. She felt him harden even more, feeling like she was about to burst. And damn her, she wanted to be filled with his release.

She pulled his lips to hers, kissing him, inviting him in.

His lips glanced against hers as though he were uncertain of what to do next. As though he hadn't claimed her many times before. But then his kisses grew as hungry and feverish as his thrusts, and she allowed herself to fall into his touch, feeling every bit of his desire.

Starlight burst inside of her, and she cried out.

As she came, something inside her hitched, as though a chord in her chest had been strummed. If she was his instrument, let him play her—in any way he liked.

Essence flowed from her chest, up her throat, and into her

mouth until it flooded out of her. He sucked, drinking in the blue wisps. As he did, another orgasm rocketed through her.

As the phantom fed on her desires, he continued thrusting into her until his movements became jerky, desperate. Then he was coming undone.

The expression on his face was both pain and pleasure, misery and ecstasy. It was a male preparing to fall into the deep—and never return.

Tears streamed down his cheeks as his eyes fixed on hers, his lips moving.

Heart drumming, she opened her mouth to speak. But he'd pulled out of her and was on his feet. Somehow, he was fully dressed once more.

Glancing down, she noted that there were long slashes in his shirt, which had traces of blood. Then her eyes found his tear-streaked face, which mirrored the anguish flooding her chest.

"Wait!" she called out, finally finding her voice.

But he was gone, leaving her alone in the dark landscape.

For a long moment, she remained where she was, utterly still.

If this was just a dream, why did it feel so real?

Chapter Three

ARABELLA

A force collided with what Arabella thought was her face. Her body felt distant as she swirled between dreams and waking. There was a distinct throbbing in her jaw. The pain had the hushed voices around her solidifying into words. But no matter what she did, her eyes remained firmly shut.

"If you hit her again, Brynne, I swear I will punch you in the face."

It was Jessamine's voice. It sounded both nearby and like it echoed across a great hall.

"What's wrong with her?" came Cora's voice. "Could it be Elias again?"

Arabella tried to open her eyes again, tried to speak, but her body felt foreign to her. It was as though—in that place of endless darkness—she'd shirked her flesh. And now that she was forced to don her skin, muscles, and bones once more, everything felt unwieldy.

It was all just a dream, she realized. *None of it was real.*

Why did that thought hurt so much?

Her head throbbed even as hunger burned in her gut. As her stomach rumbled loudly, the enchantresses fell quiet.

"Are you fucking with me, Arabella? Did you really just pass out from *hunger*?" Jessamine's voice was closer now, just above her. Fingers pressed against her forehead.

Why did it feel like Elias just fed on her? When he'd taken too much of Arabella's essence in the past, he'd given her snacks and told her to rest. She'd quickly learned that being with an erox meant she needed to eat more to keep up her strength.

But Elias was in Magnus' camp. There was no way he could have fed on her. She could feel the tugging in her chest, pulling her toward the forest and wherever Magnus' army hid their encampment.

Even still, the hunger in her gut felt all too real.

After several more attempts, she managed to open her eyes.

Blinking, the first thing she noticed was that she was lying on the ground outside the main doors to the castle. There was a grassy clearing with a path to the stables in one direction and the gardens in the other. A few hundred feet beyond both, the forest loomed, enclosing the clearing with dark, branching fingers.

Jessamine and Cora knelt on either side of Arabella while Brynne stood a few feet away with one hand resting too casually on the hilt of her sword and positioned her body toward the castle doors.

"I *am* hungry," Arabella admitted, her mouth feeling strangely dry. For a moment, she thought she noted a lingering scent of citrus and pine on her skin.

Cora helped her to a seated position and passed her a piece of bread. "Have this."

Arabella bit into it. "Breckett...?"

She doubted the erox was the reason she'd blacked out, especially after Jessamine's reaction. If he'd attacked, the enchantresses would have had him trussed up, or they'd be in pursuit if he'd fled.

Jessamine shook her head.

Fuck.

If Breckett hadn't knocked her unconscious, that meant there were yet more unanswered questions.

Tentatively, she felt down the bond.

Compared to before, it was strangely quiet on the other end. She couldn't sense pain or any strong emotions. Had Elias passed out? Some part of her hoped that he was unconscious if only to give him a respite from whatever Magnus was doing to him.

She took another bite of bread, not bothering to stand from where she sat in the grass.

"Will you use it?" Jessamine asked, nodding to where Arabella had sheathed the syphen.

There was no accusation or disapproval in Jessamine's gaze.

Like Arabella, Jessamine had been forced to make hard decisions in Shadowbank. Sometimes, saving loved ones meant hurting—or not protecting—someone else's loved ones. There was so much gray in survival.

"Maybe," Arabella said, chewing.

Once, she'd thought Elias was an enemy for the simple fact that he was a demon. But he'd shown her that actions were what made someone.

Some of the erox in Magnus' army were far from innocent. A few had tried to kill her when she'd been a captive in Magnus' camp—to rape her and consume her essence until there was nothing left. It was possible some of them hadn't wanted to be turned. Some could be in the army against their will.

But there was no way of separating the good from the bad.

Until Elias was safe from Magnus, these other erox weren't her priority. She'd protect her mate, and then she'd free them. She wouldn't become like Magnus and use the males against their wills for longer than it took to rescue Elias. But she wouldn't hesitate to use everything—and everyone—at her disposal to protect her mate.

However, to find their way out of the forest, they needed Breckett.

Elias had stepped between shadows when he'd brought her to his castle in the forest, and he'd done the same for the other enchantresses. While she estimated Shadowbank was within a day's ride, they had no way of knowing which direction the village was.

Damn her for not thinking of that earlier.

She didn't regret taking the syphen, but she also knew she owed Breckett an apology. If a blade could take free will from her or those she loved at a moment's notice, she'd be possessive of it, too.

For the first time, she wondered whether Magnus had turned Breckett with this particular syphen or if Breckett had been made with Elias' syphen.

Swallowing the last of her food, Arabella said, "I don't like how close Magnus' army is to Shadowbank." She ran a hand over her hair. "Maybe the head enchantress will have some ideas on how to take down a sorcerer."

When Elias had gone to Shadowbank for help to get Arabella's memories back, he'd given the head enchantress the amplifier—and whatever power remained within it to strengthen the village's failing ward. It had been that very magical artifact that had caused her so much trouble. It was why she'd bargained away her memories to the Witch of the Woods—in hopes of saving both the goblins who hid within Elias' castle and the humans who took refuge in the village at the edge of the world.

Arabella hoped the head enchantress, the woman who'd been like a mother to her, would have some guidance.

As Arabella rose to her feet, she noted a flash of movement in the line of trees in the distance. It was beyond the gardens—to the right, near the lake.

Squinting, she tried to make out whatever had caught her attention. But the line of trees was distant. It could be a trick of the shadows. Stranger things had already happened that day.

But there was another flicker of movement as though the deeper shadows stirred.

On instinct, her feet were moving.

Something was beyond the ward. Could it be another

alabaster, a type of demon that fed on sexual shame? She didn't have Elias to save her this time if it sucked her into its clutches.

Or had the worst happened—had Magnus found them? Had he tortured Elias until he revealed the castle's location? No. Elias wouldn't have broken so quickly.

As she neared the line of trees, her shadows bloomed beneath her until they were thrice her size. Then they surfaced from the earth like colorless vines sprouting from liquid black. Veined with darkness, they curled around her feet, moving in twisting waves as she walked.

The shadows had changed since she used the amplifier before she'd been captured by Magnus. It was like the artifact had unlocked something in her—unleashing the shadows from whatever had tethered them. Then they had changed again when her memories had returned. They were stronger now and far more wild, as though they had a will of their own. They responded to her baser emotions—fear and anger—and were eager to serve.

Instead of reaching for the shadows, she sought the earth's magic. Outside the forest, the earth held a golden hue of light as though infused with sunshine. It was the power of growing things and new life, which was so unlike the shadows. However, in the demons' territory, the earth held a darker hue. The natural magic within the land had been corrupted. Pulling several strands of the sticky earthen magic into her, she wove them together, prepared to lash out at whatever might move in the dark beyond the ward.

Something moved in the trees to her left, and she spun toward it.

Jessamine and Cora were at her heels and mirrored her movements, blades drawn. Where had Brynne gone?

"There's more than one," Jessamine said, voice low.

Arabella's eyes narrowed as she scanned the trees.

Suddenly, a sound like an explosion beneath water sounded from her right.

Turning, she saw the very thing she'd feared.

An ogre the size of a two-story building had emerged from the forest and slammed a fist into the ward.

For a moment, she was back in Shadowbank on the day the soulless had broken through Shadowbank's ward. The same day she'd gone with Nemera to rescue Rowan on the road beside the forest. A horde of the soulless had appeared and chased them back to Shadowbank. The demons had climbed over each other like insects to get into the village, uncaring of their burning bones as they touched the magical barrier. It had bent inward before tearing—and the demons poured in.

She was jerked back to the present as the castle's ward stretched. It thinned out where the ogre's fist had connected with the magic. The color leached from that section. For a moment, the ward appeared as little more than a thin film of water. Waves rippled in every direction, making the dome appear to shiver.

"Fuck," Jessamine hissed at her side.

They found us.

That one thought kept circling through Arabella's mind even as fear laced her veins. Magnus had taken Elias, and now he'd come to claim the syphen Breckett had stolen—and likely to kill her for all the trouble she'd caused him.

"They can't see us," Cora whispered, her two short swords drawn. Uncertainty laced every syllable. "Breckett said this ward keeps them from seeing the castle."

"Yeah, and it's also supposed to turn you around the moment you attempt to approach it," Brynne hissed, coming to stand beside them. "Either the magic doesn't work on ogres, or they figured out how to get past it." She pressed something into Arabella's hands.

Glancing down, Arabella's eyes widened. "Where did you get my swords?"

She hadn't had her blades since she'd left Shadowbank and gave herself to Elias as his next offering.

"Brought them with," Brynne said. "When Elias came to get us from Shadowbank." She removed a few of the smaller blades stashed in her jacket before sheathing them in some of Arabella's empty ones.

"Thank you," Arabella managed, sudden emotion tightening her throat.

They weren't as heavily armed as they'd normally be. But at least they now all had their swords and some daggers and throwing knives.

Brynne nodded. "How much time do we have?"

Footsteps sounded from around the bend in the castle. Moments later, Breckett appeared, moving so fast as he turned a corner that he slid and nearly fell. But he managed to remain upright as he ran toward them.

"Ogres!" he called. "Dozens of them just beyond the ward."

Arabella tilted her head back, closing her eyes as she rubbed the bridge of her nose.

She, Jessamine, Cora, and Brynne were some of the strongest warriors in all of Shadowbank, but they'd be no match for *dozens* of ogres—especially if they were a similar size to the monstrosity several dozen feet away, which landed another blow on the rapidly thinning section of the ward.

"Can you repair the ward?" Arabella gestured to the rippling dome. "Or strengthen it?"

Breckett eyed her incredulously. "Even if I had an amplifier, I can't wield essence. Only Elias can."

Not all erox had special abilities. For those who did, their gifts were as unique as each demon. Breckett could turn himself and anyone he touched invisible, which came in handy when trying to escape an adversary without being detected...

A thought struck her.

"Have the goblins returned?" she asked.

At best, they had minutes until the ogres broke through. She thought she heard more pounding in the distance, and she wondered if other ogres were trying to break through different sections of the ward.

"No," Breckett said simply. "They're gone, and they're not coming back."

Mind racing, she thought through their options.

They couldn't portal out of the castle grounds without the goblins' help.

There were only five of them; so, they didn't stand a chance of battling more than a few ogres head-on. They could try to sneak through the forest and hope that Magnus' army didn't catch them. That hadn't worked so well for her last time.

They couldn't travel by horse while utilizing Breckett's invisibility, and travel would be slow if they were on foot. If they were forced to run through the forest, they'd be far more vulnerable to not just being discovered by any creatures Magnus sent after them but to any demon with the ability to sense life around them.

Neither Breckett nor the enchantresses were as strong as Elias in sheer magical ability. Thus, their mere presence wouldn't deter the demons from approaching. The moment they stopped to rest, they'd be fucked.

Even as her mind raced, something blossomed in her senses. Glancing around, there was nothing there. Though perhaps the shadows were somewhat... darker. Belatedly, it struck her that it felt like the presence from her dream.

"What's your call?" Jessamine asked, her eyes never leaving the ogre nearest them as another boom rippled through the clearing and the ward bent dangerously inward.

"We run," Arabella said, turning to Breckett. "Can you shield all of us?"

Slowly, he nodded. "I've never shielded so many at once. I don't know how long I'll be able to hold it." After a moment, he added, "There will be a price, of course."

Arabella waved a hand. They didn't have time to argue over the syphen now. "Keep us hidden long enough to get past the—"

Before she could finish the sentence, there was a tearing sound before a monstrous bellow shook the air.

Her shadows hissed, forming into thorny vines as black as midnight.

The darkness was eager to fight.

An ogre the size of the House of Obscurities pushed through a tear in the ward near the lake a few hundred yards away. One of the tusks extending from its too-wide mouth was broken off. It glanced around, taking in the castle and clearing. Then its gaze swiveled toward them. A single eye narrowed as its lips peeled back, revealing several rows of razor-sharp teeth. Then a roar rent the air, and it charged toward them. As it moved, the ground shook. Loose pebbles bounced along the path near them.

"Breckett, get them out of here," Arabella said as she loosed several bolts of her earthen weaves at the ogre with the precision of a crossbow. "I'll buy you time."

"Fuck that," Jessamine snapped as she loosed her own golden weaves, which punched through one of the ogre's shoulders. The creature stumbled to the ground, dark blood leaking onto the earth.

Too quickly, it got back onto its feet, running toward them once more—uncaring of the blood trailing down its body.

"There isn't time to argue," Arabella shouted. "Get out of here now!"

The creature was two stories tall and had to weigh more than ten carriages stacked on top of each other. She wove as fast as she could and loosed bolt after bolt of her earthen magic. But the magic barely slowed it. It didn't even flinch as a weave sliced down its arm. She didn't hesitate as she formed more weaves, glaring at the creatures that were doing their damndest to block out the morning sun from the sky.

She spotted more ogres pacing through the forest beyond the ward, likely trying to find the tear or some way to get in. There had to be at least a dozen of them.

There was no way they could get past so many. Not unless they bought themselves enough time to slip away without being detected.

We are so fucked—

A hand enclosed around Arabella's arm, hauling her back.

"Quit daydreaming," Brynne hissed as Arabella released several bolts of magic at the ogre in front of her. "Or you're going to get us all killed."

It roared and brought down a fist toward them.

"Heads up," Cora shouted in her lilting voice as she formed a shield of earthen magic above them.

Jessamine was beside Cora in an instant, arms waving above her head as she reinforced Cora's shield with her magic.

It shattered upon impact, sending the weaves in every direction before sinking back into the earth. The ogre wailed, clutching its broken hand and stumbling backward.

Arabella's thoughts raced.

Brynne was right. She needed to come to a decision. Now wasn't the time for hesitation.

An idea blossomed in her mind.

"Breckett," Arabella said, spinning toward him. "We're going to fix the tears."

He stared at her dumbly for a moment. "I already told you, I can't repair the ward—"

"Not you," she interrupted, glancing down at her shadows. "My enchantress magic isn't compatible with the ward, but my shadow magic might be. And you're going to shield me. I can't fight the ogres and repair it at the same time."

There were many different types of magic in this world. And she'd learned from her time repairing Shadowbank's ward that a wielder had to use the same magic that created a ward to repair it. If Elias had dark magic from being a demon and he'd repaired the ward before, perhaps her shadow magic would be able to form a patch over the tear.

"Keep the ogres distracted," she shouted to the enchantresses as she reached for Breckett's hand, which he held out to her begrudgingly as though accepting soiled undergarments. "We'll be back soon."

Ears popping, the world blurred as though she stared through a pane of glass. It was one of the side effects of Breckett cloaking her with his invisibility.

The ogre charged again.

Gripping his fingers, she ran forward, ducking beneath the ogre's arm as it swung a meaty fist toward them. Skidding beside her, Breckett nearly fell. But there wasn't time for any hesitation or mistakes. She leaped forward and slid beneath its legs, dragging the erox behind her.

"Keep up," she hissed, careful to keep her voice low.

The male was moving like an infant.

"I am," he bit back as the ogre moved toward the enchantresses.

Jessamine and the others could handle one ogre, but if more came through the tear, they'd be overwhelmed if they didn't get to higher ground.

I can't worry about them now, she thought. She had to focus on fixing the ward.

She and Breckett got off the path and moved through the gardens toward the lake. As they crouched low, she heard Breckett's labored breaths.

"Are you winded?"

"Of course not."

She raised an eyebrow.

Relief flooded her as they came to the tear.

At least for now, there weren't any more ogres in sight. They must be in the forest somewhere or hadn't discovered the castle yet. She wasn't about to second-guess their luck.

She turned her gaze down to the shadow vines at her feet, which had returned to a translucent-like state when Breckett had touched her.

Exhaling, she shifted Breckett's hand to her shoulder, and he didn't object as he tried—and failed—to cover his gasping breaths.

Closing her eyes, she reached for the shadows.

Instinctively, she lifted her arms and spread her fingers out to summon the shadows from the ground, similar to what she did with earthen magic. Inky black licked up her body, twisting around her legs, abdomen, and up her arms until they writhed in her palms.

For a moment, she paused, staring at them. More shadows twisted up her body. It felt like a river's current flowed all around her.

Then she willed the chaos into weaves.

The shadows hissed, fighting as she tried to form them into long strands and pull them together into a patch as she'd done so many times before on Shadowbank's ward with her earthen magic. Immediately, sweat beaded on her brow as she felt what she could only describe as *resistance*.

The dark had a will of its own. Shadows couldn't be tamed.

A sudden realization struck her, and an icy fear filled her chest.

If she couldn't manage to repair the tears, then her friends would be putting themselves in danger for nothing. This would be a colossal waste of time when they could have fled on foot into the forest immediately.

They were relying on her to help them. She wouldn't leave them to die pointless deaths. Or worse, be taken prisoner by Magnus.

But she was so woefully undertrained in her shadow magic.

The time she'd spent working with Lucinda, a former apprentice of the Witch of the Woods, in Shadowbank seemed so long ago. It felt like another lifetime. It was before her powers had been unleashed, and she had so much she still needed to learn.

And no one to teach her.

Again, she tried to will her shadows to plait together. The vines writhed around her arms, and she felt the stinging kiss of the thorns puncturing her skin.

"Tell me you're doing something," Breckett hissed.

Frustration swelled in her chest and a growl escaped her lips. "I'm trying."

"Try harder," he said, voice low as he glanced around.

Beyond the tear in the ward, she thought she heard rumbling footsteps.

Sweat poured down the sides of her face as she moved her arms in a sweeping motion, forcing bands of shadow, one by one, into the air. It was like trying to force a tornado in another direction or to contain the power of the oceans with her bare hands. As the shadows slowly acquiesced to her will, she tasted blood, belatedly realizing her nose was bleeding. But she ignored it along with a dizziness forming in her vision.

The shadows formed a crisscross patch that she slowly brought up to the tear in the ward that was nearly two stories in height.

Just then, an ogre emerged from the trees.

It didn't look at them, unable to see them through Breckett's invisibility cloak. But it marched with purpose toward the castle and through the tear—and directly into her shadow weaves. They stuck to its cheek like a spiderweb, the thorns clinging to its flesh.

The ogre roared, its arms waving.

The shadows seemed to grip tighter as the creature's fingers tore at its own flesh in its desperation to free itself from her weaves.

"Did you mean to do that?" Breckett asked as they watched in horror as the shadow vines began creeping up the ogre's face. In agonizing slowness, the vines plunged into the creature's eye. Blood spurted everywhere before the ogre fell to its knees with a loud crash and then collapsed onto the ground, unmoving.

The dark weaves dissipated before the shadows at her feet grew thrice as dark as they should be.

She swallowed thickly. "No."

"Remind me not to piss you off," he muttered.

"Too late," she said, careful not to look at what remained of the ogre's head and swallowing back bile.

He cleared his throat. "Now what?"

"We try again." She wiped back the remnants of blood beneath her nose with the back of a sleeve.

There was no other choice. Not for her. Not when it came to her family.

Before she could summon the shadows, two more ogres appeared before the tear in the ward, their single eyes narrowing—as though they could sense her and the erox behind his cloak of invisibility.

Slowly, she sought out the darkness beneath her feet, coaxing it out of the ground. The shadows resisted her at first, feeling like they were vexed with her. When they slowly acquiesced and extended out around her, she realized the ogres weren't looking at her but something behind her. Breckett must have realized it at the same time because they turned around together, careful to keep a point of connection between them.

What she saw took her breath away.

A fae warrior with wings the color of midnight descended from the sky, ripping through the daylight and bringing starlight upon the land. Power thickened the air, leaving a faint humming on the wind. The ward opened willingly for him as he flew down. His wings stretched out on either side of him and were twice his massive height. He landed on the ground behind her with unmatched grace, a sword in a fist. It was then she noticed a faint shimmer of colors on what she'd initially thought was pitch-black wings of countless feathers.

When he looked up, his eyes weren't the deep brown she'd expected but glowed a dark blue.

The color of the Twilight Court.

"Prince Hadeon," she said as she released Breckett's hand. The invisibility cloak fell from them as her vision cleared. "What are you—"

Before she could finish, the fae swept his arm forward, and the ogres that had pushed through the opening in the ward instantly evaporated. There was a trail of dark blue dust in the air, and then... nothing.

As though they had never existed.

In another sweep of his arms, there was a plume of blue magic that stretched out into the air and latched on to the tear in the ward. Slowly, the magic pulled the sides of the tear inward before the ward slowly started mending itself back together.

Belatedly, she closed her gaping mouth.

So much power.

She knew the fae were powerful, and from their brief interactions in the Twilight Court, she knew Hadeon was especially so. But it was one thing to sense a wielder's ability and another to see it before her eyes.

The prince lowered his arm, and his eyes fastened on hers, shimmering faintly as though laced with starlight.

"You have ogres on your doorstep."

Chapter Four
ARABELLA

Arabella rolled her eyes at the fae prince. "Oh really? I hadn't noticed."

The body of the ogre she'd killed lay lifeless on the ground a few feet away from them, minus half its head. Dark blood pooled in the grass. The strange blue dust that had been the other two ogres hovered in the air before being swept away over the lake in a gust of wind.

Hadeon raised a brow, studying her with his midnight-blue eyes.

The fae prince had olive skin, short black hair, and his face was clean shaven. He was taller than Arabella, and his wingspan was wider than his height. His physical presence was nearly overwhelming at the size of him, let alone the assault on her senses as she felt the sheer power of his magic.

"What are you doing here?" she asked as she spared a glance toward the castle where she'd last seen the other enchantresses.

They were nowhere in sight.

Please be okay, she thought.

"I've come for my favor," Hadeon said, interrupting her thoughts.

A second tugging in her chest thrummed to life at the

mention of their deal. It was quite unlike the one she felt from the mating bond with Elias.

When she and Elias had gone to the Twilight Court for the ball celebrating the queen's birthday, they had asked the queen for an amplifier. She had refused when Elias had declined to turn her into an erox. To their surprise, Hadeon—the fifth son of the queen—had sought them out and offered an amplifier in exchange for a favor. Unfortunately, Arabella had lost that amplifier to Magnus when she'd been captured by his ogres.

"It's kind of a bad time," she managed over the incessant tugging in her chest. She didn't have time to be fulfilling a favor right now. "In case you hadn't noticed, we're a bit... occupied."

Frowning, he sniffed the air, his chin lifting as a look of confusion crossed his handsome features. His eyes closed for a brief moment before saying, "That's a scent I haven't come across in some time. You've changed, Enchantress."

"Yes, yes," she said, waving a hand. "I'm mated now."

"That isn't what I meant."

For reasons she couldn't explain, her heartbeat picked up. "What?"

"Your human scent has faded from when I saw you in the court," he said. "I thought I'd detected something unique about you then. But now, your scent is fae."

She couldn't help it. A laugh burst out of her.

For a moment, she thought she might have misplaced her sanity.

Ever since her memories returned, she'd felt different than before. Was this why she felt so filled with fury, like she was a breath away from unleashing herself on the world?

"You're mistaken," she said, though she sounded more confident than she felt. "Humans don't just become fae."

Despite her words, she couldn't help but wonder... Was it possible?

Shadow magic was rare. Most who wielded it tapped into dark magic, corrupting both the magic and their connection to it.

Then realization struck.

There was only one fae court with power over the shadows. It was the very same court that had been wiped from existence during the fae wars hundreds of years ago.

"Shadow fae." The words slipped out in a mere whisper, so soft as to be nearly inaudible. "You think I'm from the lost fae court."

Something twinkled in Hadeon's gaze, but he merely shrugged. "Perhaps."

Shaking her head, she tried to clear the thousands of questions from the front of her mind.

"I don't have time for this," she said. "I need to find my friends. They're battling an ogre. They may be hurt—"

"Of course," the fae said as he spread his large black wings once more. "Ogre first. Then my bargain."

Without another word, he launched into the air.

Arabella tugged on her braid as she watched Hadeon fly toward the castle, glaring at his back.

Until the prince called in the favor she owed him, there was every chance he could ask something that could cost her everything. If he told her she couldn't be in the same room as Elias or could never use her magic again, she would be forced to obey him.

She recalled the words she'd spoken when she'd made the bargain.

I'll be amenable to helping you at a future date within my lifetime so long as it doesn't harm those I love, doesn't require killing or endangering any humans, and doesn't violate any bargains I've already made.

Even though she'd chosen each word with care, the fae were clever and could find a way around anything if it benefited them.

I need to find a way to delay this bargain, she thought.

There was no way out of it, but maybe she could postpone it long enough to rescue Elias and get him to safety before dealing with Hadeon.

"His timing sucks," she groaned.

"From where I'm standing, that was excellent timing," Breckett said.

She leveled a flat look on Breckett before running toward where she'd last seen her friends.

"Says the male who doesn't have a bargain hanging over his head," she called over her shoulder.

Covered in ogre blood like a goddess of war, Jessamine strode across the clearing before the main entrance to the castle. Arabella ran over, wrapping her arms around her friend and feeling the press of Jessamine's blonde hair against her chest.

A few feet away, Cora and Brynne spoke in low tones.

Arabella didn't miss the worry in Brynne's eyes as she reached out and inspected a gash on Cora's arm. Brynne's touch was painfully gentle.

Like Arabella, Brynne wasn't gifted in healing magic. Most enchantresses could perform the basic healing weaves they'd all been taught during their training. But for those lacking in the skill, the weaves were often a sloppy patch job at best that could barely knit the skin back together. Still, Brynne formed the golden healing weaves, which she placed atop the wound. It scabbed over instantly, but she didn't let go of Cora's hand.

Arabella smiled, relief flooding through her.

"There are more ogres in the forest," Hadeon said as he landed in the grass near them. "If they found this place once, it won't be long until they find it again. My guess is we have an hour at best."

How had the ogres found the castle to begin with? Was Elias' ward already weakening? Or did Magnus have some spell that could penetrate the ward and its cloaking abilities? Unfortunately, there wasn't time to learn more now.

Sighing, Arabella nodded to Hadeon before turning to her friends. "Allow me to introduce Prince Hadeon of the Twilight Court."

Cora's brows shot up so high that Arabella thought they'd leap clear off her face.

"You'd told us about the ball you'd attended with Elias," Cora said carefully. "But I didn't realize you'd made… friends."

The way she spoke was almost musical. Each word was infused with a quiet gentleness. Everyone who met Cora liked her instantly, often spilling their life stories. She was the opposite of Brynne—who was as friendly as a hungry sailor with a hangover. And equally as prone to violence.

With a snort, Jessamine wiped her bloodied sword in the grass before sheathing it. "And just what do you want, Princeling? I doubt you're here for charity."

Hadeon's gaze shifted to Jessamine, his sharp eyes taking her in.

"He's here for the favor I promised him," Arabella said.

Jessamine waved a hand in the air like a magical bargain was a trivial matter. "He's *fae*. Fae lack for nothing." Then her gaze swiveled to Hadeon, her eyes locking with his. "Forcing favors out of humans is beneath you. Don't you think?"

Magical bargains were binding. As far as Arabella knew, those bound to a bargain had no choice but to comply once the terms were set. In some ways, it was like the syphen's control over erox. While she loved Jessamine for trying to get her out of this mess, this was one she'd have to wade through. There was no way Arabella could refuse, and if she tried to kill Hadeon to prevent having to fulfill the bargain, the magic would rebound and kill her.

Turning to Hadeon, Arabella said, "What is it you want?"

Rather than answering, the prince tapped his chin with a forefinger as though deep in thought. This male's mind was sharper than the blades he wore at his sides. Whatever he was about to say wasn't something he'd just come up with.

"Given that I've assisted you with your little… ogre problem, I daresay another favor is in order," he began.

"I didn't make a second bargain with you," she said, her voice dangerously low.

"Perhaps not," he allowed with a shrug of his shoulders. "But you're indebted to me all the same."

Jessamine's lips thinned beside her, and Arabella resisted the urge to pinch the bridge of her nose in frustration.

To make one magical bargain had been foolhardy at best. To bargain with the fae twice would be downright foolish. But she knew not all bargains with fae were bound by magic. Would it be possible to form an... informal agreement with this male? Did she even want to? She couldn't think of an upside to interlocking their fates more than they already were.

Unless he helped her rescue Elias.

Fae weren't known for their helpful nature or doing things out of the *goodness* of their heart. For now, she needed to find a way to fulfill her bargain *later*.

As she considered her options, she focused on three things. First, she needed to get her friends to safety. Then she needed to rescue Elias. Last, she needed to gain control over her unwieldy shadows, which seemed to feed on her darker emotions.

Arabella crossed her arms. "I didn't ask you to kill the ogres or repair the ward. You chose to do that of your own volition. So, there's no debt between us, and you can't force me into another magical bargain. That said, give me a reason to consider helping you."

The prince raised a brow, seeming to consider her for a long moment. Then he gestured to the castle with a jerk of his chin. "My sources informed me that Elias had a certain map in his possession."

"What kind of map?" Breckett interjected, which surprised Arabella. He'd been unusually quiet since their altercation with the ogres.

"An ancient one said to be created by the shadow fae," Hadeon said.

"What do you need it for?" she asked.

DEVOURED BY SHADOWS

Where did the map lead? The fae had gateways they could use to travel between the fae lands and the mortal realm. Where else could he want to go?

"I'm in search of someone who can't be reached by the usual means of travel," the prince said slowly, his eyes assessing her, almost feline. "However, this map is special. It was made by and for shadow fae. Only one of them can read it."

Brows drawing together, she said, "You're not shadow fae."

"No, indeed," he agreed. "It was a problem I'd planned to address once the map was in my possession. But now... I daresay we have a common goal."

Eyes narrowing, she began putting pieces together.

Hadeon was searching for someone who wasn't in the fae or mortal realms. To find them, he needed a map that only the shadow fae could read.

Then she made a guess.

"You're looking for the shadow fae. Aren't you?" When Hadeon didn't deny it, she continued, "Your court nearly single-handedly wiped them out of existence during the fae wars. Even mortals know the stories." Turning to her friends, she scratched the back of her head before saying, "The prince thinks I'm shadow fae."

Brynne tilted her head back and laughed. It was a deep, booming sound—and one Arabella had heard countless times in the House of Obscurities over tankards of ale.

Jessamine, on the other hand, stood with pursed lips, her eyes narrowing as though deep in thought. Then she shrugged and said, "That would explain the shadow magic."

Cora opened her mouth, closed it, and opened it again. "It would be rare for a mortal to possess fae lineage. But in case you need to hear it, we love you no matter what, Arabella."

Hadeon snorted and raised an eyebrow in Cora's direction. "Are you implying fae lineage is undesirable, Enchantress?"

"Association with your kind isn't a good thing where we come from," Jessamine cut in before Cora could reply. "Lucky for you,

49

if Arabella is part fae, she will make your kind somewhat redeemable."

"Just who do you think Arabella's parents are?" Brynne asked.

Hadeon shrugged noncommittally. "I have theories about Enchantress Arabella's parentage. And I'll gladly provide more insight—in exchange for the map."

Jessamine rolled her eyes. "I've heard better starting offers from toddlers on market day."

Thinking quickly, Arabella said, "I'll help you find the map if you assist us in rescuing Elias. He's been taken by a sorcerer named Magnus."

"No," Hadeon said, his tone grave. "I cannot be seen in open conflict with a sorcerer, especially not one as powerful as Magnus. There are too many... political ramifications for my court that I simply cannot risk."

Even having expected this answer, anger filled her.

"You killed some of his ogres," she said. "How is stealing one of his prisoners any different?"

A sad smile played on Hadeon's lips. "Killing a few ogres can be overlooked in the name of self-defense. But stealing his prized erox? Even I've heard about Magnus' infatuation with Elias."

She swallowed back the lump forming in her throat.

Getting Hadeon to help them had been a stretch. She hadn't actually expected him to say yes. But hearing that he wouldn't help her rescue her mate cut deeply all the same.

Stay strong, Elias, she thought. *I'm coming for you soon.*

"This is why we hate fae," Jessamine spat, sharp eyes fixed on Hadeon. "You only do things that benefit *you.*"

Arabella placed a hand on Jessamine's arm.

I've got this, she didn't have to say.

Jessamine nodded, understanding. Her lips drew into a thin line with the effort to *not* speak.

"I thought the fae prided themselves in having the strongest magic in realms," Arabella began, her words as sharp as her blades.

"You're right that fae are often the strongest magic wielders among the living, especially the nobility with magic they've passed down for generations," Hadeon said. "But mortals have the ability to tap into dark magic—something the fae cannot do. Our abilities are limited to the magic of our bloodlines, land, and bargains. So, while most fae are more powerful than sorcerers, it's possible that some sorcerers can become stronger than the fae—and do things that no one ever thought possible even in their darkest of ruminations. And as you well know... Magnus has already tapped into dark magic. Or else, Elias wouldn't exist."

The erox were made using dark magic. It was something she'd suspected but hadn't ever confirmed.

"You're afraid that Magnus will attack your court?" she pressed.

"I fear nothing until it's a reality I cannot overcome," Hadeon said. "But I plan for all eventualities. And an enraged sorcerer is not one I'm willing to risk—not when there are many fae in the Twilight Court who are far less powerful than the nobility. They'd be unable to defend themselves against a sorcerer and his army."

There was so much she wanted to say on the tip of her tongue, but there simply wasn't time. Not now. They needed to get away from the castle, and fast. Once they were safe, they could decide the next course of action.

"I won't make another bargain with you, but I'm willing to help you if you help us," she said. "I'll help you find this map if you get us out of here."

She couldn't let herself get tied down in more fae magic. But if she was honest with herself, they needed help escaping Magnus' army. If they had any hope of rescuing Elias, they needed to get out of this forest and find allies powerful enough to oppose a sorcerer. Maybe she could convince Hadeon to change his mind.

When Hadeon didn't reply, seeming to hesitate, she continued, "The ogres will return soon enough, and they may bring more of Magnus' army with them." She thought of the erox under his command. "If I'm taken by him again, you won't have a shadow fae to read your map."

She had to hope that Hadeon needed her enough to defy Magnus' wishes in helping her get away. The prince wouldn't be stealing Magnus' prized erox, but he would still be getting in his way.

"I can agree to this not-bargain," Hadeon said at last. "But know that I will be calling in your favor. Soon."

Great.

Turning to Breckett, she said, "I don't suppose you have any idea where Elias might have kept his maps?"

ONCE AGAIN, they found themselves in the library, digging through the tomes.

A dozen bookshelves that were three stories tall filled the space. Sunlight streamed in through colorful stained-glass windows that filled up the back wall, lighting the space in countless colors. Arabella thought the windows might depict one of her favorite fairy tales about a beast who'd fallen in love with a human woman. In this depiction, he offered her a single red rose.

Her thoughts strayed to the last time she'd been here with Elias. He'd brought her when she didn't have her memories and needed essence. Offering herself to him, she'd told him to feed on her. And he'd resisted—eventually taking just enough to assuage his hunger and keep his inner demon at bay.

What she'd give to hold him again...

Shaking her head, she forced herself to focus on the present.

Somehow, she needed to find a magical map. And a library seemed as good a place as any to begin their search.

Unlike their prior search when they'd been seeking a way to regain her memories, they didn't bother putting books and scrolls in neat piles. Instead, they moved quickly, allowing books to fall to the floor in their haste.

All too soon, they'd scoured the entirety of the library.

She tugged her braid. "It's not here."

"Use your magic," Hadeon said. "Can you sense anything? You may be drawn to it since it was made with shadow fae magic."

Taking a breath, she closed her eyes.

She had no idea what she was doing, but she envisioned her thoughts like a net and cast it out around her. At first, all she could sense was the wind outside the castle, the rustle of papers as ancient tomes of leather-bound books were opened and closed, and the ward's distant hum.

Then, for the first time, she noticed what she could only describe as a faint vibration in the air as though a storm were about to sweep through. It was the lightest pinpricks in the corners of the room.

Magic, she realized. *Those must be magical objects.*

She wondered how Elias had managed to acquire them. Or had the previous owner of the castle acquired them? There was so much she wanted to ask him.

Focus, she chastised herself. *Or you won't make it out of here alive before the ogres come back.*

She allowed her mind to roam over the room and felt her feet moving. Reaching out, she touched the places where she felt the vibration. But as she came across each—a quill hidden in a desk, a leather-bound tome in a language she didn't recognize, a small statue of a pregnant female—none possessed a magic that mirrored her own. None appealed to the shadows.

The map wasn't there. So, where was it?

Again, she cast her mind out like a net but focused it on the castle. Room by room, she felt along the energies, searching, searching...

"That's it," came Hadeon's voice, though it sounded strangely far away. "Just like that."

When she came across the room she'd dreaded returning to—

the place where she'd stabbed Elias and taken the amplifier—she felt what she sought.

Unlike the purr of the energies of other magical objects throughout the castle, this one was different. A deep hiss emanated from it the moment her thoughts touched it. At first, the energy recoiled from her. Then it changed to something akin to a caress. The energy nuzzled into her consciousness, making her thoughts swirl.

"I think I found it," she said. "It's in Elias' room."

A boom sounded outside the castle. Then there was a splitting sound that felt like the air was being torn in two.

"They broke through the ward," Jessamine said. "We need to leave. *Now.*"

Even with Hadeon cutting down ogres before and repairing the ward, it hadn't been enough. It had barely bought them a few minutes. There were more monsters to replace the ones they'd killed. Just how many creatures did Magnus have in his army?

Jessamine was right. They couldn't rely on this fae prince to stick around if shit got tough. Not to mention, Arabella had no idea how far his power went and when it would be depleted. All magic wielders grew fatigued the more magic they used. Certainly, Hadeon was powerful, but she doubted he was strong enough to hold an army at bay—even if he was willing.

"No," Hadeon said, his voice sharp. "Not before we get the map."

Arabella opened her eyes, allowing them to settle on the fae prince. His gaze was filled with fiery determination.

"If you ever want to see your mother again, it will be with this map," he said as another boom filled the air.

A second tear in the ward.

Ogres would be pouring in.

"My... mother?" Her brows drew together.

She knew she should feel something at those words. All her life, she'd been an orphaned child without any knowledge of her parentage or where she'd come from. But all she could feel at that moment was the quickening of her heartbeat.

"We have to go," Jessamine said, her fingers tightening around Arabella's arm. "There isn't time."

"Only the shadow fae can help you control your magic. If you still want to save Elias, that is," Hadeon said, knowing that he'd sealed their fates with those words.

Knowing she'd stop at nothing to rescue her mate.

Her features settled into one of perfect calm as resolution settled in her chest. "Keep up."

Then she was running through the castle, moving down corridors as she felt the pounding footsteps of ogres outside the castle. She thought she heard the flapping of great wings.

She raced down hall after hall until she reached Elias' bedroom door with the enchantresses, Hadeon, and Breckett at her heels.

Below, there was a thumping on the main castle doors. Thank fuck that Brynne had enough forethought to bolt them shut before they went to the library.

As Arabella approached Elias' bedroom door, she reached for the shadows beneath her. They formed into long, thorned vines around her arms that didn't pierce her skin this time. Instead, they stretched out, extending past her outreached hand, and lashed at the door. In an instant, they sliced through the wards Elias had put in place. The magic fell at once, and they all strode through.

There was a four-poster bed with curtains as black as Elias' eyes when he hadn't fed, which she carefully avoided looking at. She didn't dare to allow herself to think of what they had shared here—or how he'd admitted his feelings for her—moments before she'd betrayed him.

The hearth was dark and cold, and the late autumn chill hung in the air.

There was a sound of wood splintering several floors below as she cast her consciousness out into the room. Sparks of magic filled her mind, flickering into existence like stars in the night sky. One after another lit before her mind's eye—so many that it made her mind spin. There had to be dozens of magical objects here.

This was something she'd never been able to do before as an enchantress. Was sensing magical objects a gift of fae?

She longed to learn just what treasures Elias had here and what might be useful against Magnus. But there simply wasn't time. Not as the sound of pounding continued several floors below them.

She sought out the presence she'd sensed before. Immediately, she felt a caress against her mind.

"It's under the floor," she said, opening her eyes. "At the base of the bed."

Brynne ripped a floorboard free. A moment later, she pressed a rolled parchment into Arabella's palm. The presence Arabella had felt grew stronger, almost purring, as it nuzzled against her consciousness.

Releasing the map, Brynne turned toward Hadeon. Jessamine and Cora did likewise, their hands on the hilts of swords.

Their stances said one thing.

They didn't trust Hadeon enough to give him the map. They also didn't trust him to not try to take it from them.

"I've fulfilled my part," Arabella said. "How are we getting out of here—"

Suddenly, the window shutters were thrown wide and glass splintered around them as two massive shapes crashed into the room.

Instinctively, she staggered backward, throwing a hand up to shield her eyes. Shadows billowed out without her willing it, sending a gust of wind toward the oncomers. For a moment, darkness filled the room, and all she could hear was the crunching of glass beneath heavy feet.

A moment later, the shadows cleared, and she looked up.

Two figures blocked out the sun from the windows behind them. Wings made of stone, flesh, and sinew stretched out from the creatures' backs, filling up the entire back wall. They were twice the size of a human male and had bat-like wings and clawed hands and feet. Standing on hind legs, these creatures had pointed ears that vaguely resembled two curved horns. But unlike the ogres, there was intelligence in their red eyes.

Gargoyles.

Realization dawned.

When she'd lowered the shields to Elias' room for them to get in, she'd also made it possible for gargoyles and other creatures to enter—from outside of the castle.

Without thinking, she reached for her shadows.

After years of training with her earthen magic, she should have been weaving the golden magic together and unleashing bolts at the gargoyles. But the shadows called to her, singing in her veins.

The gargoyles prowled forward on hind legs.

As she unleashed a torrent of shadows, the other enchantresses loosed golden weaves, sharp as crossbow bolts. To her horror, the earthen magic did nothing. It was like they had tossed sticks at a hailstorm.

One gargoyle snarled, raising the corner of its lips to reveal razor-sharp teeth. Lashing out, her shadows embedded in its gut, sinking through flesh and stone. Red-black blood oozed onto the floor, pouring to the ground as the shadows pulled free, leaving a gaping hole in its wake.

For a moment, it was all she could do to stare at the gargoyle as it crashed to its knees.

Her shadows had done that willingly. *Eagerly.* They fed off the anger surging in her veins, seeming to gain strength and speed. But as she reached for the shadows again, she felt that strange presence tickle the edges of her senses once more—the same one from her dream. It wasn't her bond with Elias, and it was unlike the hum of magical objects. Instead, it was like a heaviness lurked in the air and draped over her shoulders.

The second creature lashed out at her as she was distracted.

Before she could react, there was a flash of movement, and something was before her.

No, not something. *Someone.*

The fae prince had freed his blade and sliced the gargoyle's head clean off its shoulders. It thumped to the ground, rolling toward the dark hearth. Then it erupted into a cloud of ash.

"The roof," Hadeon said. "Our way out is on the roof."

Footsteps sounded outside of the bedroom.

"Two hallways down," Breckett said. "There's a staircase that leads to the nearest turret."

Nodding, Hadeon moved toward the door and cut down the first ogre that appeared. It wasn't as tall as the ogres they'd faced outside, but it had to hunch over to fit in the hallway.

The creature fell backward, dissolving into a plume of dust.

What is that fucking sword?

She'd never heard of a weapon that could turn anything it touched to dust. Was it the blade itself that held this power, or was it something Hadeon's magic granted to the blade?

Breckett moved to the front of the group.

Wordlessly, Arabella and the enchantresses followed Breckett and Hadeon, racing down the hallways to the sound of drumming footsteps and splintering windows. As they rounded the corner of the second hallway, more gargoyles crashed through nearby windows. Glass sprayed in every direction.

Spinning, Arabella lashed out with her shadows.

The semi-translucent vines sunk into one of the eyes of the nearest gargoyle, which slumped onto the floor, dead instantly. But even as she moved, another gargoyle struck out. It was so fast, there was no time for her to react. Its taloned hand wrapped around her arm, wrenching her forward. Its hand felt both cold and warm, like the melding of the earth's beating core and stones after a rainfall.

Gargoyles were a type of demon, spawned either by design or chance, that had their own will—and their own need for flesh. So far as she knew, gargoyles needed to eat the flesh of mortals to sustain their life, or risk turning fully into stone.

Stony wings stretched out as the creature prepared to take flight—and take Arabella with it. But then Jessamine was there, moving an instant before the creature did. As though she knew what it was going to do.

Jessamine wrapped her blade in golden weaves and swung. With both the power of her magic-imbued weapon and the weaves, she sliced the creature's hand off at the wrist.

The gargoyle roared, and Arabella and Jessamine rolled backward in tandem, out of the reach of its other outstretched arm as it clawed for them.

"Give in, little humans," it hissed through a mouth of pointed teeth, sounding like crackling in the canyons of the deep. Blood and some strange dust seeped from its severed wrist. "There's no point in fighting our master. Not with what he plans to do next."

There was movement to Arabella's right, and Hadeon came to stand beside her, eyeing the gargoyle with a mere flick of his eyes, wearing a bored expression.

The gargoyle's eyes widened. "Prince of the Twilight Court. Why are you in this place?"

Down the hallway, shadows moved, and Arabella thought she spotted two ogres rounding the corner.

"Coming to greet former guests of my court," Hadeon said, eyeing his nails in utter disinterest. As though a powerful gargoyle didn't stand before him. "Imagine my surprise when they were rudely attacked."

Arabella frowned.

If Hadeon couldn't be seen in open conflict against Magnus' army or risk retaliation, why reveal himself to one of Magnus' soldiers? Unless Hadeon never intended to let the gargoyle live. Was the prince trying to get information out of the demon before killing it?

"We're under orders of Sorcerer Magnus," the gargoyle

rumbled. "He's instructed us to collect the enchantress called Arabella."

"Is that so?" Hadeon said, pulling a nonexistent piece of lint from the sleeve of his shirt. "What does he want with her?"

A slow, wicked smile crept across the gargoyle's features, its face nearly cracking in two. "Power, of course."

Something like fear twisted in Arabella's gut. She knew with sudden certainty that something terrible was about to happen.

"What do you mean?" she blurted before she could think to stop herself.

Narrowed red eyes settled on her. "Why do you think we're here, little human?"

She frowned.

Did they know of her suspected shadow fae heritage? But why would that matter? And how would Magnus have found out? She'd only just learned it, herself. And she wasn't entirely sure she believed it.

"It's stalling," Jessamine shouted, yanking Arabella from her thoughts. "Move!" She wrapped a hand around Arabella's wrist, hauling her backward as more gargoyles flew through the windows.

Arabella took one step forward and then another. Then they were running.

At the head of the group, Breckett pointed to a nearby door. "This way!" He pushed through it, and they all quickly followed, pouring into a twisting stone staircase.

Hadeon barred the oak door with some fae magic that Arabella was too distracted to fully comprehend. She followed Breckett up the winding stone stairs with Jessamine, Cora, and Brynne at her heels until they reached an unmarked door. Beyond it, there was a chorus of inhuman shrieks.

More gargoyles, she realized.

For a moment, she hesitated, wondering just what escape Hadeon had in mind. But with the pounding on the door to the hallway below, there was little other choice but to forge ahead.

Walking past Breckett, she grabbed the handle and pushed the door open.

Glancing around, she found herself atop one of the castle's turrets, which was open to the sky. She didn't have eyes for the smoke rising from the trees or the dozens of ogres filling the grounds below, flattening Elias' garden and knocking in the stable windows. Instead, she turned her gaze skyward to the massive tear at the top of the ward.

The blue sky filled with dark wings as dozens of gargoyles flew through. But it wasn't just them. There was another winged creature. Unlike the gargoyles with wings of stone and sinew, this newcomer had wings as dark as shadows cast by starlight. Even from this distance, she could see the long, pointed ears of the fae.

The winged fae flew across the open sky with a sword held above his head as he closed the distance between himself and a pair of gargoyles. He fell upon them, bringing his blade down and slicing through their bodies with ease. Severed limbs and heads fell earthwards.

Hadeon stood beside Arabella at the edge of the turret and raised a fist into the air.

Turning toward them, the fae who'd been battling the gargoyles flew with abandon. The remaining gargoyles descended from the sky after him—scenting prey.

"A friend of yours?" she asked.

"Yes," Hadeon said.

"As exciting as it sounds to be carried by fae like a sack of grain," she began. "I don't think two of you can carry five of us and escape this army."

Cora, Brynne, Jessamine, and Breckett stood beside her with similar looks of concern.

The winged fae landed in the center of the turret with a resounding *boom*, stones cracking around his boots and his wings tucked against his sides.

Above, the gargoyles were less than a hundred feet away.

"Do you have it?" the male asked Hadeon as he rose to his feet.

Hadeon dipped his chin. Then he raised a fist into the air once more, and night cascaded from his enclosed fingers. It lashed out, forming a dome above them, like a mini ward. And just in time. The approaching gargoyles crashed into it. Some bounced off it, hurtling backward, their wings flapping in a frenzy. Other gargoyles scraped sharp talons down it, which were blunted from a single swipe against the fae magic.

"Let's depart before I'm tempted to wipe these creatures from existence," Hadeon said, sounding entirely unaffected by the torrent of magic billowing from his fist. "Can't have the queen thinking I'm partial in any direction."

Arabella couldn't help but wonder if this display of magic was from an amplifier or his natural ability. The enchantresses were mere drops in a bucket compared to the avalanche of power coming from this fae.

"Kazimir," Hadeon said. "Call him."

"I'm here, Princeling," came a voice she hadn't heard since the moment she'd returned from Magnus' camp and learned that Elias had been hiding the goblins in his castle.

"Vorkle," she said, turning toward the goblin. "I've never been so happy to see you."

"Shadow whisperer," the goblin hissed by way of greeting. He was short, no more than three feet in height, and had long, expressive eyebrows that conveyed his perpetual disapproval. "This is why we don't get mixed up in the affairs of humans or fae. Always trouble—the lot of you. And dragging us into it."

"You want my protection now that your little erox is otherwise occupied?" Hadeon said, interrupting them. "There's a cost. Now, it's time you're off."

Surprise bolted through her.

That was where the goblins had gone—in search of someone who could provide protection for them. But why Hadeon?

With a heavy sigh, Vorkle stretched his hands out.

Interestingly, neither Hadeon nor Kazimir moved. But Breckett took one of the goblin's hands and extended an arm toward Arabella.

She reached toward him but hesitated.

"We need to warn Shadowbank," she said, turning toward the women who'd become more than sisters in arms. They were the family she'd do anything for. "I don't know what Magnus is planning, but there's an army within a few days' march of our home."

Hadeon wasn't going to let her go—not if she was the only person in existence who could read his map. And she couldn't let the enchantresses become entangled in fae schemes alongside her. Especially not if they could help protect Shadowbank when she couldn't.

Gargoyles slammed into Hadeon's shield again and again. The sounds ricocheted in every direction, feeling like they were drumming inside her skull.

Slowly, Cora nodded. Her hand slipped into Brynne's, their fingers interlocking. "We'll tell the enchantresses what we've learned and make certain everyone is prepared—for anything."

They knew as well as Arabella did that the ward wouldn't be strong enough to hold an army at bay.

Tears welled in Cora's eyes as she offered Arabella a sad smile. "Come home once you've saved your mate, okay?"

Home.

It felt like it had been an eternity since she'd been in Shadowbank.

Jessamine thumped Arabella on the back. "She won't be alone."

Arabella blinked, shaking her head. Jessamine couldn't mean she intended to stay with her. Not when it meant getting tied up with the fae...

"Are you sure you don't want to go with them—" she began.

"Knock that shit out," Jessamine interrupted. "I'm exactly where I want to be."

Arabella swallowed back a torrent of feelings along with the tears threatening to spill over. Then she turned to Vorkle and Hadeon.

"Take Cora and Brynne to Shadowbank first," she managed, her voice trembling faintly. Then she added in a quieter tone, "Please."

Vorkle looked up to Hadeon, who nodded. The goblin released Breckett before disappearing and reappearing between Cora and Brynne. He grabbed their hands and was gone in an instant.

There hadn't even been time for a goodbye.

Be safe, she thought.

A moment later, Vorkle reappeared at Kazimir's side. Again, he offered his hands, which only Breckett took. With a sigh, Jessamine took Breckett's hand in hers, which was crusted in dried ogre blood.

"I'm coming with you," Kazimir said to Hadeon, ignoring Vorkle's outstretched hand.

"No," Hadeon said. "Stay with them."

"I can't leave my prince—" Kazimir began.

"That was an order, General," Hadeon snapped, interrupting whatever he'd been about to say.

They stared at each other for a long moment, as though speaking without words, before Kazimir's lips drew into a thin line and he nodded. Without another word, he took Vorkle's other hand.

Hadeon looked at Arabella expectantly, still holding the shield above them as a dark look crossed his features.

Before she took Jessamine's hand, Arabella glanced toward the grounds below—to the place she'd begun to think of as one of her homes.

Dozens of ogres and gargoyles moved across the grounds, trampling the gardens and breaking down doors into the outer buildings. Nearby, the door to their turret shook as the creatures behind it tried to break through from the other side. Above them, the skies were filled with dark wings.

The castle was overrun.

Just as Elias had predicted.

Without a new ward, Magnus' army had found them. But despite this, Elias had risked not fully fixing the ward and gave the amplifier—and the power that remained within it—to Shadowbank.

Now, Elias was Magnus' prisoner, and Shadowbank was at risk of being overrun. Just like this place.

A strange sadness swelled in her chest as she thought of the life she and Elias might have had if things had been different. If Shadowbank had been safe from the threat of the demons and all that lay in the forest beyond. If the goblins had been safe from those who sought to use their magic for their own gain.

If there had been only the enchantress and the demon.

And all the time in the world.

"Let's go," she said, biting the inside of her cheek and tasting blood. She welcomed the pain if only to distract her from one single truth.

This might be the last time she'd see this castle.

Elias' castle.

The place she'd fallen in love with an erox.

A single tear fell down her cheek as she grabbed hold of Jessamine's hand.

"Get them out of here," Hadeon hissed at Vorkle. "Now!"

Vorkle nodded.

There was a zap of magic as Hadeon released his shield and launched himself into the sky—toward the cloud of gargoyles.

Arabella opened her mouth to yell at Hadeon and demand to know what he was doing. But then she disappeared into the space between worlds.

Leaving the fae prince behind.

Chapter Five
ELIAS

The breath was torn from Elias' lungs as he was dragged from oblivion.

"Wake up," a voice hissed as a fist landed in his gut.

No, he thought. *Let me sleep. Let me dream of her.*

He'd had dreams of Arabella every time he'd closed his eyes. Each time, she looked decadent in her leathers, and there were chains woven into her long braid.

Slowly, he opened his eyes to the sight of Flynn, one of Magnus' inner circle, standing before him in Magnus' tent.

Flynn wore a leather breastplate with crisscrossing straps and countless sheaths, metal shoulder plates, thick leather gloves with metal spikes atop the knuckles, along with trousers and tall leather boots. It was a mix of browns and blacks, a perfect blend to move stealthily in the dark forest.

Swinging, Flynn's gloved fist connected with Elias' gut again, the spikes sinking deeper. Instantly, Elias coughed up blood, gasping for air. Blood trickled down his stomach and over his cock before dripping onto the ground.

He was naked, and utterly at his captors' mercy.

He couldn't fight, couldn't move. Not when his hands and feet were cuffed to two crossing beams of wood that formed a giant X and were staked into the ground. It was a magical device that suppressed an erox's strength and powers. The only magic it permitted was his body's regeneration. His flesh could sew back together *if* he had enough essence—even if the weapon or blade was inside him.

Except for one blade.

His syphen.

If that was embedded in his flesh, his body wouldn't be able to heal. Not until it was removed.

The X was the perfect torture device for the erox. They could be ripped apart again and again, and their bodies would stitch back together. But they couldn't fight, couldn't flee.

Couldn't *object*.

He'd been tied to this torture device all those years ago beneath the mountain in Magnus' stronghold.

And now, Elias knew one thing with certainty.

There was no escaping unless someone set him free.

He'd escaped Magnus once, and the sorcerer would ensure it never happened again.

"Took you long enough," Flynn hissed as he pulled his fist back with a wet squelch that had Elias biting back a groan. Then in a mockingly sweet voice, he said, "Have we been too hard on you?"

"Just needed my beauty rest," Elias said before spitting blood onto the ground. "I trust there's a reason why you woke me?"

One of Flynn's nostrils lifted before his fist landed beneath Elias' chin. The spikes punctured his skin, and blood filled his mouth. He struggled for air as pain assaulted him. Though this was nothing new. Not since he'd given himself over to Magnus. But even as Flynn pulled his fist free, Elias could feel his wounds stitching back together.

As they did, a deep hunger—a never-ending desire to feed—plagued him.

But he didn't want just anyone.

He longed for the taste of Arabella's essence on his tongue.

Now that he'd fed on his mate, he no longer desired the taste of anyone else's essence. Still, he was so ravenous that he might give in and feed on one of Magnus' human prisoners if they offered one to him. Worse still, he feared he wouldn't be able to stop feeding if he started.

"Keep mouthing off." Flynn wiped Elias' blood from his gloves with a cloth. "The sorcerer will just work harder to break you."

Swallowing thickly, Elias tried to keep any emotion from showing on his face. But a fear that had been rooted deep in his chest was growing—spreading until there would soon be nothing left of him.

"Thank you, Flynn," came a voice from the tent's entrance. "That will be all."

Slowly, Elias' gaze turned upward, his eyes skirting across the large tent.

There were rugs and plush pillows on the ground along with a table filled with food and drinks. So many luxuries in an encampment deep in a demon-infested forest, far away from civilization. He looked past the ridiculous opulence to the male at the tent's entrance. Even silhouetted as he was from the forest outside the tent, Elias knew who he was.

Magnus strode across the tent with a mere nod to Flynn.

But he didn't have eyes for him. No, Magnus' gaze skirted up and down the length of Elias' naked body as Flynn saw himself out.

Robes as bright as Magnus' scarlet eyes swept along the carpeted floor as the sorcerer came to stand before him. "Have you nothing to say?" Trailing a finger down Elias' stomach, he swirled the blood over Elias' now-closed wounds. "Won't you beg for your freedom?"

"I've pledged myself to you," Elias said, fixing his gaze on the tent's entrance.

And you possess my syphen, he didn't add.

When Arabella had fled the castle with the amplifier, she'd

taken Elias' syphen with her. The sorcerer must have gotten hold of the blade when she'd been captured.

The moment Magnus chose to wield the syphen, he could force Elias to do anything he pleased. For reasons he didn't yet comprehend, the sorcerer hadn't compelled him. Instead, he'd kept Elias inside his tent, cuffed hand and foot to the X.

"You know I long for your undying obedience," Magnus purred, his finger swirling ever lower.

"You have my compliance," Elias said, gritting his teeth. "As I promised."

The sorcerer made a tsking sound. "One day, I'll have your loyalty."

Torturing hardly inspires loyalty, he thought.

Let Magnus scheme.

Arabella was safe, and her memories were returned to her. That was all that mattered.

"Perhaps you'll have a change of heart when you hear of what I found today." Magnus removed his finger and studied the blood on it. "That little castle of yours—the one by the lake. You didn't tell me how... scenic it was. I can understand now why you spent so many years there."

For a moment, all sounds in the room faded into the distance.

No, no, *no*. Magnus couldn't have found the castle. Not yet. Had he taken Arabella?

Elias had been careful not to reveal anything about his home in order to protect Arabella, her friends, Breckett, and the goblins. And he'd been lucky enough that Magnus hadn't forced the information out of him with his syphen. But how had Magnus found it so quickly?

Elias could only hope Arabella had left the moment her memories returned.

"But that ward... Surely, you could do better than that," Magnus continued. "It was hardly a challenge for my ogres."

Elias' mind raced.

If Magnus had captured Arabella, he'd be parading her before him. Wouldn't he?

Then Elias remembered.

The mating bond.

He reached for the constant pressure in his chest—a cord that wrapped around his heart. It was tight. Far tighter than it had been before he'd fallen unconscious.

She's farther away, he realized.

Somehow, Arabella was no longer in the forest.

"Why are you telling me this?" Elias managed, trying to push past the fear still infusing his mind—irrational fear that Magnus had somehow captured Arabella despite him knowing she wasn't nearby.

"I came across something of interest," Magnus said. "You can imagine my surprise when your friends were surrounded, were moments away from capture, and then they just... disappeared."

For a moment, Elias could only stand there, blinking.

The goblins.

They must have helped Arabella and the others escape.

He nearly wept with relief, but he forced his features into neutrality. He couldn't let Magnus suspect he knew anything about what had happened when the ogres attacked. Not when the sorcerer could use the syphen and force that information out of Elias. If he knew what to ask.

"Apparently, there were winged fae," Magnus continued, his eyes fastening on Elias' face. "My gargoyles are currently in pursuit, but... It sparked my curiosity. Why were fae at your castle?"

Elias' mind raced.

There were fae at the castle? Could it have been someone from the Twilight Court?

Suddenly, a different kind of fear filled him.

Had Hadeon come for Arabella's favor? Something akin to rage boiled in his veins. If Hadeon *dared* to hurt her...

He'd what?

There was nothing Elias could do. Not when he'd promised himself to Magnus. He was the sorcerer's creature now. He'd promised obedience.

"As you may have observed," Elias began slowly. "I'm not at my castle. So, I can't say why a—"

A finger pressed to Elias' lips. He froze as it ran along his lower lip.

"I won't tolerate lies," Magnus purred as he pushed his finger into Elias' mouth, tasting his blood.

Slowly, Magnus moved it over Elias' tongue, as though fucking his mouth. Elias swallowed back bile but didn't fight, didn't object. Magnus pulled his hand free before trailing his finger down Elias' chest. His hand moved until it was just above Elias' cock, his fingernails running over the hair there.

"Perhaps you need reminding of who you belong to," Magnus purred as his other hand wrapped around Elias' throat, forcing him to look at the sorcerer.

Magnus' hair was so blond it was almost white. The color reminded Elias of bones bleached by years under an unyielding sun. Magnus' hair contrasted his eyes, which were as red as freshly spilled blood.

Swallowing thickly, Elias knew there was nothing he could do to stop what came next.

"Come for me, Elias," Magnus purred. "Show me your *compliance.*"

Instantly, the magic of their bargain burned in Elias' chest.

The sorcerer's eyes glowed a bright scarlet as his erox powers alighted.

As the creator of erox, Magnus could feed on anyone he pleased. No one, not even erox, could deny him once he chose to use his magic. And as Magnus' erox magic swirled to the surface, demanding Elias' remaining drops of essence, it was all he could do to obey him. To let him summon it.

To spill his seed for him again.

Desire pooled in Elias' core, and his body grew pliant as he awaited what came next.

His cock hardened instantly. The pleasure was so sharp, so sudden, it was painful. Tears streamed down his cheeks even as he moaned against his wishes.

He filled his mind's eye with the picture of Arabella as he felt Magnus' lips press to his.

Although Elias lifted his chin in defiance, his lips slipped open as Magnus' tongue pressed into his mouth.

Then Elias was coming.

Magnus didn't bother to touch Elias as stinging desire bolted through his veins, loosening the essence in his core. It was the last of what he'd taken from Arabella before he'd left the castle.

His mate's essence slipped up Elias' throat and pooled between their lips before Magnus pulled it into his mouth.

A sharp pang twisted Elias' gut, and he stifled a groan as hunger burned through him.

"That wasn't so hard, was it?" Magnus' scent held a woody note with lingering amber. "Give your loyalty to me, and I can give you the world."

Seed still dripping onto the ground, Elias kept his mouth firmly shut, not bothering to pull against his restraints. This song and dance had happened too many times, and he knew fighting it was pointless.

Reaching up, Magnus swiped the tears from Elias' cheeks away with a thumb. The gesture made Elias' stomach turn. And he watched in disgust as the sorcerer licked his tears from his finger. As he did, his eyes skirted down to Elias' still-hard cock and then further down to the floor where he'd spilled his seed.

The sorcerer turned from him, walking around the tent as though deep in thought.

"Perhaps I'll share your enchantress when I find her," Magnus said.

A sudden fire filled Elias' veins, and he pulled at the restraints, but his ankles and wrists were secured in place.

"Because I *will* find her," Magnus continued, ignoring as Elias' nostrils flared and a growl bubbled up his throat. With a flick of deft fingers, Magnus removed a blade from his robes. The knife was plain and unremarkable with a simple handle and steel blade.

Fear squeezed Elias' throat at the sight of his syphen.

"Can you explain the presence of fae at your castle?" Magnus asked, still not using the syphen's power on Elias.

But why?

Could Elias wait until Magnus forced the truth out of him? To get Arabella's memories back, he'd entered into a magical bargain with the sorcerer. Would the bargain's magic permit him to withhold information? Thus far, it appeared it was limited to compliance with a direct command—not an unspoken one.

"I can't be certain without seeing them, but..." Elias began. "There are many winged fae in the Twilight Court."

It was true.

While several of the fae courts had winged fae, the court with the most winged fae was the Twilight Court.

"We attended the queen's ball not long ago," Elias continued, careful to avoid mention of Hadeon and his bargain with Arabella. "It's possible someone from court came to seek an audience."

Everything inside of Elias screamed to rip Hadeon apart for daring to leverage a favor over his mate. But if the prince had helped Arabella escape the forest, then Elias wasn't about to reveal Hadeon's ties to his mate. Not if doing so could potentially lead Magnus to Hadeon—and wherever he'd taken Arabella.

At least, not until Elias was forced to reveal the truth.

Nodding, Magnus turned from Elias, taking several steps away from him. "How very interesting." Seeming to come to a decision, Magnus started toward the tent's exit.

"You don't need her," Elias found himself saying, the word slipping free of his lips. He knew trying to reason with Magnus was pointless, but he couldn't help himself or his desire to keep

Arabella safe. "You already have a syphen. You can create new erox. Please just—"

Magnus turned to him, and something dark glittered in his scarlet gaze. "Even if the enchantress was no more than a mere mortal, I would take her."

When Elias had given himself to Magnus, the sorcerer had revealed that Arabella was shadow fae and that he intended to take her so she'd make more syphens for him. But now... It seemed that there was another reason Magnus wanted to have her under his control.

"Why?" Elias asked, feeling his heart sink.

"Because she's yours," Magnus said as though this was the most obvious thing in the world. "She's the perfect motivation to get what I want."

Elias frowned, not understanding.

What he wanted? He thought Magnus just had some strange obsession with him. Was there some other reason why he'd entrapped Elias and took special interest in him all those years ago?

"Flynn," Magnus called, and the tent flap opened. The erox strode through. "I have something to see to. Drain Elias of his essence. I want him to be on the precipice when I return."

"Yes, sir," Flynn said, his eyes fixing on where Elias was strapped to the X.

Elias swallowed thickly.

Like all demons, the erox's magic required them to feed on mortals. It was what differentiated their magic from non-demonkind. But rather than feasting on flesh or souls, erox fed on desires. Consuming essence kept the true inner demon at bay. If an erox waited too long to feed, the creature within came forth—demanding blood. And if it wasn't sated, if the erox was too far gone to hunger, there was no coming back. Everything that erox was would cease to exist as they lost their memories and humanity. They'd become a mindless creature who knew nothing but hunger for the rest of eternity.

This fate was perhaps the one thing he feared more than Magnus, himself.

"You have me," Elias called after Magnus as he grabbed the tent flap, about to exit. "What more could you possibly want?"

Magnus lingered for a moment, not bothering to look back. With a chuckle, he disappeared out of sight.

Over the pounding of his heart, Elias heard Flynn's booted footsteps as he neared.

There was the hiss of a blade being pulled free of its sheath.

I'm so sorry, Arabella, Elias thought. *This is all my fault.*

She was in danger because of him. Because Magnus had set his eyes on her. He never would have known of her existence if Elias hadn't taken her as an offering.

"I'd bet Magnus captures her within the week," Flynn purred as he ran the tip of his knife down the center of Elias' chest. Immediately, blood pooled, leaving a stinging trail in its wake. "You'll be serving the sorcerer willingly before long. Mark my words. You'll give in to him soon enough."

Flynn was right.

It was an inevitability. Elias could only last so long, even without the use of the syphen. Soon enough, Magnus would break Elias down.

And there'd be nothing left of who he'd been.

Chapter Six
ARABELLA

Arabella knew instantly she was back in the fae realm by the humming of the earth.

It was far richer than anything in the mortal lands, and it didn't hold the taint of demons. It felt like sea air carried on spring winds. She didn't sense the lingering sludge in the land that the presence of demons always left behind.

She stood beside Jessamine, Breckett, Kazimir, and Vorkle in what appeared to be a large sitting room with a myriad of sofas with velvet cushions and golden trims. Each sofa was likely worth more than a home in Shadowbank. For a moment, all she could think about was how this land was free of the threat that she'd lived with her whole life.

The demon-infested forest.

Had the demons always lived in the mortal realm? Or had they existed in all realms, but the fae had the power to kill them or force them out through the gateways?

What was it like to not live in constant fear?

After a moment, she realized that her bond with Elias was quieter somehow, though the tugging had increased tenfold. Her chest physically ached with the pressure, and she rubbed a fist to it. She wondered if the increased distance between them changed the emotions she could feel from him. But damn—this bond did not like it when they were apart.

Slowly, she looked around the room.

Lit by the sun through a series of open windows, the space was larger than the common room at the House of Obscurities. At the center of the sitting room were a series of sofas arranged in a circle, likely for hosting guests. There was also a small table and chairs near one of the windows. At another window, there was a long bench, which she assumed was a reading nook. A glance through the open window told her that they were several stories off the ground, though she couldn't be sure if they were in the castle of the Twilight Court or another location.

We escaped, she thought, her heart racing.

Magnus' army had come for her, and she'd narrowly avoided falling into his clutches.

However, not all of them had escaped. Where had Hadeon gone, and why didn't he portal with them?

"Where did the prince go?" she asked Kazimir.

The fae warrior didn't reply as he strode to a chair large enough to hold a bear. She realized belatedly it was that size to accommodate his wings. Sweat beaded on his brow, and the sun filtering through the windows made it look like his pale skin shimmered. Like Hadeon, he was tall with massive black wings and the pointed ears of fae. But unlike the prince, a seriousness lurked in the back of his gaze—as though mirth had abandoned him long before birth.

Jessamine crossed her arms, still covered in blood from the battle, not making a move to join him.

Breckett heaved a sigh from where he stood beside Jessamine before heading toward a drink cart beyond the sofas and pouring himself a glass of what Arabella assumed was fae wine.

She marched across the room to where Kazimir sat, his eyes fixed on the far wall.

"Why didn't Prince Hadeon teleport with us?" she pressed.

Slowly, Kazimir's gaze shifted up, and she realized for the first time that his eyes were violet—a rare color for anyone in the mortal or fae realms. She wondered just what that meant for his heritage or magical abilities.

"He'll be here soon enough," he said simply. "He only travels by gateway."

That wasn't an explanation, and he knew it.

"What if he's captured and taken to Magnus?" she pressed, not certain why she was so concerned for a male who held a favor over her head.

A dark fury flashed across Kazimir's gaze. "He knew the risk."

Vorkle cleared his throat. "Will that be all, my lord?"

"I'm not a lord." Kazimir turned to where the goblin stood across the room. "You and the others are free to move about the estate grounds. The staff is discreet. Stay out of sight of newcomers. It's not uncommon for the prince to receive guests from the capital."

They weren't in the city or castle, then.

Did that mean Hadeon had his own estate? She had assumed all the royalty lived at the palace or within the city proper. While she knew the basics of fae magic, there was so much she didn't know about their culture and politics.

"We'll send word if we require your services again," Kazimir said.

Vorkle's mouth settled into a fine line before his eyes shifted to Arabella.

They looked at each other for a long moment. There was an emotion on the goblin's face that she couldn't quite identify. Was it resignation? He was as dependent on the scheming fae prince as she was. Perhaps it was his version of sympathy for their shared circumstances. Or perhaps he was just cross. Then he was gone, disappearing into the air.

She opened her mouth to speak when a voice came from behind her.

"Back so soon?"

Power bloomed at the edge of her senses, and she turned

toward the figure striding toward the drink cart without pausing to acknowledge her, Jessamine, or Breckett.

Either unphased or unthreatened by them.

Like Hadeon and Kazimir, the male was breathtakingly handsome. All sharp angles and muscled confidence. But he wasn't a fae of the Twilight Court. It wasn't just his lack of wings that gave him away—though she'd learned not all fae from the Twilight Court had wings. As he reached past a stiff Breckett for a decanter and glass, she spotted faint webbing between the male's fingers. His arms shimmered as though colorful scales hovered beneath his dark brown skin.

Water fae, she realized.

If she recalled correctly, there was more than one underwater fae court. She wondered which he was from.

"The sorcerer sent a company of ogres and gargoyles," Kazimir said to the newcomer from where he sat in the chair. Although he lounged back, he didn't look comfortable. Every line of his features was as taut as a bowstring.

The water fae made a noncommittal sound. As he did, the corners of his mouth seemed intent on reaching the floor.

Kazimir gestured to the newcomer. "This is Waylen. He's a... friend of Hadeon's."

Waylen didn't bother to incline his head toward them. He simply glanced at Arabella, Jessamine, and then Breckett. His long brown hair was in many plaits and tied back in a knot, emphasizing his angular features that seemed as hard as his countenance.

"Not a friend of yours?" Waylen said, his voice holding a hint of a playful challenge as he poured himself a glass of some fae alcohol and tossed it back.

Kazimir gave Waylen a flat look. "You know what I meant."

Suddenly, the doors to the sitting room burst open.

Everyone turned toward the doors, hands on weapons, stances low.

"See?" Hadeon said, sounding more winded than she'd ever heard him. It was so unlike his usual unbothered demeanor. His black hair was damp with sweat, but he appeared unharmed. "You worried for nothing."

There was a sound like a harrumph from Kazimir, but he didn't voice an objection.

Hadeon strode over to the sofas at the center of the room and dropped into one, kicking off his boots. One of his wings draped off the edge. The entire image felt *too* comfortable.

In the oversized chair beside him, Kazimir leaned back as though finally able to relax.

"How did you get here so fast?" she asked. "The gateway is miles from the castle."

"There are gateways in the air," Hadeon replied. "Most don't know of them, and demons can't travel through them." He nodded to the water fae at the drink cart. "I see you've met Waylen." Then he gestured to the winged male beside him. "As well as Kazimir, my right hand in the Twilight Court."

That explained why Hadeon didn't seem concerned about an army so close to a gateway that led to the Twilight Court.

If demons couldn't travel by gateway, how had Elias and Breckett used it? She wondered if it was because, while they'd been turned into demons, they were once men. Perhaps the part that was once human still lived within them.

But if Elias and Breckett could travel by gateway, that meant the erox in Magnus' army could also travel by gateway. It wouldn't be the full army, but it could be enough to threaten the fae...

"Why did you bring humans here?" Waylen said, his voice was as sharp as his narrowed gaze. It was then that she realized his eyes were unlike humans' or the eyes of the Twilight Court fae. His pupils were slightly narrowed, though not quite feline.

"Because we're excellent company," Jessamine bit back before Arabella could form a reply.

Arabella tried—and failed—to suppress a smile.

Waylen turned to Jessamine, truly looking at her for the first time. "And you are?"

"Your problem," Jessamine said, entirely unaffected by the power radiating from the three fae.

Although her friend was short in stature, the dried blood coating Jessamine's face and leathers made her a fierce picture. There was no fear in the lines of her hardened features, only a smoldering flame that—it seemed—she was about to unleash.

For the first time, Arabella wondered why no one had taken their weapons.

Hadeon raised a hand, which had Waylen closing his mouth. "Why don't we all take a seat and... discuss future relations."

Waylen didn't sit but acquiesced by standing beside Kazimir's chair, leaning against it, and crossing a leg.

Arabella settled into the least-expensive-looking sofa, and Jessamine came to stand behind her.

With a sigh, Breckett tossed back whatever he'd been drinking before he joined them and sat in a chair nearest the door.

Hadeon introduced her, Jessamine, and Breckett and then provided a brief overview of what happened at the castle.

"The sorcerer will be pissed," Waylen said, once again not bothering to look at Arabella, Jessamine, or Breckett.

Kazimir nodded. "You've taken in a mortal he wants as well as a demon who stole something from him."

Breckett's eyes narrowed. "How did you—"

Waylen waved him off. "It's his job to know things."

"It's not ideal," Hadeon admitted. "But we now have the map and someone who can read it." He raised an eyebrow in Arabella's direction.

Leaning back on the sofa, she crossed her arms. "Why do you want to find the shadow fae?"

She knew her body posture screamed one thing: *Convince me to help you.*

While she found it unlikely the shadow fae were still alive, Hadeon clearly believed they were—enough to risk seeking her out when Magnus' army was close by.

For the first time since she'd met him, uncertainty flickered in

Hadeon's gaze. The scheming male who always seemed so certain, so confident in his every move, hesitated.

The fae prince shifted so that his elbows rested atop his knees as he eyed Arabella, then Jessamine, and turned back to Arabella. "Let's just say I don't like what the queen has been doing in the Twilight Court."

"What does that have to do with the shadow fae?" she pressed.

The prince laced his fingers together. "I imagine they don't like what she's done either."

Eyes narrowing, she considered his words.

There was one possible reason a prince would be making moves in the shadows to oppose the reigning queen.

"If this is some coup to usurp the throne, count me out," she said, not bothering to disguise the disgust in her tone.

To her surprise, Hadeon tilted his head back and laughed—a deep, booming sound that was faintly musical. "I have no aspirations to rule the Twilight Court." He ran a hand through his short black hair. "My mother is obsessed with immortality. There's nothing she wouldn't do to evade death—even at the expense of her court. After the erox denied her request to be turned, she grew more eager to achieve her ends." He spared a knowing glance at Breckett. "And I suspect if I locate the shadow fae, they might be amenable to assist me in stopping my mother before she does anything she can't come back from."

"This is irrelevant," Jessamine interjected. "The shadow fae were killed during the fae wars. By *your* court."

The Twilight Court had led the combined fae armies against their shared enemy—the shadow fae.

"That little tale might not be entirely true." A sudden fierceness brightened Hadeon's eyes. "I have reason to believe some of the shadow fae escaped."

Impossible.

There was no way the shadow fae not only escaped their fate but weren't found for hundreds of years.

She shook her head. "Let's pretend I believe you. You think this map will lead us to wherever they're hiding?"

"The map leads to one of the underrealms, a place called the Abyss," he said. "I believe that's where Prince Arden of the Shadow Court fled with what remains of the shadow fae army."

There were those who believed that the underrealms were the home of the demons. It was said that, long ago, someone opened a portal between an underrealm and the mortal realm, allowing demons through. Ever since, they'd feasted on mortals, and groups like the enchantresses had been formed to stop the demons from wiping humans out of existence. She had no idea if any of this held credence though.

Pursing her lips, she said, "Explain."

"Prince Arden's body was never found amongst the dead. Some of my mother's generals remarked that the shadow fae army was smaller than they'd originally thought," Hadeon said. "I'm wagering Arden is still alive and that he might be amenable to helping not just me but you as well."

"Fuck, Hadeon, what are you up to now?" Waylen rubbed his eyes. Exasperation saturated his words—like he'd been exposed to Hadeon's schemes one too many times. "Do I want to know who she is?" He flicked his fingers in her direction.

Her irritation flared. "She has a name."

Hadeon turned to the water fae before his gaze settled on Arabella. "She's an enchantress from a human village, the mate of a powerful erox, and a shadow fae-human hybrid."

"She does smell different," Kazimir said, chin lifting as though he were sniffing the air. "Not fully human."

Her thoughts swirled, and she found herself shaking her head. "I hope you can understand my skepticism that your nose holds the answer to all things. It could be the ogre blood." She waved a hand in dismissal. "While origin stories are fun at a fireside, none of this matters. Not when my mate is in Magnus' clutches. If you're not going to help me, I fail to see why I should care about some army that is most likely long dead."

A smile lifted one corner of Hadeon's lips as he leaned back, one arm stretching out over the top of the sofa, the other resting in his lap. "I can't help you openly. No one in my court would risk angering a sorcerer with an army. But the shadow fae? If they're alive, they might be itching for a fight."

She snorted. "You want me to convince Prince Arden to lead what remains of the shadow fae army against Magnus? Who's to say they won't refuse and turn toward the Twilight Court to take their revenge and slaughter everyone?"

"He might listen to his niece," he said, a hint of mischief in his eyes.

She blinked. "What?"

Waylen turned fully toward Hadeon, a similar look of incredulity on his face.

"If I'm right, Enchantress Arabella is the child of Princess Myla," Hadeon said. "She'd taken human lovers before. I have reason to believe you were brought to the human realm in secret."

If what Hadeon said was true, her mother was a princess. What did that make her?

Royalty in a kingdom that was no more.

This was all too much.

Jessamine gestured to Arabella's ears. "I think we'd know if she was fae."

A patronizing twinkle filled Hadeon's gaze. "Not all demi-fae have pointed ears. Besides, don't you find it unusual that a shadow whisperer just... *appeared* in a remote human village that happens to be near a gateway to the fae realm?"

"Stranger things have happened. Like you showing up at the very moment an ogre broke through the ward." Jessamine's gaze was unflinching. "Besides, why the Abyss? Why not one of the other underrealms?"

"It has ties to the fae realm," Hadeon said. "The exit from the Abyss leads into the Twilight Court territory. However, no one knows exactly where the entrance is. Prince Arden believed there were gateways that couldn't be seen or could only be opened by certain fae. I'm guessing the shadow fae made their final stand in the western tundra because he thought the Abyss' gateway was here. It might have been his backup plan to protect the shadow fae—or as many of them as he could." He cleared his throat before continuing. "The Abyss was an obsession of Prince Arden's when he was still alive. I can't recall the number of times he made me listen to his research on the place at dinner parties and balls."

Arabella's brows drew together. "You knew him?"

The fae wars took place at least five hundred years ago. If Hadeon had known Arden before then, that would have made him at least six hundred years old.

Hadeon waited as she put the pieces together. "I look good for my age, no?" He waved a hand. "Call it a hunch that Arden fled to the Abyss. But if I'm right, the shadow fae are there. And they might be able to teach you to control those powers of yours."

"That doesn't explain why *you* want to find the shadow fae," Jessamine interrupted. "Your mother is obsessed with immortality. So, what? Are you trying to start a civil war by bringing the shadow fae back?"

A muscle pulsed in Hadeon's jaw. "Not only is she obsessed with immortality, but my mother seeks power. She's convinced some of the fae courts will rise up against the Twilight Court. She's been in talks with some courts, forming secret alliances. I fear that she may start another war—and soon."

Jessamine sniffed. "And you think bringing back an army won't be the very thing that instigates the start of another war?"

He rubbed his hands together. "It's my hope the presence of an army will make my mother think twice before starting another war that could lead to the death of thousands. I don't want them to actually fight. In fact, I'm counting on them not fighting the Twilight Court for fear of getting wiped out of existence for real this time."

Jessamine scoffed. "Idiocy."

While Arabella didn't disagree with her friend, she had more she needed to know. "You *think* you know a way into the Abyss, and you *think* this map will lead us to the shadow fae. How do you know we'll be able to get out of there?"

While she needed allies, she wasn't about to get herself stuck in an underrealm, unable to help Elias and forever parted from her mate.

"There's an exit." His eyes fixed on her. "But I don't know how to open that particular gateway or why the shadow fae wouldn't have used it already."

"And you're willing to risk being stuck there?" she pressed.

"For a chance to avoid another war? Yes," he said without hesitation. "Not to mention any other consequences from my mother's pursuit of immortality."

For a moment, Arabella considered—truly considered—what this male was suggesting. She was up against an army of erox, ogres, gargoyles, and who knew what other kind of dark creatures. Frankly, she needed her own army to get Elias back. Stealth wouldn't be enough to rescue him. Even if she did somehow manage to free Elias, the sorcerer would just hunt them down again. They'd never be free if she didn't kill Magnus and make sure his army was dispersed.

Was this the answer she needed?

However, her need for an army to rescue Elias was separate from the fact that her shadows had become stronger since using the amplifier, and they'd become wilder since her memories had returned. If she was honest, she didn't feel entirely herself. She was impulsive, quick to anger, and more prone to give in to the wills of the shadows.

She needed help to figure out what was going on with her magic—and how to control it. Perhaps Hadeon was right that only the shadow fae could help her. Her training with Lucinda had been relatively unsuccessful. Had it been because her magic was fae and not from a mortal source of power? The idea of taking time to train—rather than push to rescue her mate immediately—filled her with guilt. How long could Elias hold out with Magnus torturing him?

At that moment, she realized there was no other option. The enchantresses couldn't aid her in rescuing Elias. They had to remain within the walls of Shadowbank to protect her home. Hadeon and the Twilight Court wouldn't help her.

Which left her with only one option.

Sighing, she said, "If we're going to the Abyss, we leave tomorrow. My mate is waiting for me to rescue him."

Chapter Seven

ARABELLA

Arabella sat atop the balcony railing of her second-story bedroom overlooking the grounds of Hadeon's estate under the light of the moon.

Leagues away, the Twilight Court's capital city loomed with its massive blue walls. At its center and visible for miles in every direction was the castle, which was nestled atop a hill. She suspected the founding fae built the city there for the vantage point. It would be indispensable should the worst happen and it was under siege.

In the room behind her—which was as unnecessarily lavish as Hadeon's sitting room—she felt the blossoming of magic and knew a wielder had entered. The feel of golden, earthen magic told her it was Jessamine.

When her friend appeared in view, a laugh escaped Arabella's lips, which she tried to cover with a cough.

"You look ridiculous, too," Jessamine's cheeks were dusted with an unusual pink. Few things got under her skin enough to make her blush. Except, apparently, wearing a short nightgown that was sheer enough to leave little to the imagination.

"You could've just worn one of the prince's shirts," Arabella said. She'd had a similar option when the staff had taken their leathers to be cleaned and chose to wear one of Hadeon's shirts. The sturdy fabric fell to her knees, and she'd had to roll up the sleeves several times.

"Never," Jessamine said as she hopped up onto the railing and swung her legs around to sit next to Arabella. Muttering obscenities, she pulled at her dress as it slid up to her hips. "What princeling has only nightgowns to offer his female guests?"

"One who doesn't often host females, I imagine," Arabella said, a smile tugging at the corner of her lips.

"Or one who only hosts those he wants to fuck," Jessamine muttered, her voice as sharp as the sword sheathed at her hip. Even in a nightgown, she'd refused to be unarmed and had tied her scabbard to her waist along with knives sheathed on her legs.

Arabella had done the same.

"If I didn't know better, I'd think you were jealous." Arabella said.

Her friend made a disgusted sound in the back of her throat. "You wouldn't catch me fucking a fae—especially not that one."

"Why?" Arabella asked, genuinely curious. "He's handsome enough."

"I wouldn't go near a male who forced my best friend into a bargain when she was in a vulnerable position," Jessamine said. "Not to mention him coercing us into coming here."

Arabella shrugged. "He did save us. We wouldn't have made it out on our own."

"Yes, we would have," Jessamine said. "And we wouldn't be stuck in fae lands."

As enchantresses, they couldn't make it through the gateways on their own. The only way home would be with help from someone who could carry them through the gateway or if one of the goblins was willing to teleport them back to the mortal realm.

"Do you want to go back to Shadowbank?" Arabella offered, feeling her heart sink as she said the words. She wouldn't stop her friend if she wanted to leave, and she could understand wanting to return home when an army was so close to the village. But she would miss Jessamine more than she wanted to think about.

"And leave you to your own devices? No. We're going to rescue Elias. Then we'll protect our home together." Jessamine nodded to the parchment Arabella had been clutching in her hands for the last several hours. "Have you opened the map?"

Arabella sighed heavily. "Yes."

"And...?"

"All that effort for a blank piece of parchment," Arabella said. "We almost got killed by gargoyles for nothing."

She'd been staring at the map for hours, which remained wholly unmarked. Only the purring of the parchment in response to her shadows let her know it was made by the shadow fae. She hoped it was the map Hadeon sought and not some other rare magical document.

They'd be royally fucked if the real map was back at the castle —and under Magnus' control.

"I've tried using my shadows," Arabella said. "But it's made no difference."

Hadeon had said the map was made by Prince Arden, and only other shadow fae could read it. She still found it strange that Hadeon had been friends with someone who'd been alive six hundred years ago—someone who was merely a name in a history book to her.

Someone who may be related to her.

That connection apparently didn't matter as far as the map was concerned. No matter what she'd tried for the past several hours, the map remained unhelpfully blank.

Jessamine nodded before turning her gaze toward the horizon and the Twilight Court. "I never thought I'd see the fae lands." Her voice no longer held the edge it had moments before. "I figured I'd remain in Shadowbank until the day a demon bested me."

"Until Elias took me to the Twilight Court for the queen's ball, I'd thought the same for myself." Arabella reached out, clasping Jessamine's hand. Calloused fingers gripped hers in return. "It's so much more peaceful than Shadowbank."

A sudden sadness swelled in her chest.

"None of it's fair." Jessamine's voice caught for a moment. "The fae leave us to die at the hands of demons when they have so much power. Even the land, itself, is more powerful here. They could wipe out the lesser demons that attack Shadowbank with a mere thought, and they don't. You saw how powerful Hadeon was. He might even be able to kill a greater demon single-handedly." For a long moment, all was silent. Then Jessamine said, "It makes me hate them—the fae. To have that much power and not use it to help those who need it is despicable."

Arabella took a deep breath. "Part of me is disgusted with them, too. But after meeting the queen, another part of me wonders just how much most of the fae know about the mortal realm."

Jessamine sniffed. "It's on them to learn. They shouldn't wait for their leaders to spoon-feed them—whether it's truth or lies."

"Perhaps they're no different from humans," Arabella said. "Perhaps they're only concerned for the welfare of those they care about. And everything else is irrelevant."

Jessamine turned to her, a hardness returning to her eyes before reluctant understanding filled them. They'd both been forced to make hard decisions in Shadowbank—deciding who to protect when there weren't enough resources to protect everyone.

Sighing, Jessamine said, "So much has changed in a short amount of time."

"Yes," Arabella agreed. "It has."

"How do you feel about trying to find the shadow fae?" Jessamine asked. "Do you think Hadeon spoke the truth about your mother?"

Shrugging, Arabella allowed her gaze to return to the dark

castle. For a moment, she thought she spotted shapes flying to and from the highest turrets. But that wasn't possible. Only a fae could see that far. Unless...

Unless there was a kernel of truth in Hadeon's claims that she was shadow fae.

"I think Hadeon is a scheming bastard," Arabella said. "But... I don't think he's dishonest. I believe he's convinced himself of my lineage—whether it's true or not."

"Big claim and no evidence." Jessamine's grip on Arabella's hand tightened slightly. "Would you want to meet them if they're still alive?"

Arabella shrugged. "I've never cared about where I came from before. They might have birthed me, but they didn't raise me. But if they happened to be in the Abyss, I'd speak to them. I have a lot of questions about my magic. My shadows are changing."

"How?"

"It's difficult to explain." Arabella shook her head, struggling to find the words. "It's harder to control them now. They respond to my fear and anger, almost like they feel my emotions."

"I hate to say it, but I think we could use the shadow fae's help—if they're alive," Jessamine said. "When we were at the castle with Breckett, you seemed different."

"I can feel myself changing," Arabella admitted.

"I wonder how much of it is the mating bond versus your magic," Jessamine said. "Maybe it's something else we aren't thinking of." She snickered. "Or this could just be the new badass Arabella."

Arabella laughed, though her heart wasn't fully in it. "Maybe."

There was so much out of their control.

Her magic, the army, and a sorcerer who wanted her for reasons she didn't yet know. Not to mention the possibility of her fae lineage, Shadowbank's patchwork ward, and no way to rescue her mate.

Restlessness filled her limbs, making it hard to remain in one place. She felt guilty allowing herself any pleasure or respite when there was so much that needed doing.

Her gaze strayed to the scroll in her lap. They'd leave for the gateway in the morning. And if they had any hope of finding the shadow fae and returning, she had to be able to read this map.

Chapter Eight
ELIAS

A tugging in Elias' chest pulled him from sleep, and he gasped awake. For a moment, he blinked, staring at the inside of Magnus' tent, nearly passing out again. As he glanced around from where he was cuffed hand and foot to the X, he heard the rustling of the awakening encampment.

It was morning.

There was another tug in his chest, and he realized it was the mating bond.

Arabella.

He could sense she was moving. There was something... different about her emotions. While her fierceness shone down the bond as it always did, there was a new determination. Or perhaps it was resignation.

What are you doing, little enchantress?

There was a flash of light as the tent flap was pulled back and Flynn walked through it with Magnus a few steps behind.

Flynn stood near the entrance, his hands crossed in front of him. "Elias is ready for you, sir. He's been teetering between passing out and going feral for hours."

That was right. He'd nearly forgotten with the tugging on the bond.

After Flynn had sliced him open for hours, bleeding him of essence, Elias had blacked out.

Now, his stomach twisted painfully, and his fangs lengthened, puncturing his lower lip.

If he didn't feed soon, he'd succumb to his inner demon.

What would turning fully into a demon do to Arabella and their bond? Would the mating bond snap? Or would she be plagued by his hunger, feeling it down the bond every moment until the final day of her mortal life?

Magnus didn't come to stand before where Elias was tied. Instead, he stood beside the table of food, popping a grape into his mouth. "Unfortunately, I don't have time this morning to see to our little experiments. I've located where the enchantress has gone to. The next time I see you, I suspect it will be with your mate in tow."

Panic surged in Elias' veins.

How had he found her so quickly?

He couldn't let Magnus find her. Not if she would soon share his fate. The sorcerer might want to use her shadow fae magic to create new syphens, but he wouldn't hesitate to torture her to get what he wanted.

"Wait," Elias said as Magnus turned toward the tent's exit.

Elias' mind raced as he desperately searched for something, *anything,* to keep Magnus from leaving.

From going after her.

Elias would do whatever he could to protect her. Even if all he could do was stall the sorcerer.

Magnus paused and turned back toward him, one eyebrow raised.

"I need..." Elias began, struggling to speak through the fear tightening his throat. "I need to feed."

Magnus nodded as though expecting this before waving a hand to Flynn. "Bring in one of the humans—"

"No," Elias interrupted. "I don't want them." For a moment, the lie lodged in his throat. But he knew there was only one thing that would keep Magnus from leaving.

"I want you."

Magnus' hand was frozen mid-air, his eyebrow inching farther up his forehead. After a moment, he lowered it before turning to face Elias fully.

"So, you've come to your senses, then?" Magnus said. "I admit, I didn't think it would be this soon. But..." He crossed the tent, stopping before Elias. Reaching up, Magnus ran the back of his fingers down Elias' cheek.

It took everything in Elias not to flinch away. "Flynn was... very convincing."

Somewhere beyond Elias' line of sight, Flynn snorted.

Magnus' scarlet eyes flickered between Elias' eyes, as though searching for the truth. Elias locked down the disgust he felt for this male behind a mental wall. Then he pictured Arabella in his mind's eye and allowed his longing for her to bleed through. He let himself succumb to his desperation to be near her. All the while, the mating bond tugged in his chest.

It was like a second heartbeat.

Slowly, Magnus nodded and waved a hand, not turning from Elias. "Flynn, there's a small unit of erox waiting at the edge of camp. Find Enchantress Arabella and bring her to me."

Flynn brought a fist to his chest before there was a flash of movement at the tent's entrance, and he'd departed.

Elias' heart dropped.

He'd prevented Magnus from leaving, but he hadn't been able to stop them from going after Arabella. As his mouth went dry, he tried to remind himself that Magnus was infinitely more powerful than the regular erox. He was both a sorcerer and an erox while the erox in his army were limited to their demon abilities and any special powers they had. It was better that the soldiers were the ones to go. This way, Arabella and whoever she was with had a chance of getting away.

Magnus leaned forward. His amber and woody scent washed over Elias, making his stomach twist. This only served to worsen the hunger gnawing at his gut.

Elias' canines pressed deeper into his lip, and he tasted blood.

"You need me?" Magnus' hand moved to the back of Elias' head, his fingers gripping on to his hair and *pulling*.

Elias gritted his teeth at the pain and nodded.

Not only was Magnus the only erox who could feed on other erox, he could also give the essence within him to another erox. It wasn't just that erox could feed on him, but that he could give them essence.

It was something he'd tried to do with Elias all those years ago. And Elias had refused.

Which was why he knew this was the one thing that would keep Magnus by his side—and away from Arabella.

"Then what are you waiting for?" Magnus asked, his lips a mere breath away.

Swallowing back bile, Elias leaned forward and kissed Magnus. His fangs brushed against the sorcerer's lips, and he traced his tongue over Magnus' lower lip, which earned him a smile.

Gripping Elias' hair tighter, Magnus deepened the kiss. As Magnus' tongue swept into Elias' mouth, the metallic taste of blood filled his senses.

His fangs had split one of Magnus' lips.

Instantly, heat swept over Elias' gaze as his pupils swelled, his eyes going fully black. Thick, heady lust and a need to *feed* swirled in his gut.

Fuck, he wasn't going to be able to hold back.

"For you, my prodigy," Magnus purred before a light crested in his throat. Elias' eyes fixed on the path of Magnus' scarlet essence as it flowed up the sorcerer's chest and into his mouth.

Then Elias' restraint slipped between his fingers like ground glass.

With a moan, he pressed back into Magnus' touch, into his

kiss, as he feasted on the sorcerer's essence. Time lost all meaning as he drank deeply, pulling mouthful after mouthful into him.

Distantly, he became aware of the sorcerer reaching between them. But he was so swept up in the feeding that he didn't fully comprehend what was happening until warmth splashed against his stomach.

With a gasp, Elias pulled away from Magnus.

The first thing his mind registered was Magnus' swollen lips. Then he glanced down to the space between Elias' naked body and Magnus' mostly clothed one.

To where Magnus had freed his cock, fisting it.

"I've been waiting a long time for that," Magnus purred, tucking his cock back into his pants before pressing a final kiss to Elias' lips.

Shame welled up within Elias as he stood there, unable to move, to fight, to *clean* himself.

Then Magnus reached into his cloak, removing a blade.

"For your good behavior," Magnus began. "You have earned some time to rest."

Something sharp sliced into Elias' mind.

"You're to remain in this tent until I return," Magnus said as he filtered his magic into the syphen. "Do not even consider fleeing, fighting, or using your magic. Self-harm is prohibited."

Elias grunted as the syphen's magic descended on him, layering over his mind, his thoughts, until the commands settled in place.

Then his cuffs unlocked.

Unable to hold himself up, Elias fell to the ground. Blood rushed back into his arms, and it felt like needles pricked along every inch of his skin.

But just as he couldn't bring himself to raise his arms, neither could he bring himself to feel relief as Magnus mussed Elias' hair before striding from the tent.

Leaving Elias alone with the memory of what they'd just done.

Chapter Nine
ARABELLA

The next morning, Hadeon was already gone when Arabella came down for breakfast, dressed in her leathers and full armor—including the syphen.

Once again, he'd refused to travel by teleportation with Vorkle and, according to Kazimir, wanted to get a head start toward the western tundra.

She shared an awkward breakfast with Jessamine, Breckett, Kazimir, and Waylen in the same sitting room from the day before.

After everyone had eaten quicker than would normally be considered polite, Kazimir stood and said, "The prince has ordered me to remain behind, and Waylen—"

"Has refused to risk my neck to find fae who are better left *not* found," Waylen interrupted. "I'd wish you luck, but... I hope your trip is far from fruitful. For the sake of everyone in the fae realms."

As the water fae spoke, something akin to anger swirled in Arabella's chest. "Are all water fae cowards, or just you?"

Waylen laughed, though it held no hint of humor. "I'm not so easily goaded, *demi-fae*."

A response was on the tip of her tongue, but she swallowed it.

One more fae wasn't going to make all that much difference against an army of shadow fae or a horde of demons.

Without another word, she turned and strode into the hallway where Vorkle waited.

The carpeted hallway was wide enough for three people to walk side by side comfortably. Like the sitting room, it had large windows with the shutters opened wide to reveal the early morning sunrise blossoming on the horizon. Around the house, there was a garden as well as some trees.

For a moment, she thought she sensed something in those trees.

As though she was being watched.

The sounds of Jessamine and Waylen's bickering echoed out of the sitting room and drew Arabella's thoughts back to the present.

"Good to see you again," she said to Vorkle, whose face was utterly emotionless. "When this is over, I daresay I'll owe you a drink."

The goblin's eyes shifted up to hers, his expression unchanging. "I'm under oath to serve Prince Hadeon and his inner circle in exchange for his protection. This is the consequence of *your* actions, Enchantress."

By stealing the amplifier to try to protect Shadowbank, she'd put Elias' castle and its secret occupants at risk. She wouldn't try to deny the consequence of her actions.

"I'm trying to make this right," she said. "But I'm curious—why Prince Hadeon? You could have gone anywhere in the mortal or fae realm. Why here? Why make a bargain with *him*?"

More bickering echoed into the hallway, the sounds drawing closer.

Something sparked in Vorkle's eyes, but he didn't reply.

She crossed her arms. "He came to call in his bargain with me before yesterday, didn't he? And you intercepted him."

Vorkle shrugged. "I saw an opportunity and took it."

Not for the first time, she wondered what arrangement the goblins had made with Hadeon, but she doubted Vorkle would tell her even if she asked outright. Either way, Vorkle had found a way to speak to Hadeon without her realizing he'd even come to the castle. But why had Hadeon left before speaking with her about the map?

Jessamine cleared her throat as she came to stand beside Arabella, apparently having tired of her verbal sparring with Waylen. The water fae turned and stormed off in the opposite direction without so much as a farewell.

Then Kazimir came into the hallway, satchels in his hands.

Breckett followed closely behind him.

Kazimir passed a satchel to each of them. "Be careful. Please keep the prince from doing anything too reckless."

Arabella glanced inside.

Dried meats, a skin of water, a blanket, and various travel supplies. Given they had no notion what the underrealms were like outside of them being the home worlds to demons, it was smart to be prepared.

"You're protective of Prince Hadeon," she said, surprised that he inspired such loyalty. "I'll see what I can do, but I doubt he'd heed my warning."

Kazimir inclined his head to her. "You're probably right." Then he turned to Vorkle. "Take them to the western tundra. The prince should be there when you arrive."

Distaste crossed Vorkle's features—the first sign of emotion she'd seen from him that morning. "That is a cursed place."

She opened her mouth to speak, but Jessamine spoke first. "Why?"

A slight stiffness lined Kazimir's features as he said, "It's where the last battle in the fae wars took place. It's where most believe the shadow fae were wiped from existence. Even if it's untrue, many died there."

"Oh good," Jessamine said, her tone dry. "I was hoping to piss off the dead today."

Arabella pinched the bridge of her nose between her thumb and forefinger. "I suppose a gateway to an underrealm was unlikely to be in a friendlier location."

"That's the spirit," Breckett said beside her, his voice laced with sarcasm.

Turning to him, she said, "Are you sure you want to come? You can stay here."

While his invisibility could be a useful tool, he'd been ill-equipped to face the ogres. She had a suspicion he'd be equally unadept at facing demons in an underrealm.

"Not with my knife in your possession, and not when there's something I can do to help Elias," the erox said.

She nodded before turning back to Vorkle.

With obvious distaste, the goblin extended a hand toward her. She took it, and Jessamine slipped a hand into hers.

Stepping forward, Breckett accepted Vorkle's other hand, shifting his satchel over his shoulder.

"Stay alert, and trust nothing," Kazimir said. "Anything that walks in the underrealms is deprived of life and light. They will try to take yours."

"Are you quite finished?" Vorkle said.

There was a flash of movement in the trees' shadows beyond the window, and she frowned. Her own shadows hummed at her feet, as though they, too, sensed the disturbance.

A sudden shouting sounded outside the house.

The hairs on Arabella's arms stood on end, and she knew in an instant something was very wrong.

Kazimir pulled his sword free of its scabbard, his eyes locking with Arabella's. "Get out of here, *now*."

Brows furrowing, she shook her head.

Something was coming. She couldn't leave them behind without helping.

There was a shifting in the shadows farther down the hallway, as though they flickered. Her own shadows hummed to life.

Erox.

Somehow, she knew. It was like a strange humming from the dark, as though the shadows had a mind and will of their own. As though they somehow communicated with her.

"Go!" Kazimir shouted as he charged down the hallway.

"Wait—" she began, but they were already portalling.

In the time it took her to blink, they had reappeared in a treeless land with sloping grassy hills dotted with boulders. In the far distance, there was a line of mountains with snow-dusted peaks.

She had no idea how far the western tundra was from the Twilight Court, but she couldn't spot the castle in any direction, nor did she recall seeing mountains near the capital. Had they just teleported to the opposite side of the fae realm?

"Erox. Those were Magnus' erox, I'm sure of it," she breathed and turned to look down at Vorkle. "You can't let him see you or the other goblins."

Vorkle released her hand.

"We suspected the sorcerer would come sniffing around the estate after we rescued you from the castle," Vorkle said, entirely too calm. "Fear not. We know how to remain out of sight."

Despite his outward appearance of indifference, she could sense his eagerness to be off. But rather than disappearing, he hesitated.

"Goblins cannot teleport to the underrealms or within them." Vorkle swallowed visibly even as he clung to his indignation. "But we have skirted along the border to the lands of the undead. Something lurks there. A devouring darkness that slumbers. Whatever you do, don't wake it." He scrubbed his palms against his trousers. "I intend to curse your name each night before I rest for forcing the goblins out of hiding, but... The master would wish for you to be safe."

"I appreciate the insight." A sad smile crept over her lips. "I'll get him back, Vorkle. Whether or not the Abyss is the answer, I'll find a way. And when I do, when he's safe, you'll have the choice whether you wish to be under his protection again."

If the goblins could get out of their bargain with Hadeon.

Vorkle harrumphed and then disappeared.

"Prickly little bastard," Jessamine muttered.

Power blossomed above Arabella, and she looked up.

Black wings filled her vision before the ground trembled as the prince of the Twilight Court landed beside her in a crouch. As he stood, his gaze turned to Jessamine. His eyes swept over her clean leathers before taking in her blonde waves, which she'd tied out of her face.

Hadeon's gaze lingered for a moment too long before he nodded to Breckett. Then he turned to Arabella. "Any progress on the map?"

With a sigh, she pulled the parchment from an inner jacket pocket. "None."

The fae scrubbed a hand through his short black hair, making it stick up in mussed spikes.

"You should know—Magnus' erox arrived at your estate when we were leaving," she said, wondering how they'd found her so quickly.

Hadeon nodded before saying, "Kazimir is prepared."

Before she could respond, something tugged at her chest—sharp and persistent—and she gasped.

Elias.

He was awake.

While she could still feel his emotions pulsing down their bond, they weren't as pronounced—as though the distance had impacted it somehow. Even with the bond being somewhat muted, a single emotion rippled down it. Then a sudden wave of a deeper emotion swept over her.

Staggering forward, she clutched her chest.

Shame, she realized. But why? What was happening?

Before, he'd been experiencing pain and fear, but this... This somehow felt worse.

I'm running out of time, she thought. *I have to hurry.*

Gasping, she struggled to stand upright. She felt the others' eyes on her but ignored them. Slowly, she managed to put one foot in front of another and walked past the prince toward the rising sun. "Let's go."

Behind her, Hadeon cleared his throat. She stopped, looking back.

"It's that way." He pointed in the opposite direction.

Of course.

She marched in the direction he pointed without a word, still clutching the map.

Anger surged through her, and the sharp edges of her emotions heightened. Even as she walked, she longed to move, to fight, to do *something*. While she understood the importance of this mission, doing anything but journey directly toward her mate had something in her chest setting aflame.

Fuck you, Magnus, she thought. *You'll die soon. At my hands.*

Shadows hissed at her feet, curling and twisting as her thoughts turned dark.

She glared at the mountain peaks in the distance as she moved in silence.

After some time, she found herself walking at Hadeon's side.

The prince had a distant look in his eyes, and she thought to wonder just what he might be thinking about. Had he been honest about his motivations for finding the shadow fae? She meant what she'd said to Jessamine the night before. She didn't believe the prince was dishonest. But she doubted he had their best interests at heart.

Even if she couldn't be entirely certain of his motivations, she couldn't help wondering why he hadn't simply forced her to help him find the shadow fae with the favor she owed him.

"Why didn't you call in the bargain?" she eventually asked, hoping the conversation might distract herself from the agony slicing down the bond. "Why this roundabout way of getting me to come with you to the Abyss?"

"Perhaps I thought it would benefit us both."

Leveling a flat look on him, she said, "You don't do anything without a reason."

Eyes scanning the gently sloping hills around them, no power winked into her awareness. There wasn't a single magic wielder nearby outside of their group. It was completely desolate. Though... as she cast her awareness further out, she thought she detected something else lingering in the air. It dusted her senses with dread, feeling like hundreds of eyes followed their group's every step.

Like they were intruding in a place they shouldn't be.

She'd never believed in ghosts nor had she encountered spirits of the dead in her time as an enchantress. All she'd had to consider were the demons that threatened her home. Most had physical bodies, and killing a corporeal form was simple enough by magic or blade. How did one fight an angry spirit?

Pushing thoughts of the lingering eyes aside, she said, "How did you meet Prince Arden?"

Hadeon shrugged. "The shadow fae weren't highly favored toward the end of their existence in the fae realm. And I've never been among my mother's favorite sons. Arden and I bonded over our mutual unfavored existence at court functions, balls, and the like."

The queen disliked her own son? The notion seemed ridiculous. But Arabella needed to know if there was more to why Hadeon wanted to stop his mother. What was their history? Why was he so desperate to stop her from securing immortality? What could the price be for one queen to live forever?

As they walked, her eyes caught on how the light reflected off sections of his wings. They didn't just have feathers like his brothers' wings, which she'd seen on the dais the day she'd met the queen with Elias. Speckled between the feathers, something glittered in the light.

Turning to the blank parchment in her hand, she said, "Any

suggestions for reading an unreadable map? Maybe something Arden said to you?"

"It was something he created," Hadeon said as he navigated around a boulder, angling downhill. "He'd been studying old texts and went on about how some realms are mirror images of each other and others were unique unto themselves. He'd been sparse with the details of how he'd created a map of a place he'd never been to. When I saw him after he created it, he looked pale and sickly. At the time, he'd been excitable and eager to tell me about it. But war was imminent, and my mother told me to end the friendship or risk us being viewed as allies to the shadow fae. So, there hadn't been time to learn much about it."

"I see," she said, though this only sparked more questions in her mind about the fae war. There was so much she didn't know—so much that was left out of the histories. How much of what she'd been taught was a fabrication or partial truth by the victors?

They walked in silence for a time while she tried to get the map to work. But as the minutes turned to hours, the parchment remained stubbornly blank.

The sun crept higher in the sky, and Hadeon slowed his steps.

Suddenly, the air shifted, like electricity just struck the ground, and she looked around.

To the naked eye, the land seemed no different.

There were unremarkable rolling grassy hills in every direction with occasional large boulders. The surrounding hills were almost entirely treeless and lacked any kind of shrubbery. In the distance, the mountains loomed.

A soundless scream ripped from the earth. It wasn't the scream of a mortal. No, this felt as though the earth itself cried out in protest at this fissure that was formed into the very fabric of this world. The sound filled her mind until all she knew was the familiar agony.

We found it.

Whether by making or happenstance, the gateway to the Abyss was before them.

She dropped to a knee, clapping her hands over both ears instinctively. But it did nothing to muffle the sound ricocheting in her mind. Beside her, Jessamine collapsed to her hands and knees before retching.

"I forgot enchantresses don't do well with gateway travel," Breckett said somewhere above her. "Elias had to haul Arabella through the gateway last time."

She managed to look up, noting panic in Hadeon's eyes. Though it disappeared as quickly as it'd come. So quickly she thought she might have imagined it.

"They can't walk through?" Hadeon pressed.

Breckett looked at her and Jessamine and then back to Hadeon before shaking his head. "Not without help."

Beside her, Jessamine had stopped retching only long enough to sway and slump onto the grass, unconscious.

Agony filled Arabella's mind as the gateway seared her senses.

Sucking in labored breaths, she struggled to remain conscious as her fingers dug into the patchy grass. But she couldn't tune out the gateway's shrieks nor the pain coming down the mating bond, which had suddenly become tinged with concern.

Could Elias sense her as well?

Spots formed in her vision, and she started to sway.

This gateway was unlike the one in the forest. It was an illness in this world—a deep wound that bore evil—and it struck something deep in her core. Distantly, she wondered if some evil entity had made a slash between realms, incrementally tainting the land with foreign energy. One that promised desolation.

She noticed then that the gateway bore a darker melody. It was a slow cadence beckoning her forward. The screeching filling her mind was gradually replaced by a trilling sound as alluring as a siren's song.

Slowly, she raised her head.

The motion had her gut whirling, and she thought she might be sick. But she managed to turn her eyes toward where the gateway materialized in the air.

It wasn't a rift in the air like the gateway in the forest. No, this was a simple dark mist hovering above the ground, about as tall as a winged fae. The mist was faint enough to be translucent. If she hadn't been looking directly at it, she might have missed it.

As she studied the gateway, its song increased, and she felt herself standing without her willing it. A presence settled on her shoulders like a cloak of night, and the agony inside her head suddenly grew distant as the lilting music overtook it. Her thoughts grew fuzzy, and she took one step forward and then another.

"Where are you going?" Breckett demanded, but she paid him no heed. "Arabella! Damn you, what are you doing?"

There was a shuffling sound behind her as she continued toward the gateway. Her feet moved of their own accord. One step and then another. Soon, she was only paces away from the dark mist.

Something in her chest tugged, urging her to stop.

Even as her thoughts grew distant, she knew the thing in her chest anchored her. The person on the other side was entwined with the threads of her destiny. He was important to her, but she couldn't seem to recall why. But even knowing that, he was too distant, especially as a song crested within her. It laced through her every sense until she was vibrating with it. It beckoned her forward.

And she would follow.

As she neared the gateway, the pale darkness of the once-translucent mist deepened and churned like a storm cloud. As if in response, her shadows blossomed beneath her feet, spreading their inky tendrils forward.

Steps sounded behind her, but her eyes fluttered closed as the dark melody swelled to a crescendo.

Come, it seemed to say. *Come to me.*

Slowly, she reached out a hand.

The moment her fingers connected with the gateway, her

braid lifted off her shoulders in a sudden gust of wind before she stepped into the space between realms.

Chapter Ten
ARABELLA

Darkness consumed her. It was everywhere, diluting her senses and thoughts until all she knew was the endless void.

One moment, she was stepping forward, an unholy siren's song lilting through her mind. In the next, tidal waves crashed over her. She tried to reach out, desperately grasping for a handhold, but she had neither fingers nor a body.

For a moment, it felt like she ceased to exist as she floated in the fathomless deep.

She wondered if it was possible to die without a body. She felt herself sink, succumbing to the weight pressing ever downward. The will to fight seeped from her, and eternal night filled her until she was forced to become one with the starless void.

Then there was a sensation like the popping of a bubble atop the surface of water.

When Arabella opened her eyes, she thought it was night.

She stood in the middle of a desert with rolling hills of sand in every direction. The inky sky bore neither stars nor moons. Yet somehow, she could see in the unlit landscape.

Suddenly, a sound came from above her. There was a scream and then a muffled *thud*.

No, two thuds.

Turning, the sand shifted beneath her leather boots as she spotted an unconscious Jessamine and a very angry, very sandy Breckett.

A moment later, wings darker than the sky spread out above them, flapping as the prince descended with irritating grace to the ground. Once he landed, he tucked his wings behind him. Then he scanned the landscape—and likely found the same thing she had.

They were utterly alone in a dark wilderness.

A crippling truth settled in her bones.

Their supplies wouldn't sustain them for long. They had waterskins, some dried meats, and other supplies, but it wouldn't be enough to even see them out of the desert. *If* there was anything other than deserts in the Abyss.

We're going to die here, she realized. *The map doesn't work, and there's no water.*

Why hadn't she gone straight to Elias? Fuck the army. Maybe she could've made a deal with Magnus to free Elias...

A sudden *wrongness* struck her. It took her a moment to place what.

"I can't feel Elias." The words came out as a whisper as fear iced her veins.

Hadeon frowned at her before realization dawned in his eyes, which was quickly replaced by confusion. "Your mating bond?"

She nodded, pulling at her jacket and leathers, desperate to remove them from her chest—as though she could touch the magical connection that tied her to Elias.

Had she broken the mating bond by coming to the Abyss? Assuming that's where they were and they hadn't stumbled into some other realm.

"I can't feel his pain, his fear," she said, her throat tightening. "When he's awake, it's always there..."

The prince was suddenly before her, extending a gloved hand

toward her chest. She felt the rumble of his magic as his eyes closed, though she couldn't see a shift in power.

"No," he said. "It's not... gone. Your scent is still mated."

She blinked.

She'd forgotten there was a fucking *smell* to fae when partners found their mates. Closing her eyes, she felt toward the tightness in her chest.

But... Hadeon was right.

Reaching toward where the bond should be, there was a tiny flower made of flickering flames within her chest. It hadn't been snuffed out. Somehow, she knew the swaying of the flames was in time with Elias' every breath.

He was alive.

Opening her eyes, she swiped a sleeve over her damp cheeks.

Hadeon extended a gloved hand toward her, and she belatedly realized he held the map. "Be more careful next time."

Frowning, she nodded. She must have dropped the map when...

Just what had happened? One moment, there was that awful screeching sound in her mind, and then her thoughts weren't entirely her own. It was like a presence, a strange drive, had filled her and willed her steps forward.

Like something wanted her here.

She shook her head. Whatever had caused her to go through the gateway—whether it was something or someone—was yet another question without an answer. And one she'd have to deal with later. For now, she needed to make sure Jessamine was okay.

Hurrying over to her friend, she felt for a pulse and breathed a sigh of relief when she felt a strong heartbeat.

Jessamine was fine.

The gateway had just been too much for her.

"You're conscious." Breckett gestured in Arabella's general vicinity.

"Unfortunately for all of us, so are you," she said halfheartedly as she brushed Jessamine's hair out of her eyes.

He was right though. She hadn't passed out from going through the gateway like she had the other times. Did repetition make traveling through it easier? Or did the destination impact the difficulty for enchantresses to travel by gateway? She suspected the reason gateways made enchantresses ill had something to do with the unnatural nature of the tear in the world. After all, enchantress magic was rooted in nature, and whatever magic had created the gateways was entirely different.

Although she'd been fine going through the gateway this time, Jessamine hadn't been so fortunate. Perhaps the reason was something else entirely—something she had yet to consider.

Breckett made a sound that she was going to pretend was complimentary.

"Fortunately for me, you're on your feet," he said as he walked away from Jessamine's unconscious form, his eyes on the distant horizon. "So, you can carry her."

"And you can read the map." Arabella scooped Jessamine off the ground and into her arms. When Breckett didn't reply, she shifted her friend over her shoulder, holding her with one arm as she opened the map with the other.

To her utter shock, the once empty map flowed with dry ink as it spread across the parchment, filling it with illustrations and a distinct, thick black line across it that led toward a large X.

How...?

But she wasn't about to question their sudden luck.

Hadeon appeared at her side. "I'll be damned."

She was about to say she had nothing to do with the map's sudden agreeableness, but Breckett spoke first.

"In case you haven't noticed, we're amongst the *damned*," the erox hissed from where he stood at the edge of a nearby hill of sand, overlooking stretches of a deep, fathomless desert. "We may very well become one of them if we remain for too long."

Right.

It was time they were off.

Biting her lip, she looked at the surrounding desert and

then glanced down at the map. There were a series of lines, which looked like waves at first glance. After a moment, she realized they were meant to be the rolling hills of sand. Across the top of the map was what appeared to be a massive mountain range. Then tiny clusters of trees were dotted throughout the desert.

Oases, she realized. *Water.*

Thank fuck.

There was a thick line that went from right to left across the center of the map. Beneath the X was what appeared to be another cluster of trees. Perhaps another oasis?

If the top of the parchment was north, it would imply they'd be journeying west to get to the place marked on the map. However, there was no way to determine how many miles the journey across the map would be. There was no scale for distance. It could be anything from a few miles to hundreds of miles.

She pointed to the nearest cluster of trees on the map. "We make for an oasis. Even in a desert as cold as this one, we won't last long without water."

Sweat gathered beneath her breasts and along her limbs, making her leather pull uncomfortably. If this desert was similar to ones in the mortal realm with an unyielding sun, travel would be much slower in the heat. At least, that's what she'd gleaned from the books she'd read. She'd never actually been to a desert before. But here, the climate was cool. Gusts of wind carried crisp air—and sand—toward them.

"Prince, can you scout ahead?" she said with a nod toward the sky.

Hadeon waved a hand. "Of course." Spreading his wings, he was about to launch into the air when he paused. "And Hadeon is fine."

She shook her head. "We can behave more familiarly around each other once there isn't a bargain hanging between us."

It would be wise not to allow herself to get too comfortable with this male. Even if they temporarily shared the same goal.

"As you wish," he said. Then he took off into the air with several beats of his powerful wings.

Breckett frowned at the prince before his gaze settled on the map. "Do you have any idea how to read that?"

"None," she said, her eyes on their surroundings.

There was no sun, no moon, no stars—nothing to indicate which direction was north, south, east, or west.

Sighing, she started walking in the direction Hadeon had flown off in, carrying Jessamine over her shoulder.

I suppose this direction is as good as any.

Before she'd taken two steps, the strange presence she'd felt a few times—the one that felt like a dark cloak over her shoulders—returned. Only this time, it was stronger than ever. The dark draped over her, and her shadows rumbled to life. The thorny vines seemed to nuzzle into the misty darkness hovering around her.

But even as her shadows moved, the hairs on the back of her neck stood on end. She froze in place, trying to steady her racing heart as she glanced around.

Other than the dark mist, there was nothing else. It was just her, Breckett, and Jessamine.

Then the pressure atop her shoulders shifted. As though it was trying to turn her. Brows furrowing, she allowed her shoulders to move with it until she faced the opposite direction Hadeon had flown.

Biting the inside of her cheek, she considered which direction to go.

It was possible whatever it was had brought her through the gateway. It was also possible not everything in the underrealms wanted to consume her soul. Or it could be a demon that was leading them to its lair and some horrible death.

She knew what Jessamine would say if she were conscious.

Beggars can't be choosers.

"Fuck," she muttered before striding in the direction the strange presence had indicated.

"It's unwise to follow anything blindly," Breckett said from where he walked beside her.

She frowned. Could he sense this strange presence, too? Maybe his being a demon allowed him to perceive more than she could in this lifeless landscape.

Distantly, she wondered if mentioning the presence aloud would draw its attention or give it more power. Some demons in the forest beyond Shadowbank couldn't take form until someone spoke their name. Then they'd gather strength as they consumed the fear of their victims—until they were large enough to consume them whole.

"I could say the same about you," she said, deciding not to mention the presence for now. Turning, she looked up at Breckett. "You leaped into a gateway you'd never gone through before. One you *hoped* led to the Abyss. For all you knew, it could have led to your death."

A twinkle of humor filled the erox's eyes. "Couldn't have my friend's mate die while he's otherwise occupied. Besides, if anyone is going to kill you, it will be me."

"Not with your combat skills."

For a moment, she thought his cheeks reddened but couldn't be certain.

"I sail on ships—or I did before this mess," he hissed, his voice full of indignation. "I don't make a hobby of playing hopscotch with ogres."

"I daresay running isn't part of any of your hobbies."

His cheeks *did* redden then. "Only you enchantresses take pleasure in that sort of torture. If you see me running, best you start running, too. Because, most likely, something is chasing me."

The sand beneath her boots shifted as she started to descend a hill, and she nearly fell. A hand clamped on her bicep, steadying her.

"Aw, Breckett." She glanced up as she shifted Jessamine over her shoulder. "If you keep doing stuff like that, I'll think you care."

He released her arm as though he'd touched open flames. "Don't get used to it."

"I would never."

While she'd rather pass time by watching moss grow than talk with Breckett, there was something about the vast darkness that unsettled her. The quiet made it feel somehow heavier.

Clearing her throat, she said, "So... What was Magnus like?"

He sighed heavily. "I wondered when you'd ask." He ran a hand through his dark hair. "Sorcerers are figures shrouded in mystery as much as power. Magnus was no exception."

They strode around a large bank of sand before he continued.

"He journeyed through the lands doing fuck knows what, turning men into erox. Willing or not. Once we were turned, he'd speak of his home. In the mountains to the east, he'd somehow built a stronghold into the earth. There was no option once we were turned, not with the syphens. It was go with him or die. Those who went with him willingly to the mountains were placed into a dormitory of sorts where we were permitted some leisure time. Those who attempted to escape or refused to follow orders were locked into cells and used as experiments."

He cleared his throat. "We'd hear screaming for hours, sometimes days, before it finally stopped. We assumed they had died because we never saw them again." Sighing, he paused as he navigated another mound of sand. "Elias was immediately locked away when Magnus brought him back. None of us even saw his face. Rumors spread when the experiments on the others stopped. Somehow, this new erox remained alive, and many whispered that he must be different from us. Some told tales of an erox with tentacles or the power of the ocean."

She swallowed thickly as she tried to imagine Elias being locked away for months or years, subjected to torture at the hands of the male who'd created him.

"I became curious," Breckett continued. "So, I used my ability to sneak into the part of the mountain where the cells were. I wanted to see the male who'd captivated Magnus'... attention. You can imagine my surprise when I saw Elias for the first time, and he seemed no different from us. Though I didn't know what his powers were at the time."

Breckett's eyes grew distant, swiveling between the horizon and the sands at their feet. "We got to talking. As time passed, we formed a sort of friendship. I'd see him when I could. Eventually, I volunteered for guard duty, and I brought him offerings. He rarely fed, and when he did, he was careful never to take too much essence."

Exhaling, he said, "One day, he just... disappeared. He'd escaped from his cell and wasn't anywhere in the mountain. He hadn't told me of his plans to escape. The fool probably thought it would keep me from getting in trouble with Magnus when we were brought in for questioning. And we were questioned. *Thoroughly*. It was some time later when I found the courage to steal Magnus' other syphen and flee. I found an opening on a boat at the nearest port and never looked back. I never stopped moving as his erox hunted me, always looking for the syphen. That is, not until I received a summons from the fae queen. Though, I have no idea how she found me."

A deep sadness filled Arabella, and she licked her suddenly dry lips.

Those males had been through so much—to be turned into demons and then forced to remain within Magnus' stronghold in the mountains and be used in experiments... It was unthinkable. Had any of them wanted to be turned? Elias hadn't. Perhaps many of the other erox hadn't as well.

She thought of the erox who'd tried to kill her at Magnus' behest when she'd been captured. Those men had been willing to do unspeakable things to her. Perhaps they'd wanted to become erox, or perhaps their once good hearts had eventually darkened over the years as they succumbed to the drive to feed.

But Elias... Her erox... He'd been at the center of Magnus' experiments.

No wonder he'd been so fearful of the sorcerer. He'd had

months or maybe even years of memories of what the sorcerer had done to him—using his body to learn whatever he could about erox.

Elias had survived, but at what cost? He'd bear those memories forever.

And I pressed him to tell me, she thought, recalling how she'd challenged Elias about his eagerness to fix the castle's ward. She'd insisted on knowing just what he'd been so afraid of and why'd he'd been keen on hiding in the forest. Now that she understood more of his history with Magnus, guilt filled her. She wished she'd been more patient with him—more understanding. But she'd been so single-minded in her goal of protecting Shadowbank.

Swallowing, she forced herself to focus on the present conversation. She needed to learn as much as she could about Magnus. Anything she gleaned could be an edge against the sorcerer.

She glanced at the map, which remained unchanged. "When did Magnus start using the erox as soldiers?"

Breckett scratched his head. "Around the time I volunteered to work as a guard, I think. We were told we'd be given the chance to serve him. Some ventured out into the world to do his bidding. That's also when the combat training began, and we learned how to feed quickly and discreetly. As well as whatever else he deemed important."

She nodded, daring to voice a question lingering in her thoughts. "Did you choose to become an erox?"

One corner of his lips lifted, and he eyed her beneath raised brows. "That's a story I only tell to friends."

"You have friends?" she said dryly.

He rolled his eyes. "Unlike you, I don't stab those I claim to care about."

Something sunk in her gut as she thought of what she'd done to Elias when she'd stolen the amplifier. While she regretted her decision, she didn't know what she'd do if she had the chance to do it all over. Shadowbank needed protecting, the same as Elias' home in the forest with the goblins.

"I did what I felt I had must to protect my home," she managed, her throat growing tight. "Elias hadn't been willing to compromise with the amplifier—even when I'd been the one to make a deal with Hadeon."

Breckett sniffed. "And you can see why he was unyielding now, yes?"

She nodded. "I wish there'd been a way to protect both our homes."

"Because of you, his castle is overrun, and the goblins revealed themselves to Hadeon," he said. "And Magnus found us."

Swallowing thickly, she said, "Yes."

He raised an eyebrow. "No objections or some self-righteous defense?"

"No." She eyed the map if only to give her something to look at as her eyes watered. "It was my actions that led to this."

It's because of me that Elias is with Magnus right now. Because he wanted to get my memories back.

"But I intend to fix this," she said, pushing back the guilt threatening to consume her. "I'm going to get him back." After a moment, she added, "I'm sorry to you, too. About the way I took the syphen."

She didn't regret taking the syphen. It was an invaluable tool. Turning a significant portion of the sorcerer's army back on him could be the very edge they needed.

At the mention of the syphen, Breckett bristled. "Have you learned nothing from what you've done? Stop taking things and doing whatever the fuck you want. It's going to *continue* to get us all into trouble." His voice hardened with each word. "If you're truly sorry, I'll accept your apology once you've returned the syphen."

She bit the inside of her cheek.

If she hadn't stabbed Elias and stolen the amplifier, she may have never come across Magnus' army and been captured. If she hadn't been captured, Elias and Breckett wouldn't have come after her, and Magnus may have never discovered either of the erox. But once he did, he'd sent his ogres and gargoyles after them and destroyed the repaired ward around Elias' castle.

Suddenly, an unspoken truth struck her.

Before the enchantresses had been her priority. Now, she had two families who needed protecting.

Elias was her family now, too.

Slowly, she stopped walking and lowered Jessamine to the ground. Placing her in the sand, she reached for the syphen hidden inside a sheath in her jacket, her hand lingering on the hilt.

"I can respect that you don't want to take free will from the erox. But the syphen is an edge in the coming confrontation against Magnus. Because there *will* be one, whether we like it or not. You don't gather an army to not use it." She turned the syphen over in her hand. "I'm sorry, but I'll do what I must to protect Shadowbank *and* Elias. I meant what I said before. I won't take the free will of the erox indefinitely. I will require their assistance only long enough to save my mate."

And she meant it.

This wasn't a world for the faint of heart or the soft. To survive meant to choose who to protect. And she'd choose Elias and Shadowbank every time.

"Why did you come with us?" she asked.

Breckett sighed. "I already told you—"

"The real reason," she pressed.

"I'm tired of running," he said. "Magnus has been chasing me for more years than I care to count. The only way this stops is if he's dead. With Magnus gone, all of the erox will be free to live as they choose."

"And you won't be constantly looking over your shoulder," she said.

"Yes," he agreed. "Magnus' erox finding us at Hadeon's estate is just the start. He will try again and again to find you—to find us both. You're a good bet as any. Besides, I don't want to leave Elias under Magnus' thumb any more than you do."

Slowly, she nodded.

A life on the run sounded exhausting. While she had every intention of looking for a way to kill Magnus, it was possible she'd share Breckett's fate. But if spending her days fleeing from the sorcerer was the only way she could be with Elias, then so be it.

"Taking the syphen makes you no better than Hadeon," Breckett said in a softer tone, the words seeped in an emotion she couldn't quite identify. "When he calls in that favor, you'll lose your free will, too. Likely only for a time, but you won't be able to refuse."

"Perhaps you're right," she said, filled with both sadness and determination. "Perhaps I'm no better than the fae prince. I will do whatever is necessary to protect those I love. In this world, we either fight to protect those we love, or we lose them."

The idea of being compared to Hadeon had something twisting inside her, but she didn't disagree entirely with what Breckett said. She forcibly pushed the guilt back.

I'll become whatever I must to protect Elias and Shadowbank.

"The ambiance of this place sucks," a female voice said from behind her. "It's so fucking dark, I can hardly see anything."

Turning, Arabella sheathed the syphen and smiled. "Did you have a nice nap?"

Jessamine spat into the sand. "No. My head aches like a gargoyle sat on it."

Her eyes fixed on something above, and Arabella followed her gaze.

Dark wings filled the sky as something descended toward them. In a burst of wind, the prince landed, sending sand flying in every direction.

Spitting into the sand again, Jessamine rose to her feet. "I think I have sand inside my skull."

"The oasis is about ten or fifteen miles from here," Hadeon said. "It's small—hardly more than a cluster of trees."

"Did you spot any life?" Arabella asked.

He shook his head. "Nothing I can see. But there's... something nearby. A presence has been lingering at the edge of my senses."

"Whatever it is will show its face before long," Jessamine said as she shook her jacket. "Demons always do. That's when things will get interesting."

"Don't instigate the undead," Breckett hissed. "It's best to avoid the notice of anything that walks these lands. Or maybe whatever it is will think we're too insignificant to bother coming after. Because," he pointed to Hadeon, "even the prince may not be strong enough to fend off what lives here."

Jessamine tied her leather jacket around her waist, crossing her arms before turning to Arabella. "Do all demons have his temperament?"

Arabella bit her lip. She'd likely just pissed Breckett off by refusing to return the syphen to him and didn't want to rub sand in his wound. And his caution wasn't unwarranted.

"Let's head to the oasis," she said. "We'll need water no matter what comes next."

"Erox don't need to drink or eat," Breckett said helpfully.

Groaning, she glared up at the starless sky before leveling her gaze on the erox. "Then you'll drag our parched asses across the sand if we become too dehydrated to walk on our own."

He muttered something in response, which she chose to ignore.

Studying the map, she eyed the line that led west—or what she was going to assume was west. As she looked closely, she spotted a marking with a cluster of trees. The oasis. The next similar marking was at least five times the distance on the map from the first one. If the first oasis was ten miles away, would it be another fifty miles until they came across water? If that was true, they'd be dead long before they reached the shadow fae on the opposite end of the map.

The opposite end of Abyss.

Hadeon came to stand next to her, gesturing to the map. "May I?"

Nodding, she passed it to him. When his gloved hands enclosed around the parchment, the ink sunk back into the map. The markings disappeared as though they never were, leaving behind a blank document.

"Fascinating," he said before handing the map back to her.

Instantly, it filled with dry ink, and markings flowed across the parchment until it was illustrated once more. Her eyes lingered on Hadeon's gloved hands and how he was careful to remain just out of reach.

Without another word, she continued westward, and the others followed.

Breckett didn't bother to start a conversation again. Instead, he remained in stoic silence. Meanwhile, Hadeon made several attempts to start conversations with Jessamine.

"What's your home like?" he asked.

"Like most human villages," Jessamine said through gritted teeth.

"Of course," the prince said as though she'd shared something of significance. "Shadowbank is the name of the village. Is it not?"

Behind Arabella, there was no reply from Jessamine.

"Do the enchantresses live within the village?" he continued.

"No, I live in the forest, and my neighbors are a belgor, the belgor's uncle, and an owl that thinks it's a shifter," Jessamine said dryly. "What do you think?"

Ignoring her quip, the prince said, "What's your role in Shadowbank? Do you repair the ward like Enchantress Arabella?"

"Why so many questions?" Jessamine said, and Arabella dared a glance over her shoulder, noting her friend's narrowed eyes and the tensing of her jaw. "Are you hoping to get a bargain out of me, too? Use my past or home against us? I'm not interested in anything you have to offer."

Arabella watched the prince's wings twitch faintly—the only outward sign of his irritation. He was careful to keep his hands at his sides.

"We're all doing what we must to protect those we feel loyal to," he said, his tone growing cold. For a moment, it was as though the color drained from his features, and he was truly the dark fae prince of nightmares. "Nothing more and nothing less."

Jessamine looked up at the male who towered over her. But even with the stark height difference, her presence billowed out around her—her sheer gumption and fearlessness making her seem far taller than she was.

"Why make a bargain with Arabella and not Elias?" Jessamine pressed. "Was it because you knew she was shadow fae?"

His eyes flickered up to Arabella as she watched them over her shoulder. "I had a feeling we'd need each other."

Jessamine harrumphed but said nothing further. It seemed the prince had finally had enough of the pleasantries as well, as he didn't attempt to start a conversation with Jessamine again.

There was no way to tell the passing of time without the guidance of a sun, moon, or stars. But what felt like hours later, they spotted a cluster of trees in the distance.

Over her life, she'd grown to associate forests with danger. But as her tongue stuck to the roof of her mouth, she breathed a sigh of relief for the first time in her life at the sight of a line of trees.

The oasis.

"About fucking time," Jessamine muttered behind her.

Freeing her swords from the sheaths on her back, Arabella ran toward the oasis. As she did, she kept her senses open, searching for any nearby magic wielders.

She passed through trees for what she thought was half a mile, and there wasn't a single sign of life. Not the pattering of small animal feet atop branches, nor the lumbering steps of demons along the forest floor. Instead, a strange quiet hovered over the earth. It felt like dozens of eyes followed their every movement.

A single well was nestled in the center of the oasis. Seeing it, she sighed with relief. She'd long since finished the water she'd packed.

They quickly drew several buckets of water, drinking their fill and refilling their waterskins. Then they explored some of the oasis, which had to be half a mile in each direction from the well. There were no signs of any other living beings—or demons. The plant life was also strange. Visually, it appeared similar to what was in the mortal realm. However, it was slightly different in color, texture, and size. She didn't trust any of them would be safe to eat.

They made camp a short distance away from the well in a cluster of trees. Arabella, Jessamine, and Hadeon nibbled on some of the rations in their satchels in silence.

"Let's take turns on watch," Hadeon said. "I'll take the first watch."

Without a word, Breckett laid down and closed his eyes, instantly asleep. Meanwhile, Arabella and Jessamine settled against a tree that wasn't quite an oak.

"Where do you think the exit is?" Jessamine asked.

It was a fair question. Even if the gateway they'd come through allowed them to pass both ways, there would be no finding it again in the endless desert.

Unbraiding her hair, Arabella said, "Honestly, I've been so focused on keeping everyone alive and reading this map that I figured I'd worry about it once we found the shadow fae. Maybe they'll know a way out."

Jessamine shook her head. "If they did, they'd have used it a long time ago. It's up to us to find the exit gateway."

"Either that or they know where it is, but they don't have the key to use it. Here's to hoping the map can show us an exit after we've found the shadow fae." Arabella patted Jessamine's arm. "Get some rest."

They settled into the coarse plants that were an unnaturally dark shade of green.

As Arabella drifted off to sleep, trying to ignore the feeling of eyes upon them, she thought about what Jessamine had said.

How would they get out of the Abyss? Would they be stuck here for all eternity like the shadow fae?

If the shadow fae were even here.

Chapter Eleven
ARABELLA

Arabella blinked, finding herself in the center of a darkness quite unlike the Abyss. She floated in a place void of light with no horizon, no sky, and no other sign of life. As her feet touched down where the ground should be, she glanced down at her hands, which glowed with a gray-white light.

The dream, she realized. *This is the same dream I had about Elias.*

Why had she returned to this place now?

Heart racing, she glanced around and scanned the surrounding darkness.

Empty.

He's not here.

Something inside her chest twisted.

Even if the phantom Elias appeared, it was just a conjuring of her mind. It wouldn't be her erox.

Instinctively, she reached for the bond in her chest. There was the faintest flicker of flames, but she still couldn't tell what he was feeling. She wondered if Magnus was torturing him at that very moment.

While she needed to learn to control what she felt down the

bond when they returned to the mortal and fae realms, she found herself missing the sensations, even the pain, because it served as a reminder that he was out there.

That he was alive.

Another thought struck her.

Would the Elias she rescued be the same male, or would these experiments forever change him?

Something tickled her cheek.

Reaching up, she was surprised to find a tear there.

Was it possible to cry in dreams? She wasn't sure she ever had before.

As tears rolled down her cheeks, she succumbed to the deep sadness filling her—and a deeper regret for the time they'd wasted at odds with one another.

Please, she thought, reaching for the flickering flames in her chest. *I need you.*

The shadows around her twisted as though awakening from a deep slumber.

Suddenly, something strummed in her chest. It was as though a harp chord had been plucked, and a single, long note reverberated. The vibration rippled out from her, and then a gray-blue light shimmered on the distant horizon.

Brows drawing together, she stared at where she'd seen the flash of light.

"Elias!" she shouted.

No reply came.

Get it together, she scolded herself. *You're an enchantress.*

Could she not allow herself a moment of weakness even in her dreams? She always had to be strong, always had to have an answer, a solution—or people would die. The humans of Shadowbank wouldn't be reassured by anything other than confidence. And that was exactly what she strived for.

Still, she longed to crumple into herself, to scream until her lungs were raw, and to just *feel.*

Unlike before, she didn't just have the safety of Shadowbank to consider. Now, she had someone she wanted to protect.

She'd found something she'd never expected to in her lifetime—her *mate*. Her perfect match in every way. Somehow, she'd found her counterpart in a demon. Would she ever have a chance to be by his side again? Or would Magnus kill one or both of them first?

Somehow, she had to find a way to save Elias and her home.

"Elias," she whispered into the darkness as more tears tumbled down her cheeks. "*Please.*"

She didn't know what she was asking. All she knew was that she longed to feel his touch with every fiber of her being.

There was a shift in the darkness behind her, and she turned toward it.

For a moment, it felt like time slowed. A single tear rolled down her cheek as her chest rose and fell with a single breath.

Elias stood before her, utterly naked.

His light brown skin shone with an otherworldly gray-blue light. A different shimmer glowed in the depths of his eyes, which turned from a dark brown to a brilliant blue—as though a flame had taken form there.

From experience, she knew what the change in the color of his eyes meant.

He was eager to feed.

Black hair came to his bare shoulders and was more disheveled than she'd ever seen it. Curls stuck out in every direction, and there were dark smudges beneath his eyes like he hadn't slept in days. His high cheekbones were sharper, and even though his beard was longer now, it couldn't hide the gauntness in his cheeks.

I'm projecting my fears into this landscape, she thought.

Even still, he was the most beautiful thing she'd ever seen.

Another tear slipped free as she said, "You're here."

He closed the distance between them in an instant.

Hands were in her unbound hair, fingers slipping between the strands at the back of her head. He pulled, forcing her to tilt her chin upward. She opened to him willingly, and his tongue ravished her mouth. The way he moved... It was like he needed to explore every inch of her. To know her body.

He ran his teeth over her lower lip, nipping gently. Then he pulled back, his arms looping loosely around her and his hands stroking.

But when his lips moved, no sounds came.

She frowned. "What?"

Again, his lips formed words, but the dark world around them was completely silent.

Lines formed between her brows. "I can't understand you."

What could this phantom Elias be trying to tell her? She studied his mouth, but she was unskilled with reading lips.

It was just a dream, she knew. But she longed to hear his voice all the same. She hungered for any words from her mate.

Elias shook his head before he crashed into her once more. His lips found hers in a feverish frenzy, moving like he intended to claim her, to remind her who she belonged to.

My heart is yours, she thought as she melted into his touch, feeling his arms wrap around her back. He pulled her in so she was pressed against him, and she felt every line of his body. The muscles rippling along his abdomen. The way his chest heaved. It was as though he was breathing her in...

Like she was the most precious thing in his world.

As he kissed her, his fingers slipped into her hair, and he *pulled*. The pressure wasn't enough to truly hurt, but she reveled in the delicious sting of it. There was something about the feel of her mate using her body, moving her as he wished. Damn her, she wanted to fulfill his every desire, just as she knew he wanted to fulfill hers.

Something flickered in the blue flames in his eyes. Pulling back, his gaze raked across her face.

That one look had her core melting.

Desire pooled in her, and she could feel herself growing wet with need. For a moment, she wondered if the phantom Elias could scent that desire because hunger filled his gaze as his nostrils flared. Then he descended upon her once more. As he kissed her, the desire in her core swelled further, and for a moment, the need was so strong that she couldn't breathe.

Spread me. Fill me. Fuck me.

She didn't want him to be gentle. She wanted a touch so intense, so consuming that she'd feel bruises where his fingers pressed into her skin. But instead of pulling off her leathers, he continued to kiss her, never releasing her hair.

Her fingernails raked over his chest, leaving marks. This only seemed to incense him further because he pulled back. His eyes glowed a brilliant blue, brighter than anything she'd ever seen.

Then pleasure was ripped from her.

She cried out as starlight burst behind her eyes. Wave after wave of pleasure crashed over her, so hard she thought she might drown. Even as the height of her pleasure peaked, she thrust against his thigh, desperate for any kind of friction.

But he didn't have to touch her for her to come.

Erox consumed the sexual pleasures of their partners, and they didn't have to touch their prey for them to reach climax. But Elias... he liked to touch her, to torture her with the promise of pleasure. He so rarely just *fed* on her.

But the telltale humming in her chest filled her as her essence swelled, flowing up her throat.

His grip on her hair tightened, forcing her to tilt her head back even more. Her essence was a brilliant blue—the same color as his eyes. And he sucked it into his mouth.

The essence that he could wield.

As he fed, she watched as some of the gauntness in his cheeks faded before her very eyes.

Releasing her hair, his hands moved to her pants, untying them at the waist before pulling them halfway down. Then he turned her around, forcing her onto her hands and knees. As though he couldn't wait long enough to pull them off.

She tried to turn around, to see what he was doing. But the moment he saw her turning toward him, his fingers closed around the back of her neck, forcing her head down.

Damn her, she wanted him to lose himself inside her—to fuck her until her body was raw from sating his need.

Something pressed against her ass, and it took her a moment to realize he'd spat and then notched his cock there.

Oh.

They'd never tried that before, and she swallowed thickly.

This is just a dream, she thought, though she wasn't sure why she needed reminding.

Even if it hurt, she wanted him to fuck her.

Grabbing her hip in one hand and his cock in another, he pressed. She gasped, her breath hitching as he slipped inch by inch into her.

It was unlike when he filled her pussy. This felt far more sensitive. The fullness of him was almost too much, but he moved slowly. She felt herself stretch as his wide cock pressed deeper into her ass. His shallow thrusts allowed her to adjust to the size of him —and the feel of him there. Gradually, she relaxed into him. As she did, she felt pleasure building in her core once more.

Again, fingers slipped into her hair as he grabbed it and pulled, forcing her to submit to him fully. She was utterly at his mercy.

His movements became faster, increasing in both quickness and... *need*. It was as if, even though their bodies were joined, it wasn't enough. He needed more of her.

And she needed more of him.

Her hands and knees pressed into the fathomless darkness beneath where she kneeled, and her shadows swirled around them. Tendrils curled around his calves and her arms, never stopping moving, as though feeding off their shared pleasure.

"I love you," she whispered into the darkness, knowing that the phantom Elias couldn't hear her. But it didn't matter in that moment.

One day, she'd tell him how she felt.

For a moment, she thought she sensed a deeper darkness within the surrounding shadows. It was that strange presence she'd been feeling since the gateway. The one that had led her toward the oasis.

But any concern slipped from her mind as Elias' pace quickened even more. He moved like a male overcome by desire, by *need*. It was all she could do to take what he was giving her. To feel him thrust with abandon deep inside, plunging into her very center. Then his movements became jerky, and there was a single shiver before he spilled his seed in her ass.

When he released her hair, her head slumped forward and her mind swirled with the pleasure of their joining. But she didn't have long to revel in the feeling because hands found her sides, flipping her over.

His lips moved again, and she thought he said, "You're mine." But she couldn't be sure.

"I'm yours," she said. "Now and always."

He growled before descending upon her.

Grabbing her pants, he pulled them roughly down until they were at her ankles. As he spread her legs further, she didn't fight. Instead, she marveled at the sight of him—completely naked—between her legs. And her, clothed except for her pants, which he'd pulled down.

His beard scratched against her clit before she felt his tongue glance over her pussy. Instantly, her back arched, and she moaned. Her shadows continued twisting around them both.

"Yes." The word slipped free from her lips, sounding utterly breathless.

His tongue pressed into her folds, skirting up and down, tracing along the outside of her pussy before returning to her clit.

Reaching down, she slipped her hand into his curls and rocked her hips against him.

As though this was the encouragement he sought, she felt him shift. A finger was at her entrance, swirling the wetness there but not pressing into her. She tightened her grip on his hair, moving her hips upward, but he remained where he was.

She longed to be filled again, needing his fingers inside her. But his tongue continued its languid strokes, moving up and down.

His presence alone had desire humming inside her.

Then his fingers pressed inside her.

The moment he touched her... It was like she'd been waiting for him, for this male, her whole life. Their bodies were meant for each other, their joining fated in the stars. And she could never get enough of him. Even as he fucked her, she wanted more of him. All of him.

For the rest of her mortal life.

It took him three strokes, his fingers curling against her inner walls, before she submitted to ecstasy.

A cry escaped her lips as her fingers tightened in his hair.

In a flash of movement too fast for her eyes to track, he was above her, his lips against hers. She tasted herself on his tongue.

This was the most vivid dream she'd ever had.

It was so realistic.

Then he was pulling essence from her. Only this time, he pulled wave after wave of it into his mouth, drinking like he was a man dying of thirst. As he fed, her mind swirled. The world seemed to spin around her, and he came in and out of focus.

Wrapping her hands around the back of his neck, she held on to him as though he was the only thing anchoring her to the earth. As though if he let her go, she would cease to be.

She kissed him back, flicking her tongue against his, reveling at the softness of his lips even as they ravished hers. All the while, his fingers never stopped moving, never stopped fucking her. At first, it was one finger, and then a second joined it. Then a third.

He curled his fingers against her walls in the way she liked. Then she thought she felt his thumb caress her clit.

And that was all it took.

She moaned into his mouth as she came undone again, and he

ate it up as greedily as her essence. Pleasure burst within her, and her eyes fluttered closed. This time, the pleasure crescendoed, lasting far longer than the other times she'd come. She trembled against his touch, her body wracked with pleasure.

It was good, *too good*.

She pulled her lips from his, gasping for air. Then he moved down to her neck, kissing and licking her skin.

The world was spinning even more now.

What's happening to me?

A pang of hunger had her stomach clenching even as desire swelled within her.

Suddenly, a familiar voice penetrated the darkness.

It sounded strangely distant, like she'd been submerged in water and the voice came from above the surface. The words were indistinguishable, but she could hear the fear in them. The desperation.

It was a woman's voice, she realized.

Jessamine's voice.

There was a slipping sensation inside her chest. As though she'd let go of a cord she hadn't realized she'd held in the first place.

Elias pulled back, brows furrowed.

She tried to speak, but words felt leaden in her mouth. It was an effort to keep her eyes open. Elias stood, a look of confusion and fear marring his features before his body began to fade from existence.

In moments, he was gone.

"Elias!" she cried out, struggling to her knees. But she was too dizzy.

Then she awoke.

Chapter Twelve

ARABELLA

"Get your ass up," Jessamine hissed. "We're being hunted."

Arabella shook her head, trying to collect herself. Trying to recall not just who she was, but *where* she was.

That dream...

It had felt far too real.

Blinking, she glanced at the trees all around them. If she squinted, she could pretend she was in the forest outside of Shadowbank with its massive interlocking branches blocking out the sky. But when she looked closely, these trees were a few shades darker green than those in the mortal realm.

Nothing moved in the space between the trees, and a strange silence hung in the air.

A few feet away, Breckett and Hadeon were on their feet, blades drawn and backs pressed to nearby trees.

Jessamine crouched above Arabella with her own blades in hand.

"Demon?" Arabella asked as she hauled herself to her feet. "Or something else?"

She didn't dare to hope it was the shadow fae.

Slowly, she pulled her blades free, but they felt strangely heavy in her hands. Hunger burned in her stomach, and her mind swirled. It was an effort to remain upright.

Rising, Jessamine pressed her back against the nearest tree, peering around it. As she did, an unnatural wind shuddered between the trees, carrying a keening cry that emerged from the ground itself. The inhuman sound hung in the air for what felt like an eternity.

Something had awakened.

Jessamine straightened. "Whatever it is, it doesn't sound friendly."

Arabella staggered to the tree beside Jessamine, pressing a hand to the rough bark to steady herself.

"Are you well, Enchantress?" Hadeon asked from where he stood, his wings tucked tightly to his sides.

"I'm fine."

For several moments, the trees were utterly still, the silence like a physical weight.

The shadows stirred beneath her feet as though sensing the oncoming conflict.

While her shadows had changed since her memories had returned, they were even more different in this place. They weren't simply a part of the world—dark extensions of anything blocking the light. Her shadows *were* the world.

There was no day but endless night. Without a natural predator, the shadows hovered over the world as though preparing to engulf it.

Darkness reigned supreme.

Whatever creature stalked the shadows was a part of the deep black as well. The darkness around her swirled, and her heart hammered against her ribs. While facing death down wasn't new, this time, she felt very exposed. It was as though something was lurking just out of sight, and no matter where she looked, something always pricked at the back of her neck.

Her arms started to tremble, and it wasn't entirely due to fatigue.

"It's feeding on our fear," she realized.

Veins bulged in Breckett's jaw. "How do you know?"

"*Breckett,*" Jessamine hissed. "Quit pissing your pants. If I can't protect you, I promise I'll kill you before *it* does."

"I've walked this world longer than you've been alive—" Breckett began but stopped short.

A sound like the fracturing of the earth's core ripped through the oasis followed by a sudden gust of wind. Shadows roared as the trees shook as though in the middle of a hurricane.

Jessamine's back was pressed against the tree. The rise and fall of her breathing never changed, even as another bellow sounded in the space between the trees.

Arabella allowed Jessamine's steadiness to give her strength, willing her limbs to stillness.

Slowly, she reached for the shadows.

As she summoned them, they were... sticky. Strands of darkness wove up her arms, but most of them hovered above the ground, plopping back down as she tried to will it into submission. She wasn't the only one commanding them, she realized.

The shadows were uncertain who to follow.

Then darkness shook as though stirred in a sudden wind before retreating into the trees.

Slowly, Arabella leaned toward the edge of the tree, glancing around it.

A body peeled from the shadows between the trees. The creature was as tall as the surrounding trees with limbs that were the length of a house. Its thin body was made of a dark sinew that was both flesh and shadow. Long, thin legs stretched upward to a torso that was unnaturally small and formless. But rather than a head atop shoulders, tendrils of shadow extended into the air dozens of feet above where its neck should be, arcing and hissing. At the end of its unnaturally long arms were four clawed fingertips.

"Oh fuck," Jessamine muttered, her body shifting—flinching away.

Arabella's stomach plummeted into her boots.

Months ago, she'd battled a horde of the soulless, creatures of bones and hunger. Those demons roamed the lands, consuming any living creature unfortunate enough to stumble into their path. All to try to reclaim a soul they'd never again find.

The first soulless had once been a human whose soul had been taken by one of the zaol.

A greater demon.

Greater demons were the first generation spawned from the darkness. They'd *made* the lesser demons who threatened the very existence of Shadowbank.

Here in the underrealms, even shadows had a face.

This was no ordinary demon. The power rippling off it meant one thing.

"Zaol!" Arabella shouted.

She'd never seen this kind of greater demon, but she'd seen illustrations and read about them. It was her job to know about all types of demons. But she had no idea if Breckett or Hadeon could identify it on sight.

And if they knew how royally fucked they were.

"A greater demon?" Breckett shrieked.

As it turned out, he did know about them.

Drawn to the sound of his voice, the creature of flesh and shadow swiped an arm out toward the erox. She threw up a wall of shadow in front of Breckett, which sent the zaol's arm flying upward at an unnatural angle. It made a strange cawing-like sound before its other arm lashed out.

An idea struck her, and she made several pools of shadows between her and Breckett.

"Jump!" she shouted.

Eyes locking with hers for the briefest moment, he nodded before stepping between the shadows. It was one of the gifts of the erox—one that Elias had used at the castle. A breath after Breckett disappeared, the zaol's shadow blasted where he'd been standing.

Breckett's body flashed in and out of existence as though his body was a skipping stone across the pools of shadow over to where Arabella and Jessamine stood.

"Thanks," Breckett gasped. "Good thinking."

While the Abyss was a realm of shadow, she didn't know the depth the darkness had to be for erox to jump between them. Maybe he could've done it without her assistance if he'd thought of it. But if he couldn't, she knew with sudden certainty that neither she nor Breckett had the strength to use their combined abilities to leap through shadows hundreds of feet at a time across the desert. They'd fatigue too quickly, especially with Hadeon and Jessamine, and they all had to save their strength.

The zaol made its strange cawing sound again, lashing one of its arms out across the entire space—slashing into the trunks of trees.

Hadeon blasted his magic before him. The power sent him backward and out of reach of the zaol, and he flapped his wings to steady himself. But with the heavy tree coverage, he couldn't take to the sky.

There was a loud cracking sound as a tree split in half. Chunks of dirt, grass, and other debris flew through the air.

Arabella rolled sideways, landing on her feet. But the world continued to spin after she was upright.

Fuck.

Why was she so weak?

She glanced over her shoulder long enough to see the zaol's fingers dig into the earth as Jessamine leapt out of the way and Breckett flickered between shadows. The zaol pulled its limb back in. As it did, it seemed to growl. But it was hard to tell without a face.

Unlike the soulless, she thought this being was intelligent. It might be driven by hunger—by the need to consume—but it did so with purpose and strategy.

There was a swelling of the shadows, and she watched as the

darkness leached from the ground, flowing toward the zaol like water rolling down a cliffside.

It's gathering power, she realized.

"Run!" she shouted, grabbing Breckett by his shirt collar and shoving him in the direction of the desert—away from the oasis. Jessamine and Hadeon turned at once, hurtling themselves forward.

Arabella threw every ounce of strength she had into each stride, willing her legs to move faster. As they all ran, the shadows trailed along the ground beneath their feet—toward the zaol.

Behind them, the greater demon bellowed.

"How do we kill it?" Hadeon shouted.

Arabella shook her head. "No one knows." Greater demons were creatures of legend in Shadowbank. No enchantress texts detailed how to end them since no one had faced them and lived to talk about it. "We could try decapitation, blasting through its heart, burning its body…"

"In case you haven't noticed, it doesn't have a head," Breckett snapped as he ran.

"Fair point," Arabella said, her mind reeling.

Her strategy in Shadowbank had always been to get behind the ward. So long as the demons didn't punch a hole through it, that kept everyone safe. Eventually, the demons lost interest and returned to the forest.

Without a ward, it was fight or die. Or outrun it.

And they were in the demon's territory, which put them at a disadvantage.

Hadeon ducked beneath a low branch—his wings barely fitting through.

She opened her mouth to speak when there was a shift in the shadows. Glancing down, she noticed the ground had turned to an ashen gray. Something rumbled beneath her feet, and she knew with sudden certainty that the zaol was about to unleash the gathering shadows.

"Behind me!" she shouted, pivoting in the underbrush and skidding to a stop.

Hadeon, Breckett, and Jessamine stopped at once and flung themselves behind her as a torrent of energy yawned open in the trees in front of them.

There were no shadows for her to pull from, nothing to form a shield, but she moved on instinct.

Darkness felled everything in its wake. Entire trees crumbled to the earth in a pile of black ashes as the power swept through.

"Arabella?" Jessamine asked, a note of warning in her voice.

But Arabella didn't respond as she watched the line of power barrel toward them.

She wasn't going to fight the shadows.

No.

The shadows were hers to command.

A few paces away, the trees exploded in a torrent of black. She knelt and pressed a hand to the earth. Then she opened herself to the dark veins of the Abyss.

The power blasted into her like a rogue wave in the deep ocean. It was so much force—more energy than had ever been in her body at a single time. It felt like she was a cup filled to overflowing. She let the shadows flow into her, soaking up every drop.

But soon, it became too much, and she directed the surplus into the ground.

She thought she heard Jessamine and Breckett shouting behind her, but she didn't register their words.

The trees on either side of her disintegrated into dark ash.

I can't take this much longer, she thought, hoping the zaol's attack was almost through.

Her entire body trembled at holding so much power. Blood trickled from her nose, and she thought she felt liquid flowing from her ears, too. Gasping, she tried to take in a deep breath, but it felt like a boulder had been placed atop her chest.

Spots formed in her vision, and she thought she might black out, when the torrent stopped.

The first thing her mind registered was a strange sizzling sound. Glancing around, her eyes widened as her gaze fell upon dozens of charred trunks where the trees had been. Only the trees that were directly behind Arabella and her friends remained in this section of the forest. Now, the desert was visible from all sides, and the shadows were returned to the earth.

She breathed a sigh of relief at the sight of Breckett, Hadeon, and Jessamine all on their feet.

All fine.

"Your neck," Hadeon said. "There's black veins."

She swiped the blood away from her nose with the back of her sleeve. "Interesting."

The zaol stood several hundred paces away. Behind it, the forest remained intact. It made a hissing sound as it took one step forward and then another.

"I think you pissed it off," Breckett said.

Jessamine's eyes narrowed on the erox. "Why don't *you* try to reason with it? Maybe if you say 'please,' it'll leave us alone."

Arabella still held on to some of the shadows from the zaol's blast of power, allowing the shadows to fill her and strengthen her. Without it, she feared she'd collapse into a heap on the ground.

She allowed a slip of shadows to wrap around her sword, which she'd scooped up from where she'd dropped it on the ground. Leaving the second sword in its sheath, she turned to Hadeon. "Let's end this now and get back to finding the shadow fae. My mate needs me." Over her shoulder, she said, "Hadeon, your blade turns whatever it touches into ash. Breckett, shield Hadeon with your magic so he can—"

"No," Hadeon interrupted. "That won't be necessary."

Her eyes narrowed. "But he could—"

"I can get close to the zaol without the help of the erox," Hadeon said.

After the greater demon bellowed again, she said, "Fine.

Breckett, shield Jessamine. Get as close as you dare. Jessamine, use your enchantress magic. Its weakness might be light and life."

Breckett nodded, not making an objection for once.

The greater demon drew closer. There wasn't time for more of a plan than that.

"Prince, kill it quickly, would you? I'll absorb its shadows," she said as she lowered herself into a crouch.

The choices before them had become simple. It was either fight the zaol now while they still had the strength or wait for it to kill them later. There was nowhere to run—not if they had another thirty or more miles across the desert before they reached the next oasis. They wouldn't stand a chance. And there was nowhere to lose the zaol in this small oasis, especially not when a quarter of the trees had been blasted in a single attack.

She watched the zaol take several lumbering steps forward, noting that its movements were slightly slower than before. Had that attack weakened it?

For Elias, she thought before launching herself forward.

The shadows around her legs released like coils, shooting her off the ground. As she flew through the air, she caught a flash of movement as Jessamine and Breckett disappeared and another as Hadeon launched into the air.

The zaol lashed out with one of its massive arms, and she slashed down with her blade. It clanged as though her blade was blunt. For a moment, she worried the sword would bounce off. But she clutched it tightly, willing the shadows around it to move more quickly. They responded instantly, and a moment later, the creature's arm sloughed off, falling to the ground and disappearing in a plume of shadow.

Roaring, the greater demon stumbled backward.

Then Hadeon was there, arcing down with his sword. The zaol managed to release a blast of shadow just before the prince's sword met its chest. Already moving, she opened herself up and reached for the shadows as they blasted Hadeon back. She absorbed the worst of the attack, though smoke trailed up from the hairs along Hadeon's arms.

Rather than releasing the shadows back into the ground, she raised her hand at the zaol, her palm forward.

And released.

The torrent spilled out from her, reminding her of dark waters as she blasted it back at the greater demon. She breathed a sigh of relief as the creature stumbled backward, roaring. Before it could retreat or make a counterattack, Jessamine appeared beneath it. She moved her arms in the motions Arabella knew all too well—summoning earthen magic to form bolts at the demon from beneath it. But rather than golden bolts appearing in the air at Jessamine's shoulders, nothing happened.

Instead, Jessamine stumbled to a knee, retching on the ground.

Sensing her, the zaol turned down to her and was about to smash them with one of its arms.

"No," Arabella screamed and lashed out with a band of shadow.

She wrapped it around both Breckett and Jessamine, looping it around their waists. With all her strength, she *pulled*. They soared through the air, narrowly missing the zaol's strike.

Jessamine and Breckett crashed into the ground on either side of Arabella. She didn't have the strength to soften their fall as she fell on her ass, gasping.

Breckett muttered something beside her as Jessamine retched again.

After a moment, Jessamine wiped her mouth with the back of her hand and said, "There's no earthen magic here. The ground is full of death."

There was no earthen magic in the Abyss? Arabella supposed that made sense, but *fuck*. That was going to be a problem. It left Jessamine with only her combat skills and Arabella with only her shadow magic.

There was a squelching sound, and Arabella looked up.

The zaol's body tumbled to the ground like a severed tree before dissolving into a plume of ash. Sword in hand, Hadeon flew to the ground, his eyes fixed on where the greater demon had been.

"He killed it!" Breckett said, his voice holding an obvious note of relief.

Jessamine sniffed, an eyebrow raised. Which, for her, likely meant she was impressed.

Arabella frowned.

Even with the magical fae sword, it was strange that a creature of legend could be felled so easily—with only a single strike. This was a demon that *made* other demons. It was the thing that haunted dreams, the fear that lurked in corners of forgotten memories. Had it just grown out of proportion in the thoughts of so many?

She hauled herself off the ground, summoning the shadows once more and lacing them around her entire body. It hid the trembling of her limbs somewhat. Why was she so fucking exhausted?

Beside her, Jessamine and Breckett got to their feet.

"That's it?" Jessamine said.

Hadeon shrugged.

They watched as the zaol's ashes hovered in the air for several moments too long.

It was then Arabella realized there wasn't any wind. But the ashes swirled in aimless circles before stilling and shuddering. Then something like a heartbeat swelled inside the surrounding shadows, which were leached from the nearby trees. The darkness flowed toward the ground beneath the ashes before it twisted in the air. As the ashes met the shadows, there was a hissing sound like a sword pulled from a forge and plunged into water.

Then two feet formed on the ground. Unnaturally long legs of sinew melded atop them as its body slowly reformed.

Breckett cleared his throat. "I don't think it worked."

"Excellent observation," Jessamine said as she shoved him back toward the trees. "Run!"

For a moment, Breckett hesitated, as though he wanted to help.

"Get out of here," Arabella called over her shoulder. "Hadeon and I will catch up with you."

Jessamine couldn't use her magic, and Breckett's magic wouldn't be helpful against the zaol. Not if Hadeon wouldn't accept the help, and she had to put all her focus on absorbing the greater demon's attacks.

Without another word, Arabella pulled the shadows from the earth around her. They hummed a delicious tune. But as she pulled the darkness into her, she noted a strange sticky sensation. As though the inky tendrils had a film atop them—something dark and menacing that filled her along with the power. Her senses became sharper and, along with it, her emotions heightened. It filled her with a sense of unyielding rage like she'd never known.

"Protect Breckett," she said in a voice that was far colder than her own.

Jessamine hesitated before nodding and running after Breckett.

Then Arabella turned to face the zaol.

Chapter Thirteen

ARABELLA

Arabella watched the zaol weave shadows and ashes together, reforming its body.

A sudden conviction filled her.

"Greater demons can't die here," she said, ignoring the faint trembling in her arms and legs. "The underrealms are their homeland... I think it will just reform."

All around her and Hadeon were the charred stumps of the trees. One-quarter of the trees in the oasis had been felled in a single blast of the zaol's magic. Now, they had no coverage, nothing to hide behind.

They had to face the demon head-on.

Hadeon's gaze swiveled between Arabella and the zaol, his sword in his fist. "Do you have a suggestion, Enchantress?"

She sifted through their options.

"I don't suppose you could fly while carrying us? Even if you bring us one at a time, we could flee and get ahead of the zaol—" she began, but he interrupted.

"Absolutely not."

She blinked, surprised by the vehemence in his voice. "Why?"

"Not an option," he said, his voice cold.

She ran a hand over her face. That was off the table, then.

Sheathing her sword, she raised an arm outward and unfurled her fingers. Then shadows exploded from her. It blasted through the zaol's abdomen, which dissipated in an instant. The legs wobbled before turning into a muddy pile of darkness on the ground.

"That should give us a head start," she said before turning in the direction the others had fled—back toward the desert. "Let's go."

She wove between the tree trunks with the fae prince at her side. He moved far lighter on his feet than he should for someone his size, hardly making any noises at all.

She held on to the shadows, letting them fill her with power. It was so much power that, for a moment, it felt like she held the amplifier. Her entire body vibrated with sheer energy. Beside her, Hadeon's magic seemed far less significant than it once had.

But she knew the moment she let go of her magic, she'd crumble. It was the only thing keeping the strange exhaustion at bay.

As they neared the edge of the oasis, there was a rumbling in the distance behind them.

It had taken the zaol mere minutes to regenerate.

If they had to stop every few minutes in the open desert to kill the zaol, they weren't going to last long. Even if they had a chance of reaching the next oasis, they'd be too fatigued and dehydrated if they had to battle a greater demon the whole way.

We're going to die.

Somehow, that thought broke through to her, and fear touched the edge of her senses. But it wasn't fear for herself. It was for Jessamine and Breckett, and perhaps even Hadeon. She felt responsible for their safety. They were relying on her to find the shadow fae, and she needed to ensure they made it.

Grabbing the map from her jacket, she opened it.

There was a line that went across the Abyss from east to west, and there were only a few oases in this endless desert. To the north, there was a series of jagged mountains.

She studied that line of mountains.

Based on the distance they'd traveled before to the first oasis, the mountains had to be about ten miles north of here. It was the next closest thing to them. While it didn't follow the path toward the west, there was a chance they could find cover there or maybe lose the zaol.

A sudden thought occurred to her as the now familiar shadowy presence settled atop her shoulders.

What if the line across the Abyss on the map didn't lead to the shadow fae? What if the spot that was marked was the exit gateway or another place? If that was the case, the shadow fae could be anywhere.

Suddenly, a trace of shadows appeared at the top of the parchment. It was so faint she nearly missed it. It hovered in a single location.

The mountains to the north.

Then the shadows disappeared, though the presence lingered.

Should she trust whatever this was? Did she have another choice? It had directed her toward the oasis. Perhaps it could lead her to the shadow fae, too.

She rolled up the map and stashed it in her jacket pocket as she ran.

Just ahead, Jessamine and Breckett lingered at the edge of what remained of the trees.

When she and Hadeon caught up, the four of them hurried into the desert, kicking up sand as they ran.

She came to a decision.

"The shadow fae found a way to avoid the zaol and survive," she said. "So, we kill it as often as we can and slow it down until we find the shadow fae—or a way to lose it."

Or until we're too exhausted to fight any longer.

"There are mountains north of here," she continued. "It's closer than the next oasis. Let's aim for those and hope we lose the zaol."

"I thought the map leads west," Jessamine said, not breaking her stride.

"It does," Arabella agreed. "But we won't make it to the next oasis on one waterskin each. Especially not if that thing is pursuing us the whole way."

There wasn't time to explain the strange presence, not as the zaol slowly took shape in the distance behind them. She hoped there'd be a chance later.

There was a long silence, and when no one objected, Arabella turned to Hadeon. "Take to the skies. Keep an eye on the zaol as it draws near."

There was a glimmer of something dangerous in his gaze. "Be careful you don't get used to giving orders, Enchantress."

"I wouldn't dream of it."

The prince shot into the sky, his black wings flapping as he ascended.

"Your neck..." Jessamine began, her voice tinged with a note of caution. "Are you okay?"

Arabella nodded.

She was well enough to do what needed to be done, and that's what mattered. Whatever these black veins were could wait.

A roar sounded behind them.

The zaol cleared the trees and lumbered across the sand toward them. As it moved, it made a hissing sound like the fracturing of dreams.

Hadeon hovered in the sky behind them, his blade held aloft. There wasn't an ounce of fear in his posture. It was the confidence of a male who'd been in countless battles, faced death, and come out on the other side.

As she ran, sweat beaded on her brows, and her limbs grew fatigued far too quickly. Whatever had happened to her in the dream had somehow affected her here. Exhaustion so thick, so penetrating filled her thoughts even with the borrowed energy from the shadows. She tried to shake it off, but bone-deep weariness remained. She felt it in the way her feet pushed one in front of the other as the sand shifted beneath her boots.

Ignoring it, she reached for the shadows.

In this place, there was neither sun nor stars. Darkness permeated the sands, lacing through the sky and the horizon.

The shadows purred as she pulled even more of them into her, humming happily as they twirled around her. Borrowing even more strength, she spun around and skidded to a stop as she aimed her arm at the zaol. It moved over the desert like a ghost—the grains of sand shifting only the slightest where it passed.

When she couldn't take even one more drop of power, she released it.

A torrent of darkness flew over the sandy hills, which parted like waves. A moment later, her shadows struck the zaol in the chest. As before, it exploded into a swirl of ash. But this time, she didn't wait to watch it reform. Instead, she turned and ran after Jessamine and Breckett.

In the skies above them, Hadeon soared, his watchful eye on where the greater demon had just been.

They ran for what felt like days. But without a sun to measure the passing of time, it could have been mere hours.

Between her shadow magic and Hadeon's blade, they'd killed the zaol countless times, but it persisted—reforming minutes later and barreling through the sands after them.

Sweat poured down her face. The crossing sheaths pulled at her back, making the skin beneath it raw. There hadn't even been time to touch her rations. She'd only managed a few small sips of water while they ran. All of them were dragging. Even Jessamine's movements slowed, and Breckett's breaths came in ragged gasps.

But the zaol had come back to life once more, sewing itself back together with whatever dark magic it possessed. It was closing the distance between them—and fast.

As she raised her arm to release another slew of shadows, the world began tilting. Then she was rolling, hurtling down a sandy hill.

"Arabella!" Jessamine shouted, though her voice sounded strangely distant.

The shadows slipped from Arabella's grasp, slinking into the ground beneath her as she rolled to a stop. Exhaustion struck her like a physical blow, threatening to consume her and nearly drowning out her fear. She couldn't raise her arms, couldn't call on her magic. It was all she could do to keep her eyes open.

Distantly, she registered a flash of wings as Hadeon fought against the zaol from the skies.

A face appeared above hers.

Jessamine's blonde hair was slick with sweat and tied back, but wisps had escaped, which she brushed back.

"Can you walk?" she asked.

Arabella managed to shake her head.

"I'll carry her."

It was Breckett.

"If that demon gets too close to us, your fighting skills will be more useful than mine."

The erox scooped Arabella up into his arms and ran northward. She was too tired to object or even feel surprised. She must have passed out because the next she knew, she felt the rumble of Breckett's voice where her cheek pressed against his chest. Blinking, she opened her eyes.

"Is that what I think it is?" he asked, his voice breathless.

Turning in the direction Breckett's gaze was fixed, she spotted a line of mountains on the horizon as though they'd pressed through the desert sands to point jagged peaks at the sky.

Jessamine made a sound of assent before turning and heading in the opposite direction. "Get Arabella to those mountains. We have to find cover and water, or we're all going to die."

"Where are you going?" Breckett gasped.

Jessamine sighed. "To help a princeling."

Before either Arabella or Breckett could object, Jessamine was running back toward Hadeon—and the zaol that had gotten dangerously close to them. It was less than half a mile away, its dark silhouette looming atop a sandy hill.

They watched as Jessamine hurdled toward where the fae prince flew at the zaol. Hadeon slashed with his sword, but the blade didn't connect. The swing was slower than it had been hours ago and missed its mark. The demon lashed out with one of its too-long arms, and it slammed into the prince's back. He was flung down into the sand, barely managing to tuck his wings in before rolling down a nearby hill.

As the demon moved to strike at him a second time, Jessamine leaped between them, her sword arcing up at an unusual angle and slicing off several of the creature's fingers before its claws could sink into Hadeon's wings.

Then Breckett turned and ran. His breaths turned into gasps, and sweat poured off him as she fought to stay awake.

"Save your strength," he rasped, glancing down at her. "I have a feeling we're going to need it if we make it to those mountains."

Reluctantly, she nodded and closed her eyes, slipping into unconsciousness.

She dreamed of dark skies and darker horizons, of Shadowbank set aflame, and Elias' castle buried beneath the sea. She raged against hordes of demons, fighting to push them back. But no matter how many times she swung her sword or released her magic, the villagers fell one by one, succumbing to sharp fangs and curved talons. Blood-strewn bodies littered the ground, and she found herself searching for one face in particular.

There was a male on his stomach, his face in the dirt. His body was streaked with grime and soot, but she knew the shape of those arms. And how they felt when they wrapped around her. As she reached toward him, the ground shook beneath her.

Suddenly, there was a sensation of her flying.

She opened her eyes.

The world spun around her before she crashed into coarse sand, rolling several times. Blinking, she tried to get her bearings, but her vision continued to spin. She shook her head, sinking her fingers into the sand and willing her vision to clear.

They were at the base of the mountain range.

It stretched in either direction as far as the eye could see, and a thick layer of mist hovered around the mountain directly before them. Far above, she thought she spotted snow on the mountaintops, but she couldn't be sure.

Unlike the mountainous forest near Shadowbank, these seemed to be mostly bare of trees. Instead, they were dotted with stones and large sections of moss.

Strangest of all, the sands of the endless desert simply stopped at the base of the mountains. Two separate terrains from completely different climates collided and formed a stark line where one ended and another began.

Glancing around, she spotted a body several feet away and crawled toward it.

Nearby, there were screams of pain along with the zaol's roar.

Fingers digging into the sand, she barely managed to haul herself over to where Breckett lay facedown in the sand. With all her strength, she shoved him sideways. When she didn't see the rise and fall of his chest, she lifted a hand and struck him above his heart. To her relief, he coughed and muttered, but he didn't open his eyes. His breaths came in a wheeze, and she didn't miss how his beauty was sharper than ever. Being near him had her desire sparking instantly, and she clamped her thighs together.

He needs to feed.

She wondered if his eyes would turn black and his canines would grow—like Elias' had when he didn't have enough essence. Because surely, he was ravenous after traveling all this way.

One problem at a time.

Turning her gaze toward another bellow of the greater demon, she spotted Hadeon on a knee, one hand pressed to his shoulder. Blood flowed between his fingers. Jessamine blocked several blows from the zaol, but her movements were slower than they should be.

They were all exhausted.

Please, she thought toward that strange, too-thick mist. *If you're here, help us.*

She hoped the shadow fae were nearby and felt her magic.

Traveling north toward the mountains had been a gamble, and they were about to find out if she had been right.

No, not her. The presence.

The weight that had settled on her shoulders slowly lifted, dissipating in the stirring breeze.

"Where are you going?" she croaked, feeling her lower lip split.

Jessamine's scream rended the air. Slowly, Arabella turned toward the zaol.

She summoned the shadows, knowing it would take all her remaining strength. But she pulled the dark from the immense desert, breathing it in until it filled her.

As before, her emotions faded to the background. The immediacy of her fear retreated until it was like the ocean's waves crashing miles away. Her senses sharpened, and she realized she could see a few feet into the mist. Were those footprints at the base of the mountain?

The strange presence returned, wrapping around her like a cloak, and she didn't question it. She welcomed the power that came with it. Something bubbled up her throat. When she opened her mouth, a language she didn't know spilled from her lips. The voice didn't sound like hers. It was harsh and guttural, and the words came out in a hiss. As she spoke, the mist stirred as though awakening.

Come, she willed. *Come now.*

Just as suddenly as the unknown language had flowed into her, the power faded. It was as though the cloak slipped from her shoulders—and with it, the shadows retreated into the sands.

The last of her strength spent, she collapsed in the sand beside Breckett.

Either they would die, or help would come. They were entirely at the mercy of the mountains.

Before her eyes fluttered closed, booted feet emerged from the mist.

Chapter Fourteen

ELIAS

With a flick of deft fingers, Magnus removed a blade from his robes.

Fear squeezed Elias' throat at the sight of the syphen. But there was nothing he could do as Magnus strode across the tent toward where Elias was bound hand and foot to the X.

While he'd been given periods of respite after feeding on Magnus where he could collapse on the tent's carpeted floor, every day brought him back to this torture device.

The sorcerer's eyes flicked up to his, as sharp as the edge of the blade he held.

"My erox found where your enchantress was," Magnus said. "She took refuge in the Twilight Court within the estate of one of the princes."

Elias' heart drummed in his chest.

Had they taken Arabella captive? If so, where were they keeping her? Was she within the encampment even now?

"But she and her friends left before we could intercept them," Magnus continued, a fire alighting in his eyes.

Before Elias could even breathe a sigh of relief, a band of air wrapped around his throat. His vision swirled, and the tent went in and out of focus. Pulling at his restraints on instinct, he tried to break free. His wrists quickly became raw, and he felt the trickle of blood down his forearms.

"Nothing to say, my prodigal son?" Magnus said as he pressed the tip of the syphen to Elias' bare chest. A single drop of blood trickled from where the blade broke his skin.

Elias gasped, unable to even get a wisp of air.

"What was that?" Magnus pressed the blade further into his chest.

Half an inch.

One inch.

Pain sliced through the panic consuming his senses, desperate for air. The syphen was one of the things that could kill him. If the blade even nicked his heart, he would cease to exist.

As Magnus pressed it in with agonizing slowness, it felt like Elias' skin was being seared by a metal pulled from flames. Unable to heal around the syphen, blood poured from the wound.

Just as Elias was about to pass out from a lack of oxygen, Magnus released the pressure around his neck—the band of air dissipating. A pitiful croaking sound escaped his lips as Elias sucked in one breath after another.

Suddenly, Elias realized one of his ankles was free. Had he broken free in his desperation to breathe? His hands were still bound, as was his other ankle. But if he wasn't fully bound to the X, he could use his magic.

"Touch your power," Magnus said as something sharp sliced into Elias' mind.

The syphen's will, he realized.

Unbidden, Elias reached for the essence swirling at his core, knowing if he used too much of it, he'd succumb to the demon within.

Heat flared behind his eyes as the room came into focus. Every time he wielded essence, his eyes burned and turned a bright blue. He focused that energy before his chest, allowing the essence to form into an orb of the same blue hue as his eyes. It grew larger between him and Magnus, but the sorcerer didn't pull back, didn't step away. Instead, he watched, transfixed as Elias' power blossomed between them.

"Hold," Magnus said, not releasing the syphen's hilt where it remained in Elias' chest.

Instantly, Elias stopped, and the orb of power hovered between them.

In his years of being tortured beneath the mountain, he'd become all too familiar with Magnus' manipulation with the syphen. He'd retreated far into himself, locking the shreds of himself far away where Magnus couldn't reach. But as he tried to protect what remained of him now, he felt himself slipping—as if shards of himself were falling through.

Into Magnus' waiting hand.

Minutes passed as Elias held on to his power, sweat trickling down his face.

All the muscles in his body strained, fighting to cling to the magic. It felt like he held a boulder thrice his size atop his shoulders. He was so weak that even this display of magic depleted his strength swiftly.

A pulling sensation came from his chest.

For a moment, he thought it was the mating bond, thought Arabella had gotten closer to him somehow. When he'd prevented Magnus from going after her, the bond disappeared hours later. Or nearly so. The tugging sensation had faded, and he could no longer sense her emotions or nearness.

He wondered if she'd escaped with Breckett through the gateway to the fae realm.

Even though he longed to feel her, he felt relief that she was far from here.

Far from Magnus.

The pulling sensation in his chest now was unlike the mating bond.

It was a deep part of him. A place he'd never journeyed. It was the well of energy at the center of his core—the very fabric that wove his being together. All that made him an erox.

My magic, he realized.

"There you are," Magnus purred. "The core of an erox's magic is in different places in each male's body. And it would appear yours is in your..."

Disbelief and then fury crossed Magnus' features as he shook his head, taking a step back. Though he never released the syphen.

"No," Magnus hissed. Then a laugh bubbled up his throat and tore through the silence in the tent. "Of course, my most sentimental erox stores his magic in the one place I can't access with the syphen."

Without warning, Magnus pulled the syphen free.

The sound Elias made was something between a croak and a cry. Blood flowed from the wound in long lines down his body, which started to stitch back together but didn't close. And it wouldn't. Not without more essence.

He'd nearly depleted all of it as he clung to the orb of magic, which he still held in front of his chest.

"Release your magic," Magnus said.

Elias did as he bid.

Instantly, the essence fizzled out, and the heat behind his eyes disappeared. He quickly breathed the orb's essence back into him. In place of the heat that once burned behind his eyes was a dark, searing pressure. He felt his pupils dilate, growing wider as hunger filled him. Fangs pricked his lips, and he tasted the metallic tang of blood.

Magnus flicked a wrist, and Elias' ankle was cuffed again.

Elias tried to form words, but the hunger was consuming him slowly, making it impossible to form individual thoughts.

"The source of your magic, my prodigal son," Magnus said as he studied Elias' blood on the blade. "Is in your heart. At present, I can't reach it—not with the syphen anyway. Can't have you dying just yet. There's much we need to do. Much, indeed."

In a flash, Magnus was before him, slicing him open from collarbone to his stomach.

Elias screamed as agony crashed over him. It felt like he was being peeled open. No, he *was* being peeled open. Glancing down, he watched as the sorcerer pulled his skin back and punched his hand into Elias' chest.

His pupils widened further as fingers touched his heart, bands of magic wrapping around it.

Soon, conscious thought faded from him, and all he knew was agony—and *hunger*.

Fangs out, Elias snapped at the male but couldn't reach him. Not bound as he was. But soon, even the hunger wasn't enough to keep him awake. He fell beneath a wave of agony, slipping into unconsciousness.

His dreams were short and filled of scarlet eyes and crows flying on bloodied wings.

When he woke, a woman was before him, and a hunger unlike anything he'd ever known burned through him. It felt like he'd stepped into flames even as they burned him from within.

Several erox held the woman by her wrists and neck.

Tears slipped down her cheeks as his gaze fixed on the essence swirling in her chest.

He called it to him, hunger driving him.

The female stopped fighting as she fell under his power, taking a step forward and then another.

Their lips crashed together, and she cried out as she came again and again. He didn't pause between feedings like he might have with other prey. No. He was too lost to the hunger and the need to *feed*. Again and again, he pulled essence into his mouth—ignoring her screams of pleasure tinged with pain—until his body was full to the brim.

All at once, his hunger was sated, and his flesh knit back together.

Thoughts returned to him, and he watched with horror as the female slipped to the ground.

Dead.

There was a tsking sound, and Elias looked up to see Flynn with a smug look on his face. "Drained her dry. I've never seen an erox kill someone so fast."

Guilt swelled in Elias' chest, and he gagged, nearly retching.

I killed her. She's dead because of me.

Flynn and the other erox turned toward the tent's exit, not bothering to remove the woman's body.

Elias' wordless screams filled the tent as he raged against his bonds.

Chapter Fifteen
ARABELLA

Something chafed at Arabella's wrists.

Even with the exhaustion weighing down her thoughts, she knew at once she was tied at her hands and feet.

"Don't touch him," came Jessamine's voice from nearby.

Peeling her eyes open with great effort, Arabella took in her surroundings all at once.

She was in some sort of cave with uneven stone walls and a single exit at the far end. There were six guards stationed at the entrance, all with dated swords or crude spears. The cave was no bigger than a guest room in the House of Obscurities, and there was no furniture. On the far wall, there was a single torch.

Breckett—also bound hand and foot—napped peacefully beside Arabella. Meanwhile, Jessamine was on her knees, spitting at a masked male who gripped an unconscious Hadeon by the throat. Her hands were bound behind her, and her ankles were also tied.

All of their weapons were gone.

"I suggest you listen to Enchantress Jessamine and put him down," Arabella rasped. "I'd hate to kill someone I've just met."

She hoped the bluff wasn't as obvious as it felt. She doubted she could summon her shadows. Not without proper rest and food.

"I'll see to you next," the male hissed in Arabella's direction. "It's because of the Twilight Court that we're here. Because of *his* kind."

Shadow fae, she thought as relief washed over her. *We found them.*

The male wore leather armor, which was tied together with handmade laces. Both the armor and his leather boots seemed sturdy. His long brown hair was braided back at his temples, and he had a dark mask that covered his nose and mouth and looped behind pointed ears.

To her eyes, he looked no different from the other fae. Like those she'd met at the Twilight Court, this male possessed supernatural grace, long limbs, and pointed ears. Though his skin was fairer than those in the Twilight Court.

As the male lifted a blade to Hadeon's neck, about to slice him open, she sighed.

It looked like he was calling her bluff after all.

Rolling onto her knees, she reached for her shadows. Immediately, a headache split her skull, and blood trickled from her nose. But she ignored it. There'd be time for pain later.

The shadows were slippery, and she nearly lost her grip on them. But she managed to weave the dark into a narrow band of magic, which she lashed out at the male and wrapped around the hilt of his blade. With a single pull, she yanked the weapon free, dropping it onto the floor. Then she fell backward, unable to hold the shadows—or her own body up—for a moment longer.

The shadow fae warrior turned on her as her stomach growled loudly.

Rather than the anger she expected to see at her interruption, shock filled his gaze. He dropped Hadeon, who collapsed on the ground, groaning.

Pausing only to grab his blade, the warrior hurried out the single opening at the opposite end of the cave. The warriors at the entrance, wearing matching leather armor and face masks, leveled narrowed gazes on them but didn't approach. Instead, they gripped spears and swords more tightly in their fists.

Turning, Arabella dry-heaved onto the cold stones. Nothing came up but bile.

"Fuck," she hissed after it subsided. "I'm so hungry, I could eat my shoe."

"Please don't," Jessamine said. In a dry tone, she added, "It won't be good with your delicate constitution."

Despite their rather dire circumstances and the fact they nearly died dozens of times since entering the Abyss, a twinkle of humor filled Jessamine's eyes.

If she wasn't so tired, Arabella might have laughed, but all she could manage was a small smile in return—which made her split lip throb. "Bitch."

Jessamine snorted.

A thought struck Arabella.

"The zaol?" she asked.

Jessamine sighed heavily. "Alive. But it can't break through the mist. Must be some type of magical ward." She nodded to the guards at the cave's entrance. "After they hauled us through, it roared for a time before turning away."

There was a coughing sound, and Hadeon pulled himself upright, wincing. "It appears the shadow fae are still holding a grudge."

By the look of him, the shadow fae must have knocked him around while Arabella had been passed out. Bruises peppered his jawline and cheeks, and one of his eyes was nearly swollen shut. He also had a split lip.

Jessamine sniffed, sparing a glare at the prince. "If you'd been stuck in an underrealm, I imagine you'd be bitter about it, too."

Arabella frowned.

The fae could live hundreds or even thousands of years. So,

some of the fae here might have been the very same who'd fought in the fae wars a few centuries ago. That was assuming, of course, that time moved the same here as it did in the fae or mortal realms. Maybe these fae were descendants of those who'd sought refuge in this underrealm.

One brow raised, Hadeon's gaze fixed on Jessamine. "Perhaps I'd be forgiving of my tardiness on account of sheer boredom. I can't imagine they receive many guests here."

Jessamine rolled her eyes before turning from him and scooting toward the wall where a stone jutted out. Eyes swiveling between the cave's opening and the stone behind her, she moved her bonds against it, pressing back and forth with slow movements.

"Thank you," Arabella said, turning to Hadeon. "For what you did with the zaol."

He raised a brow, his eyes glittering with mischief. "Are you offering me another favor, Enchantress?"

"Fuck off," she said flatly. "But since you mentioned it, I just saved you from your would-be assailant. So, let's call it even for today."

"I also saved his sorry ass," Jessamine said, not taking her eyes from the cave's entrance. "Don't let the princeling act like he did all the work with the greater demon."

"Speaking of which," he said as he turned toward her. "You have quite a knack for being in places a moment before you're needed."

Jessamine's eyes snapped up, sharper than the stone. But then the look faded as quickly as it appeared, and she returned to her bonds. "I'm good at what I do, Princeling. It's my job."

"Indeed," he said noncommittally.

Footsteps sounded at the cave's entrance, and Jessamine froze.

"It's been quite some time, Prince Hadeon."

The voice was as cool as the stones beneath Arabella's palms and laced with the power of a slumbering dragon. Something in the room shifted, and it took her a moment to realize the shadows had moved. For once, it wasn't toward her but away—toward the newcomer.

Looking up, her eyes fell upon a male with skin the color of the light side of the moon. He appeared to be in his early thirties. While he wasn't as tall as Hadeon or Elias, he had broad shoulders and thick muscles across his entire body. Like the fae warrior who'd fled earlier—and now stood behind him—his clothing was worn, but his leather armor was polished and sturdy. His pale face was clean, and his long brown hair was braided back—not unlike Arabella's braid. Only, the sides of his head were shaved from his ear to his temples, and there were smaller braids throughout the rest of his hair.

However, unlike the other warriors, he'd lowered the mask over his face, which hung around his neck.

His gaze wasn't fixed on her. Instead, his eyes fastened on Hadeon, who lounged casually against the cave wall—as though he'd asked to be bound hand and foot.

Arabella noted the rich brown color and shape of the newcomer's eyes, his high cheekbones, and his long limbs that were somewhat similar to her own.

"Prince Arden," Hadeon said. "It's been too long."

"Last I saw you, you'd dismissed my theories about this place," Arden rumbled, and something flickered in his eyes. It was like the embers of a fire before it set fully aflame. "You and so many others mocked me, acted like you were amusing me. But I was *right*."

"It would appear so," Hadeon said. "I never doubted your belief."

"But you doubted this place could be a reality," Arden said.

Hadeon merely shrugged.

"Then you left me and the shadow fae to die on that field," Arden continued, the embers in his gaze seeming to take on more heat. "You knew your mother intended to kill all members of my court over some deluded belief that the shadow fae would wipe out the other courts, and you said *nothing* during our final meeting. I should kill you for that." He gestured to the shadow fae warriors behind him—all masked, all with hate in their eyes. "My warriors are eager for your blood. For revenge for what your mother did to us. How she forced us here."

It was then Arabella realized that, even all these centuries later, the warriors who'd fought in the fae wars were very much alive. They weren't descendants after all.

"Did you ever consider *how* you learned about my mother's attack before her army arrived? How you had just enough time to decide where to take your final stand?" Hadeon asked in a bored tone. "One of your spies happened upon one of the queen's scouts, did they not?"

Brows furrowing, Arden seemed uncertain for the first time.

"I couldn't be seen aiding you, old friend," Hadeon said.

Arabella frowned.

Was Hadeon implying that he'd arranged having scouts captured to give Arden a warning of what Genoveva was doing?

Arden crossed muscled arms over his chest. "Then what took you so long to pay us a visit? It would seem after a thousand years, you've forgotten about us."

As Hadeon looked up at Arden, she could see that clever mind of his taking in this new information.

"It's been five hundred years since the fae wars," Hadeon said carefully. "In the fae realm, that is. A thousand years have passed here?"

"Lies," Arden snapped, though his tone held a hint of uncertainty. Turning from Hadeon, Arden's gaze settled on Arabella. "But he's not why I've been summoned here." Boots crunching on pebbles, the shadow fae prince strode forward. Slowly, he lowered himself so he crouched before her. "Who are you?"

She hesitated revealing what Hadeon suspected of her heritage —and her relation to this male. She wanted to see just what he was like and if he was worthy of her trust. But she did need his help if she had any hope of rescuing Elias.

"No one of note," she said carefully. "I possess shadow magic. And I was told you might be able to help me learn to control it."

Eyes narrowing, Arden's gaze lingered for a moment on her neck—where the black veins were. Then he said, "How have you survived without Queen Genoveva's notice?"

Careful not to glance toward Hadeon, she said, "As it turns out, mortals are beneath her notice."

"A demi-fae. That would explain why you weren't amongst us when the Twilight Court slaughtered civilians," Arden said, his voice growing distant. "Were you hiding among the humans?"

She nodded.

It was the truth, though all she remembered was being found at the edge of the forest near Shadowbank and the enchantresses taking her in.

In a flash, a blade was in his hand, and he was slicing the bonds at her wrists and ankles. "I'll never turn away one of my own. Not when so many of us have been hunted down simply for existing."

Rubbing her wrists, Arabella gestured to Jessamine, Hadeon, and Breckett—the latter of whom still slept.

"These are my friends. I hope you'll be equally as welcoming to them." Then she nodded to Breckett. "He's going to need to feed when he wakes. I suggest having backup when he does. Enchantress Jessamine can explain."

If she'd learned anything about Elias during the times when he'd nearly run out of essence, erox could become lost to the feeding. And fae were equally susceptible to an erox's power. Once they were under an erox's spell, they'd be unable to fight against the pleasure as their essence slipped from their lips—same as humans.

Leaning back on a heel, Arden studied her for a long moment before standing.

He nodded to the warriors behind him, one of which turned toward the cave's entrance and disappeared. Several others strode into the cave, taking positions around Breckett.

"Walk with me," Arden said. "There's much I'd like to discuss."

※

Arabella followed the shadow fae prince in silence through long tunnels within the mountain, clinging to the shreds of her remaining strength.

Like the cave they'd just been in, the walls, floors, and ceiling of the tunnel were all made of rough, uneven stone. Interestingly, there weren't torches on the walls, nor did Arden hold one. Instead, he moved through the darkness with confident familiarity.

He can see in the darkness, she realized. *Just like me.*

Sparks of magic from nearby wielders bubbled into her awareness. She didn't need to cast her awareness out. Not when hundreds of sparks lit within her mind. She could sense them through the cave walls, which led her to believe there were more tunnels and caves within the mountain that housed even more shadow fae.

Just how many fae were here?

As they walked along the rough-hewn floors that slanted upwards, she watched, transfixed by how the shadows moved around Arden just like they did for her. While it was dark within the mountain, the deeper darkness of the shadows still moved. They swirled around her feet and then his—as if they couldn't decide who to nuzzle into.

Seeing her gaze swiveling between the shadows and the cave walls, Arden said, "We used magic to tunnel into these mountains and build our home here. We needed a safe space away from the demons and creatures of this realm."

"I didn't know shadow magic could be used that way," she said honestly.

They passed several branching tunnels, down which she heard echoes of laughter.

"What do you know about our magic?" he asked.

Our.

It was so strange to meet someone else with shadow magic—especially after years among the humans of Shadowbank who looked upon this type of magic with distrust and fear. It was why she'd had to seek out Lucinda's help.

"I've only recently discovered some of my abilities," she said.

He nodded. "It's rare to encounter demi-fae. Historically, the fae have only mated amongst our kind."

"Why?" she asked cautiously.

The prince shrugged. "There weren't many humans in the fae realm. So, the opportunity didn't often present itself."

"And when it did?"

He raised a brow. "Love matches between fae and humans—or any other species—is rare. Most looked upon us with fear. But it did happen."

Turning down another tunnel, they came to what appeared to be a cave. But unlike where she'd awoken, this cave had an opening at the other end. They were higher up in the mountain, overlooking the ground thousands of feet below, which was shrouded in the dark mist. Beyond, the desert stretched out as far as the eye could see in every direction. As she followed Arden into the cave, she realized there was a steep drop-off from the mouth of the cave that led outside.

For the first time, she wondered why he'd brought her there.

As her stomach growled loud enough to wake the undead, footsteps sounded behind them. Turning, she spotted a fae warrior with something in his hands. Her mouth immediately watered. He held what appeared to be a loaf of bread and some dried meat. When the warrior approached and offered her the plate of food as well as a waterskin, she hesitated.

She wouldn't accept food if her friends weren't also being seen to.

Arden nodded toward the plate. "Please. You must be hungry."

"My friends," she began, keeping her arms firmly at her sides. "They're—"

"Being cared for," Arden interrupted. "I've instructed my warriors to see their needs are tended to."

"Even Hadeon?" she asked, annoyed at herself for protecting the fae prince who held a bargain over her head.

Lips pursed, Arden said, "Even him."

Without another word, she took the plate and waterskin from the warrior and shoved the dried meat into her mouth, tearing off a piece with her teeth.

When Arden gestured to the ground at the edge of the tunnel that overlooked the land around them, she cleared her throat awkwardly and swallowed the food.

"Thank you," she managed before sitting down, allowing her feet to hang in the open air against the mountainside.

If this place possessed stars like in the mortal and fae realms, she thought the view would be breathtaking. As it was, the landscape was made up of a dark desert and a darker sky.

The prince took a seat beside her. To her relief, he said nothing as she finished the food and took a long drink of cool water. She drank until the waterskin was empty.

Only once she'd finished did Arden speak.

"Where did you enter the Abyss?" he asked.

"To the southeast," she said. "I believe it was the same gateway you entered. The one in the western tundra."

He nodded. "I've tried to find that gateway again many times, but I've never been able to locate it. It appears to be closed from this side. I'm afraid you and your friends are now stuck here alongside us."

Her heart dropped as the realization sunk in. "When I learned of the potential of your being in the Abyss, I suspected there may have been a reason you never returned."

I will find a way to get back to Elias, she thought, clinging to the shreds of her confidence. *I won't be stuck here.*

After all, Hadeon had said he knew an exit gateway existed.

He shrugged. "We've tried to find a way out. But without my map, it's impossible to locate the exit in the west."

I'd been right, she realized. *The line across the map is to a gateway.*

"You're lucky you found us," he continued. "And that you didn't become lost in the desert."

"Yes."

She thought of revealing that she had the map tucked away in her jacket. It was a miracle the fae hadn't noticed it when removing their weapons and taking them into the mountain.

But she hesitated.

Maybe I can use the map as a bargaining tool, she thought. *A way out in exchange for their help against Magnus.*

"Why have you sought us out?" Arden asked, pulling her from her thoughts.

She considered what to say but eventually decided on partial truths. Better that than become tangled in her own web of lies.

"I need help controlling my magic," she said. "Ever since I used an amplifier, it's changed. The shadows... Well, they seem to have a will of their own."

Brows drawing together slightly, he said, "That is rare indeed."

"Not everyone can do this?" she asked.

He shook his head. "Most shadow fae can wield the shadows to some extent, but only the most powerful of our kind can *awaken* the shadows. It's even rarer for this type of magic to be possessed by a demi-fae, especially one who's part human."

Fuck.

If she had any doubts of whether she might be the daughter of some fae princess, that shattered it. Especially since most fae nobility possessed the strongest magic.

A thought occurred to her.

Was her mother there? For a moment, she longed to ask, but asking would reveal her potential parentage. And that wasn't something she was ready to reveal yet. Not if it was a card she could play in later negotiations.

"Once you've recovered, I'd like to see just what you can do," he said, his eyes on the distant horizon.

"You'll help me, then?" she dared to ask.

"If control is what you seek, I will help you," he said before looking at her, a twinkle in his eyes. For a moment, she thought he seemed genuinely happy. "But not just now. You must recover from your long journey. Eat. Rest. There will be time enough to train." A humorless laugh escaped his lips. "Without the ability to leave, all we have is time."

For a moment, guilt at not revealing that she had the map filled her. He'd been trapped here for so many years. She couldn't imagine what it must have been like to live for hundreds of years in an underrealm.

But unlike the shadow fae, she didn't have time. Not when Elias was being tortured by Magnus as they spoke.

"There's something you should know," he said, pulling her from her thoughts. "If you embrace your power, there will be consequences."

She frowned. "What do you mean?"

She shouldn't be surprised. Magic always came at a cost.

"Over time, you'll lose much of what makes you human as you use your magic," he said.

"My memories?" she asked, unable to disguise the panic bleeding into her words.

Not again. Not after what Elias went through to get them back.

"No, your memories will remain," he said as confusion crossed his features. "But your... mortality may fade."

She blinked.

"You will become more fae than human," he clarified. "It doesn't happen to all demi-fae, but most likely, you will age and look like one of us."

"What do you mean?"

"Fae can live for thousands of years. Certainly longer than the lifespan of an enchantress," he said. "And your body will become more fae. I don't just mean the pointed ears, but you will move like one of us."

For a moment, she had no words. This new information settled in her gut like stones.

She'd prided herself for so long in her abilities as an enchantress, in her abilities to protect the people of Shadowbank who couldn't protect themselves. If she was honest, she'd held fury in her heart against the fae—the very race who'd remained in their realm, behind their pristine walls or in castles, and never raised a hand against the threat of the demons in the mortal realm.

The demons who devoured all in their path.

To become fae... It was to become the very thing she'd grown to hate.

If I become fae, I won't stop protecting those I love, she thought. *It won't change me.*

But she'd already changed since using the amplifier and since her memories returned. She'd become more angry, more prone to impulses. How else would she change?

She thought of Elias, who'd risked everything to return her memories to her.

The male she loved.

The male who needed saving.

"It's worth it," she said, voice cool as the mountain stones.

Arden merely nodded. "Good." He rose to his feet. "I'll show you to your room, then—"

"Tomorrow—" To her surprise, she grabbed the prince's arm. Realizing what she'd done, she quickly dropped her hand. It wouldn't do if he saw the gesture as a threat. "Please... I'd like to begin my training right away. Tomorrow."

There wasn't a moment to waste.

She'd give herself one day to rest, and then she'd throw herself into training and learn everything she could. Somehow, she'd find an edge that she could use against Magnus and his armies.

Lines formed between Arden's brows, but he nodded. "Of course."

Then he turned, and she followed the prince down the tunnels into the deep.

First, she'd learn to control her magic. As she learned from Arden, she'd determine whether he could be trusted. Then she would see whether she could convince Arden and the shadow fae to join her in the fight against a sorcerer.

Chapter Sixteen
ARABELLA

Arabella woke up to a world as dark as her thoughts.

A strange sort of panic swelled in her chest. She couldn't quite identify the cause, but she had this sense that she was running out of time. For a moment, she wondered whether she'd dreamed of Elias again. But she couldn't recall as her dreams slipped between her fingers like the sands of the Abyss.

She sat up from where she slept on the ground, pushing aside her pile of blankets and animal skins. Or at least, she pretended it was animal skins. The idea of sleeping on the carcasses of some furry demons made her stomach turn.

The shadow fae had given Arabella, Jessamine, Breckett, and Hadeon a room farther up in the mountain as their shared sleeping quarters.

Similar to the cave she'd sat in with Arden, this one had an entrance from within the mountain as well as an opening at the other end that overlooked the desert. There was a steep descent from the mouth of the cave, which carried a constant cool breeze. If they were to flee this place, she supposed they could try to climb down the mountainside. But from this far up, they'd just as easily fall to their deaths, tumbling thousands of feet to the base of the mountain below.

"What's wrong?" Jessamine asked from where she'd been sleeping beside Arabella.

Beside Arabella, Breckett snoozed happily after Jessamine begrudgingly let him feed on her the night before. That had been after they'd been given a hearty meal of some kind of stew and waterskins.

"It's nothing," Arabella said, shaking her head as if that would clear the feeling of doom from her thoughts.

Jessamine gave her a flat look.

Sighing, Arabella said, "It's just... The mating bond... I've hardly been able to feel it since we came to the Abyss. But now, I have this awful dread I can't shake. And I don't know if it's coming from the mating bond or if it's my own fears."

Jessamine squeezed Arabella's shoulder and opened her mouth to speak when another voice came from the far end of the cave.

"Don't rush anything. Or else you might lose any alliance you'd hoped to gain."

Turning, Arabella spotted Hadeon sitting against the stone wall, his wings tucked in close. As ever, he lounged with such ease. It was as if he were in his own personal throne room. His feet were stretched out before him, arms crossed, and his head was tilted back as he leaned against the curved stone wall.

If his face wasn't covered in bruises and one eye swollen nearly shut, she might have believed his bravado.

"Didn't sleep?" she asked.

With a chuckle, he said, "No." Then he leaned forward. "I meant what I said. Don't rush Arden into an alliance. He won't take kindly to his hand being forced."

Breckett made a delightful little choking sound in his sleep before rolling over.

"I understand wanting to get back to save Elias, but maybe..."

Jessamine began, her tone oddly hesitant. "Learn as much as you can from the fae before we try to find a way out. It could be the difference between life or death in the battle to come." Again, she hesitated. "The sorcerer wants something from Elias. He sought him out for a reason. If that's the case, he wouldn't kill him off so quickly." Her eyes locked on Arabella's. "We may have some time yet."

Arabella tried to ease the tightness in her throat as she braided her hair and donned her leather jacket. "I hope you're right."

Footsteps sounded at the cave's entrance, and a shadow fae warrior appeared, his face brightened by the lone torch mounted on the wall.

"Prince Arden wishes to speak with you," the warrior said to Arabella before placing a tray of food down.

Eyeing the food, she assumed it must be morning in this world without a sun. But there was no way to truly know. All the same, this was likely meant to be their breakfast.

Belatedly, she realized it was the same male warrior who'd nearly killed Hadeon the day before. The one who'd retrieved Arden after she'd knocked the knife from his hands with her magic.

Standing, she grabbed a slice of bread from the tray, waved farewell to the others, and then gestured toward the tunnels behind the warrior. "After you."

She followed the male down long corridors as she quickly ate. The previous day, she'd spent eating her weight in absolutely anything the shadow fae offered them—from stews, to breads, to dried meats. Once she'd finished eating, she'd fallen into a deep sleep.

Even now, weariness seeped into her bones, but she couldn't let that stop her from training. There was no time to waste.

Like the day before, she felt bursts of magic through the cave walls. It felt like fireflies moved just beyond her line of sight.

Just how many shadow fae are here?

After they'd turned down several tunnels, two fae appeared, walking in the opposite direction.

Toward them.

She held her breath, uncertain of what to do with her hands.

How would the shadow fae feel about some demi-fae appearing suddenly in the Abyss with several other rather unusual companions? They'd probably never come across an erox or a human. And any encounters they'd had with the Twilight Court fae were likely less than friendly. As such, it was possible they viewed Arabella as an enemy given that she'd appeared in Hadeon's company.

For reasons she couldn't explain, she found herself wanting these fae to like her. To accept her.

These are my people.

The thought slipped into her mind. As it did, she blinked, uncertain what to make of it. Once, the enchantresses of Shadowbank had been her only family. Then Elias had come into her life and changed everything. Now, how she viewed the world was being challenged once more with this new kinship with shadow fae. Did she owe them any loyalty?

She fixed her eyes on the cave floor where the shadows swirled playfully at the feet of the oncoming fae. There were two pairs of feet. One walked with purpose toward them, and the other pair was far smaller, turning and jumping toward the first fae.

It was at that moment she realized one of them was a child.

The too-loud whispers of a small voice echoed down the tunnel.

"Who's that?"

Looking up, Arabella's gaze fell upon a middle-aged female with blue eyes as piercing as shards of glass. Like the fae guards, she was garbed in worn leathers and animal skins and boots made for hard labor. Instead of carrying a spear or sword, she held a basket of what appeared to be laundry. Beside her, the child bore a smaller basket of similar fabrics and bounced on their heels.

Both had long, pointed fae ears.

Similar to Arabella, they had pale skin, long limbs, and a fellowship with the shadows.

"Mom," the child whispered again, loud enough to wake sleeping ogres. "Who's *that*?"

Uncertain what to do, Arabella offered them a small smile.

"A guest of the prince," the female responded, eyeing Arabella.

She didn't miss the accusation in her gaze.

What do you want, outsider?

Why didn't you come before?

If Arabella had been stuck in the Abyss for countless years, she'd probably feel similar—a mixture of curiosity, hope, and fury at no one coming sooner. For them, it had been a thousand years. Plenty of time to build distrust and resentment.

She shrugged off the lingering stares as they passed, feeling the spark of their magic grow smaller as the distance grew between them.

Arabella passed several tunnels that led to rooms filled with fae. All of them were busy with their work or talking with each other as they sat cross-legged on the ground. Some spared looks her way, but many kept their eyes on their tasks.

It felt strangely... domestic.

She hadn't expected the fae to have found contentment within one of the underrealms. Part of her had thought they'd be starving or hardened from the environment. She hadn't even considered there'd be children there. But it made sense that some of the warriors could have fallen in love over time and might have wanted children.

Clearing her throat, she said to the guard, "What can I call you?"

She studied the way the cave walls and floors sloped downward and wondered if they were headed toward the base of the mountain.

"Colton," he said, not looking back at her.

"Were you part of the army that fled to this place?"

Or were you born here?

She realized she had no idea how quickly fae children aged.

But if she had to guess, Colton was about the same age as Arden, who looked like he'd be in his thirties if he were human.

"I fought in the fae wars," he said, his voice cold. "And I followed my prince when he gave the orders to retreat."

She considered her words for a long moment before saying, "Why do the other fae courts hate the shadow fae?"

Part of her disliked asking the question so bluntly. She didn't want to imply that the shadow fae held some sort of blame for the terrible predicament they were in. They were victims to unspeakable violence. But why? How did the other courts convince themselves that such an atrocity was acceptable?

Colton paused mid-stride, and she nearly rammed into his back but managed to skid to a stop before colliding with him.

Slowly, he turned toward her.

She realized that, like Arden, his long brown hair was pulled back in a series of smaller braids, which he'd woven into a single long braid that fell down his back. Perhaps this was customary for shadow fae males. Unlike the prince, however, he kept the mask over his mouth and nose at all times.

Colton's eyes narrowed on her in the dark tunnels. "Indoctrination."

"What do you mean?" she asked.

"The shadow fae were always among the least liked in the fae courts," he said. "There has always been a mistrust of shadow magic. Many called it dark magic even though no fae can wield dark magic. Over time, the mistrust turned into hate. There was a slow trickle of misinformation. It was a carefully constructed narrative that the shadow fae were no longer satisfied in our own lands, that we'd take over other courts. That no one was safe so long as we were in power. One moment, it was simple prejudice, and the next we were being hunted down."

There was no missing the bitterness and the hurt in his words, and she had to try not to flinch at the vehemence in his tone.

She dared to ask, "Who came up with this narrative?"

"Someone who wanted an enemy to unite the fae against," he said.

She frowned. "What would Queen Genoveva gain from uniting the fae courts?"

He turned back toward the tunnel, speaking over his shoulder. "Ask Prince Arden. Perhaps he'll be interested in rehashing fae history."

A deep hurt was woven into every syllable as he spoke. It wasn't just the shadow fae's genocide, though that was an atrocity all on its own. There was something about the other fae courts—how they'd turned on the shadow fae—that had created a wound in Colton. She wondered if he'd had friends in the other fae courts. Friends who hadn't defended him when it counted.

Without another word, she followed Colton into the dark.

Eventually, the tunnel opened to a massive cavern several stories high and was as long as two residential homes in Shadowbank side by side. There was a pool on one side. Steam rippled from the surface, and there were branching sections of the pool that she thought might lead into another cave somewhere beyond the wall. But most of the room was completely open, and the distant walls sloped gradually downward.

It lacked furniture or something that would denote the room had a specific purpose. If she had to guess, this must be where they held large gatherings or perhaps where the warriors trained.

A male kneeled beside the pool, his hand outstretched over the water.

Hearing them enter, he straightened, turning toward them and lowering the mask over his nose and mouth.

Like the day prior, Arden wore leather armor that was identical to what Colton and the other warriors wore. If it wasn't for the warriors' deference and an air of authority about him, she would have had no way to identify this male as a prince.

He again wore his hair in a single braid down his back. But most striking of all was his dark eyes that seemed to swallow the light around him.

"You're here. Good." Arden nodded to Colton. "Thank you for bringing her."

Colton bowed before retreating the way they'd come.

"How did you find your accommodations?" the prince asked as he turned back toward the water.

She strode to his side, following his gaze.

The pool's steam swirled, filling the air with a moist heat that had her relaxing for what felt like the first time in an eternity. Shoulders drooping, she felt her muscles going pliant. For a moment, she longed to close her eyes and forget everything. But the looming dread hovering at the back of her mind pushed to the forefront, and she forced herself to focus.

"We're grateful for your hospitality," she said. "We were ill-prepared for a long journey across a desert."

One corner of his lips lifted. "An understatement, perhaps."

She smiled. "Perhaps."

"What is it you hope to learn?" he asked, his eyes following trails of steam.

She considered her next words.

Somehow, she needed to convey her need to control her magic without revealing her heritage or that she had the map. At least, she couldn't reveal either of these yet. She also needed to forge an alliance. But first, she had to determine whether she could trust these fae.

All the while, she intended to keep an ear to the ground to see if she could glean any more information about how to get out of the Abyss when the time came.

It didn't matter that the shadow fae hadn't found a way out. She was going to forge a path back to the fae realm even if the map was useless and she had to build a way by herself with twigs, sweat, and sheer stubbornness.

"I want to learn to control the shadows," she began. "I need any edge I can get... So I can rescue my mate."

He turned to her then, brows arching toward the cavern ceiling. "Mate?"

She nodded.

"Mates are exceptionally rare amongst full fae. Even more so for demi-fae." He nodded as though having just come to a decision before turning back to the water. "And Hadeon told you of the Abyss."

It wasn't a question.

"Yes. He wanted to find you, too."

"For some scheme of his, no doubt," Arden said dryly, and she thought she saw him start to roll his eyes.

Lines formed between her brows as she realized that, although he was her uncle, he didn't act like her senior. There was a spiritedness about him that made him seem youthful. But if he knew Hadeon before the fae wars, which happened five hundred years ago, and one thousand years had passed here... Didn't that mean he was at least a thousand years old?

Shrugging, she said, "Hadeon is many things, but he seems to be a male of his word."

Why am I defending him?

Arden made a sound in the back of his throat that might have been a scoff. "I intend to speak with him at length very soon. But for now, tell me more about your mate."

She licked dry lips, hesitating.

Did she dare reveal what Elias was? Had they figured out what Breckett was yesterday? She'd assumed Jessamine had told them when he needed to feed.

But more than that, Arabella wondered how the shadow fae viewed demons. They had likely faced countless demons since coming to the Abyss. Perhaps the dislike they'd had for the creatures of the dark had turned to hate—especially if the demons in the Abyss killed their friends and loved ones.

But if Arden agreed to help her, he'd soon learn what Elias was. There wasn't a point in hiding it now.

"My people knew him as the Devourer," she said, thinking of how—not so long ago—she'd run out of Shadowbank in pursuit of Elias when he'd returned Scarlett to them. How she'd wanted to kill him before he could take one of her sisters again. "Every ten years, he took an offering from my village. The enchantresses usually volunteered, and I was his latest offering."

Head snapping toward her, Arden's eyes widened. "Are you saying your mate is a *demon*?"

Rather than the disgust she'd expected to fill his tone, there was only surprise. Was that a hint of excitement she detected as well?

"He's an erox," she said. "A demon who feeds on the sexual desires of their prey."

For a long moment, the prince stared at her, blinking in what she assumed was disbelief.

He's in shock, she thought. *Either that, or he's thinking about kicking us out of these mountains at this very moment.*

She wondered whether she'd have to fight her way back to her friends.

"Fascinating. Truly fascinating," he rumbled.

She cleared her throat. "What?"

"Never in my twelve hundred years of existence have I heard of a demi-fae finding a mate, let alone mating with a demon," he said, an odd twinkle in his gaze. "I'd always been told mating bonds were only possible between the fae—and occasionally demi-fae as well. Certainly not with any of the other races."

"Um, thank you," she said, uncertain how she was supposed to respond. After a moment, she added, "Can you tell me about mating bonds? I admit, I don't know much about them."

"They're rare, as I said before," he said. "Most mates can sense each other—how they're feeling and where they are."

She nodded. Those were things she'd experienced.

"They can also speak to each other, mind to mind," he continued, and it took everything in her not to gape at him. "Or at least, full fae can. Perhaps demi-fae don't have the same abilities. Or perhaps these things are only possible between two fae mates."

A thought occurred to her.

"Is there a choice to accept a mating bond?" she asked. "Or is it fated once the bond is in place?"

His eyes turned to her, twinkling. "There's always a choice. If one or both parties reject their pairing, the bond fades. But most of the time, the bond is accepted, and it forms a connection unlike anything in the natural world. I like to think of the mating bond as a sign that the pair is well matched."

She nodded as countless questions peppered her thoughts. Before she could voice any of them, Arden spoke.

"Tell me about your parents."

She opened her mouth to describe Iris but closed it. That wasn't what he was asking. He wanted to know about her biological parents.

"I didn't know them," she said. "The enchantresses raised me."

Rising, he started walking around the springs, and she followed him.

"I see." After a moment, he gestured to the pool. "This water is what keeps us alive in this place. There isn't another body of water for miles around, and there's no place to hide from the demons in the nearest oasis. It was by pure chance that we stumbled upon this mountain. Once we did, we created the mist spell that you saw surrounding this mountain. It's not a permanent ward, you see. The shadow fae take turns weaving the magic that protects this place. We have warriors stationed all day around the entire mountain. Without them, we wouldn't be able to live in the relative peace that we have. There are even edible plants that grow here."

"That's incredible you can use your magic in that way," she said.

As they moved, she saw that the pool did, indeed, extend to a series of what appeared to be smaller channels. The tunnels in the cavern wall were no larger than the size of a man with only inches above the water for air. But she suspected beyond this room would be where some of the plants grew. She marveled that life could exist in this realm at all.

"Can all of the shadow fae use shadow magic?" she asked.

"Yes," he said as they walked. "Some only possess mere trickles of it while others can wield the shadows like arrows or spears. Some can slip into the shadows to disguise their movements or use shadow bindings or illusions." He turned to her as they neared one side of the cavern where the water disappeared to whatever lay beyond. "Colton told me that you disarmed him yesterday with your magic."

"I did."

"Show me what you can do."

Bone-weary exhaustion still clung to her limbs and thoughts, and her movements felt slower than they normally would be. But the night of sleep and the meals they'd been given had helped her regain some of her strength. She wouldn't be able to wield shadows like she normally could, but she'd at least be able to use some magic.

Stretching an arm out, she called to the darkness.

There were shadows everywhere in this place. Without torches, lanterns, or any other form of light in most hallways and caves, the mountain was utterly dark. To summon the shadows would be as easy as breathing with so much to draw from.

Shadows around the room shifted, peeling away from the corners of stones in nearby walls and from the depths of the pool. They slunk across the water's surface and over the cavern floors until the dark swirled at her feet.

Come, she thought.

And the shadows responded.

They twisted up her body in rippling circles, moving until they encircled her legs before traveling up her torso and around her arms. To her surprise, as they inched down her forearms to her hands, the shadows stretched out past her fingertips until they formed a sort of claws.

That's new, she thought as she considered how useful it could be in hand-to-hand combat.

She swiped the air, marveling at the near-solid shadows. More shadows pooled at her feet like a black storm cloud, shifting and eager.

As she pulled in more and more shadows, a strange fury filled her—a desire to *consume*. She realized the shadows pressed against her mind, melding with her emotions. Tilting her head back, she breathed the darkness in, feeling her eyes shift and the fury within her growing.

Then her gaze sharpened.

Blood, something rumbled in her thoughts. *Desolation.*

Devour.

The prince scanned the length of her.

For reasons she didn't understand, she wanted to lash out at him, to wrap him in her shadows and demand that he send his army to the mortal realm. To save Elias. The impulse was so strong that it felt like she balanced on the edge of a blade. One push, and her restraint would shatter.

Arms trembling, it took everything in her not to unleash herself on this place.

Lines formed between Arden's brows. "Something isn't right about your magic." He circled her. "It's like something is layered on top of your shadows. Has anyone used magic on you?"

"A witch took my memories." She closed her hands into fists, forcing them to remain at her sides. As she did, rage filled her, rippling through the shadows. "And a sorcerer returned them."

Understanding dawned in his eyes. "Never let a sorcerer use their magic on you. You'll get more than you bargained for." He raised a hand toward her, palm outstretched, and then paused. "May I?"

She had no idea what he intended to do, but she managed a nod, fighting against the rising shadows that longed to be set free.

I can't hurt him, she thought past the fury filling her chest, the impulse to destroy. *I need his help.*

Suddenly, a strand of shadow lashed out from Arden's hand. Without warning, it struck her in the center of her forehead.

Instantly, pain fractured her senses.

For a moment, it felt like her head had been split open, and she nearly lost control of the shadows, nearly unleashing herself. Arden's shadow moved across her mind. His power pricked against something inside her, leaving a trail of dark agony that sent splinters of pain behind her eyes.

Gritting her teeth, she stumbled forward but managed to remain upright.

"There it is," the prince said.

Then his magic latched around something she hadn't realized was there. Something that had taken root in her mind. The strange magic had claws that sunk deep, but the shadow wrapped around it and *pulled*.

Light burst behind her eyelids as something was ripped from her mind. It was like an arrowhead or a creature's talon had been wedged beneath her skin, and the flesh had attempted to heal over it. But an infection had set in and was slowly poisoning her very being.

That infection was Magnus.

Her shadows roared as if they, too, felt her pain.

Arden balled his hand into a fist and pulled backward. The band of shadow tore from her forehead, and she staggered to a knee.

All at once, the pain stopped, but a roaring filled her ears.

Blood trickled from her nose, and her chest heaved as she took in deep, gasping breaths. Glancing up, she watched as Arden's shadows wrapped around a cloud of twisting scarlet. Sweat beaded on his forehead as he moved his arms in a sweeping motion, the entrapped scarlet hovering between his palms. Slowly, he brought his hands together. As they did, the orb shrunk. The shadows became smaller and smaller, and the scarlet raged from within. As if it knew it was about to be crushed. Pressing his palms together, the shadows and scarlet were extinguished in a puff of air.

The shadows pooling around her feet hummed.

As though happy.

"Dark magic," Arden said as he straightened, and his eyes connected with hers. "Some sorcerers can leave impressions on your mind. It's not quite mind control, but it helps make you more malleable to their will. I think this one was being used to track you."

She realized the urge to ravage everything in her path was just... gone. Her thoughts cleared, and her shadows had also calmed.

"Thank you," she said, blinking in wonder as she stared at her hands where the shadows whirled.

Then the latter part of what Arden said clicked in her mind.

Magnus had been tracking her. That must have been how he'd found Elias' castle so quickly and then located her at Hadeon's estate.

She'd endangered her friends, and she'd had no idea.

"Those black veins in your neck will fade in time as long as you're careful how much shadow magic you take into you," he said. "Give it a few days, and it'll go back to normal."

She nodded absently.

A thought occurred to her, and she looked up from her shadows. "How did you know the thing in my mind was dark magic?"

All magic wielders could sense the power of another magic wielder, but it would take a level of experience to be able to identify dark magic had wedged into her mind.

A familiarity with dark magic.

Arden looked away from her then, studying the cavern walls. "Luck, I suppose. Perhaps my senses have grown sharp where dark magic is concerned after years of being in the Abyss."

She dipped her chin ever the slightest, her eyes narrowing.

He was hiding something from her.

The prince gestured to the center of the cavern. "Let's begin our training."

Chapter Seventeen
ELIAS

Magnus must have punctured his lungs because as the syphen plunged into his chest, Elias couldn't draw a breath. Pain sliced through him as the sorcerer twisted the hilt.

"Nearly there," Magnus hissed, his voice oddly strained—quite unlike his usual stoic demeanor.

Gritting his teeth, Elias tried to stifle the scream threatening to rip out of his throat. He didn't want to give Magnus the satisfaction of knowing how deep the pain was—or how close he was to breaking.

Being tortured with a common blade or non-magical means was one thing. It was agony, but it was bearable. It was simply flesh. But to be stabbed over and over by the very blade used to create him... It was akin to having his chest torn in two, his entire being ripped open—tearing apart everything he was until there was nearly nothing left.

Blood surged up his throat, and he coughed, choking.

Panic bled across his chest with icy fingers. For several moments, he couldn't breathe. Gasping, he pulled against the restraints that bound him to the X. But all he could do was stand and bear everything that was being done to him.

Suddenly, his chest convulsed and air rushed into his lungs. Then blood spewed from his lips, and he spat scarlet onto Magnus' once-rich rugs.

The pressure in his chest eased as Magnus released the hilt and stepped back. He tapped a bloodied finger against his chin.

Elias focused on taking one breath and then the next. But each was agony. The syphen remained in his chest—piercing one of his lungs. His body tried to heal itself, but the blade's magic kept his body from mending anything it touched.

The sorcerer had changed as of late. He'd been muttering under his breath, but Elias hadn't bothered to ask. He hardly possessed the energy to remain conscious anymore, let alone fight.

But this time, when Magnus strode around the tent, Elias caught on to one word of the sorcerer's mutters—*enchantress*.

"What—" Elias began, but his punctured lung made it nearly impossible to breathe, let alone speak. He gasped, eventually managing two words. "What happened?"

A wicked smile alighted on Magnus' face. "When you and I struck our bargain and I returned Arabella's memories to her, I added a little bit of magic to be embedded in her mind alongside her memories."

Elias frowned, shaking his head. What had Magnus done?

But more than that, why had he trusted Magnus would return her memories without some ulterior motive? He'd been so foolish. And that oversight could cost Arabella her freedom.

"That magic made her more... sympathetic to dark magic," Magnus continued. "But most importantly, it allowed me to track her whereabouts."

Shock had Elias' mind spinning.

Magnus pressed his hands together. "But it would appear your enchantress is more capable than I thought. She managed to remove my magic."

Meaning, Magnus could no longer track her.

Relief swelled in Elias' chest. Before he could speak, blood bubbled up his throat once more, and he spewed it onto the ground.

Magnus sighed. "Perhaps it's time for another offering. Can't have you succumbing to your inner demon just yet."

"No," Elias snapped, the word tearing out of him. Shame bled into that single word—shame for what he'd done to that innocent woman.

I've already killed someone. I won't do it again.

But if he was presented with another mortal, he didn't think he could stop himself.

For the first time, he wondered if succumbing to the hunger was so bad. He didn't fear death—never had. But the idea of fading into the demon lurking beneath his skin, to lose his memories and be driven solely by the desire to feed... That fate had once terrorized his waking dreams. But now? He realized then that fear didn't fill him at the thought as it once had.

A smile lifted the corner of Magnus' lips. "Perhaps I've been going about this all wrong."

In a flash, the sorcerer was before him—his lips hovering in front of Elias'. If Elias moved even the slightest, they would kiss. He kept his body still, knowing what would come next.

The sorcerer's eyes glowed red, and desire churned in Elias' gut. Then the air before the sorcerer shimmered like heat above cobblestone streets in the summer.

One moment, Magnus stood there in his immaculate robes, and the next, Arabella was before him.

Tears were in the corners of Elias' eyes as he allowed himself to feel the agony in his chest alongside relief at the sight of her.

My mate. She's here.

His eyes feasted on the sight of Arabella. She was tall and lean, garbed in enchantress leathers as dark as the night itself. Her long braid was over her shoulder, and her fair skin looked like it was kissed by starlight. Even the teardrop gemstone on her forehead shimmered like it held the moon within it. But when he looked at her eyes...

They were wrong.

Instead of the brown irises he'd come to love, her eyes were a deep scarlet.

But in his current state, with a fiery hunger burning in his gut, it didn't matter.

His cock hardened instantly. *Painfully.*

"Elias," the female said as she pressed her body against his. As she did, he became very aware that he was naked and covered in both dried and fresh blood. And the syphen still stuck out of his chest.

Even still, his name on her lips had his body slackening. Blood slicked his chafed wrists as they pressed into the restraints.

A haze settled over his mind.

She reached a hand up to cup his cheek. "You don't need to fight anymore, my love. Submit to me. Give in."

His cock twitched, growing even harder.

Just being near her had his body screaming for release.

He yearned to thrust his hips forward, for any friction. One touch from her, and he'd come.

A tongue darted out from her mouth, glancing against his lower lip.

Body still slack in the restraints, he managed to tilt his chin up to her. Showing her that she could have him—all of him. He was hers for the taking.

"That's it," she purred, her breath smelling strongly of peppermint.

Then her lips were against his, pressing hard enough that he felt her teeth. Desire swirled inside him even stronger—so powerful it was painful. Then what little essence he had unlatched from deep within his chest, called to her on a soundless siren song.

That slip of energy was all that was left of the girl he'd killed.

A hand encircled Elias' cock, *squeezing.*

He grunted in pain, and sudden clarity entered his thoughts. *This isn't right.*

Arabella's touch could be hungry and laced with need, but it was never like this. Her touches lingered on his skin, pulling him in as if she couldn't get enough of him. More than once she'd raked her nails along his back, but it was never with the intention of hurting him. Anything their bodies shared was out of a desire to find the deepest parts of each other.

But this...

It was as though she was intent on consuming all that he was.

Reaching for the bond in his chest, he felt for his mate. He still couldn't sense her emotions, but he knew from the lingering tightness that she wasn't nearby.

She certainly didn't stand before him.

Something inside him cracked at the knowledge that his mate was far out of his reach. But if he couldn't see her, then neither could Magnus.

She was out of both of their reaches.

Slowly, Elias forced back the fog in his thoughts before meeting Magnus' scarlet eyes.

Dark mischief twinkled in Arabella's eyes, but the sorcerer didn't change his form. Neither did he release Elias' cock.

"No," Elias breathed.

The idea of looking upon the face of his mate *like this*, with a touch that wasn't hers, had something in him fracturing.

Please, let her touch be just mine.

He wanted to remember Arabella with her sincerity, gentleness, and fierceness. With sudden certainty, he understood why Magnus wore her face—he wanted to warp Elias' memories of his mate. To remove the safe place his thoughts retreated to during the worst of the sorcerer's administrations.

To tear him down brick by brick.

There was a flash of teeth as the female before him smiled.

Elias tried desperately to keep his body still. To keep himself from thrusting into Magnus' hand even as desire alighted in his core.

But when her tongue plunged into his mouth, his body betrayed him.

He thrust once, twice, and then his seed spilled into the female's hand. As he came, his essence shimmered up his throat and flowed into his mouth. The female's eyes glowed a brighter scarlet as she pulled it into her. The metallic tang of Elias' blood mixed with her peppermint taste and the essence's rich flavor as she fed.

Elias' fangs pressed against his lower lip as Magnus pulled back, still wearing Arabella's face. She brought her hand to her mouth, licking Elias' pleasure clean from her fingers.

A growl ripped from somewhere deep in Elias' being. He yearned to rip into Magnus' throat and tear him into shreds even as nausea filled him at the sight.

Once his hand was clean, Magnus smiled and stepped forward until his body pressed against Elias' skin. Until only Arabella's leathers were between their bodies.

"You will never be free of me," Magnus whispered into the space between them with Arabella's voice, his breath warm on Elias' cheeks. "I see now that, even after feeding on me, even with your compliance, you resist me. You guard your heart from me. So, until you lower those shields around your heart and give me what I seek, I will wear her face, keep you teetering on the edge between desperation and despair."

As Magnus' eyes glowed red once more, Elias' cock became rock hard.

"Please," Elias managed between kisses as Magnus descended upon him.

Tongue plunging into his mouth, Magnus circled slowly before pulling back and running his teeth over Elias' lower lip. "Give me what I want, and this stops."

But Elias couldn't open his heart—and magic—to Magnus.

Even if he knew how, it was the one place that he could lock away his truest self.

When Elias didn't respond, Magnus said, "That's what I thought."

Then the sorcerer's hands—Arabella's hands—were on him again.

Elias pulled at his chains. The motion was violent and filled with every ounce of rage and desperation flowing through him. Blood poured down his wrists. Soon, his arms were slick with red.

But there was nothing he could do to stop the female before him as she fed from him. Each time, she kept him teetering on the edge of humanity, a breath away from succumbing to the demon under his skin.

As day after day passed like this, a haze formed over his mind as his thoughts and realities blurred together.

Each time, he was helpless against her touch and how she used his body. Even the pleasure became painful, and he found himself flinching away at the mere sight of her. The fear bled into his dreams. Soon, the one place of refuge he had from all of this was no longer safe.

Until slowly, the faintest fissure formed in his heart.

Chapter Eighteen
ARABELLA

Over the next few weeks, Arabella trained nonstop with Arden and his warriors in the large cavern at the mountain's base.

At first, the shadow fae prince focused on her wielding shadows and controlling them in ways she could use in combat. She took to it quickly and summoned the shadows with more swiftness than ever before—blasting them at the prince, which he blocked with his own torrent of black.

Then he moved to teaching her how to hide herself in the shadows.

She quickly learned that was an ability she had zero natural ability in.

"Don't just cloak yourself in shadows," the prince said as she tried and failed for the dozenth time. "Become one with the shadows."

"I'm trying," she hissed as sweat dripped off the chains in her hair.

She stood in the center of the cavern floor. The sides of the room were a layered stone that sloped up toward the sole exit tunnel several hundred feet back. In a way, the space felt like a bowl in how it sloped down from the sides of the room to the flat area at the base where they did most of their training.

Willing the shadows to lengthen to her height, she tried to move into them. But it felt like she'd merely stepped into a dark mist.

"I can still see you," Colton said from where he lounged against a nearby wall, a bored expression visible above the black mask that covered most of his face.

For weeks, it had been Arden, Colton, her, and Jessamine in this cavern. To accommodate Jessamine's sight, lanterns were lit across the entire space and mounted onto walls.

Arabella opened her mouth to snap a reply, but Jessamine spoke first. "Then you do it."

One moment, Colton sat near the pool, hundreds of feet away from Jessamine. She sat near the exit tunnel, running a whetstone over one of her blades, which the shadow fae had returned to them. Then he winked out of existence and stood before her.

Blinking, Arabella gaped. "You can step between shadows. Like the erox."

Colton scoffed, turning from Jessamine, who'd risen to her feet and looked like she was a breath away from starting a fight.

"Where do you think they got it from?" Colton said.

Arabella frowned. Demons could take fae magic? Then realization dawned.

"The syphen," she said. "When the shadow fae created the blades, they must have imbued them with their magic—and it somehow allowed the erox to possess that ability."

"Indeed," Arden said, sounding pleased.

She'd told the prince about Magnus' involvement in the creation of erox when he asked more information about this type of demon. Though she hadn't yet revealed the sorcerer was the one who held Elias captive.

With a wave of his hand, Arden said, "After you master cloaking yourself, we'll practice moving between shadows. You cannot travel between shadows until you can meld your body with them."

She nodded. "What other abilities do shadow fae have?"

Holding a hand up, Arden ticked one finger at a time as he spoke. "Wielding shadows. Shadow binding, where you can pin an opponent in place using their shadows. Cloaking yourself, though this is less useful in broad daylight. Shadow jumping. Seeing in the darkness. Shadow illusions."

"Broad daylight," she said, her mind latching on to those words. "Is that a shadow fae's weakness—sunlight?"

"Obviously." Colton rolled his eyes, which Arabella could see even from where he stood across the cavern beside Jessamine. Then he stepped between the shadows to return to his seat beside the pool.

Arden leveled a flat look on the warrior, and Colton fell into silence.

"What's the difference between shadow jumping and portalling?" she asked.

"Distance, mostly," Arden said. "For both, you can move yourself and anything you touch from one location to another. But shadow jumping is only possible when there are shadows that are deep enough and when the distance is no more than several hundred feet apart. But portalling can take place over leagues or hundreds of miles. It's why the goblins were such valuable allies."

It was an effort to keep her face neutral, but Arabella nodded.

For a moment, there was only the sound of Jessamine's whetstone running over her blade.

"How can fae be killed?" Arabella asked.

Arden raised a brow. "Most can be killed just like a mortal—by injury or old age."

"And the shadow fae?"

It was a question that had been hovering in the back of her thoughts since her conversation with Colton about the origin of the fae wars and the prejudice against the shadow fae.

"If a wound is severe enough, the shadow fae can die by blade like any other," the prince said with obvious caution in his tone. "But fire is the most effective way—by burning the body. Without trapping a shadow fae with fire or light magic, they can continue to step between shadows and evade capture."

She had so many more questions about how this had played out in the fae wars. But by the way Arden's eyes narrowed, she didn't think now was the best time to inquire.

Arden cleared his throat. "If that's all, let's proceed with your training."

Without another word, she threw herself back into learning everything she could.

Hours later, she'd attempted to hide herself in the shadows more times than she could count, and she'd only managed to do it properly once.

Sweat poured off her, and she'd long since removed her leather jacket.

"That's enough for today," Arden said as she took a swig from one of the waterskins. "Rest. I'll see you this evening. There's something I'd like to show you."

She merely nodded, utterly exhausted.

Arden and Colton exited the cavern, disappearing into the tunnels.

She walked up to where Jessamine sat and slumped down beside her. Lying back on the cool stones, Arabella looked at the ceiling several stories up.

Jessamine nodded to the side of her head. "Your ears are different now."

Hands flying up, Arabella's fingers closed around...

Pointed ears.

"That didn't take long." She shook her head as though to dispel the surprise. "It doesn't matter if Elias is safe by the end of this."

"You're my bitch no matter what your ears look like," Jessamine said with a wink.

Arabella scrunched her nose. "Winking isn't a good look on anyone. And you can't convince me otherwise."

Jessamine snorted. "Perhaps you're right."

"You doing all right?" Arabella asked, realizing it had been some time since she'd checked in on her friend.

With a nod, Jessamine said, "I've never gone so long without actually *doing* anything. But I'm fine. Just trying to not let worry get the best of me."

This would have been the longest stretch Jessamine had gone without being home and being needed for some crisis. It had been strange for Arabella to be removed from combat when she'd become Elias' offering. She could imagine what it must feel like for Jessamine to spend so much time away from home—and the constant fear for everyone's safety.

"Why did you come with me and not go back to Shadowbank?" Arabella asked. "And I'm not asking for reassurance. I guess I'm just curious why."

"You mean, outside of the fact that we're best friends and supporting each other is what friends do?" Jessamine asked, one brow raised.

A smile played along Arabella's lips. "Outside of that."

Jessamine placed the whetstone down and sheathed her blade. "When a person's heart is whole, they are the best versions of themselves—the best friend, warrior, and people they can be. And I think when you have your mate at your side, Shadowbank will also have its best chance of surviving whatever comes next." She paused, shrugging. "Besides, not all of us are the main characters in the story. Perhaps I'm right where I need to be—keeping you alive so you can save the day."

Arabella rolled her eyes. "You can shove that main character nonsense."

Jessamine smiled, but a serious look returned to her eyes. "Shadowbank's ward doesn't have long. We knew that, at some point, we'd have to risk everything for the chance to live. And I'm choosing to bet on my friend."

Reaching over, Arabella grabbed Jessamine's hand and squeezed.

"I don't deserve you. But I appreciate you all the same," Arabella said. "What do you think you'll do when all this is over?"

"After we return from the Abyss with an army, save Elias, shove a metaphorical middle finger up Hadeon's ass, and save Shadowbank?" Jessamine shrugged. "Who the fuck knows. No enchantress has been allowed to dream outside our duties. I suppose I'd like to live long enough to figure it out."

Arabella squeezed Jessamine's hand again before releasing it and sitting upright. "I promise to do everything in my power to give you and everyone in Shadowbank a time of peace." A sudden thought occurred to her, and she asked, "How many days do you think passed in our realm?"

Jessamine sighed. "If five hundred years passed for us and one thousand in the Abyss... And we've been in here for about three weeks... Maybe forty days? Though it's hard to be certain how many days passed without the sun to tell the time."

Fuck.

Arabella had suspected as much.

"We don't have any more time to waste," Arabella said, knowing she'd spared all the time she dared to help her learn about her magic. "We need to ask them for help. Now."

"I think you're right," Jessamine said with a sigh. "And who knows how long it'll take to find a way out of the Abyss."

Resolve settled in Arabella's chest. "I'll speak to Arden tonight."

"Have you told Prince Arden about your... ties to him?" Jessamine asked carefully.

"Not yet."

Some part of Arabella still wondered whether she shared lineage with Arden. Outside of some shared features like their long limbs or the shape of their eyes, there wasn't a way to truly know if she was related to the shadow fae prince. Their physical traits could just be commonplace among the shadow fae. It might be nothing at all.

But if I don't say anything now, I may not have a chance to speak to my mother.

In the weeks that had passed, a curiosity had settled in her heart about the woman who'd birthed her—and if she was here. It was possible she wasn't with Arden's army or had been killed.

Even still, to be this close to her birth mother and not taking the chance to meet her weighed on her thoughts.

With a groan, she rose on sore muscles and extended a hand to Jessamine. "Let's get cleaned up."

There were several hot springs in the mountain, one of which was used for bathing. The one in the cavern where they trained apparently served another purpose. So, they strode up the tunnels to a smaller cave where the bathing springs were.

The light from Jessamine's torch illuminated the way her lips thinned as they walked.

Arabella tilted her head to the side. "What is it?"

"Hadeon stopped by not long ago," Jessamine said. "He and Breckett were headed to the bathing pool."

For a moment, Arabella hesitated.

There weren't enough resources, especially sources of water, for the shadow fae to be prudish about nakedness. As such, it meant anyone could bathe at the same time.

Up until now, they hadn't bathed at the same time as Hadeon or Breckett.

Arabella squeezed Jessamine's shoulder. "Come on. It's no big deal. I'm sure Hadeon's got a small cock."

They turned the corner and passed from the dark tunnel into the mouth of another cave. She knew from the dampness in the air that they'd arrived at the bathing springs.

The tunnel opened up to a cave three or four times the size of their sleeping quarters. A large pool was at the center of the room with steam pluming from its surface. The rippling surface of the water did nothing to obscure what was beneath its surface. There was also nothing in the way of furniture, and at several spots around the pool, there were odorless soaps.

Lounging at the opposite end of the pool with arms outstretched was Hadeon. His eyes followed them as they entered, a wicked curve to his lips. Utterly naked, he sat on what appeared to be a lip in the rock that acted as a seat, his legs spread wide.

As it turned out, his cock was... impressive.

"Fuck," Jessamine muttered under her breath as she stormed across the room toward a sort of alcove where bathers stashed their clothing.

In another corner of the pool, Breckett rinsed soap from his hair but looked up as they entered. Two other fae males were drying off at the far enough of the room.

Arabella followed Jessamine, offering the males a brief nod.

After her time with Elias where she'd worn dresses that barely covered her ass, she'd slowly become less concerned about covering her nakedness. But for some reason, Jessamine was extra prickly around the fae prince.

After removing her leathers with a few muttered curses, Jessamine marched into the water without acknowledging Hadeon or Breckett. The prince's eyes fixed on her as she positioned herself at the opposite end, turning from him as she washed her hair.

He soaked her in like a sailor laying his eyes upon the sea for the first time in years.

The two shadow fae males who'd just finished dressing stormed out of the room. They paused only long enough to spit in Hadeon's direction before disappearing into the tunnels.

Arabella shook her head.

That wasn't the first time some of the shadow fae had behaved unpleasantly around Hadeon. And it seemed that the weeks they'd spent there hadn't changed anything.

Whatever Hadeon and Arden spoke about since arriving must have been enough to allow Hadeon to stay in the mountains without fearing for his life, but it wasn't enough to encourage warmth between the shadow fae and a prince of the Twilight Court.

However, Hadeon seemed entirely unbothered by this latest demonstration of unpleasantries as he soaked in the water.

Striding into the water, Arabella sighed at the warmth around her. "You're looking better." She nodded to Hadeon's face, which had healed of its bruises and swelling.

Hadeon ran a thumb over his lower lip. "The shadow fae missed anything essential in their administrations."

That was a nice way of saying when they'd beaten him to a pulp but hadn't broken any bones.

He leaned farther back, not trying to cover himself.

It took conscious effort for Arabella to keep her eyes north of the horizon and not on the impressive cock between his legs.

A cock that was...

Hard. Very hard.

Don't bother, Prince, she thought as his eyes scanned the length of Jessamine's body. *She'll never look your way twice.*

But Arabella didn't say anything. Instead, she bathed in silence.

It was only when she'd finished that she said, "I intend to speak with Arden tonight. We can't linger here any longer."

Elias needs me.

Either she'd learned enough to control her new magic, or she hadn't. While she would have loved to train for years with the fae and to learn more about them, she didn't have the luxury of time. Now, she needed to focus on forming an alliance with the shadow fae—and securing an army.

Hadeon leaned forward where he lounged in the water. "I'll plan to speak to the prince about... my own propositions after you, then. Unless you'd like me to join you?"

"No." She allowed herself to relax into the warm waters for a single heartbeat, feeling the tension in her sore muscles loosen somewhat. "I think it's best if I speak to him by myself."

"As you wish," Hadeon said.

"We should discuss our exit strategy," Breckett interjected from where he lounged by the side of the pool, wearing only his shirt.

"I agree," Jessamine said. "Are we going to... follow the path to get out of here?"

Arabella nodded, understanding what Jessamine meant—the path where the map marked an X over what appeared to be another oasis to the distant west. "The shadow fae are in the mountains to the north. So, logic says it must be the exit that's marked."

"We could talk to Arden about the ma—" Breckett began.

"And risk them taking it and leaving without us?" Hadeon interrupted. "I don't intend to be trapped here."

Breckett's eyes narrowed. "Says the male who's universally disliked by the shadow fae and for good reason. You didn't even think to wonder if your supposed friend might be alive for hundreds of years. And you only sought him out when you needed something from him. Meanwhile, the shadow fae have been welcoming to Arabella, Jessamine, and I. Maybe they'll only leave *you* behind when someone who knows how to read the *document* leads us safely out of here."

Hadeon snickered. "I won't explain myself or what took place before you were born. Besides, you think you'd survive a trek across the desert if faced by the zaol or another greater demon?"

"Arabella and the shadow fae will protect our asses," Breckett said, utterly shameless, which earned him a chuckle from Jessamine at the other side of the pool. "Even I can feel that her power is comparable to yours now."

For a moment, it felt like the world stilled.

Once, Hadeon's magic far surpassed Arabella's. That had been when she'd had access to earthen magic as an enchantress and only slips of shadow magic. Then the amplifier had opened the bridge to her fae abilities. Now, as she trained with Arden, her power continued to grow and change. She may not be as powerful as Hadeon yet, and she certainly had far less training than him in her abilities, but she was no longer helpless.

And apparently, others knew it.

Arabella held a hand up, not eager for Hadeon to dangle her favor between them. "Let's see how my conversation with Prince Arden goes as well as Prince Hadeon's talk with him. He might be supportive of both our plights. In which case, none of this bickering would be necessary."

She hoped that was the case. She didn't want to consider the alternative.

Rising, she turned from them and dried off outside the pool with a rough fabric that acted as a towel. Beside her, Jessamine also toweled off.

Then there was a sloshing of water, and a glance over her shoulder revealed that Hadeon now stood behind them.

Water dripped down his body and off his wings, cascading in long rivulets over a chest and stomach without an ounce of fat. Unlike Elias, his chest was hairless, as was the path that led down to his...

Jessamine pushed one of her legs into her pants. Turning toward Hadeon, she started. "Don't sneak up on someone like that." She paused, seeming to fumble for words. "Put some clothes on," she hissed, gesturing to his manhood. "Before you poke someone's eye out."

His head tilted to the side. "Does my nakedness bother you, Enchantress?"

"Of course not," Jessamine snapped as she shoved her other leg into her pants and yanked them up.

He chuckled before turning to where his clothes were stashed in a corner. "When do you intend to speak with Prince Arden?"

"At once," Arabella said as she finished dressing. She tied her sheaths back on, checking that the syphen was there, before she quickly braided her hair and placed the chains back atop her head.

"Understood."

Arabella nodded at Jessamine, who bristled like a wet cat.

"Stay out of trouble while I'm gone." She pointed a finger at Hadeon and then at Breckett. "You, too."

Then she strode out of the bathing chamber. All the while, she mentally prepared herself to ask a fae prince to send the shadow fae into another war.

Only this time, it would be against a sorcerer.

Chapter Nineteen
ARABELLA

Arabella didn't have to go far into the tunnels before masked shadow fae warriors found her. There were six of them, each of whom carried large torches in one hand and spears in another.

She blinked at them, surprised.

Every other time she'd been summoned, the guards hadn't carried anything to light the way. They only brought torches when escorting Hadeon, Jessamine, or Breckett. So, why bring them now?

Colton stood at the front of the group of warriors and nodded to the dark tunnels behind him. "The prince asked us to bring you to him."

Swallowing her questions, she let the warriors lead the way.

Instead of walking through the usual tunnels toward the cavern at the mountain's base or toward the common areas, they led her down a series of tunnels she hadn't gone through before. The tunnels sloped ever downward. As they walked, the air grew steadily cooler until her breath plumed in the air.

Rubbing her hands against her arms, her leathers suddenly felt far from suitable for this particular journey. "It's cold down here."

Colton made a sound in the back of his throat that might have been an acknowledgment but didn't turn to her.

As they descended through countless tunnels, not only did the temperature drop, but the shadows changed.

The humming, playful shadows she'd slowly become accustomed to around the other shadow fae changed to something far deeper. The darkness grew so thick that she could no longer see more than a few steps ahead. If it wasn't for the torches, she wouldn't have been able to see at all in these tunnels.

Why was the dark different here?

They walked down perhaps a dozen more tunnels, each twisting deeper into the mountain.

Through chattering teeth, she said, "How much longer?"

The guards walked silently for another minute before stopping abruptly, placing themselves on either side of the tunnel. They tapped spears against the ground twice, their eyes fixed ahead.

Colton stood at the end of the bend of this particular tunnel, past the other guards, and said, "The prince is this way."

Eyes narrowing, she strode between the warriors, who didn't move as she walked.

As she strode past Colton, she paused, seeing that he—and the other guards—remained where they were. "You're not coming?"

He shook his head. "This isn't a place for just anyone. Consider yourself fortunate that the prince has chosen to bring you here. It's an honor."

She nodded to the torch in his hand. "Mind if I borrow that? It seems the shadows in this place are a bit... different."

He passed it to her before turning back toward the other guards. "Far more different than you could ever imagine." The words were spoken over his shoulder, and he didn't offer an explanation.

In moments, he and the other guards disappeared into the tunnels, taking the only other sources of light with them.

Exhaling heavily, she turned to where he'd indicated and began walking in that direction. In moments, the tunnel opened into a massive cavern three times the size of the one they'd been training in.

How big is this mountain?

The impenetrable dark receded to the corners of the room. But rather than mounted torches throughout the room, there were hundreds of candles lighting the space. Throughout the cavern were a series of flat stones that had been pressed into the dirt. As she took a step into the room, she realized there was a script carved onto small stones placed in neat rows on the ground.

Gravestones, she realized.

At the center of the room was a long rectangular stone slab.

Prince Arden stood before it, his back turned to her. Leaning forward, his palms pressed against the stone. She noticed then that some of the impenetrable shadows lurked around the base of the stone slab.

Placing her torch in a holder on the wall near the entrance, she strode toward the room's center, careful to walk around the candles.

"Prince." She stopped a few feet from him, inclining her head in deference, uncertain whether to bow. Although they'd never had such formalities during their training, it was clear that whatever this place was, it was akin to a holy place for the shadow fae. And she wanted to be respectful of their traditions.

Something felt different about this room, this moment.

The air felt thick with possibilities and power. It was unlike the enchantresses' earthen magic. Rather than a warm energy rumbling through the veins of the earth, this felt like shifting icebergs submerged in the northern oceans. It was the frosty core of the universe. It was the shattering quiet that sucked all light inward until there was nothing left but the unending cold.

This power was ancient. More ancient than the fae or anything she'd felt. Perhaps even more powerful than Magnus.

Was this the beating heart of the Abyss? Was this the power that had formed this underrealm?

When Arden still hadn't turned toward her, she said, "You summoned me?"

He leaned forward, his breath pluming in the air as his back slowly rose and fell. "Yes." His voice was strangely distant, as though his thoughts were far away. "I want to discuss something with you."

Ignoring the hammering of her heart, she said, "There's something I'd like to talk about, too."

Turning to her then, his eyes locked with hers.

Beyond his irises, there was a lurking pool of inky black. A strange magic surged within him, and there was a twin torrent within the room itself.

On instinct, she placed a hand on the hilt of one of the blades sheathed at her waist as the hairs along her arms stood on end.

It had nothing to do with the cold.

His gaze shifted to the cavern before settling on the stones on the ground.

For a moment, she wondered whether to voice her concern. Could she just be seeing things, or was there another type of dark magic in this place? Had she just been socialized to view all non-elemental magic as having a deep corruption?

Once, she'd believed all demons were evil. She couldn't let herself see the shadow fae in the same way. Elias had taught her better than that. In addition, Arden and the shadow fae had shown her nothing but kindness. It was past time she started to believe the best in others.

Ever so slowly, she relaxed her stance.

Gesturing to the stones on the ground, she said, "Who were they?"

"Shadow fae who fell to the demons of this realm or who succumbed to time." Lines formed between the prince's brows. "This is where we bury our dead." His hands curled into fists at his sides. "We were forced to flee to the Abyss. The other fae never liked our kind, never trusted our magic."

For a moment, she thought to ask just how many fae courts there were. What she'd learned of the fae was limited to knowledge the enchantresses had. She imagined she only knew of the most powerful courts.

Arden strode forward and knelt before a stone with script in a language she didn't recognize.

"When the fae wars began, we were hunted down by the other courts and slaughtered." His fingers lingered on the stone. "The Twilight Court queen convinced the other courts to rally and take us out, claiming we were a threat to their existence. That we possessed dark magic."

"I'm sorry for what happened to you," she said, her voice gentle.

The prince stood and walked to several more stones, touching each in kind.

"Some died from injuries sustained during our final battle with the other fae courts. Others died from exposure or from wounds inflicted by the demons in this realm." His voice was distant as though lost to memories and time. "Far too few died of old age. But those who did... They died knowing they'd never again see their homeland. My..." His voice faltered as he knelt before another stone. Unlike the others, this one had some designs around the name. It was clear someone had taken great care to memorialize whoever rested beneath the earth. "My mate died on our journey here. She was protecting me from a demon."

Turning, he looked at her, his eyes welling with tears. "I know what it means to be separated from your mate, and I don't want that for you, child."

She swallowed thickly, able to imagine all too easily Elias throwing himself in harm's way to protect her—and then having to live through the ages without him.

Coming to stand before her, the prince brushed a loose strand of hair behind her ear. "It's one of the greatest hardships to be blessed with a long life and then have to live through the years alone. Without the one who gives our existence meaning. It's because of that that I want to help you."

Thoughts swirled through her mind, but she latched on to one thing. "I'm thankful for all that you've taught me, but if I have any hope of saving my mate before it's too late, I need more than control. I need power."

The prince nodded as though expecting this. "And that's why I've brought you to this place. The place where we discovered our true power."

She blinked. "What?"

"The fae courts were right to fear what we could do with our magic—what we might become." A cold fire alighted in the back of his eyes. "It wasn't until we came here that we learned the true possibilities of our magic."

Slowly, he rose and turned to the stone slab at the center of the cavern.

Frowning, she said, "I don't understand."

"When we came to the Abyss, we were desperate for enough power to protect ourselves," he said. "We were dying far too quickly. More and more of us fell with each demon attack. We knew we'd soon perish if we didn't find another way to fend off the hordes. That's when we found the mountain." He gestured to the cavern and then to the stone at its center. "And the one who inhabits it."

Suddenly, a dark wind swept across the cavern, extinguishing her lantern on the far wall and all the candles throughout the room. Instantly everything fell under shadow. While she could still see sections of the cavern with her shadow fae abilities, other parts of it were under an impenetrable black.

Just as she'd felt when she journeyed through the gateway and first came to the Abyss, a presence hovered around her and settled on her shoulders.

Her mind reeled.

A knowing smile played over the prince's lips. "He's called the Everdark, one of the greater demons."

The presence moved from her shoulders as she shook her head.

No, it wasn't possible—

Before she could finish the thought, power blossomed around her so vast that she nearly passed out from the assault on her senses.

Her knee scraped against the ground as she gasped, sucking in air. "What have you done?" she demanded, her enchantress instincts surging to the surface. "Alliances with demons are dangerous—*especially* greater demons."

Arden raised a brow. "Given who your mate is, I thought you'd be more... understanding."

The presence billowed out into the room. As she breathed, the air grew thick, and her lungs became heavy, unable to bear the weight of this strange presence.

This demon.

"Elias showed me that not all demons are evil," she managed, still struggling to breathe. "But he's not a greater demon. They *created* the demons that plague the mortal realm. So many have died because of what they've spawned."

"Oh?" His tone sounded like he was placating a foolish child. "Are your hands clean of blood, niece?"

That one word struck her harder than a blow ever could.

He knew.

"The Everdark told me of our blood ties," he said, answering her unspoken question.

Face flushing as she struggled to take another breath, she said, "How would a demon know about my lineage when I don't?"

He gestured to the stone slab before them. "Ask him."

For a moment, she hesitated, her eyes lingering on the impenetrable dark hovering at the base of the unnatural slab of stone. It was far too angular, too perfect in dimensions to have been chiseled by hand.

This was made with magic.

And it was the perfect shape for a body to be placed atop it.

A sacrifice.

Arden believed he'd discovered true power, which meant that this greater demon could either make bargains or bestow power on others.

Elias was different, she thought. *This demon could be different, too.*

Didn't she owe it to Elias and her family in Shadowbank to at least hear Arden out? She was desperate for power and allies. If she turned down the opportunity to speak with the Everdark, perhaps the prince wouldn't consider allying with her or marching against Magnus.

But the idea of speaking with a greater demon filled her with dread. The parts of her that were an enchantress railed at the very notion of speaking to one rather than immediately seeking a way to end its existence.

As she took a step toward the altar, a single conviction filled her. She'd do anything for her mate.

Even ally herself with a demon.

Then she was before the slab of stone. No, not just stone, she realized. It was an altar.

They worshipped this demon.

"Lie down," the prince said somewhere behind her. "Offer yourself to him."

Lowering herself onto the stone, she immediately felt the cold through her leathers.

Show me what you can do, she thought. *And if you don't have a way to help Elias, I'll kill you myself.*

The impenetrable shadows in the corners of the room swelled before moving toward her. Swallowing back her fear, she forced herself to remain still as the shadows descended. A strange pressure surrounded her body—first her legs, then her stomach and chest, until it was everywhere.

Then a voice as deep and unfathomable as the Abyss entered her mind.

Hello, granddaughter.

Chapter Twenty
ARABELLA

The darkness was all around, filling her mouth and throat. It was so thick that Arabella couldn't breathe.

"Let him in." It was Arden's voice, but it sounded distant. "Submit."

She wanted to scream, to fight, but she couldn't move from where she lay on the altar. Soon, her entire body started shaking as the darkness filled her. It felt like every cell was splitting in two.

You're everything I hoped you'd be, came the voice of the Everdark in her mind, rumbling like a great presence had awoken from the deep. His voice sounded like the rippling waves from a collision of stars—and the desolation that remained in its wake.

She struggled to remain conscious as her body continued to seize.

Elias, she thought as her mind grew hazy, wanting his face to be the last thing she saw if she was to die in this place.

You're my blood, the Everdark hissed. *You must accept that you are part demon if you're to survive my entry.*

That was impossible. She was human and fae and nothing more.

"The shadows don't speak to the shadow fae," came Arden's voice. "At least, not those who are fully fae. The Everdark taught me this. It's how I knew you were different. Only those who also possess demon blood can awaken the shadows. That was how we knew you were here when the zaol chased you. You'd spoken to the dark, which summoned us."

The darkness billowing through her hummed as though in agreement.

Her mind reeled, and she wanted to ask just what it meant to speak to the shadows. But she forced her mind to focus on the present.

Allow me to unlock the demon magic within you, and you will have more power than you ever dreamed, the Everdark said. *All it needs is a key to unleash the torrent of your potential.*

Again, the darkness pressed into her, and it felt like her veins swelled with the onslaught of power.

Suddenly, her head smacked against the stones and her body began seizing. Spots formed in her vision. She was going to lose consciousness, and soon.

I'm not a demon, she thought. *I'm nothing like you.*

"You're going to kill her," Arden said, his voice closer now. Was that a hint of concern in his tone? "You must go slower. If you don't, she'll die."

The darkness blasted out into the cavern, filling every space until there was nothing but the impenetrable dark.

She heard a thud on the stones and wondered if the fae prince had been blasted backward.

She can take it, came the voice of the Everdark. *She will accept me.*

Distantly, she realized the greater demon must be able to speak into both her and Arden's minds at once.

Slowly, she slipped into unconsciousness, barely clinging to the will to fight this presence—this greater demon.

My *grandfather*?

Then the torrent closed over her.

One moment, she was on the cool stone altar, and the next

she was in a place of darkness—just like where she'd dreamed of Elias.

Black stretched in every direction. There was no horizon and no end.

Similar to her other dreams, her skin glowed with a gray-white light.

"Granddaughter."

The Everdark's voice was as fathomless as deep space. If she wasn't careful, she knew she'd fall into that dark and never find her way out.

As she glanced around, she couldn't see him in this formless landscape.

Just what kind of greater demon was he? What sort of powers did he have? She'd never heard of the Everdark before nor had she faced anything like this. Had he just tried to kill her? Was she already dead? And why was she in this dreamscape again?

"I'm not your granddaughter," she said as she turned again. But when she looked around, there was nothing but unending darkness.

Glancing down, the creeping shadow vines moved around her feet in twisting, agitated motions. They were semi-translucent and had a myriad of thorns. In the midst was a single white rose. The vine extended up to her as though offering her the flower.

She didn't accept it.

"Is this some sort of an apology?" she dared, feeling a presence shift before her. "I'll have you know I have a bad habit of holding grudges."

Glancing up, she spotted a figure darker than the night itself.

It was shaped like a man but didn't have any discernible features. There was no face, no skin, and no clothes. It was a deep shadow in the vague shape of a person, but the blackness within it swirled like a crackling thunderstorm.

Even without a mouth, she sensed that it smiled. The sensation unnerved her. Gooseflesh rippled along her skin.

"It was important that we speak without interruption," the Everdark said in that deep, fathomless voice.

It was then she realized that he spoke aloud. His words were no longer in her mind.

Hands curling into fists, she said, "You claim we're related, but I find that hard to believe. How can a shadow fuck a fae?"

Let alone produce offspring from that coupling.

The Everdark took a step forward and then another. Even though it was several paces away from her, it felt far too close. Everything in her screamed to run, to fight, but she forced herself to remain where she was. She wasn't about to show fear.

Shadows rippling, the Everdark said, "In the place between realms, anything is possible."

Her eyes narrowed. "This is a dream."

"Is it?" the greater demon rumbled, an amusement in his tone. "Have you not seen your mate in this place?"

She hesitated, countless words on the tip of her tongue.

The shadows shifted as though the demon nodded. "Have you noticed when he feeds on you that you wake feeling different? As though an erox had consumed your essence."

"How did you know that?" she demanded.

Belatedly, she realized that by asking, she'd confirmed his suspicions.

"You haven't yet learned how to shut me out of your mind," the Everdark said. "Every time you are in the in-between, I've been here with you."

"You've watched us fuck?" she said, crossing her arms as disgust curdled through her. "That's not grandfatherly behavior."

The Everdark took another step forward, and the shadow vines at her feet trembled. "I've been here your whole life. How do you think you found your way out of the forest all those years ago? Surely, you don't think a mere child could have survived on their own."

She opened and closed her mouth.

It was something she'd wondered her whole life.

Where had she come from, and how had the forest demons not devoured her?

She didn't want to believe she could have some relation to a greater demon. Moreover, just what was a demon offspring capable of? All demons fed on others in some capacity—whether it's a person's soul, life force, essence, or something else. Would she hurt those she cared about with some demon magic?

This must have been how Elias felt when he'd been turned into an erox.

She considered her next words very carefully.

"You want me to believe that we're related? Then explain."

Something sparked in the Everdark's shadows, as though he knew he had her.

"Prince Arden's sister, the princess, was held prisoner in the Twilight Court. She was forced to act as the king's assassin for centuries against her will, forced to serve him as he slaughtered the shadow fae in the fae wars. Her name was Myla," the Everdark began. "When I came to the fae realm and found her, I offered to help her escape with her human lover, one of the king's servants he'd stolen from the mortal realm. Myla was pregnant. I could scent the desperation on her. I told her there'd be a cost—that she'd be separated from her child, never able to see you again. She refused at first, but when the king was about to kill her lover, she summoned me. And I answered."

The Everdark stepped forward—only a few steps away from her now.

"I helped them escape through the gateway in the forest near your mate's castle," he said. "I held the gateway closed as I expedited your growth in your mother's belly. She'd only been three months into her pregnancy. In moments, she was swollen with child and going into labor. I pulled you from her. But your mother went back on her word and attacked. The magic of our bargain killed her at once. Her human lover lashed out in a fit of rage, but he was a mere speck of sand. He died in the forest, consumed by the soulless, becoming one of them."

For a moment, it felt like her heart stopped.

She'd never longed to meet her parents, not truly. But somehow, hearing they'd died horrible deaths—that her father had become a demon—struck something deep within her. A strange sense of despair swelled in her chest and tightened her throat.

The shadows around the Everdark trembled as he continued, "But your mother did something with her magic before dying that I'd missed. She'd used every last drop of her abilities to lock your demon magic away and place a curse on me. I couldn't speak to you nor could you see me. So, I guided you to the human village, clearing a path through the forest. This way, you could grow in power with the humans until I could contact you. During that time, I returned to the shadow fae in the Abyss. I knew you'd need an army when you took your place on the shadow fae throne."

Swallowing thickly, her mind reeled with this onslaught of information. "Why would a demon want a fae throne? Can't you rule over one of the underrealms?"

"With a shadow fae on the throne who possesses demon blood, I can bring demons into the fae realm," he said. "The fae have kept my hordes out with their magic. Only I, as a greater demon, can move as I please between realms. And I intend to claim the magic of their world. For us."

She shook her head. "If Princess Myla placed a curse on you, preventing you from speaking to me, how are you doing so now?"

"The amplifier didn't just awaken your shadow fae abilities," he rumbled. "It created the smallest fissure in your demon magic that had been locked away. In so doing, it broke the curse and allowed you to tap into some of your magic—and for us to communicate directly."

The Everdark stood before her then, and she started to take a step back. His magic wrapped around her, dark bands of ebony, forcing her to remain in place.

"How does that make you my grandfather?" she demanded,

trying—and failing—to disguise the fear filling her voice. "It just sounds like you're some power-hungry bastard."

The shadows tightened, pinning her arms to her sides.

"I brought Myla's mother, the shadow fae queen, to this place many years ago," he said, and she felt his eyeless gaze scrape over her. "Your mother is a product of our union. She was one of my many offspring with mortal females—fae or human. Some resemble their mothers and others are creatures of shadow."

"And Prince Arden?" she pressed.

"A child of the former king and queen."

So, her mother was only a half sister of Arden, then.

Without willing it, she pulled against the shadows holding her as anger fractured her senses. "You killed your daughter? Father of the year. Why not have her sit on the throne you want so much?"

You didn't have to kill her, some distant part of her thought, raging against the finality of her parents' needless deaths.

After all they'd done to find this place, her mother hadn't been here after all. She had, however, been trapped in the Twilight Court until three decades ago. That meant she would've been a prisoner for hundreds of years in the court responsible for the genocide of the shadow fae, forced to work as an assassin.

"Your mother was captured by the Twilight Court before she could ascend to the throne," the Everdark said. "When she fell in love with a human, it became obvious she wouldn't be sympathetic to my ends."

"And why would I be any different?"

The Everdark extended a shadowy arm, and the darkness wrapped around her neck, feeling like long, cool fingers. Slowly, those fingers tightened around her throat even as they caressed her neck in languid strokes.

"You want to save your mate," the greater demon said in a tone as cool and emotionless as death at midnight. "I can unlock the magic within you. Abilities you need to save him."

"What magic?" she demanded as she angled her head away from those stroking fingers.

The fingers around her neck loosened, releasing her.

"I am the master of the dead," the Everdark said, as though it were the most obvious thing in the world. "Once someone has passed from the land of the living, they are mine to use. To control."

"Necromancy," she choked out, her mind swirling. "Your power is *necromancy*?"

"I cannot raise the dead and return them to life," the greater demon said. "But I can bring the dead into a... state of living. And if I impose my will on them, they will do as I bid."

"This is the power Arden spoke of," she realized.

"All of my offspring have this ability," the Everdark said, confirming her suspicion. "But I can enable the shadow fae with enough control over the shadows to use dark magic."

For a moment, she couldn't speak. She could hardly think straight.

The very thing Genoveva had been afraid of and went to war over had come true. And all because she'd attacked the shadow fae and forced them into the Abyss. Without the fae wars, they may have never learned how to use dark magic.

But necromancy... Well, fuck.

In the darkest parts of her, the thought of being able to summon the dead to do her bidding—to fight Magnus and his army—was more than a little appealing. She knew she should feel guilt at taking away the free will of the dead and summoning them from their place of rest—just as she should feel guilt at using the syphen to control the erox. But this sounded like the very edge she sought. And like the syphen, she could utilize their assistance to rescue Elias before returning them to their place of rest. She didn't intend to take anyone's free will indefinitely.

An increasingly distant part of her railed against the potential that she—an enchantress—could be the very thing she'd been taught to protect humankind from.

"Even if I believed you and agreed to let you unlock this magic," she began carefully. "We need a way out of the Abyss."

The Everdark made a rumbling sound that she thought might have been a laugh. "And who do you think helped you find the shadow fae? To make the map work when you failed to do so?"

She gaped. "What I felt outside the gateway... The reason I wasn't ill passing through it... The map suddenly working... That was all you?"

"Yes."

It should be a knock to her pride, her capability as a magic wielder. But rather than feeling shame for not being able to use the map properly, all she felt was unfettered shock.

"You're the key to leaving the Abyss," he continued. "Only creations of the underrealms can open the gateway to leave this place—and only those strong enough."

"What's the catch?" she said past the tightness in her throat. Damn it. This wasn't the time to feel fear. Not when so much was at stake. "Power is never free. Using my shadow magic has made me become less human. What does unlocking demon magic do?"

The greater demon seemed to pause for a moment. She could have sworn it studied her intently before saying, "What differentiates demons from the other races?"

Eyes narrowing, she said, "Demons feed on life—consuming souls, essence, blood, or some other fundamental part of the living—in order to sustain their own lives or to wield magic." Realization dawned. "No. You can't mean I'd..."

The shadows that were the Everdark moved, seeming to nod. "If you fully unlock your magic, you'll awaken the part of you that is a demon. The part of you that needs to *feed*. I'll give you one day to consider. One day to choose me willingly. Until then, perhaps you need to see just what your refusal will cost you."

Sudden horror burned through her.

Before she could respond, to demand to know more, a shadow struck her in the chest. Gasping, she flew backward across the dark landscape. The Everdark grew smaller in the distance until she could no longer see him.

Eventually, she crashed into the not-ground and rolled to a

stop. It didn't hurt, exactly. But she gasped, struggling to regain her breath.

What the fuck—

Then the darkness stirred, and another shape appeared.

Sudden tears filled her eyes, and she blinked them back. "Elias?"

When her mate turned to her, he didn't reach for her. There wasn't happiness or even relief in his gaze. Instead, his face grew pale, and he flinched away.

Her heart dropped. "What have they done to you?"

Chapter Twenty-One
ELIAS

"Elias?"

It was Arabella's voice, and he peeled his eyes open with effort.

She stood at the entrance of Magnus' tent, garbed in her leathers and with her two swords in crossing sheaths on her back.

Exhaustion weighed on his limbs, and he couldn't bring himself to move from where he hung slack in the X. His wrists throbbed, and his shoulders screamed from the pressure. But he couldn't stand even if he wanted to. It was all he could do to open his eyes and remain conscious.

Arabella ran over to him, an urgency alighting her gaze. But rather than reaching for his restraints and freeing him, she cupped his cheek in a hand.

"My poor mate," she whispered. "What have they done to you?"

She stood there for long moments, her thumb swiveling over his beard, which had grown long. It was the only way he could tell time had passed. Time had lost all meaning, and he no longer knew dreams from reality. But he guessed he must have been trapped in the X for weeks or months.

In all that time, he hadn't been allowed to sleep more than a few nonconsecutive hours—and only when sleep overtook him after hours of torture.

He blinked slowly down at Arabella.

There had been too many times where he'd been filled with relief at the sight of her. But the moment he let his guard down, she'd plunged the syphen into his chest or ripped him open with magic.

"We don't have much time," she said, her voice low. "We must hurry before they return."

For a moment, he tried to speak, to tell her to get out of here before Magnus appeared, but he barely managed to part his lips before the effort became too much.

The demon inside him raged, demanding to be fed.

The idea of feeding on Magnus no longer filled him with dread. In fact, he couldn't bring himself to feel anything at all. A strange sort of numbness had settled over his mind and heart.

But when the tent flap opened, revealing Flynn, something stirred in Elias' chest.

"Run," he rasped.

But it was too late.

Flynn jumped between shadows until he appeared at Arabella's side. His hand wrapped around her neck, and she tried to fight him off. Elias watched as his mate grew pliant in Flynn's grip. In his other hand, he held a syphen.

She made a little whimpering sound that had a burning rage awakening in him.

How dare anyone touch his mate?

As Flynn leaned in, his lips nearly pressing to Arabella's as he summoned her essence, Elias managed to get his feet underneath him, pushing himself up while his ankles were shackled. He grunted as agony shot through his chest.

"The syphen," he rasped. He didn't know if Flynn had been created with the syphen in his hand or with the one Breckett had stolen, but it was her only chance of escaping. "Use the... syphen."

The effort to speak nearly had him blacking out, and his words slurred together.

Slowly, Arabella turned her head toward him, brows drawn together. "I love you, Elias."

Flynn gripped her face tightly, forcing her to look back at him as he pulled her essence from her. Glowing blue floated from her lips, which the erox sucked into his mouth. He watched as clouds of it moved from her body, watched as the life faded from her eyes.

He'd never heard his mate say those words, and he didn't want his only memory of her telling her feelings to be the moments before she died—drank dry by one of Magnus' inner circle.

"No." Elias pulled against his restraints. "Please... don't... hurt her."

But Flynn didn't look up, didn't even acknowledge that Elias had spoken as he drained Arabella dry. When the life faded from her eyes, Flynn released his grip on her neck and allowed her body to drop to the floor.

A fissure that had formed in Elias' chest cracked open further as a scream tore from somewhere in the depths of his soul.

"No!" he cried, pulling against his restraints with all his might.

Gone.

Arabella was gone.

His heart fractured into shards—his soul mere fragments of who he once was. How could he possibly exist in the ages without her? He'd wanted to share his world with her, to worship the ground she walked on and feel her love for him in her lingering touches and the way her gaze fell upon him in stolen moments.

But they'd never have the time.

Tears streamed down his face, and his strength was sapped from him all at once. His knees gave out first before his body dropped in the X. Once more, he dangled from the cuffs at his wrists. He let his head drop forward.

There was a flash of movement as Flynn came to stand before him. Then he plunged the syphen into Elias' chest. A scream tore from Elias' throat as sudden agony swelled in him, stealing his breath away.

Power flowed into the syphen, which seeped into Elias. At first, it felt like a burning sensation, as though hot oil had been spilt over open wounds.

He might have screamed again, but his ears were ringing and his heartbeat was too loud to be certain.

The power flowed into the fissure in his heart. And for the first time, that slip of power flowed inside.

"I've got you," came Magnus' voice.

Slowly, Elias managed to look up at where Flynn stood over him. Blinking through his tears, he watched as Flynn's form was replaced by the familiar form of the sorcerer. Then there was a shimmering on the carpet where Arabella's body had once been. One moment, his mate lay there, lifeless, and the next Flynn appeared, his eyes opening as he got to his feet.

They'd tricked him.

Magnus could cast illusion magic over himself and others—or their environment.

And Elias had fallen for it. Again.

Suddenly, Magnus' power flowed into Elias' chest and swelled in his heart. Without willing it, Elias' power flared to life, and his eyes burned.

"At long last, I've reached the source of your magic," Magnus purred. "Now, I can make other erox who can wield essence. My army will be unstoppable."

Before Elias could speak, shadows latched on to his mind. He felt himself slipping into unconsciousness.

Magnus pulled back, lines forming between his brows. "What—?"

His words faded as Elias slipped into endless black.

One moment, he was in Magnus' tent, and the next he was in the strange landscape of shadows.

The dream, he realized. This was where he'd dreamed of Arabella. It was one of the few good dreams he had of her. Lately, so many dreams of her had been nightmares—prolonged visions of her dying or splitting him open.

How am I here again?

When he'd come here in the past, he'd slipped into unconsciousness when his body failed him after hours of torture. This time, it was like he'd been summoned.

This was no ordinary dream.

And he wasn't alone.

Arabella knelt on the ground before him. Strands of her hair had come loose from her braid and her cheeks were flushed as though she'd just come from a fight. But the look in her eyes as she took in the sight of him had his heart dropping. It was both relief and horror, desire and despair.

He flinched away from her.

Too many times, Magnus had worn her face while torturing Elias. Now, the sight of her had fear slicing through him.

Glancing down at his body, he realized he was as naked as he'd been in Magnus' tent. Blood no longer streamed from his wrists, but he was covered in scarlet. And the syphen was still embedded in his chest.

Arabella moved in motions far quicker and more fluid than he'd ever seen. Standing before him, she wrapped her hands around the hilt and pulled. He watched, brows drawing together as she wrenched at the blade, veins bulging in her forehead. But it stayed firmly in his chest.

She's trying to help me, he realized. But he'd seen this before plenty of times in his times of captivity. Magnus was probably just tricking him again.

Even with the distrust icing his chest, he wondered if she could tell it was his syphen. The one he'd given her before she'd fled his castle.

His thoughts fragmented as he once again saw the life drain from her eyes before her body fell onto the carpet. Something inside him had broken at that sight. Even as the memory replayed in his mind, he had to forcefully push out the countless images of when Magnus had worn her face and fed on him.

She's alive, he thought. At least in this place, his mate was alive.

Despite everything that had happened to him, he allowed his broken heart to yearn for her. To enjoy the simple nearness of this phantom of her. He stretched a mental finger out to the bond in his chest and stroked it.

"The pain isn't so bad," he found himself saying.

It was an obvious lie, but he would have uttered it even if she could hear him. Anything to take away that look of devastation in her eyes as her hands dropped from the hilt and she looked up at him. He reached out, tracing her cheek with his fingers. "If I could take your worries from you, I would."

Her lips moved, but no sound came forth.

Just as every time before.

Leaning forward, he kissed her even as she continued speaking. And she melted into him.

As he did, images of Magnus glanced across his mind, unbidden. He flinched, squeezing his eyes shut.

This isn't Magnus. He wouldn't have been tender.

He'd also never tried to remove the syphen. But this phantom Arabella had.

As though sensing something was wrong, she pulled back.

Those eyes, he thought as his gaze swept over the deep brown irises. *Those are her eyes.*

For the first time, he wondered... Had Arabella found a way to reach him?

The bond in his chest brightened as if in response to the realization, and a sudden warmth flooded his entire being. All the pain in his body retreated, even the agony from the syphen lessened in the wake of her presence.

Her hands were on either side of his face as her thumbs traced a gentle path back and forth over his cheeks. The touch was so tender, so full of longing, that something in him splintered.

He staggered to a knee, tears streaming down his face.

I want this, he thought as despair swelled in him. *I want a life with you.*

He'd thought he had accepted his fate and the cost of returning Arabella's memories to her. But his heart railed against his bargain with Magnus.

Kneeling beside him, she wrapped her arms around his naked body. Her cheek pressed against his shoulder, and she was careful not to touch the syphen in his chest. His head dropped, falling to her shoulder as sobs wracked through him.

He wanted to take her worries from her. Yet he found the relief at seeing her slipping away, replaced once more by fear.

"I won't make it much longer," he rasped into her hair. "I want to fight for you. I'm trying... But he's breaking me."

It was an inevitability.

Soon, Elias would succumb to the torture, and then all he was would be no more.

Slowly, he lifted his head, not bothering to wipe his tears away as he turned toward her. He studied his mate's warm brown eyes, his gaze following the trails of tears down her cheeks.

"Live for us both," he said, somehow knowing he wouldn't see her again. Magnus would find a way to keep him from returning. Even as he spoke, he felt a pull on his body, which no longer felt so far away. "Don't think of me again. Be happy, Arabella."

Lines formed between her brows, and her lips moved.

Leaning forward, he pressed a final kiss to her lips. "You are worth it."

Then he was torn from Arabella's arms.

Chapter Twenty-Two
ARABELLA

Arabella jolted upright, a scream ripping from her throat. Sweat poured off her and tears streamed down her face.

"You're awake," Jessamine said. "Thank fuck."

Blinking, Arabella glanced around, surprised to find herself back in the cave that served as their sleeping quarters. The animal hides had become twisted around her legs. She shuffled backward until her back was pressed against the cave wall.

Slowly, her mind registered her surroundings.

Jessamine sat beside where Arabella had been asleep on her pile of hides on the ground. Hadeon and Breckett stood near the mouth of the cave that led into the mountain, wearing similar looks of concern.

Shoulders dropping in obvious relief, Jessamine scanned Arabella from head to toe. "Your whole body has been seizing on and off for hours. Are you okay? What happened with Arden?"

Arabella frowned. "How did I get here?"

"Arden carried you back," Jessamine said.

"And he didn't tell you... what happened?" Arabella asked.

Jessamine shook her head.

Leaning forward, Arabella held her head between her hands, elbows propped on her knees.

I just saw the real Elias, she thought. *I've been seeing him all along.*

Somehow, she just knew this wasn't a trick of the Everdark. Something in the bond had come alive the moment he'd appeared.

For a long moment, she could do nothing but sob. She cried so hard that her gut twisted and she leaned over, heaving up all the contents of her stomach onto the cave floor.

Jessamine extended a cloth and waterskin to Arabella, and she accepted both, wiping her mouth and taking a swig of water.

"You're not going to like it," Arabella managed. Then she looked up, her eyes connecting with Breckett's. "I saw Elias."

"How?" Breckett took a step forward so he was directly behind Jessamine.

Arabella explained about the Everdark and the hybrid children that were part shadow fae, part demon—and the power they could have. Then she shared about the dreamscape and Elias.

Breckett's light brown skin grew pale as he said, "Fuck. And you couldn't communicate with him?"

Arabella shook her head. "Neither of us could hear the other. But he disappeared before he could feed. I'm sure of it. He looked..." She faltered, a tightness forming around her throat. "Like he was close to breaking."

Before Breckett could reply, Hadeon spoke up. "And these descendants... They can control the dead?"

"Apparently."

"And you could do the same?"

"If I agree to let the Everdark unlock my gift, I suppose so."

Hadeon ran a hand through his hair, which made it stick up in spikes. But he didn't bother fixing it. "Breeding with greater demons is forbidden, and for good reason. It's dangerous. No one should be able to control the dead. I need to call in that deal of ours." A panic grew in the prince's tone as though he'd shirked any facade of having his shit together. "I can't let you unlock this power or let the shadow fae leave the Abyss. Not when they could attack the Twilight Court, let demons into the fae realm, and control the dead—"

There was a flash of movement, a flicker between the shadows, and Breckett stood behind the fae prince. Syphen in hand, he brought down the hilt on the back of Hadeon's skull. Hadeon crumpled to the ground, unconscious instantly.

Arabella's mouth hung open. "Breckett! What are you doing—?"

But as she spoke the words, her mind registered what Hadeon had started to say.

He was going to use their bargain to keep her from unlocking her demon magic.

Slowly, Breckett lowered his arm before sheathing the blade. "The fae like to pretend they're so much better than the rest of us." He nodded to where Hadeon lay on the ground, wings splayed. "He'll just have to call in that bargain another time." Then he looked up at her, determination in his gaze. "Do what you must to save Elias. And be quick about it."

Her lips twitched, and she glanced down at the syphen. "I expect you to return that later."

Bastard had probably taken it from her while she was passed out.

"Find Arden," Jessamine said. "We'll stall Hadeon as long as we can."

Arabella was on her feet at once. "Thank you."

Before she could leave, Jessamine caught her wrist. "Whether you're human, fae, demon, or all three doesn't matter. It's never been about the type of power you have but how you use it."

While the idea of feeding on anyone went against everything she'd been taught as an enchantress, she allowed those teachings to slip between her fingers. Those beliefs had served her once. It had allowed her to find the strength to protect her people. But she understood now that it was so much more complicated than that.

To protect those she loved, she needed to get more power.

Leaning down, Arabella pressed a kiss to Jessamine's forehead. "I know that now."

Then she turned toward the tunnels and ran.

Arabella followed the tunnels the guards previously led her down. But the mountain was so large that she quickly got turned around. Eventually, she came to the cavern where she'd done most of her training with Arden. Only this time, Arden and his warriors were nowhere to be seen. Instead, shadow fae civilians lingered near the water.

Skidding to a stop, she growled, and her shadows twisted in agitation.

The shadow fae didn't look up from their work as she tried to steady her breathing. Some filled waterskins and others drew water for laundry. Nearby, there were fae weaving baskets and others preparing food in large pots.

A few of the fae were children—perhaps in their teens. Outside the roundness of their faces and their generally youthful demeanor, the young ones appeared no different than the other shadow fae. They had pointed ears and long limbs, and the shadows danced around their feet as though a bonfire whipped in the wind at their backs.

She wondered how many of them were part demon.

If they possessed the Everdark's magic, were they born with the power to control the dead? Or was that something that had to be unlocked in them, too? Was only hers locked away because of the magic her mother had used before she'd died?

The idea of asking a greater demon for help—the very same one who'd killed her parents—repulsed her.

Warriors strode into the cavern, and she hurried over to them. "I need to see Prince Arden at once. It's urgent."

All the warriors wore masks over their faces and eyed her with disinterest.

The one at the front, a male, said, "He's hunting with some of the warriors. He'll be back in a few hours."

She didn't have time to wait. Hadeon might be awake by then.

If he found her before she found Arden, he'd use his bargain. Depending on what bargain he called in, she wouldn't be able to acquire the power of the demons, or she might not be able to bring the shadow fae back through the gateway.

"Where did he leave from?" she asked. "Can you bring me to where he'll be when he returns?"

Somehow, she knew if she asked the warriors to lead her down into the heart of the mountain where the Everdark dwelled, they'd refuse. It seemed that it was akin to their holy place, and they wouldn't bring an outsider there alone. But maybe she could catch Arden as he returned, and he could bring her directly to the Everdark.

The guard who'd spoken frowned at her but made no objection as he led her down more tunnels to one that opened at the base of the mountain and the dark mist surrounding it.

To her dismay, no one was there.

"Wait here." He turned toward the tunnels with the other warriors. "If you leave the mists, the demons will set upon you, and you'll die."

She nodded.

Little did they know, a greater demon lived in the heart of this very mountain.

A thought occurred to her. If the Everdark was breeding with some of the females, then the shadow fae most likely knew of his existence.

She didn't intend to venture into the desert—not yet. If she left the tunnels, there was a chance Hadeon could fly above the mountain and spot her. No, she wouldn't make it that easy for him. Hopefully, Arden would return soon and bring her to the Everdark. She wasn't sure that she could find the altar room on her own. And hopefully, Hadeon would be asleep for a good long while. But in case Breckett hadn't struck him nearly hard enough, she needed to exercise caution.

For a moment, she wondered whether Hadeon would do anything to Jessamine or Breckett when he awoke. He was going to be pissed. And perhaps he was like Arabella—willing to do anything for those he'd sworn to protect.

If he hurts them, I will make him regret the moment he laid eyes upon me.

The magic of the bargain might keep her from killing him until she'd fulfilled her favor, but she'd find a way to make his existence a living nightmare.

As the warriors disappeared, she pressed her back against the cave wall and tugged on her braid.

Did she dare to risk waiting for Arden to return? She had no idea if the hunters went into the mountains or desert, and it was possible it could take hours for them to come back.

Could she summon the Everdark on her own? The greater demon had claimed that he'd been watching her for years. What if his presence hovered around her now? It had helped her to get into the Abyss. Perhaps he was close by.

Closing her eyes, she let her mind slip into the awaiting shadows.

She stretched out her senses like she had in Elias' castle when they'd been looking for the map and cast it like a net around her.

Instantly, she recoiled.

There was so much power in the mountain and around it. The existence of the mists alone was an assault on her senses. It was a constant flow of power from a rotation of shadow fae who filtered their magic into it.

There was far too much power for her to pinpoint anything.

Growling in frustration, she paced back and forth at the cave's entrance.

Unbidden, her mind wandered to her dream of Elias.

He'd been naked and covered in blood, and his features were ragged as though he hadn't slept in weeks. A knife was plunged into the center of his chest. Immediately, she'd reached for it, desperate to pull it out. But no matter what she did, it remained as though it was embedded in stone.

And when he kissed her...

Damn her if it didn't feel like he was saying goodbye.

She needed to save him, and now.

Taking a steadying breath, she cast her mind out again. Power assaulted her senses, making her dizzy, but she didn't stop.

I just need to go down, she thought. *If I can locate the tunnels into the deep, perhaps I can find the Everdark.*

She let the magic all around wash over her—the hybrid fae-demon children, warriors with magical artifacts, hides of demons that were still infused with dark magic, and magic wielders using spells in their caves. All the while, the power of the mists swelled in the background, blasting her like a blizzard carried on the northern winds.

She staggered, struggling to remain upright. The power was too much. But she didn't stop. She couldn't. Stretching out her senses as far as she could, she eventually felt a single dark heartbeat in the deep.

There you are.

Then she was striding into the dark. She moved down more tunnels than she could count until the air grew thin and her breath plumed in front of her. When she descended into a darkness that even her shadow fae senses couldn't penetrate, she knew she'd found the Everdark's stronghold.

She didn't stop to find a torch. Instead, she pressed ahead, using her hands along the walls to feel her way until, eventually, she rounded a corner.

The impenetrable black receded to the room's corners, and she realized she'd made it.

She stood in the shadow fae graveyard.

When she spoke, her words echoed like a drum in the deep. "Release my magic."

The impenetrable darkness in the recesses of the room shifted as though awakening.

Inky black sloughed off crevices in the stone, slipping into other shadows as it moved down the walls and across the floor. Slowly, the black gathered until a dark cloud formed above the stone altar.

Welcome back, granddaughter, the Everdark said into her mind. *I knew you'd see the appeal of my offer.*

"How is it done?" she demanded. She didn't care about his games or goals. Not right now. Not when her mate was near to breaking.

So impatient, the greater demon rumbled. *How very human of you.*

"You saw my mate in the dreamscape, I assume," she said. Not waiting for a response, she continued, "Then you'll understand my need for haste. Tell me how it's done."

The swirling black that hovered above the altar rippled before she heard the Everdark's voice once more.

I am the darkness that stalks the night. I am what mortals fear in the recesses of the deep. I am seduction and shadows.

It seemed to pause.

I will coax out your inner shadows with my own. Then you will be able to access your truest power. You will be a child of demons.

Still not understanding, she said, "Tell me what to do."

The Everdark hovered in the air and seemed to gesture to the altar.

She hesitated, a hand reaching toward a knife sheathed at her side—a weapon that would be utterly useless against this demon. For a moment, she thought about refusing. But as the image of Elias from the dreamscape returned to her mind, she nodded.

Swallowing past the fear that had her heart thundering in her chest, she lay down on the altar. The stone felt like ice through her leathers, and she bit back a shiver that started to work its way up her spine.

Do you submit to me?

The Everdark's voice was all around her. She felt it in the earth's shadows and deep within her—as though something inside her responded to his magic.

"How will I feed?" she asked.

There was a rumbling in the shadows, almost like the greater demon laughed.

You will see in time.

That wasn't an answer. But did she dare to press him? She needed to unlock her magic before Hadeon could find her. There wasn't time to delay.

"Do what you must to awaken my magic," she said. "I won't fight you."

The swirling black above her shifted until it took on the shape of a man.

It looked similar to the form the Everdark had taken in the dreamscape—a faceless shadow in the vague outline of a human. But then the shadows peeled back and something unearthly stepped forth.

It was utterly naked with skin that was a deep gray like decayed flesh. Sharp nails protruded from its fingers and toes, and on its face were two slits that opened to reveal eyes as dark as pitch. It didn't have a nose or ears or any other human feature.

Slowly, a maw opened below its eyes, revealing a too-large mouth filled with countless sharp teeth that were narrower than mortal teeth but also far longer. At the center was a long, thin tongue that lashed out like a snake.

Without meaning to, she flinched away, tilting her head away as it flicked its tongue toward her.

This is a manifestation of my magic, the Everdark said, and she thought she sensed his magic in the darkness hovering above the altar. As he spoke, bands of darkness wrapped around her wrists and ankles. It pulled her arms over her head.

Resist, and this will not work, the Everdark continued as she pulled at the bands of shadows holding her down. Even her shadows were being subdued by some inky darkness beyond her sight.

You want to save your mate, do you not?

Gritting her teeth, she swallowed back both fear and pride before saying, "Just do it."

As the demon lowered itself so it hovered above her body, she didn't flinch, didn't dare move as its claw-tipped fingers clicked against the stone as it placed its hands on either side of her head.

Then a piece of the Everdark's magic moved.

Reaching a hand up, it pressed a single claw to the center of her forehead. Magic speared into her, and a single tear slipped down her cheek as pain sliced into her center.

Elias, she thought. *I can do this for Elias.*

Tendrils of shadow enveloped her, spreading out until they filled her, until there was only the darkness.

Slowly, she felt herself separate from her body. She watched as the creature knelt above her. Shadows rippled around the stone altar, coming off the demon in waves as it reached a hand up, sinking clawed fingertips into her chest.

She watched as her body convulsed and tendrils of shadow filled her veins, moving out from where the creature's hand was. The darkness bled up her throat until she felt it caress her mind, her memories.

For a terrifying moment, she was back in the cottage in the woods as the witch entered her mind and tore her memories away. The memory assaulted her senses, and she felt herself tremble above her body, nearly descending back into it.

No, she thought as terror rippled through her senses. *I'm not in that cabin. I'm no longer helpless.*

But the demon didn't flip through her memories. Instead, it moved around them to the deepest recesses of her mind, to a corner she hadn't even known was there. Where there was a single box of shadow that was encased in bands of twining silver.

There, the Everdark purred.

His voice was everywhere and nowhere all at once.

The searching darkness formed a key before her mind's eye. A single dark key with an onyx stone. In a flash, the key was before the box, entering the lock. With a single click, the box opened.

For a moment, nothing happened.

Both she and the Everdark's magic waited in silence, eyeing the dark box that had creaked open. Then a shaft of shadow lashed out, and a torrent of magic burst forth like a dark tornado. It lashed onto the Everdark, clasping the shadows and forcing it back, back, *back*.

Suddenly, she crashed back into her body.

A power unlike any she'd ever known swelled within her. Inky tendrils extended out from that recess of her mind, filling her thoughts, her chest, her entire being until it was all she was.

Then the magic of the Everdark was forced out.

There was a flash of motion, and she blinked, finding herself atop the demon. The creature lay on its back, the stone altar cracked beneath it. Her fingers were wrapped around its neck. And at the tips of her fingers were long, sharp nails the color of night. There was a strange heat behind her eyes as blackness swallowed them whole. She felt her canines sharpen and let out a low growl.

Welcome, granddaughter, came the voice of the Everdark. *A princess of fae and demons.*

As the demon magic swelled inside her alongside the shadow fae power and the earthen magic of the enchantresses, she knew what the Everdark said was true.

Like her mate, she was a demon now, too.

And that demon would be what saved both him and Shadowbank.

Chapter Twenty-Three
ARABELLA

As Arabella rose from the stone altar, she felt the Everdark's impenetrable dark receding, slipping into the cave walls. *You are the key,* the Everdark said into her mind. *To open the gateway.*

"What?" she asked over her fangs.

Only a greater demon or a being with greater demon blood can open the gateway, and only for its own kind to go through. I could not let the shadow fae out because I am not fae. But one of my offspring can open it for the fae, he said. *Only the royal line is strong enough.*

In an instant, she understood why the shadow fae had never been able to leave the Abyss even with the help of the Everdark. And since she was human, fae, and demon, she was the only one who could open the gateway to let Hadeon, Jessamine, Breckett, and the shadow fae through.

"Where's the gateway?" she asked, needing to confirm whether her suspicions had been right. As she spoke, she could feel the Everdark's voice grow strangely quiet, as though slipping into some faraway darkness.

Follow the map.

Then the Everdark was gone.

She ran a hand over her neck. Where was he going? Had he become tired from awakening her magic?

Before she could dwell on it long, Arden appeared in the cavern.

A knowing smile traced the corners of his lips. "I see you've made your decision. We're glad to have you as one of us."

She ran the tip of her tongue over her receding fangs until they were normal size, which made her think of Rowan back in Shadowbank. "Vampire fangs. Interesting."

Glancing down, she noted that her black nails didn't retract. Instead, they stuck out in sharp points just over the tips of her fingers.

Arden shrugged. "Where do you think vampires got it from?"

"I suppose I assumed they always existed," she said honestly. "That they weren't a product of demons."

Perhaps some foolish sorcerer thought to make them in hopes of using and controlling them just as Magnus had with the erox.

"I need your help to learn my new abilities," she said. "Teach me how to control the dead."

"I wish I could help you," Arden began. "But since I don't possess demon blood, and the other fae-demon hybrids amongst us are only children, there's no one I could call upon to teach you."

Well, fuck.

All that effort to gain power she'd have to figure out on her own.

Nodding, she moved to the next portion of her plan. "What would you do if you could get out of the Abyss?"

A fire bloomed behind Arden's gaze as though a deep fury reawakened in him.

"That's a question I've pondered for years—just what I'd do if given the chance." Arden's gaze fixed on the far wall where the Everdark's deeper shadows had been. "The Twilight Court must pay for what they've done to the shadow fae."

Part of her understood his thirst for revenge. If someone

marched on Shadowbank, she wouldn't stop until they were wiped from the earth. But she didn't have time for his thirst for revenge—not to mention what it would do to her crumbling alliance with Hadeon.

In a softer tone, she said, "Would you consider helping me save my mate?"

Gaze shifting to her, Arden's brows furrowed. "I told you the only way out of the Abyss is with the aid of my map, which was lost to me many years ago."

She had to navigate this with caution.

One wrong move and Arden could try to kill her and take the map. Did he know that her magic was the key to open the gateway? And at some point, Hadeon would find her—and use his bargain to stop her.

It was at that moment she realized her abilities far exceeded Arden's. His power felt like a trickling stream compared to the torrent now pulsing in her veins.

"If I find a way out of here, will you help me rescue Elias?" she asked.

The prince crossed his arms. "What are you not telling me?"

Exhaling, she said, "The Everdark revealed I'm the key to getting out and opening the gateway. But I need your help, and so does Hadeon. It's why we journeyed here together. He wants to stop Queen Genoveva. She seeks immortality, and she's willing to pay any price. Hadeon fears that cost. Apparently, she's also preparing for war again. As for myself... I need help against a sorcerer—and his army. Magnus holds Elias captive."

Turning, Arden strode toward the wall nearest the entrance. He chuckled, which vibrated strangely in the cool air. "I knew Hadeon was planning something. He always is."

"Will you help us?"

For a long moment, he didn't move. She watched the rise and fall of his back as he breathed. At his hip, he wore an ancient fae blade with markings in a language she didn't understand.

Then he turned toward her, a dark shimmer in his gaze. "I

would be a terrible uncle to deny my niece the aid she needs. But I can't promise anything to Hadeon. Not when I can't trust his motives."

She stretched out her senses to see if the greater demon had returned. When she didn't feel the weight of his presence, she said, "What's your agreement with the Everdark?"

She wasn't sure whether a formal magical bargain had been struck, but at the very least, Arden and the shadow fae had formed an alliance with the Everdark—something that allowed them to use dark magic. The moment the greater demon taught the shadow fae new abilities and impregnated their females, he'd intertwined the fates of the shadow fae with the Everdark.

One corner of his lips lifted. "You know what he wishes."

Demons in the fae realm.

And he needed her to make that happen. More specifically, he needed a shadow fae of the royal line who possessed demon heritage on the throne.

By himself, the Everdark could only allow greater demons through the gateway. The other less powerful demonkind couldn't pass through the gateway into the fae realm with the help of the Everdark alone.

But she could let the demons through.

If the Everdark wasn't a factor, did she even want a place among the fae, and one of royalty? Besides her need for power to save Elias and Shadowbank, she'd never considered it. Political power had never been something she desired.

But she did know the demons that plagued Shadowbank and the mortal realm would cause harm in the fae realm if unleashed. The fae could push them back with their magic, but there would be a cost. Hadeon had mentioned that some fae were weak in magic, and they'd be vulnerable.

A terrifying thought struck her.

Would the fae cast the demons into the mortal realm if they couldn't kill them? There wasn't currently a way for demons to portal between the mortal and fae realms since they couldn't use the gateway. But not long ago, there also hadn't been a way to portal to one of the underrealms.

"If the Everdark gets his way and demons enter the fae realm," she began. "Many will die."

Arden raised a brow. "Many have already died." He stepped toward her, studying her eyes as though searching for something. "Join us, Arabella. You're shadow fae. The fae will be overjoyed to know a daughter of Myla lives. Help us to reclaim our homeland. It will likely be rubble or overtaken by another fae court."

What did the shadow fae lands look like? They had been one of the great fae courts. But when the fae wars occurred, had their lands been destroyed? What happened to their cities and strongholds? She had no way of knowing.

"This—us working together—is what your mother would have wanted," he continued.

For a moment, his words fell upon her like she shouldered the weight of a mountain.

Or the fate of a realm.

Part of her felt sad for her mother, who'd been held in captivity for years against her will. At the same time, Arabella couldn't bring herself to prioritize what her biological mother might have wanted. Because she already had a mother, and her name was Iris.

Still, the shadow fae were her people. And perhaps it was a side effect of awakening her new abilities, but she realized she felt responsible for them.

No one deserved to be trapped for an eternity in the Abyss.

"I must see to the safety of my mate and the humans of Shadowbank." She licked suddenly dry lips. "I can't save my village from the threat of demons only to bring that very same threat to someone else's home."

He nodded as though in understanding. "Tell me, have the fae courts done anything to protect Shadowbank? Have they reinforced your ward or brought their armies to slay the creatures?"

She didn't answer.

"Did they build new wards? Did they go out of their way *at all* to ensure the mortal realm was safe?" he pressed. "No. The Twilight Court is selfish, as are the other fae courts. They look after their own needs first and don't raise a hand to help those who don't impact them. Those they consider beneath them."

He took a step toward her and then another until he was before her, their chests nearly touching.

"Join me, and not only will your mate be by your side, but Shadowbank will be protected. We will reinforce the wards before returning to the fae realm," he said. "Then we will return to the Shadow Court and rebuild until we are strong enough that none can threaten us ever again."

His offer was tempting.

Did she dare unleash that darkness upon another realm? For the first time, she allowed herself to truly consider.

He's right. The fae never lifted a finger to help us, a darker part of her thought. *Perhaps it's their turn to face the unyielding dark.*

There was still so much to consider.

"Don't forget that you're part demon, too," he said. The sharpness of his tone felt like she teetered on the edge of a blade, ready to tip over with one wrong word. "The other courts will never accept you. They will see you as a threat and take you down. Especially if they learn about your ability to control the dead. You and your mate will never be safe."

Fists clenching at her sides, she considered his words. Before she could respond, he was already speaking.

"Join us, and my armies are yours. I don't fear a sorcerer, and neither should you." In a softer tone, he added, "You're one of us. No other court will accept you, but we will."

Every instinct inside her screamed to say yes, to accept his offer at once. But then she thought of her looming bargain with Hadeon.

"Hadeon will want you to consider mercy," she said. "To direct your spirit of vengeance to stop the Twilight Court queen from hurting the fae in her search for immortality or starting another war."

If you don't spare the Twilight Court, Hadeon will keep me from allying with you.

"Consider mercy for the Twilight Court," she said as Arden opened his mouth to speak. "And I'll consider my role amongst the shadow fae."

For a moment, Arden cast his gaze at the far wall, nodding as though deep in thought. He crossed his arms behind his back as he took one step forward and then another. Without turning around, he gestured toward the cave entrance. "Perhaps you'll think differently when you speak to Hadeon, yourself."

Fear sliced down her center as a dozen shadow fae warriors dragged Hadeon into the cavern. His gloved hands were bound in front of him, and his face was covered in bruises. There was a gag in his mouth. Dark eyes stared at her with a ferocity she'd never seen before.

It was then she registered that Breckett and Jessamine stood beside the warriors. Their hands were bound, and they had gags in their mouths as well.

Arabella noted the faintest shake of Jessamine's head.

"Why are they tied up?" Arabella demanded.

"Breckett told us of Hadeon's plan to leave the Abyss—without us," Arden said, his voice laced with venom. "The erox and the enchantress are restrained as a... precaution."

Arabella's eyes narrowed.

Arden knew as well as she did that Breckett could escape at any time he wanted with his ability to shadow jump and his invisibility powers. It would be easy for him to evade the shadow fae. But perhaps he was complying with them in hopes of securing their good will—and escaping the Abyss with them. If what Arden said was right, he'd aligned his fate with theirs.

But Breckett wouldn't know that Arabella was the key to getting out of the Abyss.

"I would have preferred that you told me about the map,

yourself, but we can move past that," Arden continued. "We are new to you. You didn't grow up amongst your kind as you should have. In time, you'll learn to trust us."

She leveled her gaze on Breckett.

Once the erox had been pissed at her for acting on her own. But now, he'd done the very same thing—acting without her. Had Jessamine approved? Breckett knew that letting the shadow fae back into the fae realm meant demons would be unleashed. Arabella didn't disagree with his actions. She wasn't even certain what she intended to do. But she wanted to understand his reasons.

"I want to hear from Breckett his reasoning," she said.

Arden nodded to one of the guards, who lowered Breckett's gag.

She didn't look away, didn't flinch, as she said, "Why?"

"Outside of the fact that Jessamine and I can't keep Hadeon at bay by ourselves for long," he said, his eyes full of fierce determination. "We need an army to defeat Magnus, and I refuse to go home without one. Not when he could rip my free will from me at any time." A muscle pulsed in his jaw. "The real question should be—why are you hesitating? They're offering you everything you wanted. Could it be that you don't want to rescue Elias after all?"

She flinched as though slapped. "Of course, I do."

"Then what else is there to consider?" he demanded.

Fists clenching, she opened her mouth to reply, but Arden spoke, pulling her attention back to him.

"There's one other thing you should know—about your mother," Arden said. "Myla was a prisoner in the Twilight Court for hundreds of years. The king had captured her at the start of the fae wars and kept her as his personal assassin." He turned to Hadeon, who'd been forced to his knees by the shadow fae warriors. "Isn't that right, Hadeon? You knew Myla *personally*."

Lines formed between Hadeon's brows, but he didn't shake his head or try to deny it.

The room grew quiet as her heartbeat drowned out all other sounds.

She'd known that her mother had been captured and held captive in the Twilight Court. And logically, if Arabella was in her thirties, her mother would have been alive in the recent past. That meant Myla would've been in the Twilight Court at the same time as Hadeon.

She shook her head.

Why hadn't she thought of that? She should've put the pieces together.

"Has he told you about the potential *cost* of immortality?" Arden continued. "His mother is pursuing immortality for not just herself, but her entire court. Which means the cost will be even greater—especially with a spell of that magnitude."

Belatedly, she realized her mouth hung agape, and she snapped it shut.

Arden nodded. "I see he hasn't told you. It's no wonder it's been a challenge for you to trust the fae when you've been exposed to the likes of Hadeon. He shared with me over a private dinner just what the cost could be for immortality. But you don't have to believe my word. You should hear it from Hadeon, himself."

One of the guards reached for the gag in Hadeon's mouth. The motion felt like it was in slow motion.

"Don't—" she began, but it was too late.

"I'm calling in our bargain," Hadeon said the moment the gag fell from his lips. "Take Jessamine and I out of the Abyss and no one else. Strike down anyone who gets in our way."

An electric charge pulsed through her like a single heartbeat as the bargain's magic settled over her.

Arden's eyes drew wide. "You had a bargain with him—?"

Apparently, Breckett and Jessamine hadn't revealed that fact to the shadow fae before they'd been restrained.

Unbidden, Arabella drew upon darkness throughout the

room, letting it infuse her. With a single step, she moved between shadows.

It was as natural as breathing.

It was as if her demon powers being locked away had prevented her from fully embracing all of her shadow fae magic. And now that they'd been unleashed, anything she willed was a breath away from reality.

She reappeared in the shadows beside Hadeon, blasting back the shadow fae warriors surrounding him with a torrent of black. With a flick of her fingers, she'd unsheathed one of her blades and cut Hadeon's and Jessamine's bonds.

Arden shouted somewhere behind her, calling to his guards.

"Get us out of here," Hadeon said as Arden's shadows surged. They had a heartbeat before his magic would descend upon them. And even if Arabella's power was stronger than his, he had years of experience and training.

"The syphen," she began, gesturing to where Breckett had rolled away from the guards—and outside of Arabella's reach.

Even as she spoke, she knew there wasn't time. Especially if Breckett gave her chase and leapt between shadows or turned invisible.

But the magic of the bargain clamped around her chest, keeping her from leaving Hadeon's and Jessamine's sides.

"Now, Enchantress," Hadeon hissed.

"Hold on tight," Arabella said, stretching out her arms.

Jessamine grabbed Arabella's hand. Hadeon hesitated for a moment before his fingers latched around her wrist over her jacket. Immediately, Arabella's stomach turned, and she nearly retched on the floor. Then she stepped between the shadows into the tunnels. Behind her, she cast a solid wall of black at the exit tunnel, locking the shadow fae and Breckett within it. It wouldn't last long, but it would give them a head start.

Moments later, they'd moved hundreds of feet up the tunnels and had returned to the main passages.

"Get us to the base of the mountains," Hadeon whispered. "I have provisions stored for us there."

Of course, he did.

Several heartbeats later, they were outside the mountain.

Jessamine pulled the gag from her mouth. "I'm sorry. Breckett disappeared after you left and told me to stay with Hadeon. I should've suspected—"

Arabella shook her head. "There isn't time to discuss this now."

A strange electric current pulsed through her, demanding she fulfill her portion of the bargain, urging her forward.

Hadeon grabbed four packs from where he'd stashed them at the base of the mountain under a pool of starlight. He tossed one to Arabella and another to Jessamine before shouldering two.

"You've been planning this," Arabella realized.

"I like to be prepared for all eventualities," he said.

As he strode before her, she spat at his feet. "You're damning the shadow fae to remain in the underrealm."

Unless she found a way to return, they'd be trapped here. And she had a suspicion Hadeon would try to keep her from going to the gateway in the western tundra.

Hate as hot as the sun's surface filled her veins, and she felt black filtering over her gaze, sharpening her sight. He'd damned the shadow fae to live in the Abyss, perhaps indefinitely. He'd also eliminated the chance of saving Elias with the only army willing to face Magnus.

His gaze raked over her, lingering on her dark nails with tips as sharp as a blade's edge. "I see you've unlocked your magic."

She didn't deny it. "I did what I had to—to save my mate."

"Surely, you can see how dangerous it would be if demons were in the fae realm," he said. "Would you make the fae suffer the same as your home?"

"It's a fate I wouldn't wish upon anyone," she said. "I'd also never wish an eternity in this place for anyone."

"Get us out of here alive, and I'll speak to my mother. I'll convince her to help save your mate and Shadowbank."

Something inside her hardened.

If he'd offered this to her before, they never would have entered the Abyss. But he hadn't taken her concerns seriously when she'd requested his help. It wasn't until she was a danger to him that he truly cared about the safety of Shadowbank or her mate.

"You're only offering this because I can kill you the moment we step through the gateway," she said, her voice cold.

"You should be thankful I spared your friend when she could have easily been left behind." He grabbed Arabella's jacket and pushed her toward the desert. "Get that map out, Enchantress. Or should I say Demoness?"

Stumbling forward, she glared at him with every ounce of hatred she felt. But he was right. The shadow fae would be flooding out of the mountain soon. Would Arden be able to stop them? He knew she couldn't hold the gateway open for the shadow fae even if she wanted to. Not with her bargain with Hadeon and the wording he'd used.

Unless Hadeon is dead.

If the prince wasn't alive, would that nullify her bargain with him? She could only hope.

"I'll never forgive you for this," she hissed through the hate filling her heart.

For a long moment, his eyes shifted between hers. "This isn't what I wanted. But it's what I must do to protect my home."

Then they ran through the desert. She would have leapt between the shadows, but she had to save her strength in case any demons appeared. Not to mention, using magic would draw the attention of any demons nearby. It would be the same for Breckett and the shadow fae if they tried to shadow jump.

She slowed her steps as much as she dared as they ran over rolling hills of sand. All she could do now was hope Arden and his warriors could catch up to them in time.

Otherwise, she'd take Hadeon and Jessamine through the gateway—and leave the shadow fae behind.

Trapped in the Abyss forever.

Chapter Twenty-Four
ARABELLA

"Demon isn't a terrible look on you."

From the playful tone in Jessamine's voice, Arabella knew her friend was trying to cheer her up, but her mood was as dark as the skies of the Abyss.

Arabella shifted her pack over her shoulder as they ran through the desert. Her eyes strayed to where Hadeon flew half a mile ahead of them to scout out the land in case any demons were nearby.

"Do you think there's any way to let the shadow fae through?" Arabella asked, careful to keep her voice low.

Jessamine shook her head, not sounding winded at all. "Not this time. But... we could come back to the Abyss if we can find the entrance again. Then we can lead them out."

Damn it, they didn't have time to make the journey again.

When Arabella spoke, her words were barely more than a whisper. "Elias won't make it that long."

Suddenly, Hadeon turned from the skies and landed beside them.

Jessamine offered him a glare and nothing more.

None of them stopped as Hadeon ran beside them.

"Do you feel guilty for not trying to rescue Prince Arden

sooner?" Arabella dared, her voice sharp. "Oh wait, you don't *feel* guilt. Do you? Or else, you wouldn't be leaving them to this fate a second time."

He sighed heavily. "I thought Arden was dead until the moment I met you."

"What?"

"Before my mother's ball, I'd thought the shadow fae were dead. I'd forgotten of Arden's map and talks of the Abyss. There had been so much going on during the fae wars with most of the courts preparing for war that it wasn't at the top of my mind." Pausing, he eyed her with that strange, knowing look of his. "Then I laid eyes on you. And you looked just like *her*."

"My mother," she said, bitterness evident in her tone.

"It was you who made me recall my discussions with Arden," he said. "I wondered where the map might be. Because if Arden had it, surely, he would have returned by now."

Understanding clicked inside her, bringing with it a tide of fury.

"You made a bargain with me, knowing I was a shadow fae."

"Suspecting," he corrected. "But yes."

"Are you trying to give us more reasons to hate you?" Jessamine spat.

"Myla was kinder to me than my own mother," Hadeon said, surprising Arabella as true sorrow filled his voice. "I didn't help her escape, but I wish I had."

"If you had, the Everdark wouldn't have killed her and my father," Arabella said.

His brows rose. "I'd always wondered what happened to them. One day, they just... disappeared. My father never explained what happened to her. I had assumed she'd died on one of his missions."

Something in her chest twisted, and it was all she could do not to lash out with her magic. While she knew she should press Hadeon for answers, she was too fucking tired. Everything she'd learned from the Everdark and about the shadow fae had been... a lot. And she now had to figure out just what ramifications her new demon magic would have—and how she'd need to feed. She couldn't raise a hand against Hadeon while her bargain hadn't been fulfilled. That meant, if she became *hungry*, she might be tempted to feed on Jessamine.

And she refused to let that happen.

She turned her focus back to the sands and moving one foot in front of another.

Unlike their previous trek, they didn't encounter a demon in their days of travel—or at least what they estimated was the passing of days. They were also able to journey farther without the need to seek out an oasis since Hadeon had packed extra supplies.

As they journeyed, she wondered if the demons didn't approach them because her demon magic had been unleashed. Maybe they wouldn't encroach on the territory of another demon.

A foolish part of her hoped they'd come under attack if only to slow them down. It would give Arden and the warriors more time to catch up with them.

But they didn't encounter any opposition.

Far too soon, a deeper darkness materialized on the horizon.

As they neared it, she realized it was a leafless forest. Hundreds of trees of varying heights clustered together in the sand. Some were taller than the Quarter in Shadowbank and others were twice the height of a man. The largest trees' trunks had deep grooves as though a great beast had clawed them. But they weren't dead. Instead, the trees appeared as though they'd just shaken the leaves loose in preparation for winter—that life would return in a few short months.

Frowning, she studied the line where the desert met the trees.

Unlike before, she didn't need the Everdark's magic to make the map work, which was fortunate for Hadeon since the greater demon had been scarce since awakening her magic. She wondered if it had done something to the Everdark—perhaps temporarily weakened him.

She gestured with the tilt of her chin. "The gateway is ahead."

Hadeon motioned for her to walk forward, and she did, eyeing the trees' twisting branches. But even as she tried to remain vigilant, she felt her limbs and eyelids grow heavy. They had traveled for days with little rest. Hadeon had pressed them to keep moving to ensure they stayed ahead of the shadow fae.

As she walked through the trees, she said over her shoulder to Jessamine, "If you feel sick, let me know."

Jessamine made a sound of assent.

For once, their growing ill at the nearness of a gateway would be helpful to locate it. Since the map only marked an area, there was no way of telling where exactly it would be. But she anticipated both she and Jessamine would grow faint soon.

Frankly, she didn't want to think about it.

Without the Everdark to assist her through the gateway, she'd likely lose the contents of her stomach very soon.

As they walked through the trees, something tingled at the edge of her senses. It was like a dissonant melody purring just beyond her sight.

"We're getting close," she said as she pushed back interlocking branches.

The further she walked into the trees, the less she could see the desert—even though she should have been able to see it between the bare branches. Instead, all she saw was darkness.

"Stay close," she said. "I have a feeling getting separated in here wouldn't be ideal."

A hand was on her shoulder, and she glanced back. Jessamine nodded to her and then glanced back at Hadeon.

"Absolutely not," he said. "I can keep up just fine."

"It wouldn't be the greatest inconvenience if you remained trapped here, fae prick," Jessamine said. "I mean, fae *prince*."

His lips twitched, but he didn't respond.

Arabella turned forward, following the dissonant chorus that slowly increased in volume as she strode across the dark sands. As she neared where the sound was loudest, she didn't feel the onslaught against her senses, like the realm was splitting in two. Pain didn't split her skull nor did nausea swell in her stomach. Instead, the hum felt like a rumbling purr, and she strode toward it.

Sadness swelled in her as she wondered just how much of her human self had been lost to her training in shadow fae magic. Perhaps she wouldn't be sick by the gateways after all. Not if she'd lost what made her human.

Outwardly, she'd changed. Her ears were pointed, just like Hadeon's, and she noticed that her movements were more... fluid. Graceful like the fae.

Stretching an arm out, she allowed her eyes to flutter shut as a film of black fell over them. On instinct, she leaned into her newest magic, and her shadows sung.

Something hissed in the trees, which rustled as though a wind had just passed through. But all was still.

The night awaits.

Eyes snapping open, she scanned their surroundings to see who—or what—had spoken. A flash of motion caught her eye, and she glanced down at the wisps of darkness at her feet, which dug into the sands, forming grooves. Her shadows continued to shift into something more... corporeal. They'd possessed substance before, but they'd felt like an extension of the dark. Now, it was some spirit of the deep that seemed to respond to her emotions—and her commands.

"I think I'm going to be sick," Jessamine said behind her before there was a gagging sound.

Hadeon cursed.

Turning, Arabella caught Jessamine as she passed out and heaved her over a shoulder. There was no way she was trusting Hadeon to carry her friend through the gateway. Not that he would have offered to help.

"Hang in there, Jessamine," Arabella said, uncertain whether her friend could hear her. "We'll be back home soon."

"It's fortunate the gateways no longer affect you," Hadeon said behind her. "Otherwise, we wouldn't be able to read the map. Getting home would be much more difficult."

Your home, she thought.

Unwilling to speak to the fae prince any more than she had to, she kept her gaze ahead as she followed the hissing sound. Without willing it, her shadows pushed through more interlocking branches, creating a path for her.

A weeping willow tree with long draping branches appeared before them. Unlike the trees in the forest, this one bore leaves the color of decayed flesh. A clearing had formed around it as though this tree were a disease that sucked life from the land.

"There," she said. "That's the gateway."

She wondered whether she needed to do something with her magic to open the gateway, or if her mere presence would be enough to allow them passage through.

Suddenly, there was a rustling behind them.

Spinning, she faced the sound, holding Jessamine with one arm and shadows licking up the other. Beside her, Hadeon held his sword before him, his dark power billowing around him.

Did a demon live in this place? Was this tree its nest? Or could it be the zaol again?

Tell me what comes, she commanded to the dark on some new instinct.

A few of the shadows that had taken the shape of thorny vines around her pulled away and fell back into the ground. Then they stretched forward toward the trees—back in the direction of where they'd just come. They darted back and forth from one tree's shadow to the next, moving like spilled ink down a cliffside.

The shadows hummed in her mind, and she could feel them move and what they sensed. It was how she knew who they were up against the moment the dark encountered what stalked them.

For a moment, she hesitated. Was there a way she could avoid telling Hadeon?

But the prince must have sensed something because he raised his sword and said, "I knew you'd catch up eventually."

Then Arden and his warriors appeared between the trees.

Arden's eyes darkened as they fastened on Hadeon. "You *dared* to force my kin into a bargain? The levels you're willing to sink to never cease to amaze me."

Hadeon didn't lower his blade as he spoke. "She made the bargain willingly."

"Be careful," she said as shadows sparked in Arden's eyes. "I don't want to hurt you."

There were far more of the shadow fae. A dozen warriors spread out in the clearing, forming a semicircle around her, Jessamine, and Hadeon.

Arden managed a brief nod in her direction before his gaze returned to Hadeon. "Were you ever intending to help us? Or was this all some farce to assuage you of your guilt for never helping us during the fae wars? Why bother coming here?"

Hadeon had angled himself between Arabella and Arden. When he stepped back, she was forced to do the same or let him run into her. But he angled them in one direction.

Toward the tree—and the gateway somewhere within it.

"I'd hoped for your help to stop my mother from acquiring immortality and starting another war, but it became clear you wouldn't listen after weeks of the same hostility," Hadeon said as he took another slow step backward. "When I learned about your intention to unleash demons in the fae realm, I knew it was too late for you to see reason. Do you know how many fae will die?"

A humorless laugh escaped Arden's lips. The sound was so raw, so full of emotion that both she and Hadeon stilled.

"What of the shadow fae who were slaughtered?" Arden demanded. "No one considered mercy for the civilians, the *innocent*."

As Arden stepped forward, the shadows swelled from the earth. They weren't as solid or as large as the thorny vines at her feet. But translucent tendrils rose from the ground and pointed toward them.

No, towards Hadeon.

She glanced around as the shadow fae surrounding them also summoned the dark. Some formed inky tendrils while others formed the shadows into bolts.

"I should've spoken up or aided you more openly," Hadeon said, taking a step backward and forcing Arabella to do the same. "It's one of my biggest regrets, and that's something I'll have to live with."

"*Live* with. You've lived safely in the fae realm for centuries while the shadow fae have been fighting for each breath we take." Arden raised his arms to either side, and the shadows moved in response, pooling beneath his fingertips. "The thing about magical bargains is they're only between the two who make them. If I kill you, Arabella will no longer be bound to your demands."

Arabella was nearly beneath the tree's branches when she paused, breathing a sigh of relief. She'd been right—if Hadeon was dead, she'd no longer be bound to their bargain. But would it be possible for Arden to kill Hadeon? From what she could sense, Hadeon's magic exceeded his. But there were more shadow fae.

As her own shadows swelled, unbidden, she knew with sudden certainty there was no hope of Arden surviving a head-on attack. Not against both her and Hadeon.

"Don't," Arabella warned. "You can't win against us both. And Hadeon forbade me from letting anyone else through the gateway." When Arden's shadows swelled even further, she said, "Return to the mountain. Survive."

I won't forget you.

If she somehow survived rescuing Elias and Shadowbank, then she'd return to the Abyss. Somehow, she'd free these people.

Her people.

She couldn't openly promise to return to them—not in front of Hadeon. The exit gateway was somewhere in the Twilight Court, and he held sway there. Even if his mother didn't like him, he could insist on them imprisoning her. He could keep her from getting to Elias.

Arden's eyes narrowed, and she hoped he understood her meaning.

There was a strange humming coming from the tree as her shadows stretched out toward it, unbidden.

Somehow, thanks to the bargain, her magic was unlocking the gateway.

The shadows slid along the ground like snakes. As they inched toward the willow tree, the sound grew louder until she realized it wasn't a humming but whispers. It wasn't in any language she'd heard before. The words were deep and guttural, and it wasn't one voice but many.

"Was it worth it?" she said, looking up to Hadeon. "You went to all this trouble to find the shadow fae, and you've left with more enemies than you started."

Slowly, Hadeon raised his hand toward her, his gaze never leaving Arden. "I may hate my mother, and my brothers may despise my existence, but the Twilight Court is still my home. And I won't let the shadow fae destroy it in a quest for vengeance."

Hadeon loosed a plume of wind from his hand, which struck Arabella in the chest.

She gasped, nearly dropping Jessamine as she flew backward —toward the tree.

And the open gateway.

Somehow, her shadows had connected with the tempest at the base of the tree trunk, and a slice in the universe had opened.

She watched in horror as Arden and the soldiers unleashed their shadows upon Hadeon. The fae with wings...

Like a dragon, she thought.

Before their shadows could touch Hadeon, a torrent of magic billowed out from him, forming a swirling storm that exploded in the clearing.

She released a whisper of shadows as she flew through the gaping wound in the air.

And the gateway swallowed her and Jessamine whole.

Chapter Twenty-Five
ARABELLA

Arabella's palms slapped cool stone as she rolled to a stop. Glancing up, she was surprised to find herself in a dungeon cell. There were three walls of stone, while the fourth wall was a gate of iron bars. There were no windows, but there were a few lanterns with magic-infused light in the hallway beyond the cell.

Jessamine groaned where she'd landed beside Arabella.

Then Hadeon appeared through the gateway at the center of the dungeon cell, his face the manifestation of fury itself. Not bothering to look at them, he spun back toward the slash in the air and raised his arm toward it.

A sudden realization struck her.

"No!" she shouted.

But it was too late.

He never intended to let the shadow fae leave the Abyss. Not when he planned to close the gateway from the outside.

Even as she lashed out with her shadows, enveloping him in vines of night—letting the thorns sink into his arms, body, and wings—it was too late.

The slash in the air disappeared a moment before her shadows threw him to the ground, encircling him so he could no longer raise his arms. She let them enfold his legs, strangling him like a snake with its prey.

"Release me," he said, a deep weariness filling his tone, his eyes fixed on the back wall.

"Be careful, Prince," she hissed as she rose. *Daring* him to try. "You no longer have a bargain to leverage over me."

His eyes locked with hers, and he nodded to where Jessamine lay unconscious as he said, "You forget we aren't alone, Enchantress. There are still those you want to protect."

Anger and fear swelled in her chest in tandem. "Controlling me by threatening those I love makes you no better than Magnus."

Hadeon's power bloomed, pressing against her shadows. For a moment, she almost lost her grip on them. But she held firm, keeping the prince pinned on the floor. Her abilities surpassed his in sheer power, but she had a long way to go to learn to control her new magic.

"I'm nothing like him."

She laughed humorlessly before releasing him with a flick of her wrist.

What was the point? The gateway was sealed shut. There was nothing she could do for the shadow fae and no way to open it again. He'd killed them without ending their lives, himself. Her shadows retreated into the ground. "All fae are the same—selfish liars. If only there was a way to force you to tell the truth for once in your life."

For the first time, she wondered whether this meant the Everdark and other greater demons were also trapped in the Abyss.

Blood plopped onto the floor from where her dark thorns had sunk into Hadeon's skin and wings. But he didn't flinch or make any indication that he felt anything as he stood.

"I'm not your enemy, Enchantress," he said as he moved to her side, towering over her.

"But now, you're mine," came a voice from behind her.

Arabella blinked, her mind not fully registering the words as the prince went from looming above her to falling to the ground. She watched in stunned surprise as Jessamine swept a foot beneath him before landing an elbow on his chest. His wings splayed as he crashed backward onto the stone. He reached for where his sword had fallen beside him, but Jessamine was already there, her arm coming down on his. The blade skittered out of reach. He lashed out, trying to strike Jessamine, but she was a moment ahead of each of his strikes, blocking one and then the next.

"You shouldn't touch me," he hissed as Jessamine straddled him. "You won't like what happens next."

Rage filled Jessamine's gaze as she held a dagger to his throat. "Lucky for me, I won't have to learn. Not when you're going to be dead. This is what will happen to all fae who are so obscenely selfish. You locked away innocent people in an underrealm forever. Fuck you, and fuck your court."

He tried to block her, to force her back. But again, she merely swatted his hands out of the way each time with the side of her arm, garbed in leathers.

"How did you do that?" he grunted. "It's like you knew what I was going to do before I did."

Jessamine's lips pursed before she schooled her features into neutrality. "It's nothing you need to concern yourself with, fae prick."

As Jessamine plunged the blade toward Hadeon's chest, a sudden power bloomed outside of their cell. It was at that moment Arabella wondered just where they were—and why the exit from the Abyss was in this place.

Starlight lashed out from the hall beyond the bars. Jessamine's blade flew backward, coming to a stop in the hand of Genoveva, Queen of the Twilight Court.

"I wasn't expecting visitors." The queen studied the dagger

with obvious distaste. Behind her, there were two dozen fae guards, all heavily armed. "But you can imagine my surprise when I felt the gateway open—one that hasn't been used in an age."

Arabella nearly groaned.

The gateway leading out of the Abyss wasn't in just any dungeon. It was within the castle of the Twilight Court.

Of-fucking-course.

Jessamine didn't move from where she straddled Hadeon. Instead, her hand was already reaching for another blade inside her jacket.

"I wouldn't," the queen said, not looking at her. "I won't spare you a second time, *human*."

"Mother," Hadeon said as he leaned up on an elbow. "This is a mere... misunderstanding. Allow me to introduce my comrades."

Arabella's eyes narrowed.

Was he trying to protect them?

The queen, likely thinking the same thing, raised a brow.

"This is Enchantress Jessamine," Hadeon said, nodding to Jessamine—who still didn't move to get up. With a pause, he gestured to Arabella. "You've met Enchantress Arabella as well. But much has come to light since."

"To think a shadow fae entered my court under my very nose." The queen spoke as though she'd sniffed a rotten corpse, nodding to the twisting shadows at Arabella's feet. Genoveva's gaze traveled up and down the length of Arabella in her leathers—filthy from days traveling through a desert. It was quite unlike the queen's midnight-blue gown, which had an outer sheer fabric with interwoven silver thread that looked like shooting stars.

"I was only recently made aware of my heritage," Arabella said.

"And what heritage is that?" the queen asked.

Arabella's eyes narrowed as she wondered whether the queen was implying she knew about Arabella's demon heritage or if she was wondering who her shadow fae parent was. Did she suspect Arabella's ties to the royal family?

Crossing her arms, Arabella nodded toward the locked cell door. "Perhaps you'd like to invite us to a more comfortable place to discuss such matters?"

While Arabella could step through the shadows and get out of the cell easily, she was too far away from Jessamine to be able to escape with her friend before the queen or Hadeon could attack. It was either escape alone or risk losing Jessamine by trying to get to where she straddled Hadeon on the ground behind her. And she wasn't about to risk Jessamine's life.

Genoveva turned to Hadeon as though Arabella had never spoken. "What's at the other end of the gateway? Where did it lead?"

Hadeon frowned. "You don't know?"

There was a gateway in the Twilight Court, and the queen didn't know where it came from? Why not seal it herself, then? Why risk leaving it open if she didn't know where it came from?

The queen's power—which exceeded her son's—bloomed in Arabella's mind's eye. A single strand flicked out from Genoveva's extended hand.

The door to the cell swung open.

Behind Arabella, there was a shuffling sound, and she hoped Jessamine had dismounted from Hadeon. She loved her friend for her fierce loyalty, but now wasn't the time to deal with Hadeon's betrayal. Not if they were in the Twilight Court. They were at a severe disadvantage and could be imprisoned at any moment. As such, it was too risky to do anything but play along for now.

It was clear the queen didn't have eyes for Jessamine or Hadeon as they strode into the hallway. Instead, her gaze fixed on Arabella as she left the cell.

Again, her nostrils flared, one lifting higher than the other. "Why do you smell like a demon?"

"The gateway comes from the Abyss. We encountered a number of demons on our journey," Hadeon said, moving to

Arabella's side. "You'll have to excuse our appearance and... scents."

Arabella bit the inside of her cheek in an attempt to keep her facial expressions from revealing more than they should.

What was Hadeon's angle? Why try to protect her and Jessamine? He'd shown that he was no friend of theirs by forcing them through the gateway and sealing it behind them. And then threatening Jessamine.

She allowed her senses to stretch back toward the cell—where the gateway had been.

And was no more.

Somehow, the prince had found a way to close the gateway permanently.

Not for the first time, she was overcome by frustration at her lack of knowledge. She had no idea how gateways were created or destroyed. The only thing she could tell with certainty was its existence.

Turning, the queen strode down a long stone hallway illuminated on either side by a series of torches on the wall. It wasn't unlike the dungeons beneath the Quarter in Shadowbank—cells in a place of stone, which neutralized many different types of magic.

As Genoveva walked, her dress trailed on the ground behind her.

Arabella glanced at Jessamine, who looked at her at the same moment. It was clear her friend had the same thought as her.

Just what was in store for them?

Then the queen spoke. "I expect a full explanation soon. But for now, I have another visitor."

※

THE GATEWAY LET out in the dungeons beneath the castle in the Twilight Court—the very same castle she'd fucked Elias at not too long ago.

Longing filled her alongside a deep ache.

It was at that moment she realized that she could feel Elias' emotions down the mating bond. The tugging in her chest had returned the moment she was in the fae realm. Unlike the last time she was here, his emotions felt far sharper. They were no longer muffled.

Fear filtered down the bond but not pain. He wasn't actively being tortured by Magnus. That was something, at least.

The last she'd seen him in the dreamscape, he'd been near to breaking. She knew at that moment she had precious little time before the male she loved was no more. Either he'd be broken by Magnus, forever changed, or worse.

As guilty as she felt about the shadow fae being trapped in the Abyss, their plight was secondary to her mate's.

But why could she feel him so clearly now? What was different?

As they followed the queen and her guards in silence up winding stone staircases and through the dungeon's magical wards, her mind raced. How long would it be until she could go back to the mortal realm?

I'm coming, Elias. It won't be long now.

Without the shadow fae as allies—and not trusting Hadeon to come through with his vague promise of aid—she intended to face Magnus' army head-on with her new abilities. As soon as she could get out of the Twilight Court, she would descend upon the sorcerer and his army, and fuck the consequences.

More fae guards with dark blue armor surrounded them as they emerged into the hallways above the dungeons in the main castle. Like Hadeon, the feel of their magic was star-kissed. Their power was weaker than hers, Hadeon's, or the queen's, but there were enough of them that it would keep Arabella and Jessamine from making a break for it.

Each guard had a sword sheathed on a hip along with a dagger on the opposite. It wasn't much in terms of weapons, at least compared to how many blades the enchantresses wore. Perhaps the fae relied mostly on their magic in combat.

Just like her first time in the castle of the Twilight Court, the show of wealth was painfully apparent—it was in every crystal chandelier they passed, every curtain laced with silver and gold thread, and in the empty silver trays the servants carried as they hurried in the opposite direction.

A sudden pang struck her in the gut, and she brought a hand up to her stomach. She hadn't eaten very much with their limited supplies, but this wasn't like any hunger she'd felt before. This was somehow different.

Then realization dawned.

My demon power, she thought. *I need to feed.*

But just how would she do that? Would she consume essence like the erox or blood like the vampires? Either way, she couldn't let the queen see her feeding, or else risk revealing what she was. There wasn't time to deal with this right now.

With significant effort, she pressed the hunger back, forcing herself to focus on the present.

As they walked along silk carpets, she couldn't help but marvel at how the mating bond changed. The tugging in her chest had loosened, and she no longer felt like she was on the balls of her feet, eager to move toward where her mate was. Instead, the tension had eased, and she could sense his feelings more clearly.

Like he was nearby.

Then they rounded a corner and strode into another hallway, and her heart nearly stopped.

"Elias."

Standing before her was the male who'd captivated both her dreams and waking hours. The male she'd sworn to burn the world down for.

Elias stood next to an open door to what appeared to be a throne room. Beside him were a dozen erox with magic that was a similar strength to her mate. Magnus stood at the head of the group in robes rich enough to make a king blush.

Eyes fixing on Elias, she blinked and then blinked again.

The erox all wore simple leather armor with crisscrossing straps and sheaths, metal shoulder plates, and gloves with metal spikes atop their knuckles.

All except Elias.

He wore black trousers, tall black leather boots, and a black long-sleeved shirt that dipped low on his chest. While he still felt larger than life and his body rippled with muscles, there was a hollowness to his features that she'd never seen before. She also noted his hair and beard weren't as long as they'd been in the dreamscape, as though he'd been recently groomed.

His eyes, too, seemed different.

They were still the rich brown color she'd come to love—the color his eyes were when he wasn't using his magic. But there was a vacantness there. Like his body was present, but his mind was somewhere far away.

For a moment, she wondered whether she was dreaming.

How was he here?

Glancing to her side where both Jessamine and Hadeon stood, she noted their rounded eyes and knew this wasn't an illusion. They looked as shocked as she felt.

But Elias didn't look at her. He didn't even raise his eyes as she stopped mere feet from him. His face was utterly expressionless, appearing like the perfect soldier.

Look at me, she thought. *Please.*

The queen inclined her head to Magnus. "Sorcerer."

The erox around Magnus hummed with power—power she once would have thought was immense.

But Magnus' power...

It boomed throughout the room like a thunderclap.

Power cascaded off the edges of his robes like an extension of him. It was like he stood at the eye of a hurricane that he could command at will. It moved around him in scarlet waves. Once, it had appeared as a gray mist, and she wondered what this change could mean. Most magic wielders' abilities were only discernible by other wielders. However, Magnus' power was so vast, so unfathomable, that it was visible to the naked eye.

Her heart sank as she realized that, even with her new abilities, his power vastly exceeded hers.

What was happening? Why were Magnus, Elias, and the erox in the fae realm? Had they sought an audience with the queen?

Some distant part of her knew she should be quiet, knew she should watch and assess as things played out. But rage filled her, and words tumbled from her lips.

"You keep questionable company, Your Highness." Her insides roiled like a tempest about to be unleashed.

Hadeon stiffened before falling completely still. Even Jessamine didn't dare move as they all awaited the queen's response.

"You are deeply mistaken if you think I care for your opinion, *child*. You're lucky I deigned to let you live." The queen's tone snapped like a whip. "The sorcerer is here with a proposition I intend to hear."

Arabella's mind reeled.

What could Magnus possibly want? Did this have something to do with another fae war or the queen's pursuit of immortality?

"Mother," Hadeon began, taking a step forward so he was between Genoveva and Magnus, forcing her to look at him. "There is much we need to discuss that can't wait."

"You went into an underrealm without consulting me," the queen said. "If you value my insight so little, then I fail to see why I should prioritize yours. Whatever it is can wait."

If Arabella's eyes hadn't been fixed on Elias, she might have missed it. But as she watched Elias, she noted a very distinct, very long blink at the queen's words when she mentioned the underrealm. It was the most expression she'd seen on his otherwise cold exterior.

At the same time, fear spiked down the mating bond.

Since she'd last seen Elias in the in-between, she lived in terror of what Magnus was doing to him and if he'd broken her mate—

stripping him of all he'd been and leaving him as a shell of himself. Perhaps even taking his memories like the Witch of the Woods had done to her.

But at the mention of the Abyss, Elias had felt fear, which meant he not only knew what the underrealm was, but he worried for her safety. He wasn't ignoring her out of indifference or because he didn't recognize her. Magnus must be controlling him with the syphen. Had the sorcerer found the blade she'd dropped in the forest?

Fury roiled through her, and her leash on her shadows shortened.

If Magnus was holding the syphen beneath his robes, he could force Elias to do anything.

Even hurt himself.

Magnus swept an arm forward. As he did, she thought she spotted the glint of a blade. "If this isn't a good time, I'm happy to return at your convenience..."

"No." The queen placed a hand on Hadeon's chest, forcing him to step back. "Now is the perfect time."

Dipping his head in deference, Magnus followed the queen into the adjacent throne room. Elias was at his heels, moving with near-silent footsteps.

Arabella wasn't about to be parted from him. So, she strode after Elias—as though she had every right to be in a private meeting with the queen of the Twilight Court.

To her surprise, Elias paused in the doorway. She tried to stop, but she bumped into him from behind, his shoulder brushing hers. The touch was like electricity shooting down to her toes, and she gasped. But as she started to look up at him, he walked forward, not looking back.

It was then she got her first look at the throne room.

Part of her had expected more of the similar opulence she'd seen in the castle hallways, but it felt like she'd stepped atop a still lake that reflected the starry night sky. The floor was made of dark, glittering tiles with swirling illustrations of moons. She couldn't tell if the images were painted within the dark tiles or if magic had been imbued in them.

The room itself was long and had at least a dozen archways on each side with columns wider than most tree trunks in the forest outside Shadowbank. Near the base of the columns was a ledge that held candles of varying heights. They emitted a soft glow in a room that felt infused by starlight.

Guards were stationed beneath each archway.

At the opposite end of the room was a dais with steps that led to a throne made of a clear crystal with twisting silver patterns that swept up on either side until it formed a skewed crescent moon ten feet high.

Rather than feeling awe at the sheer majesty of this place, fury raged in her heart.

So much wealth had been put into making this throne room —resources that could have been allocated to helping others.

Finding her courage, she strode into the throne room after Elias, who followed Magnus and the queen. A glance over her shoulder told her that Hadeon and Jessamine stood behind her just inside the doorway.

"This once, I'll not remark on your insolence, human," Genoveva said in a dangerously low tone, turning from where she was at the base of the dais. "Despite your newly pointed ears, I know what you really are. Get out of my throne room before I—"

"If I might make a request," Magnus interrupted, which had the queen quieting. "I'd like for Enchantress Arabella and the others to join us. If that is acceptable to you, of course."

Arabella frowned and might have objected to doing *anything* Magnus wanted. However, if it meant that she'd remain near Elias, she'd gladly attend any meeting.

For a long moment, the queen said nothing as she studied the sorcerer. Then she walked up the dais. As she did, she flicked her fingers, and a wisp of magic shot across the throne room and closed the doors behind them.

Turning back to them, Genoveva lowered herself onto the

throne, appearing as though she lounged atop a crescent moon. "I'll permit it."

"While we're placing requests, I have one of my own," Arabella snapped as she marched down the center of the throne room. It was an effort to keep control over the blackness filtering over her eyes and prevent her fangs from emerging as rage churned through her. She pointed a finger at Magnus. "He's taken my mate hostage and tortured him for weeks. I can't imagine what there is to discuss besides telling him to fuck right off."

Sand trailed the floor behind her, and her dirty boots and leathers squeaked in the unnaturally quiet room. What felt like an eternity later, she came to stand at the base of the dais, opposite Magnus and Elias. A moment later, Jessamine and Hadeon were by her side.

Genoveva's gaze settled on Arabella's clawed fingertips. "I failed to hear a request."

Get a hold of yourself, Arabella thought. She needed to get a leash on her anger if she had any hope of navigating whatever political labyrinth she'd stepped into.

Magnus raised his hand as Arabella opened her mouth to speak. "If I may provide context to Your Majesty." He gestured to where Elias stood behind him. "Elias offered himself to me of his own volition. I wasn't aware they were bonded. However, under the terms of our agreement, his life is mine."

Arabella watched as one of Magnus' hands disappeared in his robes before Elias spoke.

"He speaks the truth," Elias said in a tone so cold, so emotionless, that it was nearly unrecognizable. "I offered myself to him."

A sudden, hot fury seared in her veins.

He is using the syphen.

She'd suspected it, but to see it happen was something else entirely.

Instinctively, she reached for the shadows. But before she could unleash them, Hadeon caught her wrist.

Rather than telling him to fuck right off, she found herself looking up at the fae male.

Ever so slightly, he shook his head.

Don't, his gaze said.

Did she dare trust him after everything? What if this was some trick, too?

A simple fact made her pause. She was woefully outnumbered.

Even with her new powers, she wouldn't be able to take down Magnus, Genoveva, and the guards, steal the syphen, and escape the Twilight Court with Elias and Jessamine. But damn it, she wanted to try.

It took everything in her to not look over to where Elias stood behind the sorcerer. Even still, Elias' presence alighted her senses with a static energy. She felt more alive than she had in the weeks they'd been apart. It was like he awakened something in her magic. Even the shadows rumbled at her feet, shifting like rolling waves.

"If I may be so bold," Magnus said with a false humility infusing his voice. "I'd like to hear about their journey to the underrealm. I've never ventured to one, and I'm curious to learn more about it."

For the first time, Arabella wondered whether the sorcerer intended to reveal how Hadeon had come to Elias' castle and fought his army. Was that why he'd asked for them to stay—to reveal what Hadeon had done in front of the queen? Despite the prince's claim that killing the ogres and gargoyles could be labeled as self-defense, Arabella had a feeling the queen wouldn't see it that way. Not if it jeopardized whatever good will she had with the sorcerer. It was clear Magnus had the queen's ear and that she possessed disdain for Hadeon. But why?

"As you wish." The queen turned to her son with a gaze far colder than a mother should look at her child, her fingers drumming on the throne's armrest. "Speak."

A muscle pulsed in Hadeon's jaw. "Recently, I heard rumors

that the shadow fae may still be alive. When I'd heard of a gateway near the western tundra, I asked Enchantress Arabella to join me in a journey to the Abyss. As it turns out, it's a one-way entrance into the underrealm."

"How did you know where to go?" Magnus pressed. "And why bring the enchantress?"

Hadeon hesitated before saying, "Before the war, Prince Arden created a map of the Abyss, which only shadow fae can use. The enchantress was able to read the map, and we located the shadow fae."

"What aren't you saying?" the queen demanded, her eyes narrowing. "The child's magic didn't feel like this before. Something has changed."

Again, Hadeon seemed to consider. "While in the Abyss, she trained with them and unlocked some of her shadow fae abilities, which is likely why you can sense her powers now and couldn't before."

Arabella was careful to school her features into neutrality.

It didn't miss her notice that Hadeon specified unlocking her shadow fae abilities and not her demon magic. Yet again, why did he protect her from the queen?

I'd probably never be allowed to leave this court if Genoveva knew of my demon magic, she thought. *I'd be held hostage just like my mother or executed.*

Even now, she may not be allowed to leave since the queen knew she was part shadow fae.

For a moment, she wondered if she should have tried to flee the Twilight Court. Even with the guards, she and Jessamine could have made a run for the gateway in the forest. They might have stood a chance of succeeding.

And leave Elias behind?

No, she couldn't have left without him.

If she was to be trapped in the Twilight Court alongside her mate, so be it. But maybe she could avoid having Jessamine trapped alongside her.

"What I wish to discuss with you has to do with the shadow fae," Hadeon said. "Specifically, what they intend to do if they ever return to the fae realm."

The queen raised a perfectly manicured eyebrow.

"They made a deal with a greater demon called the Everdark," he said. "It will help them in their quest for revenge on our court. In exchange, the shadow fae will help the demons gain entry into the fae realm."

The words seemed to hover in the air, and the room remained utterly quiet as though no one dared to breathe.

Then the queen spoke.

"And?"

Lines formed between Hadeon's brows as he said, "*And?* Demons could run rampant in our realm, feeding off the land's magic, killing those with weaker magic—"

"You sealed the gateway, did you not? They are trapped in the underrealm with no way out. As such, there's no reason to concern ourselves with the shadow fae any further," the queen said with a wave of her hand. Her gaze flicked to Magnus. "I presume the reason for your presence here today is because you have good news."

Hadeon's eyes widened. "What have you done?"

Countless emotions swirled through Arabella, but all she could do was look between Elias and the others.

Magnus didn't speak right away. Instead, he looked at the queen, who nodded—granting him permission to speak further. Then he turned to Arabella, Jessamine, and Hadeon. "Her Majesty has requested my assistance on a specific matter. She knew I'd found a way to grant immortality to my erox, and she asked if it was possible to grant immortality to an existing race. I'm happy to report, I found a way, but there will be a price."

"Did you not hear me, Mother?" Hadeon said, interrupting Magnus. "The shadow fae want to return. They could find another way and attack the Twilight Court. Surely, this matter with immortality and the sorcerer can wait."

"All the more reason to forge new alliances," the queen said, not meeting her son's gaze. "Did you discover other exits from the Abyss?"

"There are none that we know of—" Hadeon began.

"That's good enough for now," Genoveva said.

Hadeon spoke again, but Arabella didn't hear the words. Even as he tried to get through to his mother, she knew it was no use.

"What's the cost?" Arabella said, her voice low.

The queen leaned back in her throne, her hands draped over the armrests. "Something that doesn't concern you. That is between the sorcerer and I."

Jessamine crossed her arms, speaking up for the first time. "You do realize that the sorcerer has an army of erox and creatures of the dark on the other side of a gateway that leads into *your* territory, right? Most of the demons and monsters might not be able to pass through the gateway for now, but the erox can. They can feed on the fae—not just mortals. With enough erox, your kingdom wouldn't stand a chance."

Turning to Jessamine, the queen leveled a patronizing look on her, like she was placating a foolish child. "Don't you worry about that, human. We've come to an agreement."

Magnus cleared his throat, drawing all eyes to him. "As a sign of good faith for our alliance, I'd like Enchantress Arabella."

For the first time, the queen's gaze narrowed on the sorcerer. "You want the only shadow fae in the lands of the living? Why?"

"I need her magic for my final preparations to grant your request," Magnus said.

Belatedly, Arabella found her voice. "I'm not some pawn to be bargained off—"

But the queen was already speaking. "You're a fugitive in my court who came here without my invitation. What comes next is at my discretion." Then she turned to Magnus. "What is it you want with her magic?"

"Only the shadow fae can create syphens, which are essential to creating new erox." Magnus paused, leveling a knowing gaze on the queen. "To achieve immortality for the fae, I'll need a more powerful syphen. One that can... make exchanges."

Genoveva sniffed. "You intended this all along." She waved a hand. "Create the syphen. Now. And you will give a demonstration of what it can do, or our deal is off."

Magnus turned to Arabella, his eyes full of dark promise.

"Let's begin."

Chapter Twenty-Six
ARABELLA

Instinctively, Arabella lowered her stance and took a step back—away from the dais and the sorcerer standing at the base of it. Rather than reaching for the blades at her back, she summoned the shadows beneath her feet.

Through windows several stories up in the back of the throne room, she could see that night had fallen.

It was a time when shadow fae were the strongest.

When the darkness reigned supreme.

The shadows hummed to life, emerging from the floor in an eager tempest. The light from the candles at the base of each of the pillars flickered, half of them extinguishing in an instant and sending the room into partial darkness.

Wrapping a band of shadows around Jessamine's waist, she pulled her friend behind her, positioning herself between Jessamine and Magnus—and the dais.

Hadeon stood beside her, unmoving.

A thought occurred to Arabella.

While she had no desire to help Magnus, this was a unique opportunity—one she may never find herself in again. There was something the sorcerer needed. Something only she could provide. As such, this could be her only chance to bargain for Elias' freedom.

Maybe—just maybe—there was something Magnus wanted more than her mate.

"Free Elias and give me his syphen, and I'll consider making you a replacement blade," she said as her shadows whipped at her feet.

"If you think—" Genoveva began, but Magnus raised a hand.

"If it pleases Your Majesty, I can take it from here," the sorcerer said.

The queen dipped her chin.

Everything after that was a blur.

One moment, Jessamine was behind Arabella. In the next, a blast of scarlet enfolded Arabella and her shadows, and Jessamine was hauled across the dark tiles—toward Magnus.

"No!" Arabella screamed as she fought against the wall of scarlet that pressed her down, down, *down*. She unleashed her shadows against the scarlet, which bounced off the wall without making an indent. Growling, she clawed at the red with her talons. To her relief, she felt them tear. Grabbing on to the tear, she pulled it apart, widening it until she leaped through.

Magnus raised a brow, a flicker of surprise marring his features for the briefest of moments.

But she didn't have eyes for him.

Instead, she fixed her gaze on Elias, whose hand was wrapped around Jessamine's throat. Jessamine's feet barely touched the floor, the toes of her boots scraping against the tiles as she struggled to free herself. With a flicker of blue in his gaze, Jessamine went pliant in his grip. She dropped the earthen weaves she'd been forming, which dissipated instantly.

"You made a mistake in trying to protect your friend before," Magnus said. "You revealed what you care for—and what you're desperate to protect. It's too late for you to protect Elias, but we'll see about your friend. Now, you have a choice: do as you're told, or she dies."

Arabella's eyes flickered between her mate and Jessamine—whose eyes had glazed over with the pull of desire from Elias' erox magic. Elias still didn't look at her, and his face was devoid of emotion.

It was as though he were nothing more than a soldier taking orders.

He's still in there, she thought. *Or else he wouldn't have felt fear at the mention of the underrealm.*

But even if Elias was in there somewhere, he could still be forced to kill Jessamine, and Arabella could never allow that.

Somehow, she had to save them both.

First, she'd separate Jessamine from Elias, and then she would unleash her new magic. It was clear the queen wasn't going to let her go. She'd have to fight her way out.

For now, she'd play along until there was an opening.

She lifted her chin. "How can I make the syphen?"

A trace of humor flicked across Magnus' eyes. "I knew you'd see reason. A new syphen can only be created under the power of the black moon. As it just so happens, the dark side of the moon will be revealed tonight."

She wasn't certain how much time had passed while they were in the Abyss, but what awful timing. Magnus would wreak havoc if he had some all-powerful syphen. And there was no way he could use this weapon to grant immortality without there being a steep price for it.

A slip of scarlet plucked one of her daggers from her waist. It trailed in the air before coming into Magnus' outstretched hand.

"You can create a blade from scratch, infusing the metal with magic as it's being forged, but the theatrics are unnecessary," Magnus said. "And finding a shadow fae blacksmith is a rarity these days. But I've found making a syphen with an existing blade is equally effective." He gestured to Arabella's dagger, which was a simple blade of steel with a black handle. Like Elias' syphen, it was unremarkable in appearance—neither embossed or covered in gemstones. "However, there's one thing I'll add." Reaching into his pocket, he pulled out what appeared to be a round glass ball.

She gaped.

It was the amplifier she'd gotten from Hadeon at the ball and lost when she'd fled Elias' castle and was captured by the ogres.

A bright light burst from Magnus' hands. It was so bright that she flinched away, unable to look at where he held her knife and the amplifier. As the light receded, she turned back to find Magnus had somehow fused the amplifier to the end of the handle.

"There we have it," he said before flipping the knife, grabbing the tip of the blade, and throwing it at her.

She lunged out of the blade's path while throwing up a wall of black. Rather than the blade punching into her shoulder, it was enfolded in shadows. She raised it with her magic, holding it by the tip just as Magnus had.

It was then she realized that the amplifier was utterly empty of magic.

No wonder he hadn't been concerned about handing over an amplifier to her.

Magnus strode over to where Arabella stood at the base of the dais.

As he did, Hadeon looked up at Genoveva. "Mother, I must insist. We can't—"

"That's enough," Genoveva snapped. "Interfere or speak out of turn one more time, and I'll throw you into the dungeons."

A vein in Hadeon's jaw bulged, but he didn't object.

As he spoke, Arabella allowed her shadows to stretch upward from the ground, obscuring everything from the waist down. As she did, she pulled one of her hidden knives free from a scabbard at her back. She moved slowly, careful not to show signs of movement.

If she was lucky, Magnus' focus would be entirely on the blade with the amplifier or on attacks from her magic. She hoped an attack with a simple knife would be beneath his notice.

A moment later, he stood within arm's reach and gestured to the dagger with the fused amplifier that she held with her shadows. "You must infuse a blade with the power of the dark side of the moon in order to make a syphen."

Her eyes narrowed. "I'm going to need a bit more than that."

The corner of his lips twitched, and he leaned forward. For a strange moment, she thought he might kiss her cheek, and she recoiled. Instead, his cheek pressed against hers as he whispered in her ear. "I'd put that little knife you're holding behind your back away if I were you. Else, I might allow Elias to feed on your friend. What's her name... Jessamine, isn't it? Elias was due to replenish his essence today. But we didn't have the time before our journey here. I'm sure he's eager to feed. But that would be awkward, wouldn't it? Your lover and best friend."

For a moment, she considered taking her chances and trying to stab Magnus in the heart then and there—to throw everything she had at him.

Then her gaze shifted to where Elias stood a few feet away with his fingers around Jessamine's throat. Her blinks grew slower as she hung slack in his grip, unable to fully touch the ground. Arabella sheathed the blade before shoving Magnus in the chest so he was forced to take a step backward.

"Tell Elias to release her with that other syphen in your robes," she demanded. "Or you're on your own."

Something glittered in Magnus' gaze as a hand disappeared into his cloak. But as he spoke the words to Elias, his eyes never left Arabella's face. "Release Enchantress Jessamine. But keep her within reach. The minute Enchantress Arabella or anyone else tries to... delay or prevent this new syphen from being made, drain Jessamine dry."

Elias dipped his chin before he complied.

There was a squeak as Jessamine's boots touched the floor, and she gasped, gripping her throat.

"Let's begin." Magnus made a sweeping gesture with an arm,

and the remaining lit candles throughout the throne room went dark in an instant.

Arabella could still see the entire throne room and those in it with perfect clarity, but by the mutters of nearby guards, she knew that visibility for them was greatly diminished. It was then she realized Magnus' magic, the scarlet clouds pooling around his feet, hadn't gone dark as well. Instead, they *glowed*.

His magic plucked the knife with the amplifier from her shadows, floating it until it was within the palm of his hand. With his empty hand, he grabbed her wrist, turning her hand so her palm faced up. Then he ran the blade over her palm. She gritted her teeth, biting back a hiss, but didn't object. Blood beaded along the cut before dripping over the sides of her hand onto the tiled floor.

As he ran the knife over his own palm, he said, "It takes shadow fae years to learn how to create a syphen. Unfortunately, I don't have the time to train you. Luckily, I can access your magic for a limited time and... perform the spell for you."

She started. "Dark magic? You can use it to control my magic?"

There was a reason both fae and humans were fearful of dark magic. It was nearly limitless in what could be done—with the right sacrifices. It was perhaps even more feared than demon magic.

"Blood spells are convenient for such things." The sorcerer's scarlet eyes glowed bright as his power surged. "The trick is the participant must be *willing*."

That explained his swiftness in taking Jessamine. He knew Arabella wouldn't have given him access to her blood without leverage.

Magnus pressed his bloodied palm against hers and began chanting in a language she didn't understand. When their palms touched, their blood floated up and wrapped in a circle around both of their forearms. A moment later, both Arabella's shadows and Magnus' scarlet power banded around their arms as well.

He paused his chanting and said, "Your Majesty, do you object to my... borrowing one of your guards?"

"Do what you must," Genoveva said from her throne.

With a flick of his wrist, the sorcerer sent a band of his magic flying to the soldier beneath the nearest archway. There was a distinct tug somewhere deep within Arabella as her magic was summoned without her willing it, flowing into Magnus. When the fae screamed, she turned toward him, watching in horror as her and Magnus' combined magic wrapped around the soldier, starting at his feet and entwining up his entire body. As it did, blood flowed down the band of magic toward the fae. When it collided with his chest, the man's head jerked toward the ceiling as his screams grew to a feverish pitch. His eyes and mouth glowed a brilliant white, which solidified into a burbling liquid and poured out of his mouth. Then it flowed out of him and up their combined magic until it swirled around their bloodied palms.

The guard crumpled to the ground, dead instantly.

"What the fuck?" Arabella hissed. "You just killed him."

Magnus had begun chanting again, but he paused to say, "You didn't think a syphen came into existence without sacrifice, did you?" He made a tsking sound before returning to his chanting.

As he wove his dark spell, the flow of magic coming from her changed. At first, it felt like something tugged at her core, stripping pieces of her away as she was siphoned of energy. Like a human amplifier. Power flowed from her like a trickling stream until there was a burning sensation and then a *tug*. Then it was like the damn on her power had been decimated as the current poured from her.

Gasping, she stumbled forward, catching herself and bumping into Magnus. He ignored her as he continued the spell, and she watched as her shadows swirled around them both, mixing with the sorcerer's scarlet magic until she could no longer differentiate the two. Some of their combined magic flowed into the once-empty amplifier.

Then he held the blade into the air, and a strange darkness swirled down from the windows.

It wasn't the shadows. She would've been able to feel their humming if it had been. This was entirely different. It felt like a pulsing of deep space, an otherworldly dark heartbeat.

The dark moon, she realized. *He's summoning its magic.*

She watched as the dark moon's power twisted in the air, flowing toward the knife. Its movements were jerky, almost child-like, as though it was curious.

As though it was somehow alive.

Hadeon, Genoveva, Jessamine, and Elias watched in silence as that dark crept ever downward.

The only sound that could be heard was Magnus' chanting, which had softened to a low rumble.

Clenching her teeth, she took several deep breaths, trying to steady her swirling vision. The flow of Magnus' dark magic was quickly depleting her energy. It was an effort to ignore the way her slick palm slid against Magnus' as he gripped her hand too tightly, his attention focused wholly on the new presence whirling toward them.

Then it was a breath away, stretching out toward the knife.

The moment the energy collided with the hilt, a burst of unnatural wind swept through the throne room.

"Yes," Magnus hissed as the energy... *stuck* to the blade.

Somehow, she could feel its sudden fear, how it tried to pull away, but it couldn't separate itself from the knife.

The sorcerer's chanting grew to a crescendo, and suddenly his voice was no longer one, but many.

The magic spinning around their bodies swept upward to meet where the dark moon's magic was being sucked into the blade. Then all three powers moved in a combined current of magic, billowing in circles that soon became too fast for her eyes to track. As it did, she felt a tickling sensation from her ears and nose. When she brought up her free hand to swipe it, she realized it was blood.

Then the torrent began to slow as their powers flowed into the amplifier at the hilt.

In moments, the magic was sucked into the amplifier until nothing remained.

The room was utterly silent, and the dark moon's magic had changed. No, that wasn't right. It wasn't just magic. It was a piece of the moon, itself.

No longer did it hover in the air. Somehow, the sorcerer had trapped the magic within the blade.

Magnus released her abruptly, and she staggered backward, nearly falling on her ass. He looked up to the queen on her throne, whose eyes flashed with sudden fervor.

"Now, I shall prove to you immortality is within reach." He turned back to Arabella. "But first..." He reached within his robes—grabbing Elias' syphen. "Elias, restrain Enchantress Arabella. If she resists or tries to break free, kill Jessamine and then yourself."

Arabella blinked, her mind not wrapping around his words as Elias stepped between the shadows. He appeared beside her and grabbed her arms, forcing them behind her back.

"Elias—" she began but stopped as she watched in horror as Magnus pressed the tip of his new syphen to the center of Jessamine's chest. His scarlet magic banded around Jessamine's entire body, pinning her arms to her sides. "No! Don't touch her—"

Elias' lips pressed to her ear, and Arabella thought for a moment he might speak, might say something—*anything*—to make this better. To make this madness *stop*.

But she knew with devastating certainty that Magnus had forbidden him from speaking to her as Elias shook his head. The gesture was so faint, and she felt it in the way his cheek pressed into her hair.

Don't, he was trying to say.

If Arabella tried to use her magic or break away, Elias would kill both Jessamine and himself. In a single instant, she'd lose both her best friend and her mate.

Tears cascaded down her cheeks as she watched Magnus hold the syphen to Jessamine's chest, chanting once more. Blood plopped onto the floor beneath his hand, but he ignored it as a golden magic swirled from Jessamine's chest and out her mouth.

Her magic, Arabella realized.

Somehow, Magnus had detached the earthen magic from Jessamine's body. How was that even possible?

Jessamine snarled at Magnus as his power lifted her off the floor, making her hover in the air. She spat in his face as her magic wrapped around the syphen and filtered into the amplifier at the base of the hilt. For a moment, the black glass orb glowed golden. Then, the sorcerer's magic wrapped around Jessamine's neck and pulled.

The sound of Jessamine's neck snapping cracked across the room, echoing unnaturally loud.

A scream tore from Arabella's throat as she felt the blossoming light of her friend's magic—Jessamine's *life*—go suddenly dark.

No, no, no, this couldn't be happening.

Jessamine was her sister, her best friend. She couldn't even comprehend a life without her in it—without her laugh, her sharp tongue, and her constant reassuring presence.

Arabella screamed and screamed, the shadows surging from the floor in a torrent.

As her knees slammed into the floor, she distantly registered that Magnus' chanting continued.

One moment, Jessamine's body hung limp in the sorcerer's magic a few inches off the ground, and the next, there was a loud gasp.

Blinking through her tears, Arabella watched as the shimmering gold energy from the syphen flowed over Jessamine from head to toe. As it did, light animated her features, but it also *changed* them. Jessamine's cheekbones grew sharper, her muscles swelled within her leathers, and her ears became pointed.

Like the fae.

Jessamine fell to the floor, gasping.

In an instant, Arabella stepped between shadows, crossing the space and knelt before her friend.

Running her hands over Jessamine's face, she couldn't believe her eyes. Jessamine's neck had been broken—twisted unnaturally to the side. Now, she was not only whole, but a magic unlike anything Arabella had ever sensed from another magic wielder blossomed in her senses. No longer was there the telltale golden energy of an enchantress. Instead, Arabella felt the booming power of something else entirely.

"Unbelievable," Jessamine groaned. "He turned me into a fucking fae."

She was right. Or, Arabella thought she was. The magic *felt* fae but also more than that. It felt like it was somehow tied both to the beating heart of the earth and the fae realm, itself.

A sudden realization struck Arabella as she sensed the pulsing of her friend's new abilities.

Jessamine's magic had surpassed all the fae in the room, including Hadeon and the queen. Only Magnus' power was stronger than hers. Somehow, she'd become…

"Immortal," Magnus said as he strode over to the base of the dais. "She's a new type of fae—an immortal race that doesn't grow old or become ill. The only way she can die is by blade, poison, or a… similar means."

The queen rose, striding down the dais steps and coming to stand before Jessamine. Genoveva's eyes drew wide as she studied Jessamine, likely coming to the same conclusion Arabella had—feeling the complete change in her magic.

Then the queen turned to Magnus. "Find a way to keep my magic and grant immortality, and you have a deal. But…" She pointed to Arabella. "The shadow fae will remain in my custody. The moment you fulfill your half of the bargain, she's all yours."

Magnus bowed his head. "As you say. I'll make my final preparations." Without another word, he turned toward the door with Elias at his heels.

Arabella stood in stunned silence, her mind reeling, before her feet were moving. She pointed a finger at Hadeon and then at Jessamine. "Help her. Now." Then she ran after the sorcerer as he strode down the long throne room toward the doors. "Wait!"

This couldn't be happening. Not only had Magnus done unspeakable things to Jessamine, but he was taking Elias away again.

When Magnus and Elias didn't stop, she skidded to a halt and summoned her shadows. She formed a wall of impenetrable black before the door.

Magnus turned on a heel and walked back to her, his robes trailing on the ground. Blood no longer dripped from his hand but had dried around his fingers. Elias followed at his heels, his arms crossed behind him, his eyes on the sorcerer's back.

Look at me, she thought, not for the first time.

It was a foolish thing to wish. She knew why he wasn't looking at her, why he was so cold, acting as though he didn't know her. It was the syphen. It was Magnus—all of this was his fault. But even knowing that, her heart twisted when he didn't meet her eyes, when she couldn't find the reassurance in them that she sought.

Even if she could see some recognition in his eyes, that would be enough. Just to see the male she'd fallen for was still there.

He'd been so close to breaking in the dreamscape.

She longed to know that he was okay, that he was still *him*.

"Why?" she demanded.

As she spoke, she thought of the enchantress she'd once been —the confident woman who'd been accustomed to giving orders and having them obeyed.

She needed to be that woman now.

The sorcerer stood before her, just out of arm's reach. "You'll have to be more specific, Enchantress."

"For one, why Elias?" she said, grabbing hold of the anger

alighting her senses and allowing it to bolster her courage. "Why can't you find some other twisted hobby to occupy your time? For another..." She lowered her voice so that even the fae couldn't pick up the next words with their hearing. "What do you hope to gain by allying with the Twilight Court?"

The sorcerer's face remained impassive as he said, "I was ending kingdoms long before you were born. I cannot be goaded so easily." He glanced over his shoulder to where Elias stood. "As for your questions... All in due time."

She crossed her arms. "You want me? Then I want answers, and I want Elias free. Otherwise, I might be tempted to trip and fall onto a blade before the queen hands me over. Then I'll be of no use to you."

Maybe the sorcerer needed her to make more syphens. Perhaps he wanted to kill off the last of the shadow fae still walking within the lands of the living. Or it could be something else entirely. But she made a bet it was the former, hoping she could use her life as leverage.

Jessamine came to stand beside Arabella. Her footsteps had been so quiet that Arabella had completely missed them.

Arabella's heart twisted at everything that had been taken from her friend in a single moment. She'd been unable to protect her.

In the room behind them, there were a series of footsteps. A glance over her shoulder revealed the fae guards had moved from their posts beneath the archways, hands on the hilts of swords. But none drew closer. For some reason, the queen was letting them have it out in her throne room and didn't lock Arabella away immediately.

For now, it was enough that the Twilight Court guards were staying away from her while she faced down the male who held her mate captive.

Magnus took a lazy step back until he stood beside Elias. He ran the back of a finger down the side of Elias' face. The gesture was intimate, like one of lovers. "My prodigal son has always been unique. His power is unlike his brothers."

She frowned.

Elias' ability to feed off mortals and weaponize essence... That was what Magnus was after? Then she understood the implication. If all his erox could use essence as a weapon, they could take over the mortal realm, going from village to village and turning the men into erox. No one could stop them.

"What do you want with Arabella?" Jessamine demanded.

Magnus turned from Elias, who never moved, never objected to the sorcerer's touch. "I can only control so many erox at once with a syphen. I can make them do my bidding, true, but to give them each their own task and ensure they make each step in the way I want... Well, that requires a lot of concentration. More than I'm willing to devote." He took a step forward so that he whispered in Arabella's ear—so low that she almost missed it. "But if my erox each had syphens, they could control armies, and I could control them. I'd have legions at my fingertips."

"What could you possibly want armies for?" she demanded.

Slowly, the sorcerer leaned back so he could study her eyes. "Let's just say I have some unfinished business with The Ten."

The Ten were said to be the original sorcerers in the mortal realm. They'd been the founders of the great human cities and created so many of the technologies used there. But they'd been alive thousands of years ago. Surely, they were long dead.

Arabella frowned, shaking her head.

None of this mattered. Not right now when her mate was before her and needed her to rescue him.

Enough holding back. Enough *talking*.

Jessamine was safe, and if Arabella could attack before Magnus was ready, maybe she could get Elias' syphen from him.

She lashed out with her shadows. They arced in the air toward the blade.

As the thorned vines neared the sorcerer, they crashed into a wall of power. The shadows became less corporeal, melting into mere dark smudges as they pressed against the shield the sorcerer had formed around himself and Elias.

Her heart dropped.

Even after everything she'd gone through, the sorcerer was still so much more powerful than her.

Magnus pressed the syphen to Elias' throat. "Try that again, and I'll slice your mate open."

Chapter Twenty-Seven
ELIAS

Elias didn't have control over his actions or his body as he stood in the queen's throne room, Magnus' syphen pressed to his throat.

He was utterly at the mercy of the sorcerer's whims, and his mate would be the one to suffer the consequences.

Arabella stood before him, but he wasn't permitted to look at her.

Prior to leaving the camp and journeying to the gateway, Magnus had used the syphen to forbid Elias from interacting with Arabella in any capacity. Magnus had prepared just in case they'd encounter Arabella and her friends.

Somehow, they'd crossed paths in the Twilight Court.

Elias allowed himself to marvel at her nearness, at the glorious energy pouring down the bond. There was terror in her heart and so much anger. But it didn't take away from his joy at seeing her again—to marvel at these few precious moments in her presence.

Unbidden, his body started trembling faintly.

The fissure that had formed in his heart widened further. Even feeling how the bond hummed in his chest, his body and mind recalled all the times Magnus had worn her face—and killed

Elias or tortured him. Rather than feeling only happiness at seeing his mate, he also felt fear.

This isn't a trick of Magnus', he thought. *This is my mate.*

But even knowing it was her by the way the tightness in his chest eased, he couldn't shirk the doubt lingering in his thoughts.

Elias stared at the far wall, able only to glance Arabella's face in his periphery. He could make out the strands of her hair that had pulled free of her braid and her black leather streaked with... Was that sand?

Beneath the smells of sweat, leather, and dark earth was the faint scent of lilacs and peppermint—which is what her essence tasted like.

Fuck, he'd do anything to taste her again.

Those dreams had been the only solace during the long weeks with Magnus. But now... He longed for her touch more than anything in this world.

But I can never touch her again. And I can't let Magnus use me against her.

There was a sharp sting as the blade broke his skin and blood trickled down his neck.

Let me die, he thought, hoping Arabella could understand the desperation filling him.

He'd just kept her from protecting Jessamine, and he couldn't let Magnus use him against Arabella and her friends again.

For the first time, he wondered what Hadeon was doing here and why he'd been with Arabella. Had he used the bargain with Arabella? What would he have taken from her, and to what end?

There was so much Elias didn't know.

"Remain still," Magnus purred as blood flowed more freely down Elias' neck.

The words were infused with the syphen's magic. Instantly, Elias froze in place. His skin knit back together, leaving a pang of hunger in his gut.

Fuck, he needed essence so desperately.

"Free Elias, hand his syphen over, and I'll come with you," Arabella said as he was forced to fix his gaze on the far wall.

No!

He wanted to scream, to tell her to run far from here. But all he could do was to stand in place and await whatever Magnus ordered him to do next.

"Where you go is no longer within your power to bargain," Magnus said. "You're a guest of the Twilight Court now. But don't fret. I'll have you and Elias under my care soon enough. Speaking of my syphen…"

A burning rage filled Magnus' eyes. "You have something of mine." His voice lowered. It was a tone Elias had become far too familiar with. One that promised violence. "Where is Breckett?"

Elias swallowed thickly, his mouth suddenly dry. If Magnus hadn't ordered him to remain still, his knees might have given out.

Run, Arabella.

The blade pressed against his throat once more.

"I don't need Elias to have his memories now that I've found a way to duplicate his magic and give it to my other erox," Magnus purred. "He remains as he is only because it suits me. For now."

Fear seized Elias' veins, and a tightness spread through his chest, making it hard to breathe. While the idea of succumbing to his inner demon had terror ripping through every fiber of his being, there was one thing he feared more—something happening to his mate.

"You wouldn't," Arabella hissed somewhere beyond his sight.

A deep, haunting fear flowed down the bond so strongly it nearly drowned out his own. Even after everything, Arabella worried for his safety.

"I would," Magnus said. "In fact—"

There was a flash of movement as Magnus' arm moved before pain exploded in Elias' gut.

He felt his mouth open but couldn't get a wisp of air. Agony exploded from his center, and his body tried to slump forward, to fall to his knees. But he couldn't move. Not with the syphen's magic holding him in place. It wouldn't be until the moment he died that he could disobey any orders the holder of the syphen gave.

Gasping for air, blood poured out of his gut and pooled on the floor.

His body tried to heal the wound but couldn't through the syphen's magic. Instead, the essence in his body worked to replenish the blood in his veins and to heal the damage to his internal organs around where the blade was. In moments, his essence depleted until almost nothing was left.

His grip on reality slackened and his fangs emerged, puncturing his lower lip. A metallic tang filled his mouth.

Somewhere, he thought he heard screaming.

Arabella, he realized.

No, some distant part of him thought. *Don't cry for me.*

He'd chosen this. And despite everything he'd endured, he'd give himself over to Magnus a thousand times over if it meant she was herself again—free to live her life and with her memories back once more.

"Breckett is in the Abyss."

It was Arabella's voice.

"He's trapped there with the shadow fae," she added.

There was a flash of movement before Elias' vision went dark. He was either going to black out or the demon would soon come forth.

And he'd be no more.

Magnus laughed, the sound piercing the air. It echoed down the hallway, and it seemed like all other sounds ceased.

"I answered your question. Now, take the syphen out." It was Arabella again, her voice raising in pitch. "Let Elias feed on me before it's too late."

There was a sudden pressure at his center and then a squelching sound as the blade was pulled free from his gut.

He felt Magnus' magic through the syphen as the sorcerer

said, "For this moment only, you're permitted to move, to look at her. Feed, my prodigal son, to your heart's content."

Through his darkening vision, he thought he saw the silhouette of his mate before him. Was this some dream? As he felt her arms loop under his and her lilac scent washed over him, he raised a hand and brushed loose strands of hair back from her face.

"You're beautiful." The words came out like a strangled sound, further garbled by his elongated canines. But they were two of the truest words he'd ever spoken.

As he spoke, his body started trembling again. But he was too weak to flinch away, to give in to the fear Magnus had instilled in him at the sight of her.

"You can write sonnets for me later," Arabella said. "But right now, you need to feed."

No, he didn't want to feed. Not when it meant that the moment he finished, he'd have to leave. Magnus would force Elias to go with him when this little game of his was over. And even if some part of Elias was terrified that she'd suddenly rip out his heart, he also longed to remain in her presence—for as long as time would allow.

Broken as it was, his heart would forever be hers.

"Kiss me, Elias," she said, her voice cracking. "Please."

Please.

Once, he would have given her anything if she uttered that one word. He would have granted her any pleasure she'd wished if only she'd promise herself to him. Denying her anything had been difficult then. And he found himself unable to deny her even now.

Then he was kissing her.

Her lips were salty from sweat and dirt—from whatever travels she'd undergone in the Abyss. And he'd never tasted anything so perfect. Her lips were soft, divine. She was everything he'd wished for and more.

He moved his tongue into her mouth, exploring her, wanting to feel her softness.

Perhaps for the last time.

Her tongue moved against his as she explored his mouth in return.

I love you, he wanted to say. *I will love you long after my last breath.*

But he was far past the ability to speak, to form words. His hunger surged, and his power swelled, stretching out toward his mate.

His magic stretched out without his willing it, caressing against her very core—where her essence lived deep within her. It wasn't her soul nor was it strictly her physical energy. It was the energy of her spirit and body intertwined in one. Everyone's essence tasted different. And as an erox, he could only access it when her spirit and body were one in pleasure. At the peak moment when her body succumbed to ecstasy.

And if he could give her nothing else before he was gone, he wanted to give her that.

He wanted to go slow, to touch her and coax her over the edge. But his hunger was too vast and his body too weak. It was all he could do to hold on to her, to kiss her and pull her essence forth.

His power latched on to her, and he felt her being pulled to the brink of pleasure.

I love you, he thought again.

Then she was moaning into his mouth, and the beast took over.

His power fastened on to her essence, summoning it from deep within her. It needed no coaxing as their bond had her essence flowing faster than ever before. Then it was pooling in his mouth, tasting of lilacs and a cool autumn breeze. There was something else there, too. Something that hadn't been there before. But he was too far gone to wrap his mind around what.

He felt his cock harden, and he nearly came just from the taste of her.

He sucked the essence in, pulling one draft and then another.

As he did, his vision started to clear, and he felt steadier on his feet, leaning on Arabella less. Then his hands were moving, cupping her face before sweeping across her back like he couldn't pull her close enough. Like he couldn't get enough of her.

Even if they spent hundreds of lifetimes together, he'd never have enough of her. Though they wouldn't even have one.

"That's enough," came Magnus' voice.

A slice of scarlet magic pressed between them before it burst, and Elias was forced backward.

Looking at his mate for the first time with clear eyes, he studied her face, memorizing her swollen lips and her large brown eyes—eyes that fixed on him like she could see the core of who he was. He also saw the purple smudges under her eyes. Guilt swelled in him that he'd taken from her when she likely needed rest more than anything else.

He wanted more time. But time was something they'd never have.

Elias stared at Arabella, his tongue heavy with unspoken words. And she stared right back, her chest heaving beneath her black leather corset like she'd just run miles to get to him.

He knew what came next.

"My previous orders are to be obeyed." Magnus' words were infused with the syphen's power.

As the sorcerer spoke, Elias' eyes were torn from his mate. Once more, he was forbidden to look at or interact with Arabella.

"It's time we were off," Magnus said, turning.

Elias' feet moved on their own accord—each step taking him farther away from his mate.

Magnus lingered as the doors swung open, Arabella's wall of shadows gone.

"Enjoy your stay in the Twilight Court," the sorcerer said over his shoulder. "I'll see you again soon."

"You fucking bastard," Arabella called somewhere behind them. "I'll kill you for this."

"Unlikely," Magnus said. He started to move but paused

again. "There's something else you might not know since you're still so new to this world. I'll share a little-known fact with you. Many know that a mating bond will be broken if the couple don't accept it. But did you know that a mating bond can be severed if the bond isn't *consummated* in the waking world? Funny the way magic can be. It's so *unpredictable*."

As Magnus strode out of the throne room, the other erox closing ranks around them, he spoke the words that shattered any hope remaining in Elias' heart.

"Enjoy what time you have left, Enchantress—just in case that little thread *snaps*," the sorcerer said. "And before I march on that human village of yours."

"What?"

It was Arabella's voice. She sounded so small, like the lost girl she'd once been in the forest.

Magnus didn't turn back to her as he said, "I'll be at the gates of Shadowbank in three days' time. My erox who can wield essence will take down the ward. It will be like child's play."

Elias' heart nearly stopped.

Magnus was marching on Shadowbank? But why?

Sudden realization dawned.

Magnus needed more men to turn into erox to grow his army. He'd also found a way to give other erox Elias' ability to wield essence. And now, he had another, more powerful syphen.

That's why Magnus wanted me, he realized. *He wanted to find a way to take down wards—including the wards around the great cities.*

Without those wards, demons could march into human cities without any resistance.

But first, Magnus needed more erox.

Tears streamed down Elias' cheeks as he walked down the castle hallways to the sound of his mate screaming.

Then they were gone.

Thanks for reading Devoured by Shadows*!*

Click here *to preorder the third book in The Wild Shadows Series,* **Forged by Gilded Night,** *or go to:*
bit.ly/ForgedbyGildedNight*.*

You can also check out the prequel novella in The Wild Shadows Series, **Auctioned to the Vampire***, or go to:*
bit.ly/AuctionedtotheVampire*.*

If you'd like to be considered for an **advanced review copy (ARC)** *of my future books, please* ***fill out this form*** *(e-book) or go to:*
bit.ly/ReadRosalynStirling*.*

To be considered for the ARC team of Forged by Gilded Night *(The Wild Shadows, #3), please* ***fill out this form*** *(e-book) or go to:*
bit.ly/ForgedbyGildedNightARC*.*

Acknowledgments

As a newbie author who's never written a sequel before, I nearly shat my pants at the idea of writing one. It was a huge project that I wondered if I could do justice.

I'm not sure if I could have found my courage without the endless support and encouraging words of my partner. Thank you for your endless faith in me and all the times you listened to me with patience and grace.

To my editors, beta readers, and cover designer, thank you for helping me make this book the best it could be. Your eyes and expertise are invaluable.

To my patrons who've shown me so much support, I appreciate you so very much. Thank you for believing in me. I'd like to give a special shout-out to Idris Danley and Trisha Huang.

To my readers who've shown me so much love, thank you. You're why I continue to write the stories I do. I look forward to reading your DMs, emails, and comments. (For those who've asked, yes, absolutely send me your real-time, play-by-play reactions as you read. I eat that shit up.)

To everyone else who's impacted my life and stories in any way, thank you.

And stay tuned for the next book, *Forged by Gilded Night*.

About the Author

Rosalyn Stirling is an author of steamy fantasy romance. In her free time, she enjoys reading and watching stories where love wins against all odds and the lovers find their happily ever after. She can be found at your nearest bookstore, tea in hand, dreaming of other worlds.

Want to stay up to date with everything Rosalyn is doing? Join her newsletter! You'll get first access to cover reveals, teasers, and giveaways.

bit.ly.com/RosalynStirlingNewsletter

Connect with her on social media:
Instagram (@rosalynstirling)
Facebook (Author Rosalyn Stirling)